AWEN RISING

O. J. BARRÉ

PEACEMAKERS PUBLISHING COMPANY

PEACEMAKERS PUBLISHING COMPANY, JULY 2019

PeaceMakers Publishing
14505 N Presidio Loop
Nampa, ID 83651

droherrell@yahoo.com
ojbarreauthor@gmail.com
www.ojbarre.com

For information about special discounts available for quantity purchases and orders by trade bookstores, wholesalers, book clubs, etc; or for film options, translation rights, etc, please contact the publisher at one of the above addresses.

PeaceMakers Publishing Trade Paperback ISBN: 978-1-7332736-1-9

Cover Design © 2019 by Lauren Willmore
Edited by Charlie Knight

First Printing, 2019
Printed in the United States of America

IN MEMORY OF BUGSY

who taught me animals are people
with better dispositions.

&

TO VILLA RICA

who raised me as a child,
and welcomed me back when I needed to heal.

ACKNOWLEDGMENTS

First of all, I'd like to thank my mama and daddy, Jean and Yank Herrell, for doing the deed that brought me into this world. Daddy, thank you for instilling your love for the earth and its glorious creatures; Mama for passing on your love of the written word and for always being there when I needed you. To my brothers, Bill and Jon, you have left this planet to join our parents, but you will ever live inside my heart.

To my sister, Cherry (whom everyone calls Cheryl), thank you for being my childhood reading buddy, my lifelong friend and sounding board, and a shining example for us all. Your and Don's undying love and support have kept me going through good times and bad.

Grandmother Willoughby Herrell, you always knew that I was special. Thank you for encouraging my curiosity, answering my endless questions, and for teaching me the names of every plant, flower, and growing thing in your vast yard. But more, thank you for being a veritable force at a time when women weren't allowed.

To my ninth grade English teacher Mrs. Lucy Harris, thank you for recognizing my gift with words. I wish I had understood the import of your revelation, rather than waiting a lifetime to start writing. To the college English Comp teacher whose name I don't remember, thank you. You raised my hackles *and* my awareness, and taught me to write an essay or argument that can stand the test of time. I only hope that holds true for novels.

To Andrew Post, Roland Yeomans, Eric Trant, Elliot Grace, and all the other authors and kind souls who read my blog, That Rebel with a Blog, thank you. Your feedback helped me find my voice, that elusive quality every writer must have. To you, I owe my writing life. Without you, this book would not exist in its present form.

For those who read the early versions of *Awen Rising*, your feedback helped shape the final story. Thank you to authors Liv Rancourt, Charlotte Gruber, Eric Trant, Lara Bujold Clouden, Amanda Helander, and Lauren Willmore; writing partner Debra Holm; and friend and fellow bodyworker, Janine Willey.

Thank you to Philip and Stephanie Carr-Gomm. Your book *The Druid Animal Oracle* provided inspiration for *Awen Rising's* animal characters.

And finally, to my publishing team, Editor Charlie Knight and Cover Artist Lauren Willmore, thank you for treating my manuscript with love and respect. You took *Awen Rising* and made it shine like a bestseller, and for that, I am forever grateful.

Table of Contents

AWEN:

*Life Essence, Inspiration,
Divine Creative Energy*

December 21, 2012

The scroll was delivered to the White House in the wee hours of the morning by an old woman demanding secrecy. High-ranking officials were summoned from bed, and after a flurry of activity, had declared the scroll authentic and "threat-free". Only then was the message copied and deciphered, the age-delicate original stored in an acid-free environment for preservation.

The president's polished shoes sank into the rug as he crossed the Oval Office. He had engineered a rare moment alone and used it to remove the file from the hidden alcove in the Resolute desk. Withdrawing its contents, he read through the report and studied the map at the bottom of the reproduction.

Outside Caen, in the north of France, was a town called Falaise. It was here the message had been discovered, under the ancient ruins of a castle that once belonged to William the Conqueror.

The cave itself was a significant find, containing pictographs and vault-like chambers that held an entire library of scrolls and tablets, and a treasury of precious gems and metals. But in an inner chamber, sealed away from all else, was a priceless sculpture of a woman with long, curly hair, flanked by an inordinately large hound and wildcat. In the photograph, the woman's arms were lifted to the heavens in supplication with the rolled parchment resting in one hand.

The president considered the lacy writing and the meticulously drawn symbols. Carbon dating and writing-style analysis had traced the parchment to the early eleventh century, corresponding to William's reign.

The Mayan calendar ceased its countdown today, making the find more significant. Translated, the missive warned of a world-ending event. The White House stood prepared for the worst.

But if truly a prophecy, it also declared the existence of a champion. And therefore, hope. He polished his glasses with a soft cloth and put them back on to reread the cryptic message.

When Armageddon threatens,
The sleeping one will wake.
Along the same meridian
The fallen steps in place.
One coast will gather light and kind
The other dark, despair,
But each will yield its suffering
To a world laid waste with fear.
The call will soon be answered
Old wounds doth fester e'er,
The battle begun before
Earth was wrought
Must be won in the helm
Of the sufferer's heart,
And from thence
She leaps forth
Once again.

The president slumped deeper into his regal chair and tapped the sheet of paper against his chin. The words meant nothing to him. He was a politician and understood legalese, not prophetese. But the nation's top minds were working on the cipher. With the clues supplied by the mysterious crone, he was certain they would come up with something of use.

The intercom squawked, jarring him back to his hectic day. He folded the prophecy and stuck it in an inside pocket, then replaced the file in the hidden drawer.

One Thousand Years Ago

The druid Awen focused on exiting Belafel's body and returning to her own. With a deep inhalation, she invoked the magical waters and separated from the mare. The spear from the battle had been expelled in the shift and floated nearby, handle up. Blood from the wound in the mare's haunch stained the waters a bright red.

Leading Belafel to the shallows, Awen examined the injury. In moments the rapidly-healing gash was gone, replaced by healthy tissue and hair. Patting the mare, Awen murmured thanks and released her to the wild, then turned to attend the fallen royal.

Mercifully, he'd remained unconscious for most of the difficult journey. His head rested on a mat of lotus flowers with his youthful face floating above the surface. The rest of the duke's body lay submerged in the pool.

Awen studied the finely chiseled features and wondered again that he'd been sent to her. Had she not intervened, William, Duke of Normandy, would have died with the others.

She had awakened at daybreak and known the duke was in danger. The tea leaves had given confirmation. Later, as Awen bathed in the pool, his gaunt features appeared in the reflection of the clear water. She'd gazed into eyes the color of steel and a knowing had come upon her: this man would unite nations and take all she held dear.

Of course, that was predicated on Awen saving him. She did have a choice. But it was a fool's choice and against Awen's nature to do otherwise.

She grunted as she drew the creaking mail from the broad chest and muscled arms and shoved it aside. Summoning all her strength, she dragged the duke inch-by-faltering-inch out of the water, then leaned close to probe for injuries. The wounds had closed, save those that kept him from waking.

3

With an ear to his bloody gambeson, Awen listened for the beat of life. It was faint, but steady. A good sign. Placing her cheek above his mouth, she felt his breath, shallow and hurried. Turning her face to examine William's color, her lips accidentally grazed his.

The eyes flew open, stared without seeing, and closed again. His body was waking but his spirit still wandered the Otherworld.

Worried he might not make it back from that dark, treacherous world, Awen touched her lips to his cold, white ones. The eyelids flickered. Encouraged, she placed her hands on either side of the handsome face and kissed the duke in the way of the druid: forehead, nose, chin, eyelids, cheeks, then back to his lips.

This time they were warmer and breath tumbled from them like the water that sprang from the rocks of Luftshorne. Awen waited, face inches from the fallen warrior's. But the death sleep was unrelenting.

Uncertain as to what to do next, Awen sat back on her bare heels. The glade would soon go dark. She must set a fire and heat the kettle.

But first to wake the almost-dead. Shaking the shoulder that had not been pierced, she urged, "Arise!"

The handsome head lolled away. Cradling it gently, she eased it toward her to repeat the kiss of life. This time, the princely lips parted on hers and strong arms snaked out to encage her.

Awen jerked away in protest, but her lips softened of their own accord and yielded to the duke, whose eyes never wavered. No veil could hide the soul of this man, no shroud could cover hers.

Betrayed by her own body, she melted into the warrior's embrace. Her heart thumped against his gambeson. His answered and beat in sync with hers; slowly, steadily gathering strength. When the heat between them was too much to bear, Awen squirmed out of the duke's grip, eager to escape the unfamiliar feelings.

Gloom had settled heavy upon the clearing. She must get him inside.

"Come," she commanded, ignoring the blush riding high on her cheeks.

William clasped her outstretched hand and let her drag him upright. With a long moan, he wobbled on unsteady legs. Awen crooked an arm around his waist and one step at a time helped the weakened leader to her simple hut.

His heavy-lidded eyes masked the effort Awen knew it must cost. The healing waters had mended his outer wounds, but the toll on his psyche was another matter.

William ducked through the doorway, swaying when she let go to close the door. Reacting quickly, she grabbed his out-flung arm.

"You're shivering," she exclaimed. "Can you strip out of those wet things while I light a fire?"

The duke got the tight inner-armor over his head and his knees buckled. He staggered into Awen and dropped to the floor, arms pinned overhead.

She bent to free them from the sopping gambeson. "We'll get you in bed, your grace. But first we must remove these wet breeches."

The duke rolled his eyes, but obliged. He pushed the lot to his knees and slumped back to the plank floor. Water sloshed from his royal boots as Awen shucked them off. The sodden breeches followed.

"That way, my lord." She pointed with her chin, eyes averted. A blush stained her cheeks as she helped the naked man stand.

He took two stumbling strides across the room and collapsed on the tiny bed in the corner. Relieved, Awen rushed to bolt the door and close the curtains, then added wood to the fire until it blazed. The chill hinted of an early winter.

She turned to the man draped across her bed and gasped. The young Duke of Normandy had fainted again, leaving the glory of his aroused manhood on display.

Awen shivered and covered her eyes. This morning's vision had not prepared her for the raw attraction that sparked her breath and made it ragged.

She hurried to the cot and arranged the pelts over the duke's frame, then leaned close to feel his feverish brow. William wasn't out of the woods yet. The night ahead would be critical.

**

William woke to a distant roll of thunder. Without opening his eyes he knew he was somewhere other than the Chateau. Then horror and grief tore at his heart.

Percival. Vesuvius. All were dead. Even Shaen, his page, brilliant beyond his nine years, had fallen to the murderers. How could William have survived? It was impossible.

Thunder rumbled, louder this time. A storm approached. But where was he?

They'd been traveling north with Vesuvius in the lead, on a hunting expedition in the wild lands. A gift from his uncle for his seventeenth birthday, William had been suspicious. But all had gone well for the first two days, and he'd lowered his guard. Then the heathens fell upon them, attacking his small party from all sides.

Ferrach had reared, taking a spear meant for William, then crashed to the verge. William had rolled free and whipped his sword from its scabbard. But an arrow knocked him rearward and a spear struck him in the back behind his heart. From there, William had no recollection. Was he dead?

Nay. A flame seared his back where the spear had hewn, but his heart beat strong. His shoulder ached where the arrow had found its mark. Yea, William lived.

But where was he now? How had he escaped? And how had he come to cheat death of its rightful quarry? No man survived such a mortal wound. Not even William, Duke of Normandy.

Yet here he lay, on a pallet of soft feathers with naught but a fur covering his loins.

A glance told William he was in a one-room hut that felt oddly familiar. And he wasn't alone. A woman huddled by a lowing fire. A great wolfhound lay at her feet and a wildcat curled in her lap. The cat's yellow eyes were trained upon William, alert and on guard.

He examined the room without moving his head. There was a door and two windows. Should need arise, he could escape.

But why was he here? Why was he not dead? And who was this mysterious woman?

Pushing up with great effort, William slowly maneuvered his legs over the edge of the bed, dragging the pelt with him. The room swayed and he felt slightly nauseous.

The wolfhound scrambled to plant its body between William and the maiden. She sat up in consternation, fire dancing in crystal-clear eyes the color of Oriental jade. He had seen those eyes before. In a dream, perchance?

"Who are you?" he demanded. "Where is this place? And what magic has kept me alive?" William swung his arm as if brandishing a sword. "My shoulder and back bear no mark. What magic is this that my heart yet beats?"

"Druid magic, my lord. I am Awen."

"A witch! I have been magicked by a witch?" William recoiled.

The woman leaned forward and held a candle between them. Cerise hair shot with gold tumbled over her shoulders and cascaded to a compact waist. Long-lashed eyes gazed into William's soul. Heat gathered in him. He stared, mesmerized.

She tossed her fiery hair and laughed. "A witch I am not. I am a daughter of Earth, as you are its son. My powers come from her and can be used only for good. You know this. You have the gift. Search your heart."

William tried to stand, but his legs betrayed him. He collapsed on the bed and studied the witch through narrowed eyes. Though alarmed, he did feel comfortable. Safe even, in spite of what he'd been taught of witches.

He closed his eyes and studied her energy. William felt no evil, nor malice. No duplicity, either. Still he was wary. The church despised pagans and had fought long and hard to wipe them out. How had this one survived?

"I fled my home in England," the woman answered his thoughts. "My mother and father were murdered, along with our servants. Luckily, other druids happened upon me: a childless couple leaving England. They brought me along and raised me here. Strong magic hides this glade. It can be found only by those who know it."

She paused and William motioned her to continue.

"I foresaw your uncle's treachery. He betrayed you and sent you riding to certain death. I could not let that happen."

"My uncle? It is no secret his loyalties lay elsewhere. But why would a druid witch care about my fate?"

She stared at a point just over his head. "This morning I dreamt of your ambush. You were killed by the spear that pierced your heart, bleeding out as one of your own turned his back. He betrayed you, Sir. And relished striking the killing blow, this man of fair face and foul heart."

William's guts twisted into a knot. He suspected he knew who had done the deed.

"Then Normandy rebelled and neighbor slew neighbor. The madness spread throughout France, England, and Europe, then on to the Orient and the rest of the world. Civilization fell and anarchy reigned as humans laid waste to our earth.

"So, Earth fought back. Great cracks appeared all over the land. Fiery pits opened and spewed lava until the sea boiled, and the air filled with fumes too harsh to breathe. Earth died. And took all life with her."

William stared at the sultry witch. Her story sounded much like the Armageddon prophesied in the Christian bible. But she couldn't be right. As much as he would like to think so, William wasn't important enough to have such an effect on history.

"And what has this to do with me?" he asked.

The woman blinked, as if waking from a trance. "Only you can stop it. How, I do not know. But the vision was clear. If you die, Earth and all she mothers dies too. I could not let that happen. So, with the help of a brave mare, I rescued you. And brought you here. The waters did the rest."

"The waters?" he hiccupped, touching the shoulder that had been wounded. "The healing Waters of Luftshorne?" The witch nodded.

"That's a legend," he sneered. But something had healed his mortal wounds. Something very powerful.

"Aye," she agreed. "A legend based in fact. When you're strong enough, I will show them to you. But tonight, my lord, you must rest."

Something in her dusky tone made William aware of how drowsy he felt. In the middle of a yawn, he tried to remember what he'd been going to say, then decided it didn't matter. He sighed, then sank to the feather mattress and burrowed beneath its soft furs.

On the precipice of slumber, a thought pierced his mind. He was in a druid's lair, under the spell of the druidess. He must escape, or all would be lost.

**

William woke with a start. The cabin was empty, save for him. Moonbeams played on the thin curtains and bathed the hut in a purple light. The storm had passed. And he felt stronger. A dulcet voice wafted to him from outside.

He rose and wrapped a pelt around his waist. What had the witch done with his clothes? His legs held and carried him to the side window.

Through parted curtains he spied the maiden in the center of the meadow, clad in nothing but a simple robe. It hugged her body and flowed to the rhythm of a slow, provocative dance. A fire flickered at her bare feet and she swayed, unaware William watched from the window.

A need sprang within him, so sweet and so sharp that his heart pounded against his ribs. Leaving the confines of the hut, he approached the siren, averse to interrupting her sensual dance but unable to stop his feet from advancing.

She turned in William's direction, slender arms twirling overhead, punctuating Celtic words he didn't understand. But her welcome was unmistakable. He reached for the maiden and let the pelt fall between them.

Awen swayed like a reed in the circle of William's arms, singing of the earth and its countless blessings. The tune filled him with something he couldn't name and memory stirred William's feet in long-forgotten steps. He gave himself to the primitive dance.

The melody washed over and through his body, entering the wounds the waters couldn't reach. One by one, William felt them heal.

Gratitude filled his heart to overflowing. He bent to graze Awen's lips, ending her song mid-verse. For a fleeting instant he was aware he was at the witch's mercy, then decided he didn't care.

He guided her to the fallen fur and settled her gently upon the curls that tumbled around her alabaster shoulders. Awen's eyes filled with hesitation and William faltered.

She pulled him closer. Slowly, he drew her robe from her shoulders and feasted on her beauty. Her body trembled as he traced liquid lines from her navel to her chin, then back again.

Breath ragged, William claimed lips as hungry as his own. The need poured between them and the kiss deepened. The world disappeared and all that existed was their exquisite, mounting need. With a desire greater than any he had ever known, William rose above the druid priestess and pierced the veil of her forbidden kingdom.

The fire roared, stoked by winds whistling down on godsbreath. Crimson sparks leapt in the night air to dance around Awen, last druid priestess, and William, the young Duke of Normandy.

It was an unlikely union. Awen was a witness to the obliteration of both her realm and people. William was a product of the ones to blame, the bastard destined to bring the veneer of civilization to an unruly kingdom.

Rain sprang from the mushrooming clouds. Eager grasses ripened on autumn's sharp tongue welcomed the benediction. The expectant sky exploded in a thunderous display of pyrotechnics and a bolt of lightning struck the oak beneath which the lovers lay.

Ripped asunder, the monarch of the forest shrieked, and thunderclaps shook the vault of the heavens before rolling across the land.

Faraway in Falaise, nobles bolted upright in privileged beds and peasants rose from rick and cot to wonder if judgment day was upon them. How close to the truth their suspicions lay, not one amongst them would guess.

For that night in September 1042, a noble seed was planted in fertile druid soil and blessed by elemental divine. The blending of ancient energies was wrought.

Humankind's hope would survive.

A Thousand Years Later

Emily Mayhall stared out the window, determined to ignore the letter. Below her the Pacific Ocean sparkled Caribbean-green in the early afternoon sun. A stiff onshore breeze whipped whitecaps on the waves and hungry pelicans dove for lunch, while the homeless of Venice Beach worked the boardwalk. Or at least, what was left of it.

Most of them lived in the block-long chasm that loomed in the distance; an area once known as Muscle Beach. Her team had been the first on-scene after that chunk of coastline had vanished. Emily shivered. It was one thing to chase disasters for a living. It was another when they happened in your own backyard.

In spite of her intentions, Emily's gaze drifted to the registered letter that mocked her from its perch amid the clutter on the counter. It had been there all week and at the postal store before that. Sighing, she decided she had suffered long enough. Opening it couldn't be worse than imagining what misery it might bring.

Rising from the overstuffed armchair, she crossed to the counter and lifted the official-looking envelope in the air. For the umpteenth time, she gazed at it intently, trying to divine the message within.

As usual, Emily divined nothing.

It grated that she'd thrown away precious dollars to develop a sensing ability Shalane had insisted she possessed. That she had listened to the shaman in the first place was part of the rub. Regaining the self-esteem her mother's tongue had taken from her was difficult enough. Avoiding others with the same agenda was harder still. On the surface, they looked like everyone else.

Emily eyed the letter. If it was a debt that hadn't been listed in her already-discharged bankruptcy, the creditor was up shits creek. That's what her Canadian friend would say if Emily were to solicit her advice. Of course, she hadn't. And couldn't. Not without giving her new identity away.

Dismissing the guilt, Emily ripped open the envelope and searched the solitary sheet of linen for an unpaid balance due. There were no numbers, just a request to contact the office of Mitchell Albom Wainwright III Esquire, whose address was in Atlanta, Georgia. The letter was dated January 11, 2042, more than a month ago. What did Mitchell Albom Wainwright the Third want?

She folded the paper, stuffed it back in the envelope, and tossed it on the counter. Outside, the surf broke over the jetty, sending spray dancing high against the blue sky.

The wave washed inland and surged back toward the sea, stirring a need in Emily that was palpable. It was a crystal-clear day and she could think of no better cure for the fear that plagued her. She needed to run.

Fishing sunglasses and a lone key from the bottom of her purse, she stopped to hug Ralph. He mewed and blinked sleepy amber eyes, pretending to be annoyed. His purring told her otherwise. She planted a kiss on the spot between his cheek and ear.

"Bye, Ralphy. I'm going for a run."

He yawned and stretched on the back of the armchair, then set about licking the fur she had mussed. He was OCD like that, a compulsive washer. The two of them made a fine pair.

Scanning the tiny apartment, Emily dug beneath papers to retrieve a worn headband. Only a few boxes dotted the floor of the three rooms. The furniture was gone except for the bed and armchair. The maintenance guy had promised to take those.

"Back soon, Raf-feller!" Emily called as she turned the two bottom locks and the deadbolt.

A damp wind greeted her, lifting curls the color of crimson and gold, and with them, Emily's spirits. Inhaling deeply, she savored the briny tang of the ocean air.

An aging gull landed on the railing beside her, mewing as if greeting an old friend. Another swooped down and started a ruckus, no doubt sensing a mark in the making. Disappointed when Emily had nothing for them to eat, they raced to the beach screaming challenges at one another before continuing the search for a handout.

Smiling at their antics, she braced her hands on the low stucco wall and leaned against it to rise on tippy-toes, stretching her calves. A long, high whistle shrilled from the nearby Bottle Brush tree. Amid its fluffy red blooms, a parrot mimicked Emily's movements, yellow head bobbing up and down.

She placed her foot midway up the wall, leaned into a thigh stretch, and squatted before stretching her abdominal muscles. The entire warm-up took only a minute, just long enough for more parrots to join her audience.

"Hello lovelies," Emily called to the chattering birds. She zipped her jacket and fixed the headband over ears too sensitive to endure the Santa Ana winds.

Fingering the Taser in her jacket pocket, she said a silent prayer she wouldn't need to use it and dashed down the three flights of stairs to the street. Turning away from the beach, Emily jogged a short block to Pacific Avenue and followed it to the park.

She was sweating by the time she entered the gates, but the cursed letter dogged her, attached to her psyche by a thread of her own weaving. Determined to outrun it, she increased her pace, counting to sync her breath to her stride, "One, two, three, four. Five, six, seven, eight—"

Her toe caught on a lifted corner of sidewalk. Quick reflexes and cat-like agility kept Emily on her feet, but she chomped down hard on her bottom lip, drawing blood. Crying out in pain and frustration that had nothing and everything to do with biting her lip, she ran even faster.

Though buckled and broken by myriad quakes, the neighborhood survived, unrepaired by a government that had run out of money and leadership long ago. Emily spat the blood in the sand beside the trail.

"Budget cuts, my ass." It was the bullshit reason they'd given for firing her. But it was really because Emily had identified a pattern in the chaos. No sooner had she shared her theory with her boss than she'd been out on her ass with barely a severance package to show for her years of service.

But not before Cyclone Charlotte literally ripped her fiancé from her arms. Emily pressed her tongue against her jagged lip, not wanting to think about Trey. He had saved her life, but it had cost him his.

"Think of the government. Think about Chester. Be mad, goddammit!" Her ex-boss, ex-friend, and one-time lover had sold Emily out. His betrayal wasn't limited to her dismissal, either. Chester made sure Emily would never work again by having her blacklisted.

She zigged around a barrier and caught a flash of movement. Yanking the Taser from her pocket, Emily dropped to a crouch, heart thudding. It turned out to be her favorite homeless lady, wearing layers of warring colors. Emily relaxed.

The grinning Maude waved and threw her head back in a cackle, revealing gums sporting nary a tooth. Pocketing her weapon, Emily hailed the leather-faced woman and left the erstwhile actress with a crumpled dollar bill.

A fresh gust of wind whipped the flags overhead. They were stacked atop one another and lowered to half-mast. Who had died? Keeping up with politics was a past-time Emily had never pursued. Or politicians, either.

"Actors, now, are a different story," she muttered to herself, passing the building Caleb MacLaine had reclaimed. She eyed the Einstein posit emblazoned on the side: "Imagination is More Important than Knowledge."

As a scientist, Emily had no trouble with Einstein's theories of motion and relativity, or even gravitational waves and wormholes. But she couldn't fathom how this maxim could possibly be true. Seeking knowledge had been her lifelong pursuit.

At the Muscle Beach Chasm, she detoured through an alley between two mansions. Riotous masses of coastal geraniums and hot-pink bougainvillea spilled over every surface of the patio to her right.

On her left, coastal oaks trailed Spanish moss. One had been given a whimsical face, complete with lips and nose. She waved to the tree-man, grateful Venice Beach had mostly been spared.

Many coastal cities were wiped out completely, leaving gaping sinkholes and putrid pits of ash and rubble and dirty salt water. Chunks of the California coastline had succumbed to the advancing sea. Nearby Manhattan and Huntington Beaches were both gone, with a million people lost and presumed dead.

Emily had worked those disasters and consulted on others. Pre-Charlotte. Pre-Trey. She had participated in recoveries around the globe, even led a few.

She'd been told she was bossy, but got the job done, working longer and harder than most of her peers. Until six months ago when she'd been handed her walking papers. She snorted with disgust. She'd had her fill of studying disasters anyway.

Which really only meant Emily had lost her nerve.

She cut across an eerily-vacant Bel Air Avenue, fingers gripping the Taser in her pocket. Had more of the locals packed up and left? Many wouldn't, or couldn't, in spite of the continued and constant warnings.

Either they'd fooled themselves into thinking the worst was over or prayed it wouldn't happen to them. Shame stung Emily, knowing she could be counted in their number.

At the precarious shortcut, she slowed to pick her way through the debris to the beach, then jogged a while in the shifting sand. All but the ocean and its wildlife faded. Gulls cavorted in the crashing waves and pelicans dove for an afternoon meal. The salty spray soothed Emily's soul. The sun coaxed a smile to her lips.

Then the stench of old death assaulted her senses and she stumbled and retched. Unable to not look, Emily bit back a sob for the innocent sea lion rotting on the beach, even as her rapidly-sorting, cataloguing brain compared the reek of old death to the shambles of her life at the present.

"Shut up, dammit," she cried in anguish.

Keeping an eye out for obstacles, she settled into a blistering pace, anxious to escape both life and death. It was something Emily pondered a lot—escape. Change your name, use cash, stay off the grid. With a new identity and tricks her mother had perfected, even a novice could disappear.

So, reeling from Trey's death and Shalane's unwanted advances, Emily had assumed a new identity. One taken from the ledger in her mother's box. She had chosen the first name on a long list of aliases they used over the years, and Ebby Panera became Emily Mayhall.

But she wasn't her mother and living this way felt wrong. On New Year's Eve, alone and lonely, Emily had resolved to find her true self and to be it no matter what. So far, she hadn't a clue what that was.

Unease stirred in the pit of her stomach. She glanced over both shoulders and detoured inland. Unbidden, a puzzle she'd been pondering earlier snicked into place. Her mother's box, the registered letter, and the recurring dreams were all connected. They had to be.

The day she'd signed for the registered letter, Emily had tossed it on the counter unopened. But a compulsion to retrieve her mother's wooden box from its hiding place had seized her and wouldn't let go.

She had fallen asleep leafing through a remarkably-preserved papyrus tome contained within. Delicate hand-drawings of dragons, birds and animals, along with maps of places that no longer existed filled the pages in a flowing, lacy hand. The language was so cryptic Emily had yet to discover its origins. Not that she had tried very hard.

Upon falling asleep that night, the dreams had come in fits and spurts so urgent Emily woke in a sweat. Each time she had fallen back asleep, the dreams continued.

In every dream, she was a druid priestess in times gone by, fighting to save the life of one man. A royal who would be both her destiny and downfall. An unknowing diverter of disasters.

Clearing the last line of beach cottages, Emily faltered when a curtain of sand pelted her face. Sputtering, she brushed the grit away, along with the haunting dreams, the box, and the letter. She would think about those later.

She pounded the boardwalk, lungs laboring, and avoided the eyes of the few locals who scurried to let her pass. In the distance, her destination bobbed into view. Battered and shorter than its original length, the Venice Pier jutted reassuringly into the agitated sea.

Pumping harder, she ignored the pain that pierced her side and rounded the point. A woman with blond, flyaway hair appeared in her path. Unable to stop or even slow down, Emily plowed into her, ears assaulted by a sharp squeal as they tumbled to the ground. Fire shot up Emily's forearm as her palms bore the brunt of her fall.

Beneath her groaned a female version of the Pillsbury Dough Boy, eyes clenched tight. Fear turned Emily's innards to liquid and her adrenaline spiked. Leaping to her feet, she dashed away pulling her hood over her head.

Of all the french-fried luck. The woman she had bowled over was none other than her stalker, Shalane Carpenter. Shaman, sorceress, evangelist, creep.

"Come back, you fucking lunatic!" Shalane screeched after Emily. "Come back here, you—" Wind and distance garbled the rest.

Emily sped for the cover of the decrepit pier, praying Shalane hadn't seen her face. When the path dumped her on the far side of the jetty, she bent to gulp air, lungs blazing. On legs of rubber, and guts threatening to hurl, she sidled to a bench and doubled over in pain.

"I think I ruptured something," she gasped.

An unkempt veteran leapt from the bench, accusing eyes frantic beneath black, bushy brows. He backed away quickly, putting several cracked spans of concrete between them.

If Emily could have laughed, she would have. Instead she sucked in air and fought to keep from losing her meager lunch. She collapsed on the seat the homeless man had vacated and tucked chilled hands beneath sweaty armpits. Soon the fuzziness faded from her sight and she no longer felt like puking.

When there was still no sign of Shalane, Emily told herself the run-in was coincidental. The shaman hadn't known it was her.

Though far from convinced, a satisfied sigh escaped Emily's lips. The jog might have brought her close to discovery, but it had eased the unbearable tension building in her chest since the dreams began.

Slouching low, Emily stared at the sea. Waves broke angry against the reef a hundred yards out, whipped to a frenzy by yet another storm brewing in the Pacific Ocean. Swells upward of ten feet slapped the underside of the pier before rushing to the beach. Onlookers gathered to watch a pair in wetsuits battle the big surf.

Emily dug a fist into her side and groaned when the letter popped in her head.

"Go away!" she demanded, wishing her brain would obey.

It wasn't like Emily had any credit left to ruin. Not after losing her job and the resultant bankruptcy. She had a little cash from the sale of her stuff. But come Friday it was official—she would be out on the street with no job, no home, and nowhere to go.

And now, in spite of all her many precautions, Emily's stalker likely knew her whereabouts. She swiveled to search both ends of the boardwalk. No Shalane.

But her relief was short lived. The deeper, primitive ache of destitution twisted Emily's gut. She wrapped her arms around her scuffed knees and buried her face, willing the dam not to break. If it did, the tears might never stop.

"*Ahhh-wen.*" At the edge of awareness, a musical voice crooned the name from Emily's dreams.

Her head jerked up, startling a gull that was picking through a metal waste can. On a shriek, it took flight and wheeled toward the sea. Shivers danced along the nape of Emily's neck. Who else knew about Awen?

The number of surfers and spectators was growing, but no likely culprits there. Maybe it was a snatch of song on the salt-laced breeze. Or was Emily hearing things, on top of everything else?

"Stay in the moment," she muttered with a calm she didn't feel. "Now is all that matters. Those people are okay. That gull is okay. That homeless man is okay. Shalane didn't see you, so you're okay, too. Now quit the waterworks and stop freaking."

In defiance, her mind conjured the aqua clunker Emily had purchased after the bank repossessed her sexy little coupe. Tears blurred her vision and Emily rubbed her face briskly in her hands. The salt-eaten sedan had a large back seat. Which was good, considering her collision put the kibosh on her plan to seek refuge at the Venice Mission.

Replaying the crash in her head, Emily had to grin. It'd felt good to deck that sadistic bitch, even if by accident. Only now she would have to get away from here, money or no money. And as Emily Mayhall, she didn't know a soul. Not here or anywhere else.

A long-forgotten scent jolted her awareness and was gone before Emily could give it a name.

"Ahhh-wen." More thought than sound, the druid moniker tickled her inner ear. Baffled, she stood to search the boardwalk, the beach, and the sea.

A new and different foreboding crept upon her, more disturbing than Shalane or homelessness. Like molten metal, it trickled slowly down Emily's spine and spread through her body, triggering her instinct to run.

Water Dragon

At the end of Venice Pier, a dragon lurked in the deep water, tail anchored in the pylons. Draig Ooschu's eyes broke the restless surface, intent on the humans. She envied their bright-colored raiment as they paddled boards from the rocky shore and battled to the calm beyond the breakers.

Not one of the humans noticed Ooschu, whose scales and saucer-eyes reflected the ocean's hues. She was invisible to all but the most discerning, and even they wouldn't remember having seen her.

Like all dragons, Ooschu carried a built-in forgetfulness curse. Any species who gazed upon her forgot right away. All but the dragon master, though it appeared Awen had fallen prey to the larger memory veil.

As had Ooschu. Ooschu had no idea how long she had slumbered. Or what magic had lulled her to sleep. But she did remember that she answered to Awen.

Ooschu also remembered the last Earth War, when the dragons were tasked with keeping the humans in AboveEarth and the reptilians in UnderEarth. The memory veil was instituted at that time to ensure the two opponents would forget one another.

It had taken ten thousand years for the dragons to find and seal all the portals, after which they went into hibernation. All except the handful of Keepers assigned to watch the borders.

Draig Ooschu was one. As a water dragon, her duty was to guard the sea portals. There were three others—an earth dragon, an air dragon, and a fire dragon. But as time went on, even the Keepers had succumbed to sleep.

Since waking several years ago, Ooschu had crisscrossed the seven seas searching. She found Draig Talav asleep in a cave and managed to rouse the earth dragon. Together, they located

21

Draigs a-Ur and Tienu. But something was wrong with the air and fire dragon. Both were transfixed. Neither could they stir.

On the other side of the world, Talav stumbled upon the Awen's energy signature. With naught but a certainty that another Earth War was imminent, the two Dragon Keepers had pursued her ever since. Now time was running out, but Ooschu was close to making contact.

She poked her head above the waves to scan the shoreline and spied a blaze of gold-tipped crimson. The owner was bent double, face hidden from view.

"Awen," Ooschu called telepathically.

The woman raised her head and looked around.

"Awen," the dragon tried again.

The flaming head looked directly at Ooschu, but the gaze held no trace of recognition, nor flare of comprehension. Instead, Awen leapt from her perch and sprinted north, covering the tell-tale hair.

Disappointed and confused, Ooschu struck out for deeper waters to avoid harming the humans. Treading lightly, she trailed the Awen until the woman turned inland and disappeared again.

Ooschu paddled beneath a pod of dolphins and spied a harbor seal struggling against the tangle of a discarded net.

Anger surged through her. The humans' arrogance would kill them all. Diving, she used a razor-sharp claw to free the pinniped. With no thank you or acknowledgement, the seal swam away.

Ooschu winced. After all this time, she should be used to the rude behavior. But dragons were sensitive, especially water dragons. And Ooschu was more sensitive than most.

The forgetfulness curse allowed dragon-kind to survive, and with them, the Earth and her many species. But it made Ooschu's life thankless, not to mention lonely. And infinitely boring.

Of course, lonely and boring were preferable to the precipitous end they all faced. The reptilians were restless and seeking a way out of UnderEarth. It was up to the druids and the Dragon Keepers to stop them. But with their memories lost,

AboveEarth was in danger. And only Ooschu and Talav had a clue.

Underworld Encounter

Her spirit guides woke Shalane in the middle of the night, which usually happened when they wanted to deliver a message. She would rather sleep than receive transmissions. But Divine never asked her opinion.

She sat up and stacked pillows behind her, groaning with each motion. Her back and head, hell, her entire body ached from yesterday's fall. Or from being tackled by a lunatic. One who'd dashed off without bothering to see if Shalane was hurt. Anger surged, hot and impotent.

She took several deep breaths until it passed, then prepared for meditation. On the third out-breath, Shalane imagined sending energetic roots into the earth and rode them down. Slicing through the bedrock, she descended the tendrils to their endpoint.

Once there, Shalane turned for the surface, but a flash of silver caught her eye. The size of a firefly without the blink, it shot toward her and stopped. Another light followed, joining the first to hover at eye level a few yards away.

Were they studying her? Their behavior indicated sentience, but her probe encountered nothing familiar. Shalane hesitated, then gathered to her full energetic height, bowed deeply and straightened.

"Greetings, beings. I am Shalane; sorceress, priest, shaman, and channel, beloved of Archangel Michael."

No sooner had the words exited her mouth than the lights vanished. Goosebumps crept up the back of Shalane's neck. She could no longer see the entities, but she sensed them, along with something else.

Nerves jolted, Shalane continued, "I reside above Earth, though my spirit travels where it will. Who are you, oh creatures of Earth's inner realm?"

No reply. No visible sign of the beings either. Time to leave. Shalane tried to ascend, but something held her in place. She couldn't break free.

Sick fear burgeoned. She was stuck in the Underworld. Shalane called on Archangel Michael, but her panicked pleas sounded garbled to her own ears.

Casting about, Shalane searched for what had trapped her spirit. Shimmering beyond reach, an amorphous blob pulsed in alternating shades of quicksilver, charcoal, ebony, and slate.

Was it fixed to the bedrock? Or translucent and hovering? It had locked onto Shalane's energy body. Her leg disappeared into the rock in some kind of vacuum.

She took a deep, centering breath and focused her powers on escape. The creature fell back, and her leg reappeared. But she was still stuck. Redoubling her efforts, she called again on Archangel Michael and felt a welcome surge of energy. The hold loosened and Shalane's foot slid free.

Shooting to the surface, she came to with a gasp in her own bed and opened grateful eyes to survey her surroundings. Everything was in its place and all was as it should be, though her body ached and she was trembling. From the room next door came Cecil's rhythmic snores, the reason they no longer slept together.

Shuddering, Shalane sank lower in the bed and drew the covers to her chin. Her failure to sense danger was worrisome. Those creatures had been intent on keeping her prisoner in the Underworld. Though her grandmother had warned her repeatedly over the years, Shalane had never encountered anything like this.

Afraid to continue the meditation, she rose gingerly and wrapped a silk kimono around her girth. She resisted the urge to check her reflection in the mirror. The extra pounds gained since Thanksgiving were a mystery. She had taken the pills her doctor prescribed and neither ate nor drank more than before. She got plenty of exercise, thanks to Cecil and her various lovers. Yet still Shalane's figure ballooned.

Making her way to the wet bar, she poured several fingers of her favorite Glenlivet. Cecil had stockpiled cases of the single-malt scotch before it went scarce and prices skyrocketed.

Sipping it like a liqueur, Shalane carried her glass to the expansive terrace overlooking the San Fernando Valley. The mansion's upkeep was monstrous, but the panorama was worth every penny. She sank into a fancy cushioned chair and pulled her robe tight against the Santa Ana winds.

Lights littered the valley before her. Traffic buzzed along the 101, speeding in and out of Los Angeles even at this hour. In the far distance, Shalane could just make out the light-trail that would be cars climbing the El Cajon pass, heading north out of the valley.

Behind her, the Pacific Ocean glistened diamonds under the moon, but no headlights there. That particular section of iconic Highway 1 had been gobbled by the sea.

Shalane rested her drink on the ledge of her protruding belly and thought of Ebby Panera, as she often did. The weight gain had started after the woman vanished. Was it coincidence or connected?

She'd had plans for Ebby, though fat good it had done. The woman had dropped off the face of the earth. Shalane missed her spunk and her keen intellect. And the trail of gardenias that always followed in her wake.

Gardenias. Wait. The scent still clung Shalane. Was the runner Ebby? Her thoughts flashed to the day before, to the whirlwind that had knocked her flat, giving her a slight concussion.

The fuzzy details sharpened into focus. The hair was different—an almost startling shade of red—but the compact shapely figure and the enormous energy belonged to Ebby Panera. Elated, Shalane put her glass on the patio table and danced around the terrace. She had found Ebby!

Or had she? It had happened so fast and Shalane never saw her face. But deep down she knew, and the certainty grew. Casting an imaginary circle, Shalane walked around it three times and stood in the middle, facing south toward Venice Beach.

"It's been too long, Ebby darling," Shalane muttered aloud. "You won't know this is from me, but you will wish for protection and that's enough for now. You thought you could run away, but no one walks out on Shalane Carpenter. Not even you."

Reaching out to the energetic universe, Shalane gathered a ball of ether between her palms and poured her intention into creating an Elemental. She cackled and widened the distance between her hands as the throbbing orb grew.

When the Elemental reached the size of a beach ball and threw off sparks the color of night, Shalane pictured Ebby on the boardwalk, crimson hair whipping in a gale. On a whispered curse, Shalane hurled the Elemental in Ebby's direction.

Satisfied, she reclaimed her drink and lifted it to the heavens in a toast. She took a long swig and welcomed the burn as the liquid raged down the back of her throat and blazed a trail to her stomach. Sweat beads erupted, and the faltering east winds cooled her brow.

Turning a slow circle, Shalane soaked up the view. She would miss this place while away on tour. Twenty weeks was a long time to be gone.

Nergal

Deep within the Earth's crust, Reptilian General Nergal watched the Fomorian writhe on the onyx bench. The creature had identified and tagged a human target, one that he hoped could be used to overthrow the humans.

As the information downloaded from the Fomorian to the main server, Nergal's anticipation grew. He tapped a clawed foot, picked meat out of his pointed teeth and checked the console again. The computer was taking a long time.

Uncomfortable in the laboratory, Nergal inspected his digits and scraped away the dried flakes. He admired the ripple of the new olivine scales along his three long fingers and opposable thumb. Most Dracos' claws were short and blunt. Deadly enough, but Nergal kept his meticulously sharpened.

A glance at the console told him the data wasn't ready. He sucked in his gut and ran his claws over his torso. The ventral plates covering his abs had peeled and shone a pale flax. He cocked a snakelike head and ran a foredigit up each of the bony ridges that flared from above his eyes to the back of his skull. He caressed the two top horns—reminders of his lofty status and the Elohim from which Nergal had descended.

The computer pinged as Vice Major Ishkur swept into the lab and saluted. Nergal returned the gesture and joined his assistant at the monitor.

Ishkur was shorter than most Dracos, though similar in appearance. He a larger head and vertically-slit black pupils rather than Draco red. Ishkur was a crossbreed, a scientist reared for its intellect, and an exception to Nergal's half-breed rule.

It was Ishkur who'd perfected Nergal's idea to harness influential humans to overthrow AboveEarth. But the targets kept dying. Time to find out if this one was viable. Ishkur's wide mouth stretched, his flat nose flared, and his eyes blinked rapidly as the target's memories tumbled across the screen.

"General, I believe we have our first success."

Nergal read through the scrolling data. It appeared the Fomorian had come through. Shalane Carpenter was an important human with a substantial following and a penchant for perversion. She was an evangelist, but also a sorceress proficient in both white and dark magic.

According to the data, she was born in a witch's colony in Northern California. Her parents were a well-known actor and actress who left the commune and abandoned the precocious child to her grandmother. She had risen through the ranks, stripping the leadership from older, wiser witches—apparently along with their clothes.

Nergal noted the last with interest. "She is strong, this human," he grunted.

Noticing something else, he glared at Ishkur. The target was a mixed breed, one of the religious zealots spawned from the reptilian-human matings.

It was part of the master plan to bend human light around Draconian darkness, but Nergal found the practice revolting. Admittedly, before the portals had been sealed, he had bed more than one human female in his youth. But his intention had always been recreation. Not procreation.

To Nergal and the few remaining purebreds, humanity was a scourge. Yet the reptiloids had been relegated to UnderEarth with the "lesser" races. Now, ten thousand years later, the Dracos had thrown off the memory veil imposed by the Old Ones and plotted to gain control of the entire planet.

They had almost succeeded a time or two, but one major obstacle stood in the way: the reptilians were as effectively sealed inside the globe as the humans were bound to the top of it.

Until now. By using influential leaders like Shalane Carpenter, they would manipulate the humans into destroying one another and opening the portals between the worlds.

Soon, very soon, the reptiles would take control of AboveEarth, and with Nergal in command, rid its surface of both humans *and* mixed-breeds. Then Earth would belong to the Reptilian Nation, once and for all.

News from Afar

S ince Emily's run-in with Shalane and hearing the eerie voice, the feeling of being watched was ever present. Something out there wanted her. Something, or someone, who knew about the dreams.

The wind had changed overnight. It howled, shaking the shutters and interrupting Emily's practice. She peered out the window, careful to stay hidden behind the closed blinds. Dawn crept over the seascape, revealing thunder clouds on the horizon. A storm was brewing, and it looked to be a bad one.

She returned to her yoga routine, the last she would enjoy in this seaside apartment. But rather than relaxing, her mind was busy planning Emily's future. She needed a home and a job. Disaster hound was out of the question; she would likely rabbit at the first sign of trouble. Plus, there was that blacklist thing.

But surely someone needed a scientist. Even one with a doctored resume.

By the time she made it to corpse pose, Emily was ready to make the call. She perched on the arm of the worn chair and entered the attorney's number in her iBlast, then mumbled a quick prayer.

By the second ring, a honeyed voice answered, announcing the law office of Mitchell Albom Wainwright the Third. Emily's throat closed around a wad of fear. The voice repeated the salutation, louder this time, and with less of a Southern accent.

Swallowing hard, Emily blurted, "Hello, this is Emily Mayhall. I received a letter from Mr. Wainwright. Could you please tell me what it regards?"

"Emily Mayhall?" The voice went up two octaves. "Thank you for calling. Please hold the line for Mr. Wainwright."

"Oh. Okay. I guess." She listened to the jazzy recording and stuck a finger between the slats to stare out the window. The red-feathered fronds of the Bottle Brush tree thrashed in the wind and scrubbed against the railing.

A husky voice clicked on. "Ms. Mayhall? Emily? I'm Mitchell Wainwright. Thank you for contacting my office. We've had one helluva time finding you."

Emily's thumb covered the mic as she sucked in a breath.

"You are the daughter of Janis Alexis Mayhall Mobley, as stated in your bankruptcy petition?"

An icy numbness stole through Emily's limbs. She had buried her mother a long time ago, along with the accompanying memories. That she had used her name in the bankruptcy proceedings now appeared to be a bad idea. But who would be looking after all these years?

"Who wants to know?"

"Are you sitting down?"

Heart thudding, Emily responded, "I am, why?"

"Alexis Mayhall married Hamilton Hester in Atlanta and bore him a daughter on June 21, 2012. I have the birth certificate in front of me. We believe you to be that daughter. Your father still lives in Druid Hills and would very much like to see you."

Like hell. "That's impossible. My father is buried in a cemetery in California."

Unbidden, a photograph popped into Emily's mind, the one she had found long ago in her mother's box. The box. The shot portrayed happy people around a picnic table at what appeared to be a family gathering. Her mother had a red-headed baby on one hip. A smiling man had his arm around them.

Her mother had snatched the picture from Emily, saying it was her best friend's family, taken the day her friend died. It made her sad, her mother said, and she wouldn't talk about it—ever. The photo had disappeared, but until Emily got older, she had pretended those people were the extended family she never had. One that actually liked and wanted her.

"This may be hard for you to fathom, but your mother left with you when you were four. Your father has been searching ever since. Last month we caught a break when Alexis's name popped up in an ongoing records search."

Emily's heart beat faster. They had moved countless times over the years, taking new names and discarding old ones like yesterday's underwear. Her mother had blamed it on debt collectors, and always gullible, Emily had believed her.

"Your father wants you home. At his expense, of course. Please, say you'll come. Mr. Hester's heart is set on seeing you."

Not knowing what to think, much less to say, Emily stared at her trembling hands. Maybe this was the answer to her prayers. Or it could be a load of hog manure. A trap of some sort.

"I am authorized to secure first-class passage on the next flight to Atlanta, should you agree. My office will make the arrangements."

Something stirred in Emily. A memory? Or the instinct to run? "Look, are you sure you have the right person?"

"You have a small, paw-print-shaped birthmark on your left lower shin and a scar beneath your chin where you had stitches when you were two. You have a dent in the middle of your forehead where your brother Sean hit you with a, um, stick when you were three," Mitchell Wainwright read.

Emily's thoughts raced. She had a brother. And that *was* her daddy in the picture. Her real father. *And* her family. She had known it, even at eight.

Thrilled beyond her wildest dreams, Emily jumped up and circled the room. Her heart beat a staccato solo, a million and one questions crowding her brain.

The voice went silky, almost smug, like the attorney had sensed her reaction from the other end of the phone. "Did I describe your identifying marks?"

Swallowing around a new lump clogging her throat, Emily admitted against her better judgment, "Yes. You did."

"Your father has been trying to find you for twenty-six years." Wainwright sounded relieved. "He wants you to come home. Let me send you a ticket." And excited, too. Probably in line for a big bonus.

Hot tears brimmed and trickled down her cheeks. Talk about a miracle! But she had to be sure. "Did you say you have a birth certificate?"

"I do. Check your email. My assistant sent you a copy."

"You have my email address?"

"We have current records, yes."

Her records. The bankruptcy. The foreclosure. The repossession. Her eviction, too? Probably her bank accounts, her medical history, and who knew—her pooping habits?

Emily opened her inbox and clicked the email to see an official-looking Certificate of Live Birth with a Georgia seal. The mother's name was Janis Alexis Mayhall Hester, the father's Hamilton H. Hester. The baby's birth date was June 21, 2012, 6:21 a.m. Her eyes were hazel, and she had tiny footprints. The baby's name was Emily. Emily Bridget Hester. Well, hell.

Opening another email, Emily stared at a formal portrait that had obviously been taken at an expensive studio. It was a couple with a baby—her mother and the man from the old photograph. The child he cradled had wide green eyes and a head full of fiery hair tipped with a halo of gold. That and the grin gave her away.

"Omigod. That's me." Through the slats of the faux-wood blinds she stared at the noisy parrots in the Bottle Brush tree. Her brain barely registered the thick clouds overtaking Venice. They pressed against the windows like a wet shroud, obscuring the seascape and cutting Emily off from the rest of the world.

Dread-tinged anticipation joined the sick feeling in her gut. Getting out of California was imperative now. She might as well go first-class.

"How soon can you leave?" Wainwright asked. "And do you need a car to the airport?"

"Yes, to the car," Emily said. "And I can leave today. I just need an hour to get ready." She looked around the room. She had tidied the apartment the night before and her few remaining clothes were packed.

"Excellent. My assistant will email your itinerary when the arrangements are made. I will see you at the Atlanta airport."

Emily ended the call and went to the bathroom to stare at her reflection. She inspected her eyes and smile, and the red hair.

Dyeing and straightening it had been a once-a-month ritual in the Mayhall house. One Emily had continued into adulthood, until recently at high-priced salons.

She had chopped it short and let it go native after changing her name. She stared at the unruly curls and strained to recall the first time her mother had straightened and dyed it.

A forgotten scene burst into consciousness and the weed of knowing bloomed in her gut. It was the night of her fourth birthday—the day Alexis had taken Emily from her father.

Nauseated, she sank to the toilet and rested her brow on the porcelain sink. Memories played across the theater of her mind, a thousand and one incidents, coincidences and lies.

Once upon a time she had known there was more and had ached for it with all her heart. The memory of that feeling was strong and visceral. But nowhere in the shadows of Emily's mind was there a whisper of the man with laughing eyes.

Possession

Shalane shivered. The salon was cold, but it wasn't that. At forty-five years old, hormones had her cranking down thermostats wherever she went. She trusted her team to take care of such details; they were handpicked to follow orders.

Her teeth chattered as ice coursed through veins more used to hot flashes. The cold penetrated Shalane's core and the shaking started in earnest. She wrapped her arms around her shoulders and doubled over, rocking back and forth to break the grip of the chill.

This time, Shalane had been meditating before the show. Another wave of chills tore up her back and neck. Cold sweat gathered over lips gone numb. As from faraway, the orchestra played the opening strains of her introduction. The crowd responded. She must get up. She must go on.

Shalane focused on the wispy threads of thought emanating from the crowd. She followed first one strand, then another, drawing energy from the emotion carried within each until the icy cocoon shattered and fell away.

With no time to spare, Shalane rose from the sofa and inspected her appearance. Her china-doll face appeared whiter than usual, her pupils too large. Platinum hair framed her cheeks and brushed her shoulders. Her cobalt robe hid a waist not as tiny as it had once been.

The robe was fashioned from the finest black-market silk by a generous devotee. For Shalane, the Exalted. She Who Grants Boons. She fingered the soft, hand-stitched material gathered at her neck and resisted the urge to rip it from her throat. She'd better pull herself together.

Shaking like a wet terrier, Shalane shoved the last tendrils of ice from her. The orchestra pounded out the crescendo. Thirty-eight thousand, five hundred, and twenty-three pairs of hands and feet clapped and stomped in unison, begging the Reverend Carpenter to appear.

She opened the dressing room door and hurried toward the stage. The attendant who had interrupted the trance by pounding on her door now stood guard in the hallway.

Shalane nodded and paused short of the curtain. She cupped her bejeweled hands and inhaled deeply from the vial of Dragon's Blood oil she kept for such purposes.

The applause swelled. The crowd shouted, "SHA-LANE, SHA-LANE!"

Gathering power to her like a cloak, Shalane thought of her adopted grandson Ned and a smile spread across her face. She stepped through the curtains, only to slam into an invisible wall.

Was that the roar of the crowd? Or had some outside force planted itself in front of her? She wavered, paralyzed, unable to move, see, or hear.

Commanding the force to leave her in the name of the Lord of All, Shalane blinked, and the world reappeared. An arena full of people stood before her shouting "SHA-LANE!"

Whatever she had meant to say was gone. Fear squeezed her throat shut. She invoked Archangel Michael and clawed at the otherworldly veil. She was God's emissary, was she not?

Out of Shalane's throat came a joyous whoop, followed by a blood stirring, "Hallelujah!"

Then she broke into her signature song and surrendered to rejoicing in the Lord. The audience joined in and the orchestra played along, kicking off Shalane Carpenter's First Evangelical Tour of America.

To her devotees, Reverend Carpenter appeared inspired. Unflappable. But fear burrowed inside the woman Shalane. Finding a spot behind her left eye, it drilled a hole and took up residence, leaving her orbit throbbing like an infected tooth. But worse was the panic rippling through her. What if she blacked out on stage? The consequences to the tour could be disastrous.

**

The human addressed an auditorium filled to capacity. Nergal's instructions to the searchers had been simple and explicit. Find a spiritual leader with psychic powers and a penchant for perversion.

Seeing Shalane in action confirmed Nergal's suspicion: she was the perfect vehicle for disseminating the Draco's plan to take AboveEarth.

The woman bowed and he sent a tickler through the Fomorian linked to her mind. He chuckled when she raised a fist to the heavens. The fool human didn't suspect a thing.

While she postured onscreen, Nergal reveled in his good fortune. He would delay notifying the Draconian Council and keep an eye on this one. The previous targets had proved too fragile. Nergal had an instinct about this one.

Stretching to change bandwidths, his claw halted mid-air. The woman's angelic voice was reminiscent of his forebears. Nergal was far removed from those hallowed ancestors, but the song reverberated in a wistful corner of his memory nonetheless. He'd obviously been stuck in this hellhole too long.

With renewed interest, he studied the screen. Something about the woman niggled at him. The melody rose and his vision went soft.

Rubbing his head to clear the fog, Nergal studied the round face. Tilted eyes barely contained large brown pupils split by irises on the vertical plane.

The scales on the back of Nergal's neck crawled. He knew those eyes.

Zooming in for a closer look, Nergal gulped. Shalane Carpenter was not just a human-reptile mix. She was a rare, earthbound Reylian. The Draco had known only one in all his years—his old consort, Camille.

Nergal had met Camille during a long-ago mission to AboveEarth. Afterward, they used an idle volcano chute to rendezvous until a double-crossing firedrake blocked the passage.

Much time had gone by, but Nergal never forgot his shameful attraction to the Reylian-humanoid, even after he heard Camille was dead.

Nergal rose from his seat, horrified. Was Shalane Carpenter a descendant of his consort? If so, the sorceress-priestess could be Nergal's indirect spawn.

Gagging, he staggered to the loo.

A New Start

Aswarthy man in a dated plaid suit and holding a sign met Emily and Ralph at the airport escalator. Now she stared out the window of the white limo and examined the miserable feeling swirling inside her.

She had known her birth father wasn't scheduled to pick her up. But Emily had not realized how much she'd hoped he would. And, not for nothing, but the attorney *was* supposed to be there. Even he left the job to someone else.

The weather had turned nasty in Los Angeles, but the sun shone in Atlanta and the traffic moved along fairly well. Sniffing back tears, Emily focused on the tents and cardboard boxes dotting the green space along the route. Housing for the displaced and homeless, she guessed. Here and there, decaying buildings were surrounded by chain-link barriers or left to the mercy of scavengers.

Just short of downtown, the interstate ended. Her driver looked in the rearview mirror and informed her a sinkhole had taken out all eight lanes of Northbound I-75. Emily cringed a little when they detoured through a crumbling neighborhood and moved at a crawl on the congested street.

She opened a game on her iBlast, hoping to take her mind off the depressing surroundings. But when she heard loud voices, she looked up. The light was green, but the limo was swarmed by a sea of bodies yelling in protest.

"What's happening?" she asked the chauffeur.

"Nothing, ma'am. Just street people looking for a handout."

Emily opened her wallet and extracted several one-dollar bills. The limo inched into the intersection. The rabble pounded on the glass. Emily tried to roll the window down, but the driver flipped a switch and it went back up.

"No'm. That's not a good idea." He frowned in the mirror.

"Unlock my window, please. I'd like to give them what I can."

The driver shook his head. "No'm. It's not ever enough, no matter how much you give 'em. And I promised Mr. Wainwright I'd bring you home safe." The limo picked up speed and the crowd parted to besiege the car behind them.

Emily stuffed the money back in her purse. The signs of deterioration were less obvious once they got past the horde. Fifty-five minutes after leaving the airport, the limo arrived at Wainwright's office.

The quaint three-story edifice faced a bustling street, across from the high walls of Emory University. Wainwright's assistant showed them to his suite. The driver settled Ralph's carrier and her luggage. With a gracious nod, he dismissed the tip Emily tried to give him and backed through the door smiling.

The assistant returned with a cup of steaming water and an assortment of teas, along with lemon, honey, and creamer. A few minutes later, she came back to announce the attorney was stuck in traffic.

Emily settled in one of the not-so-comfortable wing chairs and sipped Earl Grey while studying the décor. Classic style downplayed rich furnishings, as did eccentric touches here and there.

Most intriguing was a painting in which a full-canopied oak towered above a dark forest. A diminutive deer danced in the foreground before a cave that drew the eye to enter. Emily shuddered. Caves were not her thing. Nor was the dark.

She thought of her little apartment overlooking the beach. If she focused hard, she could almost imagine the cars rushing by on the street below were waves crashing over the Venice breakwater.

Her stomach growled and she checked the time. Where was the attorney?

She shivered and held her lapels together. She'd not been prepared for this kind of cold. Her coat was too thin and her shoes were open-toed, leaving her pink-tipped toes exposed.

A built-in bookcase loomed behind the mahogany desk. Emily circled to examine its leather-bound books and stone carvings. She reached for the closest stone and turned it over in her hand.

Flat and carved with a stick figure, she recognized it as a rune. What kind of lawyer played with runes? She traced the vertical line and top right-ray. Emily's rune-reading skills were on par with her divining abilities—basically nonexistent.

But she did know a thing or two about stones. Some of the runes were moonstone, others labradorite. Both were worth a pretty penny on the open market. Like gems, the price of semi-precious stones outstripped many currencies.

She shuffled through the runes and noticed something else. The lines were similar to the hand-written symbols in the manuscript in her mother's box. Emily weighed one in each hand. Could there be a connection? She placed one over each closed eyelid and let the cool, polished surfaces calm her rising irritation.

Her stomach growled louder and her composure crumbled. Where was Mitchell Fucking Wainwright? She put the stones on the shelf and flounced to the outer office. She needed to eat thirty minutes ago.

"Excuse me, miss." Emily hated the high-pitched tenor of her voice. The woman looked up and beamed. "Will Mr. Wainwright be here soon? I'm sure Ralph's ready to get out of his cage, and I haven't eaten since breakfast."

"He just texted that he's five minutes away. I have nuts if that would help?" The smiled widened.

"No." Emily turned away, then changed her mind. "Well, actually, yes." The attorney might be close, but she had reached the weepy stage. If she didn't eat soon, the mean would follow.

The secretary held up a canister of nuts. "Tamari almonds?"

Emily thanked the woman and returned to the inner office, where she munched and wandered. She noted framed degrees and business licenses, awards, and even a medal from the USAF. Mitchell Wainwright had been in the service. Huh.

In a place of prominence on the wall in front of the mahogany desk hung a large portrait of Wainwright in a judge's robe. He was flanked by an older couple, his parents Emily assumed. The woman was adoring, the man cold and distant. She could imagine the attorney sitting at his desk, reliving what would have been a glory moment, tempered by a taciturn father.

A picture-lined alcove led to a window that had been left slightly ajar. The sound of drums drew Emily's gaze. Against the high walls of Emory, a band of scruffy Rastas grinned and played. She bounced to the rhythm and smiled when the youngest finished a solo with toothy flair.

The sun pierced a cloud and glinted off a frame. The picture was of a young boy held aloft by a man and displaying a stringer of fish. Emily leaned closer, surprised that it was the man from her mother's photograph. She looked from boy to man and back again. Their eyes were the same. But what would her birth father be doing with the attorney? Were the Wainwrights family friends?

Emily returned to the window. Clouds scurried across the pale blue sky and the sun rode low. A BMW convertible, sleek and sexy, cleared a security gate and screeched into the parking lot on two wheels. Mitchell Wainwright. Emily would bet her last dollar.

The top went up and the door opened. A man with wind-tossed hair the color of sun-licked straw unfolded from the front seat. He tucked his shirt into tailored trousers, straightened a red power tie, and buttoned a svelte, charcoal jacket.

Emily approved. Suits and ties might be considered old-fashioned, but they were still apropos in her opinion. He hefted a thin briefcase and jogged to the entrance, disappearing from view.

**

Draig Ooschu rolled from side to side in the storm-fraught sea. No matter how keen her sensing abilities, the water dragon could find no trace of the Awen. Her trail had gone cold again.

Against her deepest instincts, Ooschu contemplated defeat. She needed help. But Draig Talav was on the east coast, as were the sleeping Keepers. If Ooschu could fly or walk, the nearest wormhole would be a quick trip. By water, it was thousands of miles.

Ooschu couldn't shake the vague premonition there was a faster way. But when she tried to focus, it eluded her grasp. There was nothing for it but to start swimming.

She sank beneath the stormy surface of Catalina Channel and headed south. She could ride the swift California Current to the tip of Baja, then turn north and make for the cleft in the Gulf of California.

**

Emily was in the bathroom repairing her makeup when the attorney finally pushed through the door of his inner sanctum. Heavy footfall announced his presence outside the bathroom door.

"Ms. Hester? Are you in there?"

For a moment, Emily froze. She met the reflection of her eyes in the mirror. Gulping, she mouthed, "you've got this", then fluffed her hair and opened the door.

Wainwright stood, jaw agape as if Emily was some mythical creature. A cherubim, or mermaid, or something of that ilk. Something the lawyer had never seen.

She, on the other hand, had seen the look before. Mostly from men. It was the hair.

When the stare continued, the heat rose in Emily's neck and face. An attorney should know better, especially one that had kept his client waiting for way too long.

The heat of cortisol surged through Emily's body. Her blood sugar crashed. And God help them, the mean took over. Her bottom lip pooched out and she unloaded on him.

"About time you got here. And one hears so much about southern hospitality. Do you always leave your clients waiting for hours? Bet you don't have many, do ya?"

Pleased when Wainwright's jaw dropped a half inch further, she flounced out of the bathroom and pushed by him. She reached the middle of his office, wheeled and planted her fists on her hips.

The attorney almost smiled, but the look in her eyes must have stopped him. Smart man. She could be dangerous when provoked. Lethal, if you factored in the years of jujitsu and aikido her mother had forced her to take.

Wainwright's ears reddened. "I am truly sorry." His tone matched his hue. "I did try to get the case postponed or expedited, but the judge wouldn't do either. If it helps, she took delight in torturing me all afternoon, then tore me a new one before we recessed."

Emily huffed, only a little mollified.

"I had every intention of picking you up at the airport." Condescension crept into the attorney's tone. "I'm sorry if you were inconvenienced." The dark eyebrows lifted. "You are my top priority, Ms. Hester, but you are not my only one. Did Rochelle not take care of you?"

"It's explanations I want," she spat.

The attorney winced. "How about I answer your questions over dinner?"

Now that was something Emily could get behind. Food. And answers. At last.

"Jocko's is not far. And I promise it's the best pizza you'll ever put in your mouth. What do you say?" He flashed a conciliatory smile, no doubt trying to diffuse the bomb ticking in front of him.

But…Jocko's Pizza. That was worth reining in the mean.

Emily blinked and tried her best not to glare. Failing, she looked down and mumbled, "I'm sorry. My blood sugar hit the floor twenty minutes ago." Looking up, she extended a hand, embarrassment warming her cheeks. "Hi. I'm Emily Mayhall. And I very much need to eat."

"Mitchell Albom Wainwright the Third." The attorney took her hand and a jolt of electricity sizzled up Emily's arm, straight to her heart.

Startled, she let go and backpedaled, retreating to the comfort of a purring Ralph, who eyed her from his cage. She had read about such jolts but had never experienced one. What did it mean? That this man was her soulmate? Surely not.

The thought sent an unpleasant shudder through her. She was certain the attorney had felt something, too. His soft hand had recoiled at the same moment and the blue eyes had sparked with astonishment, then something not unlike knowing.

A surreptitious glance told Emily he rifled absently through papers on his desk. What did the attorney know that Emily didn't?

**

Back in his quarters, Nergal perused the details of Shalane Carpenter's dossier. If reptiles could blush, Nergal would. He had never seen a human female with the voracity this one exhibited.

Nergal paged through the information, most of which pertained to her life after priesthood. There was little information on Shalane's family. He pored through the list of friends and acquaintances, cross-referencing ages and addresses, looking for a clue.

When he saw Camille's name, Nergal's lizard heart thudded. And when he found more references, it nearly burst from his chest. Camille had definitely been something to this woman.

Paging up to Shalane's birth data, Nergal found what he was looking for. Shalane Carpenter was born to Lila Snow and Lloyd Carpenter, but lived with her maternal grandmother, Camille Bernstein Snow, from age eight until age eighteen. This woman was descended from his Reylian lover.

A pain shot through his chest and he glanced at the syncranometer. It was not feeding time, so no hunger pang. Striding back to his PC, Nergal stared at the mixed-breed humanoid that likely carried his blood. The pain pierced him again, a dagger that twisted and ripped at his heart.

For one crystalline moment, the Draco knew—he was no better than the humans he reviled. But swift was denial. Hate replaced the aberrant weakness. Nergal slammed his scaled fist into the screen.

The mixed-breed woman repulsed him. When he was done with her, he would tear her to shreds, one excruciating bit at a time. Only icy determination kept him from pulling the plug now.

Shalane Carpenter knew magic and had a large following. Through her, Nergal could manipulate many humans. Then, when Nergal was done and AboveEarth belonged to the reptiles, the abomination would die. Along with all the humans and mixed-breeds.

Jocko's Pizza

Jocko's Pizza was an institution. Emily had seen it featured on a food network years before and added it to her restaurant bucket list. On the flight from L.A., she'd opened a magazine and there it was, one of the top five pizza restaurants in the country.

What the article failed to mention was that Jocko's manager was smoking hot, and as yummy as the pizza. He approached the table and spoke to Mitchell. But his eyes were on Emily.

"Good evening, Mitch. Glad you stopped by."

To Emily he smiled. "Welcome to Jocko's Pizza. Is this your first time here?"

She nodded, tongue-tied. He was just her type, dark and sultry with wavy black hair that flopped in his eyes. He shoved it back and extended his hand.

"My name is Lughnasadh MacBrayer, Lugh for short. And yours, mi'lady?" His black eyes lingered on Emily's lips.

"E-Emily," she stuttered. "Emily Mayhall. Nice to meet you, Lugh." She ignored the butterflies fluttering in her stomach. "I'm looking forward to trying your famous pie. Mitchell tells me it's the best pizza ever."

The pirate-manager beamed and nodded at Mitch. "So, we're told. Thank you for bringing Emily in." The aroma of steaming pizza preceded the waitress, who held it aloft in one hand. Lugh stepped back.

"Genevieve will take good care of you. But if you need anything, I'll be around. Enjoy." Eyes on Emily, he backed away.

The waitress settled the pizza pie on the tall holder and dished slices before retreating.

Emily took her first bite and sighed. "Mmmm." She rocked in her seat as the flavors exploded. "Mmm, mm, mm, mm, MMM!" Moaning, she took another bite.

By the third slice Emily was beyond full and stopped to wash it down with Coca-Cola. The pizza was living up to her expectations and then some.

The attorney fleshed out details in between bites of pizza and swigs of beer, but not enough to satisfy Emily. He would only say that his instructions were to deliver her to her new-found father's home, where all Emily's questions would be answered.

"Will I stay at the house or a hotel?" she pressed, thinking of her meager funds.

Wainwright smirked. "*That* I have been authorized to tell you. Your father's estate includes a carriage house that will be at your disposal. So, no, a hotel will not be necessary. You know. Southern hospitality and all."

Emily couldn't help grinning. He had cheek. She would give him that.

He steepled his fingers under his chin and watched her next bite with fascination. "So, I was right, wasn't I?"

"About what?" she mumbled, mouth full.

"The pizza being the best you've ever tasted."

"Oh. Well. At least second best."

The offhand remark earned her a searing scowl from Wainwright, and a concerned glance from the sexy manager who was behind the bar serving drinks.

She blinked coyly. "Possibly first. But at least second."

Mitchell Wainwright's square jaw dropped. "Not first? Really? You mean California has something that can beat this? Name it."

Emily grinned. Turned out the attorney was sensitive and didn't like to be wrong. She filed that away for future reference. But he did know good pie.

"I was a kid and don't remember. I *do* remember it was the best thing I'd ever tasted. Mama thought so, too, because I remember she raved."

Emily dabbed a pizza bone in parmesan cheese and stuffed it in her mouth. "This is kinda like that." She jumped when Mitchell slapped his hands on the lacquered tabletop.

"Because it's the same pizza. Think about it. You lived only a few blocks from here and you were four when she ran off. Old enough to remember pizza."

Though his remark rankled, awareness dawned. Emily thumped her forehead with the butt of her palm. "Shit. You might be right. Or…nah," she waffled.

She tried to shove the idea from her mind, but it anchored and took hold. Something ancient stirred inside her. A lock opened and a velvety richness spread through her body. She looked around the pizza parlor, seeing it anew.

"Why not?" Mitchell watched her through narrowed lids. "Jocko's opened in nineteen-seventy, long before you were born. That slice of pie you're referring to, little lady, was eaten right here in this dining room, maybe even at this table." He jabbed his thumb at his chest. "Which means I am right. Jocko's is the best pizza you ever put in your mouth. Admit it."

Emily crowed, "Dude! I've got chill bumps on my chill bumps! Do you know what this means? I remember being here. Maybe this whole fairy-tale malarkey you've been feeding me is true. I wanted it to be, but I've had serious doubts. In spite of that birth certificate and the pictures and whatnot." The attorney looked annoyed. "Those can be faked. I've seen it enough. But the pizza is concrete evidence. Omigod!"

Mitchell thrust an index finger at her. "Hold that thought." Smugness riding his triumphant lips as he whipped his cell phone to his ear. "Mitchell Wainwright."

The light faded from the intense eyes. The cornflower hardened to grey steel. Mitchell glanced at Emily and then stared at a spot just above her head. The bold features, expressive before, stiffened to stone.

"We're on the way." A quick gesture brought Lugh MacBrayer scurrying.

Butterflies bloomed in Emily's gut as he approached, black eyes fixed on her. A smile warmed his quixotic face. For an instant, she forgot both Mitchell and the fear-alarms clanging in her head. Then the attorney cleared his throat, recalling her attention.

"What's wrong?" she hissed in a low voice. "Why are we leaving?"

Wainwright ignored her and shoved a fifty-dollar bill at Lugh, who asked, "Is everything okay?"

Mitchell's brusque, "Not now, Lugh. We have to go. Keep the change," shut down any further discourse.

Skimming her coat and purse from the back of the chair, Emily nodded in apology to the handsome man. She hurried to the door and galloped for the car.

"What is it?" she asked again.

"Your father is in an ambulance en route to the hospital." Mitchell disarmed the alarm. "For everyone's sake, you better hope he pulls through."

Horrified, Emily fell into the passenger seat and fumbled for the safety belt. "My birth father is dying?"

Wainwright slid into the driver's seat. "We'll know soon. The hospital is less than a mile away."

But it was five after five and almost dark. Traffic was at a standstill. Wainwright tried first one street and then another, but each avenue was clogged. The attorney finally settled in the line of unmoving cars, mumbling, "Come on, come on, come on."

A haunting tune drifted from the stereo, familiar, but not. An electric guitar whined, an organ toned, and a plaintive voice warned a rabbit to run.

"What is this?" she asked the now saturnine man thrumming his fingers on the steering wheel.

Without bothering to glance her way, he mumbled, "Pink Floyd. Dark Side of the Moon," and shoved them a few car-lengths closer to the light. He almost made the yellow before slamming his brakes at the red. Emily's seat belt grabbed and held fast.

"Hey!" She rubbed her shoulder. "You damn near put me through the windshield."

No response came from the stony profile.

Glaring out the side window, Emily wondered what kind of mess she was getting into. A fountain caught her eye, shimmering silver in a grove of white trees. Then the light changed and the attorney punched the accelerator. She craned her neck, but the fountain and grove vanished when they cleared the intersection.

The sports car cornered a tight turn. Emily clutched the overhead strap and swayed, but in her mind's eye she was in that fountain on a summer's day, giggling and chasing an older, freckled boy with strawberry hair.

Chills crept up Emily's spine and along her scalp. She had been in that fountain as a little girl. Was the boy Emily's brother? Was that him in the photograph in Mitchell's office?

Palm Springs

After a bumpy start, the first day of Shalane's Evangelical Tour went off without a hitch. Every seat was filled. Overflow crowds crammed into two nearby buildings to witness a larger than life Shalane on closed-circuit TV. The rest huddled under huge tents dotting the Palm Springs landscape, watching on strategically placed screens.

For the most part, Shalane had managed to relegate her fears to the nether regions of her brain. But the headache persisted, progressing in intensity with each passing hour. White willow bark had dulled it enough to finish the previous day, but this morning her eye throbbed like a mother-fucker.

Inspecting wider than usual pupils, Shalane wondered if she might have a brain tumor. Fear blossomed raw, sharpening the agony. Desperate, she dug for the pain pills she had hidden in the bottom of her luggage. Just in case.

Catching her grimace in the mirror, Shalane sighed and shook her head. Why must she always be her own biggest critic? Breaking the seal on the prescription bottle, she removed a tiny yellow Tapentadol and chased it with a sip of spring water.

Her manager would be furious. He had said he never knew if one pill would lead to two, or two would lead to four. Or how many it would take before Shalane was off, running toward addiction, needing more, more, more.

This one was necessary, she justified. She couldn't hear God through a raging headache. Plus, what her manager didn't know wouldn't hurt him. Or at least he couldn't use it as a tool against her.

At the thought of her bossy, but sexy, manager, her twat twitched. She leered at herself in the mirror, then closed her eyes to "see" him better and tweaked her nipples until they were hard. She would like to use his tool all right.

But it was time to go on stage and give the people what they paid for—day two of a three-day audience with God. Channeling the newly erupted sexual energy through her root chakra, Shalane forced it up her sushumna all the way to her crown, before blowing it skyward through her stargate chakra.

Breathing deeply, Shalane allowed the iridescent particles of descending energy to suffuse her with golden trails of shimmering light. Fully charged, she strode from the dressing room, down the hall, and out onto stage without missing a beat.

Shalane faced the howling crowd, body vibrating to the roar of adulation; clapping hands, stomping feet, and voices calling Shalane's name as if she was the God they'd come to worship. Riveted by sixty-thousand hungry eyes, Shalane laughed—a deep, throaty yodel with, some would say, a donkey-like bray.

When the band rose to play the opening chords of *Hallelujah* and Shalane commenced to sing, a hush settled over the stadium. In rare form, she rendered a poignant version of her pièce de résistance, teasing the crowd like she would a lover, softly and sweetly, then finishing with a fiery frenzy.

The crowd went wild, wolf whistles and all. After another minute of tumultuous applause, the auditorium quieted.

Shalane spoke into the mic attached to her collar. "Welcome to the beginning of another glorious day with God."

The applause and catcalls resumed. Arms thrown wide, Shalane pushed back at the pain behind her eye and basked in the adoration.

The Hester Family

For the second time in as many hours, Mitchell Wainwright found himself speeding into a parking lot, this time at Emory University Hospital. His family, the Wainwrights, had helped build this place. Then, after the war in 2029, they helped rebuild it, erecting new stone walls that stood ten-feet high. When manned, it was a formidable fortress.

Good old Emory. Mitch's alma mater. The affiliated teaching-hospital was the finest in the country. It was also where, Mitch was convinced, he had been abandoned by his real father. The same birthday and hands were not the only things Mitch shared with Emily Hester.

A shadow flickered across Emily's shuttered face and fear jolted through him; a fleeting, yet alarming thought that she'd read his mind. Shaking it off, Mitch scrambled from the car.

If the rumors were true, Emily's mother kidnapped her to keep her away from magic. He and his cohorts were relying on that.

She caught up to Mitch at the elevator and crowded in behind him. "What should I do when we get there?"

"Do nothing and say nothing until I tell you."

Daggers flashed from the jade eyes. Emily wrinkled her nose, dug a lipstick from her purse, and used the mirrored wall to stain her lips.

Mitch kept one eye on the numbers flashing over the door and the other on his half-sister. Half-sister, bah! He lowered his eyelids to hide the familiar surge of resentment as the white-hot bubbles expanded to fill his chest.

In spite of the bitterness, Mitch had been meticulous in his search, and couldn't help feeling pride in finding Emily. The other firm hadn't come close in twenty-four years.

Now he was delivering his half-sister to Hamilton Hester, the man who had yet to acknowledge Mitch's identity, much less welcome him to the family empire.

Frustration fueled Mitch's hatred. It had taken all of his considerable acting skills to be cordial over pizza. Emily was the one person who had what Mitch wanted—claim to the Hester Empire and the Druid throne. But more importantly, the power that came with both.

**

Emily stepped from the elevator and ducked behind the attorney as a cacophony of sights and smells assailed her jangled senses. A muttering medic wheeled a man past them on a squeaking gurney. Sniffles rose from another left alone in the hallway. The smell of antiseptic mingled with the rot of illness.

At Emergency Admissions, a harried mother with two crying toddlers cuddled a screaming baby whose arm stuck out at an unnatural angle. An old man clung to a frail woman who wheezed and hacked, like Ralph chugging a hairball.

Ralph. Shit. He needed out of his carrier. Instead, she was at the hospital with skinheads and winos and sick people. She peeked around the corner of a wavy glass wall, where a baby cried feverishly in a waiting room filled to overflowing. The suffering pressed against her from all sides. Emily wrapped her arms across her chest and whimpered.

"We can't wait, dammit," Mitchell growled. He elbowed his way to the window, ignoring the protests from those waiting in line.

"I am Mitchell Albom Wainwright the Third. I need to locate Hamilton Hester. He arrived a short while ago by ambulance."

They were directed to a different desk by a flustered clerk. There they waited for an impatient ten minutes while the staff located Hamilton Hester.

Turned out, he had been admitted on arrival and whisked to surgery. More than that, the attendant refused to divulge, even though Emily was his daughter and Mitchell played both the attorney and the Wainwright-name card.

When they were on yet another elevator, heading for the surgical wing, Emily broached the subject of Ralph. "I need to

56

get back. Ralph's been in that cage all day. He needs a potty break." Remorse twisted in her chest.

"Good God, woman," Mitchell spit as the door opened. "Your father could be dying, and you're worried about a stupid cat. What is wrong with you?" He stomped from the elevator with a backward scowl.

Primed to give him a piece of her mind, Emily stormed the door Wainwright had entered. "For your information, Ralph *is* my family—" She stopped short. Strangers surrounded the attorney. They all turned to stare at Emily.

"Who is this?" barked a sloe-eyed woman cozying up to Wainwright. The strident voice belied her petite form.

"I would think that'd be obvious, my dear," another drawled. She resembled the first but was taller and heavier of girth.

The second woman glided toward Emily, merry eyes dancing and delight painting every feature of her face. "You must be Cousin Emily, come back to Georgia after all these years. Welcome home, Cuz."

Before Emily could react, she was engulfed in a bear hug. She fought the urge to struggle as her new cousin rocked her back and forth. She was released to arm's length for the buxom brunette to give her a once over.

"I know you don't remember me, sugar." Emily was sure she would recognize that drawl had she heard it before. "And I don't expect you to. It's been a long time and we were girls when you left. I'm Becca. This is my mama and your aunt, Morgan Foster. The mouthy one here is my sister, Dana."

Dana backhanded her sibling on the shoulder.

Morgan pulled Emily close and rocked her against her majestic frame. "My sweet Emily, how I have missed you." Morgan let go to beam at her. "The Hills haven't been the same since your mother took you away. But we never gave up hope. We knew our little wren would come home to roost. Now here you are, against all odds. And there'd be no mistaking you, either."

"Mama!" Dana gasped.

A frowning Wainwright cleared his throat.

"Spoilsports," Morgan grumbled, but her eyes twinkled. "Come meet the rest of your family."

"The whole family's here?" Emily squeaked. She hadn't expected to see anyone but her father. Not today. Not this soon.

The others leaned in Emily's direction. She fought the panic squeezing her chest. Besides Becca, Dana, and Morgan Foster, there was a tall, sandy-haired man; a thickset ruddy man, bald of pate and welcoming; and two young girls, one blond and blue-eyed, the other dark.

"Not all of us," Morgan assured. "Just those in the vicinity."

"I hate to interrupt the welcoming party, but can you tell us what happened?" Mitchell was as brusque as ever. Emily glared. The man's rudeness knew no bounds.

Morgan drew to a height that rivaled Wainwright's and stared down her regal nose into his cold, steel eyes. Her voice dripped with disdain. "My brother wanted tea and a game of chess. I was winning, too, until the bugger started clawing at his shirt collar and collapsed."

Emily's head swam. She hugged her purse like a life raft and leaned against a chair back for support.

"I had Mary call 911 and thank God the ambulance arrived within minutes. I rode with Ham, and Finn was waiting when we got to ER. They took him back to run tests, then into surgery fifteen minutes later."

Mitchell pressed. "What have they found?"

"They think he had a stroke—" Morgan's voice broke, and she fidgeted with a slender gold wristwatch. "That was forty minutes ago." Tears brimmed in Morgan's eyes.

"How bad?" The attorney almost sounded like he cared.

"It's touch and go. Finn says he'll give us an update once he's out of surgery."

"At least Grandpa is here at Emory." The sandy-haired man spoke. "If anyone can save him, it's Uncle Finn." He took a step closer to Emily. "I'm Sean Jr, your nephew. My daddy was your brother."

"Was?" The thrill Emily had felt since learning she had a brother snaked around her heart and squeezed.

"Daddy died two years ago. It was all very hush-hush, but I personally think he was murdered." He stared defiantly at the others. None spoke, but sadness and disapproval played on their faces.

Emily took his long hands. "Sean, I'm so sorry. I'm sad I won't get to know my brother. But I'm grateful to know you." She hugged her nephew. He looked like the boy in the fountain.

Over his shoulder, her eyes met those of the rosy-cheeked man. The two little girls nipped behind him and peeked at Emily. Sean squeezed her and let go. The man took her hand.

"I'm your Uncle Don, Morgan's husband. I was stationed in Iran when you were born, then Afghanistan after that. It's a pleasure to finally meet you, Emily." He bowed with a flourish.

Emily smiled. "Uncle Don, the pleasure is mine. Are these your children?"

The girls tittered. The younger, dark-haired one hid behind the older, who hid behind Don.

"You darling girl, no. These are my granddaughters. Maria, Sirona, come meet your cousin Emily."

The blond took a hesitant step forward, but the little one held her back.

"It's okay, sweetie. Emily won't hurt you," Don cajoled. "She's from California."

A light sprang on in both little faces and they rushed Emily, words tumbling out and jumbling together. "California! We love California! But the news said it fell into the sea. Did you live by the sea? Were you in the earthquake? What did it feel like? Was it scary? Is California still there? Did you get hurt? Is that why you came to Atlanta?"

When the barrage slowed, Emily addressed the eldest. "I'm Emily. Are you Maria?"

"No, I'm Maria." The youngest jostled her sister out of the way and thrust her hand and chest out.

"Well, hello, Maria. It's nice to meet you." Emily took the tiny hand and extended her other. "Then that would make you Sirona. Hello, Sirona."

The girl hesitated, then took Emily's outstretched hand and peeked up from beneath lush, dark lashes. "Hello," she whispered.

A doctor swept into the room, dressed in burgundy scrubs and reeking of apprehension. He was tall and lanky with spiky, walnut hair that sprouted around a face that would do a wolf justice, yellow eyes and all. Fascinated, Emily stared over the girls' heads. The doctor made a beeline for Morgan.

The little ones twisted away and squealed, "Daddy!"

"Mother," Finn uttered and stepped into the circle of Morgan's arms. The girls threw themselves at his legs. He patted their heads and looked around the room. The wolf-eyes widened when they fell on Emily.

He nodded in acknowledgement and said in an official voice, "Uncle Hamilton is out of surgery, but still unconscious. We ruled out a stroke. But he'll be in intensive care, at least until morning. You should all go home. I will call if anything changes."

Everyone spoke at once. "What happened?" "Will he be okay?" "What if he dies?" "I'm staying." "I'm not leaving."

Maria's high-pitched whine shrilled above the voices. "Daddy, is Uncle Ham going to live?"

The doctor bent to scoop Maria in his arms. "Sweetie, that's the plan. In the meantime, I want you to go home with Nana and Bop-Bop. You can see your Uncle Ham when he wakes tomorrow. Deal?" Finn tickled her under the chin and Maria giggled.

He handed her off to Don and lifted Sirona, who danced impatiently with her arms in the air. Finn buried his face in her silken hair, then set her back on the floor.

"You be good for Nana and Bop," he told them both.

"But I want to stay with you," Maria whined, leaning away from Don to reach for Finn.

The doctor touched his shaggy brow to hers. "Honey, Daddy's got to work."

"Please, Daddy. Can't we stay and help Uncle Ham wake up?" Sirona wrapped her little arms around his leg. "You know we can."

Finn glanced at Emily. "No, sweetie, not this time. You haven't had supper and bedtime's soon. Tomorrow's a school day, remember?"

He peeled Sirona's arms from his legs and placed them around his neck. He lifted her off the floor and swung her around, singing, "Good night ladies, good night ladies, good night ladies, I'm going to leave you now." The tune tickled Emily's memory.

"No!" Maria shrilled.

"Sweet dreams ladies, sweet dreams ladies, sweet dreams ladies…" Finn held the last note and planted kisses on both girls' cheeks.

Sirona relented first, but her words dragged out in a pout. "Ohh-kaay. If we have to." Then the girls promised everyone, including Emily, they would see them.

They left with Don and Morgan and Finn addressed Emily. "I'm Finn Foster, proud father of those two little vixens. And you're our long-lost Emily, come home after all this time."

Dana pinched her brother.

"Ouch!" Finn yelped, rubbing his arm. "What'd you do that for?"

"I owed you one." Dana cut her eyes toward Emily. "Cuz, this here is the great-hope of the Foster clan, Finn Hester Foster, Emory neurosurgeon-extraordinaire."

"A brain surgeon. Wow. It's nice to meet you." Emily was impressed.

The outstretched hand engulfed hers. "And you as well. Welcome to Atlanta. The timing sucks, but let's hope tomorrow is a better day." His demeanor was gracious, as were his words.

"Amen to that." Anything from Emily would sound trite or self-serving, but she had to try. "I haven't met my father, yet. But please, Finn, don't let him die." Tears rendered her last words unintelligible, but the yellow eyes conveyed understanding.

"We're doing everything we—" His voice broke, too. Swallowing hard, he continued. "You must be exhausted after flying all day and meeting this crazy family for the first time.

61

Why don't you go on over to Wren's Roost and get some rest. We'll let you know if anything changes. I promise."

Finn looked around at the stragglers. "That goes for all of you. Now skedaddle."

Carriage House

The attorney delivered Emily to Wren's Roost with a promise to touch base if her father's condition changed. Ralph was happy to be out of his carrier and found a patch of grass near the rear door. He did his business and scurried to the kitchen in search of food, none the worse for the cross-country flight and crazy-long day.

Emily opened a can of cat food she'd packed for the trip. Hungry meows and the scent of salmon gravy filled the air. When the can hit the floor, Ralph dove face first.

"You'll be fat by the time I make up for this one, huh?" Moist smacking noises were Emily's answer.

Grateful for her cat's familiar presence, she ruffled his fur and wandered to the front bedroom. She'd chosen the red room, as she had dubbed it, for its freshly-laid fireplace and the view of the forest.

The four-poster bed and flat-screen TV were both pluses, though other than WebFlix, Emily hadn't watched television in years. She unpacked her meager wardrobe and put it away in the chest of drawers.

Curious about her new family, Emily meandered through the house, delight growing. Antique furniture adorned with lace doilies, glassware, candelabras, and decorative vases were everywhere.

Cases held books and objets d'art, chandeliers graced the ornamental ceilings. The walls sported elegant paintings in ornate frames, metal sculptures, and earthen sconces. As nice as this was, the main house must be impressive indeed.

In the living room, an overstuffed sofa reigned supreme, with aubergine fabric that was invitingly worn. A cheerful fire crackled in the fireplace. Emily suspected Simon or Mary, of the couple Morgan had mentioned, were responsible. She made a mental note to thank them for the hospitable gesture.

Burnished oak gleamed under Emily's caress as she ran her fingertips along the intricate pattern of leaves and vines carved into the mantel. She touched the black-enamel screen, expecting it to be hot.

When it wasn't, she ran her palm over the heavy-gauge metal, enjoying its silken texture and marveling at the artisan's handiwork. Like many of the furnishings in the carriage house, the screen was a masterpiece. The carved wooden handles matched the mantel, and though it looked quite substantial, lifting the screen to the side took little effort.

She added logs from a nearby rack and used the poker from a matched set. The dry logs caught and blazed, filling the room with the delicate scent of cherry. While Emily worked, Ralph claimed a cushion on the hearth and curled in a ball.

"Cat hair be damned. Love me, love my cat," Emily mumbled. Squatting, she buried her face in Ralph's fur.

He had been the one constant in Emily's life since she'd rescued the lanky cat from a no-kill shelter. He was Emily's rock. Her anchor. Her companion. Inured to traveling, Ralph had that feline ability to land on his feet. Where didn't matter, as long as he was with Emily.

Now, she'd parked them in the Bible belt, home of the staunch conservatives that had commandeered the government in Emily's early years and dragged the U.S. into a war it couldn't win. Was she loony tunes for coming here?

The events of the day weighed upon her, crushing her beneath its weight. What had she done? Why had she come here?

Emily sank to the rug as anxiety rolled over her in waves, engulfing her in a riptide of fear. She drew a lungful of air and counted to eight before letting it out and sucking in another. She needed air.

Rising on trembling legs, Emily gave Ralph a squeeze and went to the red room to don her sweats and jogging shoes. She glanced longingly at the four-poster bed. If the run didn't help her sleep, nothing would.

Zipping her heaviest jacket against the cold, Emily transferred the Taser from her purse to her pocket. Wainwright had assured her the neighborhood was safe, but still. In spite of the early hour, dark had descended.

**

Alone in her dressing room, Shalane Carpenter took an ice mask from the freezer and held it to her face. Her eye ached like a devil-worm was eating its way into her brain. A quiet knock sounded at the door.

"Go away!" she snapped. The knock came again, more insistent.

"Open up, sweetheart. It's Cecil."

"Go away, dammit. All I ask is five minutes. Five lousy minutes, before you or anyone else rushes in to smother me."

"Five minutes. Gotcha," her husband said a bit too thinly. "Better yet, how 'bout I change and give you fifteen?"

Shame colored Shalane's answer. "That's great, baby. I'll see you then." Fumbling in the drawer for the pain pills, she dumped two in her hand and swallowed them dry.

Fetching an Erlanger, she tipped the frosty bottle and guzzled half. Some dribbled down the dimple in Shalane's chin. Wiping it, she collapsed on the sofa and held the ice mask to her eye.

She couldn't take the pain much longer. If it didn't end soon, Shalane would either die or kill someone.

Quoth the Raven

The wind's icy fingers tore at Emily when she stepped outside. Squealing, she shimmied and pranced on the landing, then settled into a quick stretch. The main house loomed before her, its impressive outline brooding in the dark. A single light glowed in an upstairs window. The caretakers must've retired early.

A hard-pack driveway led past the main house and disappeared in the dense forest. Trees crouched on all sides, looming above the long lane and concealing the houses from the world. The hardwoods were still mostly bare, but the conifers provided protection this time of year. Mitchell was right. The estate was an oasis surrounded by city.

Closing her eyes, Emily stretched and focused on the swirling energies. The neighborhood's vibe was calm and quiet, old and rather stately. By contrast, Atlanta felt big and bawdy, like Los Angeles had back in the day.

Loose and ready, she jogged down the unlit driveway and into the night. Turning right at the road, Emily retraced the route they had followed earlier. A dog barked and she crossed the street.

Glowing street lamps provided ample lighting, easing some of her apprehension. She paused at an intersection and looked both ways before loping across. The night was quiet, save her footfall and the peripheral sounds of the city.

Houses similar in size to her father's sat back from the street, yards professionally-lit and landscaped. A few hid completely behind imposing fences, some had a visible garage or carriage house. But none rivaled Wren's Roost. And none bore any sign of the ravages of marauders or gangs.

The few cars parked on the narrow street were late-model electrics and fission-hybrids. A dog woofed and Emily missed a step, nerves on edge. Another answered from down the street. Why couldn't the buggers be quiet like cats?

Her muscles warmed and sweat moistened her brow, despite the chill. Her worries melted away as the downhill curved to hug a babbling creek. Halfway up the next hill, her mind turned to the rude attorney.

Mitchell Wainwright had been charming at first. Emily had wanted to like him. But her father's attorney was an asshole. One that wielded some sort of power over her new family. The Hesters were afraid of Wainwright, and little wonder. The man came across as a little unbalanced with an edge of crazy.

A Jeep Traveler lumbered through the next intersection. Emily crossed and settled into a slow rhythm, striding in time to the city's pulse. A raven cawed, sending chills up her spine. The night darkened. Tree limbs rattled in a high, icy wind.

Alarmed, Emily turned and picked up the pace for several blocks. She reached the creek bottom where a fine mist crept along the ground. Her shoes dampened and her nerves unraveled.

This sidewalk was different, cracked and tilted, the yards overgrown and wild. The houses were small, shabby boxes lit by garish street lights. She had definitely not come this way. In windows hung sheets, or rebel flags, or nothing at all.

A rusting car leered from the driveway of a cinderblock house. Gang symbols scrawled across it in red spray paint. Hearing a fierce snarl, Emily skittered to the centerline just in time. A skeletal Rottweiler leapt at her, yelping when it slammed against the end of its chain.

She bit off a scream and executed a perfect pirouette to sprint in the opposite direction. Chastising herself for running at night in unknown territory, she fumbled for her cell phone and had a sinking realization. She'd forgotten to grab it from the nightstand.

Of all the things to forget. She patted the reassuring Taser in her pocket.

At the top of the hill, the fog disappeared and the neighborhood took a turn for the better. Emily charged toward the glow of gas lanterns, but the street ended there.

Ahead was a grassy knoll and an entrance to what appeared to be a park of some sort. This was all wrong. Adrenaline spiking, Emily's heart pounded. Tell-tale dots clouded her vision. She wheeled in one direction and then the other. It was all unfamiliar.

Houses lined both ends of the street with the park in the middle. Sweat beaded on her forehead and her exertion-warmed hands turned clammy and cold.

A dog barked. Another bayed in answer. They sounded close. Emily squinted in the three directions, cursing herself for leaving her iBlast at the house. Clamping down on the rising panic, she covered her face and retraced her steps in her head.

A wintry wind whistled down the avenue, thrashing bony branches and exciting dead leaves that still clung to the trees. The clatter rose to a shimmering crescendo, then fell silent. In the ensuing calm, Emily thought she heard singing deep in the woods.

Into the night, a woman's crystalline soprano rose, answered by a man's resounding vibrato. The words were unintelligible, but Emily found herself moving in the direction of the melody, her quest for home forgotten.

She stepped onto the trail and lanterns sprang to life at her feet, lighting her way. The wind shrieked. Dead leaves and dry branches rattled around her in a wanton riot, drowning out the song again. But her feet drew her onward.

Up the rise and down a vale, then up another she marched, following the snatches of song to a summit encircling a bowl-like depression. Skeletal trees circled the rim, arms lifted in supplication.

Urgency bloomed in Emily's chest; her life depended upon knowing what was happening down there in that hollow. She crept toward the edge and flattened her belly to the leaf-strewn earth, then crawled between the trees. Below her was the grove with the silvery birches.

Emily's eyes widened in disbelief. In the middle of the clearing, singers danced around the shimmering fountain. She was far from Wren's Roost, indeed.

**

Bran the Raven Elder blinked from his perch in the leafless elm. The Awen had finally returned to the magical stronghold of Wren's Roost. Long had the rogue druid succeeded in hiding her. Long had she been denied her gifts.

Now Earth's final hours drew near. If the druids were to succeed in stopping the Darkness, the Awen must awaken. Or else.

To that end, Bran had resorted to trickery. A rite had been assembled in the local grove. It'd been up to him to lure the new Awen to the glade. Here, the Animal Elders—the collective receptacles of the Awen's memories and magical powers— would confer them upon her.

Bran spread his ancient wings and circled the clearing, swooping low over the initiates to settle on the rim of the fountain. He faced the once and future-Awen and summoned the Elders. Animal magic pulsed through the clearing and smoldered in the hills, thrumming to the synchronic beat of the drums.

One by one, the Elders appeared—Shevug the falcon, Primus the lion, Cu the wolfhound, Muc, Torc, Cat, Tarv, Faol, E-ach, Corr, Art, Ron, Dobhran, and the others. All but the dragons did Bran muster; they answered only to the Awen and themselves.

The ghostly animals surrounded the dancers, filling the grove's sacred space. Magic rose into the night and hung like a veil, enshrouding the clearing and sealing the participants inside a magical world invisible to prying eyes.

**

In a semi-circle around the couple, fifteen robed figures chanted and swayed to a drum pulsing from an unseen source. A raven whooshed past Emily, drawing her gaze. It circled the clearing and landed on the fountain.

The maiden's song continued uninterrupted, low and sweet and haunting. The male's tenor answered, a deep, dulcet tone of longing and need. Tears sprang to Emily's eyes and sadness filled her until she was one big, throbbing ache.

**

The couple whirled, feet flying above the ground as the drums beat faster. When the dancers were little more than a blur, Bran let go a loud shriek that split the night. Halos of magic emanated from him and the other Elders. The hums, hisses, roars, and chatter joined forces, and the individual spells coalesced into a magical glowing mass that swirled overhead.

When it filled the hollow, a thin silver channel formed at the bottom, spiraling like the tail of a cyclone. It searched and found the woman on the rise. Attaching to her, the funnel anchored deep into her psyche, and with a blinding flash, the Awen's magical powers poured into the waiting vessel.

**

Longing pierced Emily's heart as she watched the play being enacted below. Only she was the girl. And it wasn't a play. She was wise and ancient, yet young and fair of face. The man was dark and ruggedly handsome.

They were drawn together by some irresistible force, then melted into one. Conscious thought fled as they were whisked away on a steed of black night. Through an inky sky they flew, memories flashing in kaleidoscopic fragments. A blazing fire. A thin white robe. Soft fur pelt. Thunder crashing. A coupling, wild and passionate. Then suddenly, violently, they were ripped apart.

Unable to hold the vision any longer, Emily's eyes flew open. Where the dancers had been, a multitude of ghostly animals gazed upwards—at her. The raven chattered and flapped in their midst. Emily recoiled and hid her face in the musty leaves. Surely she was seeing things.

But when she peeked, the animals were still there. One by one the apparitions bowed to Emily and disappeared. The raven cawed, loud and long, and took flight. As it did, the moon wavered and dipped behind a cloud. Dark settled, leaving Emily alone in the woods.

Lost and Found

The ghostly figures had barely faded when a series of high-pitched yelps exploded from somewhere behind Emily. She scrambled upright and dusted leaves from her belly and legs.

She didn't much care for dogs. In fact, she abhorred them. They tended to fall into one of three categories: too accommodating, too needy, or too freaking scary. This one sounded the latter. Just her luck she had to go that way.

But where was the trail? She shoved through a tangle of bare bushes she didn't remember and wished for her phone and its powerful flashlight. An automatic sensor flicked on at her feet and she nearly screamed. She followed the lights toward the barking dog.

Tree limbs formed a canopy overhead, menacing in a way Emily hadn't noticed before. The heebie jeebies grabbed hold of her, and she bolted, grateful for the sensors that flicked on at her approach.

When an owl hooted over her head in a cry that echoed the north wind, she ducked, half expecting it to turn into a ghost and disappear. Near the edge of the woods, she came to an abrupt halt. The dog had stopped barking.

Heart pounding, she held her breath to listen. All she heard was the wind in the dry leaves. Then a snuffle came from the bushes to her right. She wheeled as a tall creature parted from the shadows and reared to attack.

Emily juked and backpedaled, but the animal's huge paws landed square on her shoulders and knocked her flat. She yelled and wiggled free, only to be pinned again.

"Help!" she hollered, covering her face. But instead of ripping her throat out, the dog slathered her hands in wet kisses. Squirming away, she made it to all fours and leapt upright.

Pointing a shaky finger, she commanded, "Stay!"

Miraculously, the dog obeyed.

A kid bundled in a chartreuse ski jacket and stocking cap crashed through the bushes and grabbed the giant dog's leash.

"Bad Cu! Bad! Heel!" the boy scolded.

The dog did.

"Are you okay? Cu wouldn't normally hurt a fly. I don't know what got into him. I'm really sorry."

"Just keep him away from me," Emily snapped. But the dog whined forlornly. Its shaggy face looked like a terrier's, only it was tall, a good three feet at the shoulders. She touched its wiry hair with a tentative hand and scratched gently.

The boy wrinkled his nose. "I'm Brian. And this is Cu."

"I'm Emily. Nice to meet you." The prancing dog led them to the road. "Any idea which way Wren's Lane might be?"

"Thataway." The boy pointed in the one direction Emily wouldn't have suspected—the way she had come.

"Are you sure?" She edged away when the dog tried to lick her face.

"Yeah, it's near my house. Well, my uncle's. I'm staying with him. Want us to show you the way?"

Emily hesitated only a second. He might be a kid, but his dog was scary. It'd be good protection, especially through the run-down neighborhood. "That would be great."

Neither of them spoke for the first block, or the second. But as they crossed to the third, a dog barked behind them. Cu wheeled abruptly and galloped to the fence, dragging Brian with him. A car horn blared, speeding toward the intersection.

Emily leapt into the street and shoved Brian just in time. They landed in a heap on the shoulder of the road. Cu barked at the retreating car and ran circles around them.

"They almost ran me over!" Brian gasped, trying to stand. But the leash was wrapped around their legs. He stumbled and fell on top of Emily. Cu pounced, licking his face.

"Stop!" he moaned. He thrashed about and the leash tightened around Emily's legs. Cu's warm tongue found her cheek.

Cringing away, she snapped at Brian, "Stop moving. We're tied together and your bony elbow is jabbing me."

Cu danced to the other side and the leash loosened. Emily untangled one leg and then the other. Scrambling to her feet, she freed Brian. He stood, eyes wide in the purple street light, rubbing his shoulder.

"You okay?" she asked.

"Yeah. No. Cu 'bout yanked my arm out of its socket." He bent forward to stretch and laughed a little shakily. "And my bones are bruised from where you tackled me. How 'bout you?"

She fingered her sore chest and ribs. "I have an elbow-sized dent, but I'm pretty sure nothing's broken." Another car whizzed by, going too fast.

The cold wind penetrated Emily's thin jacket and her teeth chattered. She pointed toward Wren's Roost. "The house I'm staying at is over there. Want to come let me check you for injuries?"

"Nah." He tugged a cell phone from his yellow parka and pointed to the left. "I'm only a coupla blocks thataway. I'd better get back before Uncle Lugh gets home."

Emily stared at the wavy black hair and Roman nose. "Your uncle's not Lugh MacBrayer, is he?" The dark eyes grew bigger.

"You know Uncle Lugh?"

"I met him today at Jocko's. Small world." This day had been full of surprises.

"That's his restaurant. We'd better get going. He'll shoot me if I'm not home when he gets there."

"I'm sure he worries. Are you positive you're okay? I can walk you home." Maybe she'd get lucky and see Lugh. If she had known they were related, she could've pressed Brian for details. Like whether Lugh had a girlfriend. Or shit—a wife. Though he hadn't been wearing a wedding ring.

"Yeah, I'm good. Let's go, Cu. See ya, Emily." He tugged the dog's leash and they hurried down the street.

A vague disappointment gnawed at Emily's gut. "Be careful of cars," she yelled after him.

The kid threw up an arm as one growled past.

Emily turned toward Wren's Roost rubbing her sore breast. She jogged the last block, pondering the scary neighborhood. It had vanished without a trace. Like the singers in the park. And the ghostly animals. Where had they gone? Or was Emily going crazy?

She reached the dark driveway and hesitated. Was this the right place? There was there no security light. Or mailbox. The wind whipped around Emily and whistled down the tunnel formed by the tall pines and naked hardwoods. She was almost certain this was Wren's Roost.

Shivering, she followed the narrow lane. Limbs swayed and creaked, twanging her nerves. The driveway curved and the lights of the carriage house blazed ahead. Thankful, she jogged past the brooding main house.

"HOLY HELL!" she screeched, skidding to a halt.

An enormous striped cat leapt from the woods in front of her and crouched in the road hissing. Emily teetered on tiptoes, not sure what to do. The cat growled and arched its back, then ran to the carriage house and up the steps to pace the landing, meowing.

Emily drew the Taser from her pocket and approached with caution. The cat plopped in front of the door and eyed her expectantly. She mounted the steps slowly. The cat turned to lick its shoulder.

"You're kinda big for a house cat. But you don't act feral."

It ignored her and purred, busily washing its hindquarters. So, it wasn't a wildcat.

"Do you belong to a neighbor?" She moved to the side and gestured toward the driveway. "Shoo! Go home."

But the striped cat cocked its large head and stared at the door, at Emily, at the door, then back at her again. Like Ralph when he wanted to be let in. She let go an exasperated breath.

Getting lost at night had been freaky enough, the spectacle in the clearing more so. She'd been attacked by a dog, saved Lugh MacBrayer's nephew from death by car, and now the biggest domestic cat she'd ever seen wanted in her father's house. This, she had control over. Here she drew the line.

"Thank you for not attacking me. I'll bring you some food, but you are not coming in. This isn't my house."

The cat moved to let her retrieve the key from its hiding place. "Thank you," Emily cooed and opened the door. The cat shot through.

"What the hell?" she shrieked, chasing it down the hall to the kitchen. The cat buried its wide nose in Ralph's kibble dish and crunched loudly.

"You can't be in here."

Ralph trotted in and spied the interloper. He arched, hissing, hair on end and tail ballooning.

"It's okay, Bubbe." She bent to ruffle his fur. "I think this fella might be lost."

Ralph's growl changed from threatening to annoyed. He sniffed the air around the visitor, not sure whether to attack. Then the tabby stopped eating and sashayed over. Ralph hissed and stood his ground.

When the tabby crouched and folded its front paws beneath its bulk, Ralph moved between it and the bowl and mirrored its pose. His growl quieted to an anxious hum.

Unperturbed, the cat set about cleaning its body, starting with the wide shoulders and back. Ralph mewed a capitulatory sigh. The interloper ignored both human and pet as if this were its domain and it had every right to be here.

"Oh! Do you live here?" That was the likeliest answer. Maybe the cat was her father's. It was cold outside, so she would let it stay the night. She could find out tomorrow if it belonged.

Leaving the cats to sort things out, she dressed in the pink-plaid flannel pajamas she'd found in the dresser and slid her feet into matching fuzzy socks. It was ten-fifteen, seven-fifteen Pacific, but she was worn ragged. This day had been a doozy.

Her new-found father might not survive the night. Mitchell Wainwright had been a roller-coaster ride. And there was a tension present with the rest of the family that ran just beneath the surface. They'd been nice enough. But all was not as it seemed in Atlanta.

Adding wood to the fire, Emily climbed into the high bed, sighing when the mattress cradled her like a cloud. She smoothed the covers so that nothing touched her skin but soft flannel, then fluffed her feather pillows. Powering on the flat screen TV, she ran the channels with the remote.

Nothing caught her interest until she came across a California station. A powerful storm clobbered the Los Angeles coast. Overhead views showed water flooding the runways at LAX and an inundated shoreline up to Malibu.

Emily gasped at the footage of the storm surge pounding Venice Pier and splintering it to smithereens. When the camera panned to a wave overtaking an apartment building, Emily immediately recognized her Bottle Brush tree.

She leaned toward the screen, screaming, "NOOOOOO—" as the sea engulfed her building and kept going, sweeping inland.

The picture shifted to a scrolling list of shelter locations and contact information. Emily switched off the TV and hunkered beneath the covers. Her body trembled. If she hadn't agreed to fly out that very morning, she would be dead.

She wept for Maude and the homeless people living in Muscle Beach and prayed the authorities had evacuated them.

A scratch and a thud signaled Ralph had joined her in bed. She dragged him to her and hugged him close, rocking and crying for Venice and Maude.

Ralph squirmed out of her arms and kneaded the bed beside Emily's feet. She dried her eyes and shoved the images from her mind. She was on a slippery emotional slope already.

She couldn't think about this latest disaster. Not now.

An ember popped and whistled before joining the gentle crackle of the fire. Emily concentrated on the shadows on the ceiling and emptying her mind.

In spite of her twanging nerves, a blessed peace filled the room. Little by little, her frame relaxed. Soon, she heaved a sigh of release.

The last few days had been bizarre. Now by all accounts, she should be dead. But for the first time since Trey's freak accident, Emily felt safe. Why had she doubted? Why did she ever?

Ralph purred at her feet, and somehow Emily knew that the big cat in the living room was purring, too.

Discovery

The day had gone well for the paying public. As usual, Shalane remembered few details. She seldom did when channeling spirit. At her direction, the staff videoed each session, taking pains to film her from every angle. Shalane pored over these videos, ever amazed that God chose her to deliver his message.

Some called Shalane the Messiah, but she harbored no such illusion. The religious right asserted she was riddled with original sin. But in Shalane's world, sex wasn't bad. Or sinful.

Sterilizing and euthanizing undesirables? Forced abortions? Infanticide? Genocide? Slavery? These were evil. Buying up the world's banks to unleash financial collapse and ruin? Sinful. Fouling the food supply and manipulating the skies? Unconscionable. Killing the bees? A death knell for all.

But sex? What could be more natural? When the great Beings seeded Earth, they ensured the perpetuity of bloodlines by bedding many, not just one. Successful civilizations continued this practice into the last century. Kings and reigning monarchs of some countries still took several wives.

Add in untold courtesans, concubines, and mistresses, and the net outcome meant a rapid rise in the number of descendants bearing royal blood, thus ensuring the furtherance of those lines. Shalane had no such bloodline to further, but she figured what was good for the gander was good for the goose.

She fast-forwarded through the intro and the opening song to watch her entrance. Her arms were flung wide and a smile radiated from her glistening cheeks.

Shalane jotted a note to have Grace blot and powder her before each session, then studied her movements, looking for anything to hint at the raging headache held barely at bay by the blockers.

She saw nothing. What Shalane did see was Spirit taking over and using her, moving her about the stage, putting words in her mouth, delivering the message of the ages—the end is near, but do not fear. Turn to the Father in all your actions. Give Him your troubles, your worries, your woes.

Bring Him your burdens. He'll replace them with joy. Bring Him your brokenness. You'll receive new life. Offer up yourself and your possessions, He'll absolve your sins, no matter how heinous.

Live in the sunlight of the Spirit and the pardon would be permanent—with everlasting life in Jehovah's kingdom, a place of perfection, with no suffering, no wars and no death.

By the end of the recording, Shalane had half a page of notes. Not bad considering she had been hampered by the blocker, which dulled her senses as well as the pain. It was a good thing God was God, no matter how battered or imperfect the vessel.

Done with that task, Shalane opened her laptop to check emails. Not for her official persona, but her private account. The one she used to seek companions. Her favorite screen name was 1hotvixen and it had never failed to deliver.

Yes, Shalane had gained weight. Her sugar habit seesawed between out of control and abstinence, with little territory in between. But plenty preferred Rubenesque women. Whole dating sites were dedicated to finding the perfect "plumpy".

After her failure with Ebby, Shalane steered away from hetero women. Men, on the other hand, were eager to sleep with bisexual women, ever hopeful she would bring another lady for a threesome. Sometimes, when it suited her, Shalane did.

She surfed the prospects on several dating sites, preferring the thrill of conquest over the ease of the fuck-me sites. None of the candidates aroused Shalane. She clicked off, out-of-sorts, and plodded the short distance to the bathroom.

Stripping, she turned the shower on hot and stepped in, wincing when the water scalded her skin. The cascade beat against her shoulders and sensitive breasts.

Shalane plunged her head beneath the torrent, gasping as it seared her scalp and ears. Then she opened her legs, reveling in the heat. She lathered her body, paying special attention to her swollen clit, convulsing once, twice, three times, before rinsing and exiting the skinny stall.

She wrapped a heavy towel around her and peeked into Cecil's room. He snored, dead to the world. Closing the door, Shalane stepped to her cubicle and let the towel fall in a sodden heap to the floor. She inspected her body in the full-length mirror, not liking what she saw.

She had gained another five pounds and it showed. Combing her wet hair, she stared at her reflection. She was no longer the beauty she wished herself to be. Good thing she could fix it with magic.

Waving her hand in front of her face, Shalane watched it transform. Her eyes looked larger and sparkled with life. Her skin glowed, the sallow tint hidden behind the modest spell. Her teeth and nose were perfect. Shalane was beautiful to behold.

Satisfied, she climbed into the uncomfortable bed with a glass of wine and used the remote to power on the overhead screen. She wasted several minutes surfing hundreds of stations for anything that might lull her to sleep. There were infomercials, thinly-veiled lies disguised as news, and shows in which idiots did every stupid thing the emcee suggested.

In five short minutes, contestants swallowed mud, ate insects, dove into a vat of melted lard, and got slapped by an eighty-year old grandma in a wheelchair.

Craving something other than drivel, Shalane changed the station and gasped in disbelief. There on the monitor was Ebby Panera, sporting an unruly mane of jaw-length red hair. Splashed across the screen was the name Emily Bridget Hester. Was Ebby an alias?

"Well, I'll be damned. So, it *was* you the other day. Where are you, Ebby?" Shalane increased the volume.

"…the long-lost daughter of land tycoon Hamilton Hester was living in Venice, California at the time of her discovery, ending a twenty-six-year search. Miss Hester was kidnapped at the age of four by her mother, Janis Alexis Mayhall Hester of Nantucket, New York, during a trip to the local market.

"That was June 21ˢᵗ 2016, the heiress's fourth birthday. Mother and child never returned to their Druid Hills mansion where her father and family waited."

"Oh boohoo," Shalane snarked. "Where is she now?"

"Emily Hester's whereabouts were discovered by Wainwright and Associates, a local law firm, in what was described as an ongoing effort to locate the heiress. Details are sketchy, as are the facts of Emily Hester's hasty return to Atlanta."

Shalane's heart kerthumped. Ebby was in Atlanta.

"Sources say that Hamilton Hester collapsed hours before his daughter's arrival. Details are being withheld by the family and Emory University Hospital, an institution the Hester family has supported with sizable donations and endowments over the years.

"The prestigious School of Meteorology is housed in the Hester Building, funded in part by Hamilton Hester in honor of his commitment to the science. This is Dan Landover, reporting live from Emory University Hospital in Atlanta."

The photograph of Ebby Panera was replaced by a news anchor reporting on the storm in Los Angeles. Shalane watched for a few more minutes, then muted the sound. She tossed the remote on the bed and took a contemplative gulp of cabernet.

Ebby Panera was an heiress. Damn. And in Atlanta. Grabbing her eDroid, she accessed her schedule. Atlanta was six long weeks away. In the meantime, Shalane would recast her Elemental.

**

In a Draco's life the rules are simple—win you live, lose you die. This accomplished two things necessary for the survival of a space-limited species with long life-spans: population control and the continuation of the fiercest lines.

Nergal eyed his dinner opponent, a battle-scarred Ecthelion. The ugly creature's only chance of surviving until tomorrow was to kill Nergal. And that was not going to happen.

Circling the room on great, clawed feet, Nergal observed the lizard's movements. He knew its weaknesses and was about to pounce when a buzzing interrupted, breaking his concentration.

Nergal glanced at the hologram. A message awaited. The Fomorian was receiving new information from the woman.

When Nergal returned his gaze, the Ecthelion was gone. Groaning, Nergal wheeled on sturdy hind legs, regretting having heeded the computer. The creature leapt, sinking needle-sharp teeth into Nergal's throat. Pain lanced through him.

Reacting swiftly, he pried the strong jaws loose with claws of steel. He yanked and heard a grinding crack. Putting his back into the task, he tore the lizard's face apart. But dinner would have to wait.

Leaving the Ecthelion lying in a pool of blood, Nergal strode from the arena to his office. He activated the screen with a curt, "Receive incoming." An image of Shalane Carpenter appeared on the screen, caught in the act of magic.

"Rewind," Nergal commanded, "back to the beginning." Settling in his lounger, he licked his bloody claws clean. The target was watching a video of her performance from the night before. Nergal wagged his head. Humans were so arrogant. "Skip forward."

The recording changed to Shalane Carpenter conjuring an energetic spell to bedevil someone named Ebby Panera. Nergal paced his office, restlessness growing. Who was this Ebby Panera?

Hunger interceding, he returned for the fallen Ecthelion.

Catspeak

The crack of thunder at daybreak woke Emily from a deep sleep. Rain lashed against the carriage house, driven in sheets by a wind that alternately roared against the siding and moaned through the trees. Rolling to one side, Emily dragged the other pillow over her head and fell back to sleep in the swaddle of warm blankets.

It was after ten when she finally roused. Emily listened to the rhythmic melody of the rain and breathed in the scent of lavender potpourri and charred ashes. Wishing she didn't have to, she crawled from the covers, shivering in the morning air.

Sliding her feet into the slippers she'd scavenged the night before, Emily wrapped a throw around her quivering shoulders, bumped the thermostat up a couple of notches, and shuffled to the kitchen.

She set water to boil and opened the door for a meowing Ralph to go out. The tabby cat was nowhere to be seen. Did it know a secret way out of the house? Or had Emily dreamed the whole damned thing?

Back in the warming bedroom, she exchanged the throw for a long, fleece robe, also discovered the night before. She swapped the slippers for her worn knee-high Koolaburras and wished she could afford a new pair.

The teakettle whistled and she hurried to the kitchen. It was bright and cheerful in spite of the gloomy day. She poured water over the green tea leaves she'd brought from home and set it to steep in a thick, ceramic mug.

Gathering her journal and a pen, she took it all to the porch, a solarium with three Plexiglas walls that opened on a garden surrounded by woods.

Ralph spied her and loped to the storm door, eager to get out of the cold rain. Emily let him in and settled in an overstuffed armchair similar to the one she'd left in Venice Beach. Her breath feathered the air.

A tulip-shaped thermometer of the mercury kind registered thirty-eight degrees Fahrenheit. It had a ways to go to reach the forecast fifty-two. Sipping her tea, Emily blew out a breath and watched the tendrils rise.

Her iBlast buzzed and Emily jumped, anxiety spiking. It was a text from Mitchell Wainwright. Hamilton Hester was stable, but still in a coma. Mitchell suggested taking the day to settle in and asked if Emily needed anything.

Only to be left alone, though she refrained from saying so. Folding her legs in lotus position, she pulled a nubby blanket up to her chin, and cradled the mug in her cold hands. When a slightly-damp Ralph asked to sit in her lap, she put the mug on the table to make room.

Outside, the rain calmed to a drizzle. Birds lined up to take turns in a puddle occupied by a bright-red cardinal. It splashed with abandon, then flew to a branch. A cedar waxwing took its place. Delighted, Emily searched the bushes. Where there was one waxwing, you could usually find others.

Sure enough, the overgrown privets teemed. The top-knotted birds flitted to and fro in a feeding frenzy, gorging on the purple berries that had somehow survived the winter. The happy, high-pitched titter of their collective-trill penetrated the Plexiglas windows.

A thump from the kitchen startled her and Ralph. Birds forgotten, she scrambled from the chair.

"Who's there?" Emily opened the door to peek around. The mysterious tabby blinked up at her.

"Oh. It's you."

With an insulted meow, the cat wound through Emily's legs and padded to the sun porch to flop on the rug. A bowed and puffed Ralph hissed from the arm of the chair.

"It's okay, Bubbe," she assured the twenty-pounder. "You know it's you I love."

She sat, pulled Ralph into her lap, and buried her face in his thick, white fur. The rain beat down in sheets again, sending the birds to cover.

Despite her usual jumpiness, last night's feeling of safety persisted. It was an odd, but totally pleasant sensation. One Emily could get used to. She smiled, and noticed the tabby cat was smiling too.

A warmth bloomed inside her, like an oven kicking on or a sun bursting over an unseen horizon. Emily's smile deepened to a lopsided grin. Outside, a fat robin darted from the branch of a stately oak and landed with a splash in the puddle.

A floodgate let go, releasing a torrent of dammed-up emotions. Happy tears sprang to Emily's eyes. This place was perfect. If she tried to imagine a better situation, she couldn't. Other than having her father home and healthy. She wrapped her arms around her shoulders and hugged the foreign contentment close.

A sunbeam fell across her face. At the same moment the tabby leapt to the arm of Emily's chair, damn near parting her from her skin. The cat stretched its nose to Ralph, who returned the gesture.

When it presented its forehead to Emily, she reciprocated. The cat bumped her head, then startled her again by leaping over her shoulder, remarkably nimble for one so hefty.

Mushing the cushion, it lowered its girth to sprawl across the back of the chair. Ralph eyed the intruder with displeasure.

A squirrel darted across the yard, catching Emily's eye. It scattered the birds to lap water from the puddle, reminding her of last night's dream. The tabby shifted.

"It wasn't a dream."

Emily jerked up straight. The voice was feminine with a foreign accent as in last night's dream. Her heart pounded. Had the words come from the no-longer-purring cat?

"Of course, silly girl. Nothing wrong with your hearing, is there?"

Emily's stomach lurched. The cat *had* spoken. Which made it no ordinary cat. Or something very out of the ordinary was happening to Emily.

"Yes, on both counts," the cat concurred in a light tone. "I am no ordinary cat. And you are no ordinary human."

Emily whipped around to face the tabby, unseating Ralph, who was eyeing the cat with newfound interest. "This is not possible. Cats do not talk."

The tabby was silent, amber eyes staring.

"Who are you?" Emily demanded, more than slightly freaked.

"I believe the real question is: who are you?"

"B-but what is your name?"

The eyes blinked. "Yours first."

Irked, Emily hissed, "Emily Mayhall."

"Really?" the cat yawned. "Before you can know me, you must first know you, *Emily Mayhall*."

"Then what should I call you?" Emily snapped, "Madam Freud?" The cat looked down its wide nose.

"Nonsense, child. I answer to many names, none my own. You, *Emily Mayhall*, may call me Hope."

So, he was a she. With a French accent. And they had something in common.

Hope lowered her head, inviting a rub. Emily massaged the delicate cheekbones with her thumbs, working her way to the muscles along Hope's throat and behind her ears. The tabby's satisfied purr tickled Emily's fingertips. Ralph looked on, perturbed.

The doorbell warbled and Emily jumped, disturbing both cats from their perch.

Earth Dragon

The two cats hit the floor running. Emily opened the door to the kitchen and they scrambled through, skittering across the polished hardwood floor to round the corner and vanish down the hall to the back of the house.

Through the peephole Emily spied her new aunt. What was Morgan Foster doing here? She stood inspecting an elegant manicure, decked in skinny jeans and a leopard-print turtleneck that hugged her ample bosom beneath a faux-fur vest.

Removing the safety latch, Emily opened the heavy, metal door. Morgan was through and wrapping her in a bear hug before Emily could say hello or how do you do.

Releasing her, Morgan announced, "We're going shopping, get dressed. Those California duds won't keep a possum warm. You need clothes and Hamilton's still—um—sleeping." When Emily winced, Morgan added, "Your daddy's paying. Courtesy the lawyer."

The prospect of new clothes and warm shoes was tempting, but Emily was loathe to leave her safe haven. Especially in the rain.

"I've barely had tea," she protested feebly.

"Which means you haven't eaten either." Morgan's cajoling tone was oddly soothing.

Emily shook her head.

"Well get a move on, girl. Time's a wasting. We'll stop at the Lullwater for brunch, then pop on over to Lenox Square to get you some clothes. It'll give us time to get to know one another. Plus, I can show you a bit of Buckhead, Atlanta's crown jewel."

Emily kissed her do-nothing day goodbye. "Could you give me fifteen minutes to get dressed and do my face?"

"Of course, sweetheart. Mind if I fix myself a cup of coffee?"

"Not at all," Emily tossed over her shoulder. The woman had grown up here, after all.

First a talking cat and now a bossy aunt. This day was shaping up to be as crazy as the last. She paused in the bedroom doorway. A talking cat. With stripes and a fat, ringed tail.

Diving into the closet, Emily yanked her suitcase off the shelf and threw it on the bed. She opened it and ran a finger under an invisible slit. The false bottom opened with a click.

Withdrawing the antique manuscript from her mother's box, Emily placed it beside the suitcase and carefully leafed through the parchment pages until she found a picture of the striped cat. Like Hope, it was broad and shaggy, with yellow eyes set wide on a face that boasted distinct black markings. Coincidence?

Emily thought not. Anxious now to get away from the house and its many secrets, she returned the manuscript to its hiding place and dressed in a hurry.

**

By the time they reached Lenox Square Mall, Emily felt she had known her aunt forever. Morgan was charming and vivacious, and in spite of her age and having children and grandchildren, easy to talk to. Emily found herself filling in details of the missing years with something akin to relief.

Until Morgan brought up men.

"You never married?"

Emily despised the blush that stained her cheeks. "No. I've had a couple of serious relationships and was engaged once. Nothing else amounted to much."

"No one's swept you off your feet?"

Her tone was teasing, but Emily blanched at Morgan's unfortunate wording. She kept quiet about Trey and the awful accident. "Well. Put it this way: I haven't met 'him' yet."

"Ahh. The elusive 'him.' I was lucky," Morgan gushed. "Mine found me in high school. We've been together ever since. You're

young, sweetie. And you're right, he's out there. I promise."
Morgan patted her arm and pointed to a designer's sale rack.

"Look! What a pretty sweater. It's your color, too. You must
try it on. And, oh look, this one, too."

**

It was late afternoon when Emily and her aunt emerged from
the mall, arms laden with bags of outer, over, and under wear,
none of which belonged to Morgan. Across the way in a parking
lot, people waited in front of a food truck that blared Country
and Western music while feeding the homeless. Guards patrolled
the perimeter, stun-guns at the ready.

It was warmer now. The sun chased in and out of gathering
rainclouds that scudded across a bruised sky. A wind from the
south drove the storm, carrying the welcome hint of spring.

Emily opened her mouth to comment on the change, when a
massive groan rose from beneath them, like the bowels of the
earth were ripping apart. She froze mid-stride, flashing back to
her first encounter with the elusive Hum in Peru. Most had
never heard of the Hum, though it had been reported on for
decades.

To Emily it sounded like giant shears slicing through metal.
She shivered as the noise rose and fell to an otherworldly
rhythm. Shouts, barely audible over the screeching Hum, came
from the vicinity of the food truck.

Guards ran across the parking lot, rushing toward them and
the eerie noise. Emily turned to yell "run," but her aunt beat her
to it.

"To the car," Morgan bleated and broke into a jog,
surprisingly agile in three-inch heels. Emily bounded after her,
wincing. She longed to cover her ears, but her arms were full.

She reached the cold-fusion powered VDub. Shoppers
scurried past trying to escape the godawful racket. Others
looking dazed were swept up in the scramble. The guards
converged on the parking lot.

"*Ahh-wen. Ahhh-wen. Ahhh-wen.*"

Was Emily going nuts? She had heard a similar voice by the
Venice pier. And that name every night in her dreams. She fell
into the seat beside her aunt and shoved the packages in the

back. Buckling in, she mouthed a silent prayer of protection. The Hum had found her again.

Morgan threw the car in gear and hastily retreated. The parking deck moaned as they exited the lot and pulled into traffic. Twisting in her seat, Emily watched the scene unfold behind them.

Sirens heralded the arrival of first responders. Morgan braked for a fire truck that wove through traffic and passed, siren blaring. A news helicopter sped through the sky to join the fracas. Pandemonium reigned.

**

Talav ceased her subterranean gyrations to listen. She sensed activity, but not the druid Awen. Why had she rebuffed Talav's advances again? Did she not know the world hung in the balance? Or had she fallen prey to the memory veil she and Ooschu were experiencing?

"Why, oh why?" the earth dragon roared, not caring whether the humans heard. None would recognize it for what it was. Nor would they remember, if they did.

Not knowing what else to do, she bellowed louder, angry at herself, angry at the Awen, and angry she had no help. Ooschu was enroute to the east coast, but it'd be days or longer before she arrived, and the other Keepers still languished under the sleeping spell.

At her wits' end, Talav sent up a request for divine intervention. Her magic hadn't done much good of late, not where the Awen was concerned.

**

The parking lot disappeared from view and Emily faced forward, keeping an eye on the visor mirror. Another helicopter approached the scene. Civil defense sirens blared danger, warning Buckhead and the surrounding areas to take cover.

She glanced at her aunt. "That was the Hum!" Morgan ignored her to maneuver the rapidly-snarling traffic. "Every time I hear it, it scares me more," Emily babbled, riding the keen edge of hysteria. "That was a big one."

Morgan checked the rearview mirror. "If we're lucky, it's nothing more than that."

"What do you mean?" Emily clung to the overhead strap as they took a sharp right.

"Geysers, volcanoes, stuff like that."

Images of Managua danced in Emily's head. "No way!"

Morgan's narrowed eyes flashed. "I thought you said you're familiar."

"I am. Or was." Emily braced her feet against the floorboard, as they took another turn. "I left that job months ago. And haven't watched the news. Whereabouts?"

"South and Central America. Mid-US. Southwest Canada. None of them in a densely-populated area. Like here." Morgan's brow knit. "That would be devastating."

Emily mused out loud, "Then they're escalating. The Hum was never linked to geologic events before. None measurable, anyway."

Maybe she was wrong. Maybe it was coincidence. Maybe the Hum had nothing to do with Emily, despite having occurred in her presence seventeen times in the last two years. Eighteen months, if you subtracted the last six when Emily no longer worked as a disaster specialist.

But she was not ready to reveal that information. "What do we do now?" Her aunt was calm.

"Now we wake your daddy from that coma. This is serious business, sugar pie. We are not prepared to proceed without Hamilton."

The blood drained from Emily's face. Her hands went cold. "What do you mean?"

"I mean, young lady, that if your father doesn't wake soon, we are going to be in a world of trouble. More trouble than we can likely handle."

"What kind of trouble?" She wasn't sure she wanted to know.

"Earthquakes. Mass destruction. Annihilation. Armageddon. The end of the world. Take your pick." With each horrible word, Emily sank lower in the passenger seat and buried her face in her hands.

"Why did I know you would say that? Good God, what have I gotten myself into?"

"Seriously?" her aunt chided, slamming on the brakes at a stop sign. All semblance of southern sweetness was gone. "Seriously? You have no idea what's happening?"

Emily wagged her head, wilting more beneath her aunt's searching stare. No way could Morgan know about the pattern Emily had found. Or that the pattern may have something to do with her.

Her dad's sister let go a long-suffering sigh and punched a button on the dash. "Damn, damn, damn, damn, DAMN!"

"What?" Emily was relieved she hadn't told Morgan her theory. "What did I do?"

"Hush," her aunt ordered, with a stern finger to her pursed lips.

Finn Foster's voice boomed from the dash. "Mom! What's up?"

"The Hum is up, Finn. A big one. In Lenox Square's parking lot. Emily and I had just come out. I would swear it was right under our feet." Morgan glanced at Emily, who nodded confirmation. "The whole parking lot was vibrating and screeching."

"Damn," was all Finn said.

Emily and Morgan exchanged looks. Their sentiment exactly.

When Morgan spoke again, ice hardened her voice. "We can wait no longer. It's beginning, Finn. You know what to do. I will call the others and meet you at the hospital in an hour."

"Bring her."

Her? Emily? What did she have to do with this?

"Of course. You just figure out how to wake your Uncle Hamilton. I'll take care of the rest."

"Yes ma'am. I'll see you in a few. And mom? Is tú mo ghrá."

"Is tú mo ghrá, my son."

Obsession

S halane hung the "Do Not Disturb" sign and slammed the dressing room door. She sank into the chaise lounge and pressed a thumb in her eye socket. As long as she held the point, it felt better. When she let go, the pain rushed back.

She dug a bottle from its hiding place and dumped the contents in her palm. The pain pills were almost gone. She'd have to call the pharmacist in Laurel Canyon.

Taking two, she washed them down with a sip of water and fished for the vial from the local Cannabis Dispensary. She rolled a bead of oil between her thumb and forefinger and dropped it in the pen.

Holding the stem to her lips, she inhaled deeply, keeping the smoke in her lungs as long as she could. Her shoulders relaxed. Shalane took another hit and drew her legs up beneath her, ignoring what sounded like a tap at the door.

That doctor was a genius. The hashish was working. Her head still hurt, but she was beginning not to care.

Taking another toke, Shalane reached for the remote. The God stuff was boring her silly today. Maybe something worldly would help. She surfed the news outlets, stopping on the Atlanta FIX affiliate, eager for word of Ebby.

She straightened her legs and back, and stretched. Sitting in her throne chair for hours on end was bordering on torture. She hadn't foreseen that when agreeing to a hectic twenty-week tour. Not nearly enough down time had been built into the schedule and every event was sold out.

If she cancelled now, refunds would be due. And that wasn't happening. Shalane Carpenter would just have to buck the fuck up.

The crawl on the muted screen caught her attention. She snagged the remote and increased the volume, "...striking at 4:12 p.m. Eastern Time, the Hum occurred beneath a parking deck at Lenox Square Mall, an upscale development in Buckhead near downtown Atlanta.

"Minimal seismic activity has been reported, but the Lenox Mall parking deck and outer lot are closed pending further investigation. Stay tuned to WFIX for breaking news and updates from Lenox Square Mall in Atlanta."

Elated, Shalane muted the volume and leapt from the chaise to dance around the dressing room. Her Elemental had found its mark.

But her spell wasn't designed to produce anything called a Hum. She stopped dancing and paced back and forth. Spying the vape pen, she scooped it up and inhaled deeply. Too deeply.

The smoke expanded and filled her lungs until it burst explosively from every available orifice, searing her mucus membranes and wringing tears from her eyes. Spasmodic coughing wracked her lungs.

Fighting to breathe, she coughed and hacked, flopping on the chaise like a fish out of water. She put her head between her knees, only to leap up coughing and wheezing. She bent at the waist, tears streaming down her blazing cheeks.

When Shalane feared she might pass out from lack of oxygen, the spasms calmed enough to sip tiny bubbles of precious air. Anything more and she coughed again, which deteriorated into another hacking attack.

This was all Ebby's fault. Two people, ever, had gotten under Shalane's skin. The first was dead. She'd be damned if she let the other get away. Not again. Slurping water to soothe her throat, she coughed and thought of the day she'd met Ebby.

Innocent power had oozed from the petite blond, along with an air of sadness and mystery. Shalane had offered a private reading in which Archangel Michael confirmed her suspicions— Ebby Panera was the real deal and knew nothing of her powers.

Unwilling to listen to her guides' whispered warnings, Shalane had given in to her desires. She would have the fae creature, no matter what. She talked Ebby into taking private lessons, teaching her simple spells and treatments.

With each class, Shalane had fallen deeper and deeper, fooling herself into believing a romantic relationship was on the horizon. But Ebby had remained naïvely immune to Shalane's advances.

Shalane had picked and prodded, honing sharp edges and correcting Ebby's moves. In the name of perfection, of course. But the look on Ebby's face the day she snapped and walked out was etched in Shalane's memory.

Never before had her methods backfired. She'd tried to recant, but to no avail. Ebby wouldn't listen, or take Shalane's calls. Texts, emails, messages, pings, all were returned undelivered.

Finally, she'd driven to Ebby's house and found it empty. A sign declared the ocean-view property "FOR RENT." Ebby Panera had disappeared without a trace.

Shalane had collapsed into a monumental funk, realizing too late she was in love with the young woman. She'd spent several more weeks trying to figure out what had happened. Had she waited too long to make a move? Been too intimidating? Too dike-y? Too overbearing? Whatever the case, Ebby had walked out on Shalane and dropped off the face of the earth.

Until now. Ebby was in Atlanta. And soon, Shalane would be, too.

The Family Business

Emily changed into warmer clothes, pulled her data on the Hum, and stuffed it in her purse. With luck, she'd have a chance to talk to her aunt about it. She hugged Ralph and gave him a treat. The talking cat was nowhere in sight.

Emily returned to the car as Morgan finished a call.

"Aunt Morgan?"

"Yes, dear?" The response was preoccupied.

"A cat showed up here last night. A huge tabby cat. It bolted in the house when I opened the door and acts like it belongs. Does my father own a cat?"

Morgan's brow scrunched and she wagged her head. "We had a big tabby named Hope. But that was a long time ago."

"That's her." Should Emily mention the talking part?

"Hope died twenty years ago. Maybe more. She was old, even then. It can't be Hope."

"But she comes and goes like she belongs," Emily insisted, keeping the rest to herself.

Morgan hesitated, as if choosing her words. "Then, it's not outside the realm of possibility." A smile broke across the regal face. "If Hope is back, good fortune may be with us." The grin widened as they rounded a curve. "Yes, that would definitely omen well for our side."

Emily's flesh crawled. "Our side?" She flinched and waited for another grenade.

"You will know soon enough. It is not my place to share that information. But I will tell you this. You're with family, Emily Bridget, and for now you are safe in Druid Hills. Wren's Roost is well protected."

Her words held no comfort. Instead dread trickled through the holes the past hour had torn in Emily's new-found security.

Dusk threw a golden sheen over Emory as they drove through the campus. Imposing high-rise buildings, some brick, some marble and limestone, graced landscaped grounds and manicured lawns. Here and there, an ancient oak spread naked limbs over sidewalks crowded with students on the way to and from class.

They passed beneath an old railroad trestle that looked vaguely familiar. Had Emily seen it on the internet? Or was it another missing piece of her childhood? Two blocks later they arrived at the hospital.

Exiting the car, Emily smoothed the hip-length coat her aunt had talked her into buying. It had been a wild splurge, even with someone else's money. But it flattered Emily's figure, and was a chocolaty shade of brown that was hard to find.

The kiwi trim was a perfect frame for her fiery hair and the reflection of it brought the green out in her eyes. The soft, luxurious material caressed her sensitive skin.

"I'm so glad you got that coat," Morgan said on the walk to the elevator. "It couldn't be more perfect if it had been tailored for you. Is it as warm as it looks?"

"It is, Aunt Morgan. And thank you. Thank you for everything. For the shopping trip and your warm welcome. You've made me feel at home. I can't thank you enough."

"Oh, honey." Morgan stopped to take Emily's hands and leaned close, till they were eye to eye. "You are so welcome. If you knew how much I have wanted this, to take my niece shopping or anywhere else, every day for the past twenty-six years, you would know it is my pleasure. Now," Morgan steered her toward the hospital entrance, "let's find your daddy and my son."

**

Emily despised hospitals. Had ever since her mother was in one, face beaten to a purple pulp, one eye swollen shut, the other a slit. The man Emily had called her father had done that to her, a too-common experience until he finally stopped drinking.

97

They followed the signs to her birth father's hospital room, dread congealing in Emily's gut. "No Admittance" announced the placard on the closed door. Undaunted, Morgan shoved it aside to enter.

Stepping over the threshold behind her aunt, Emily paused. The group around the bed turned, faces lit. All, that is, except Mitchell Wainwright, whose lips curled in a sneer. She clung to the door handle, legs refusing to carry her any closer.

Morgan had no such qualms. She marched to the bed and squeezed between her son and her husband Don, whose arm snaked around her and drew her near. Behind them, an IV dripped, and electrodes communicated with monitors beeping quietly overhead.

Hamilton Hester lay unmoving in the bed, tanned, muscular arms at his sides. Was this the father she'd yearned for? He had a fine, chiseled face with a strong chin and high forehead. It was the face from the picture in her mother's box.

A headful of dark hair threaded with gray was framed by a slightly-receding hairline. His chest rose and fell, shallow but steady beneath a beige blanket.

Finn murmured something Emily couldn't hear and her aunt's demeanor changed. She grew taller and her shadow stretched up the wall, consuming the others.

Towering over the bed, Morgan commanded in the tone she had used earlier on the phone, "Hamilton, wake up. Emily Bridget has come home. Open your eyes. Look upon your daughter." Morgan beckoned her to the bed.

Emily clung to the door.

Morgan shook the man's lifeless shoulder. Nothing happened. Finn brushed a thumb across Hamilton's brow. The lids quivered and opened, revealing sleep-vague eyes the color of a Wyoming morning.

Emily gasped and stole a glance at Mitchell Wainwright, whose own blue eyes peered down at her birth father. Please, God, don't let them be related. The man in the bed lifted his head, searching.

Without thought, she let go of the door handle and moved into his line of sight. A duplicate of Emily's smile broke over the wan face, lighting it from within.

When he reached for her, the need to connect overrode her fear. She went to his side and the others moved to let her. Finn stayed put, thumb and forefinger resting lightly on Hamilton's brow.

"Emily Bridget." The whisper was hoarse. The hand that closed on Emily's felt cool.

"Sir?" she croaked past the lump in her throat.

"It's Da, a ghrá. Remember?" His eyes probed the web of Emily's thoughts. It tickled at first, then increased in pressure when she resisted. Overcome by a compulsion to let go, Emily relented.

A dam opened and memories flooded in. Of Da bouncing a giggling Emily on his lap to Ride-a-Pony. Da chasing Emily through the back yard. Da catching lightning bugs. Da tucking Emily into bed, singing in an off-key, narcotic tone. Here were her memories of the man with the laughing eyes.

Her heart overflowed with love remembered. Here was the father for whom she had grieved.

"Da," she breathed through tender tears.

She wanted to touch him, to know he was real. Careful to avoid the tubes and needles, Emily leaned closer and laid her face on his chest. His heartbeat was fast and thready against her ear.

His free arm drew her closer, holding on as if afraid she might break instead of the other way around. When he nestled his cheek on top of Emily's head, the tears gathered around the lump in her throat. He couldn't die now, he just couldn't.

"Welcome home, my child." His whisper tickled Emily's scalp.

"Da," she sobbed and clung tighter. He stroked her shoulder and made sweet, shushing daddy sounds.

"I hate to break up another family reunion." Mitchell tugged Emily's shirt, dragging her from the embrace.

Her father's hand closed on hers and tightened. He was stronger than she would have thought, given the circumstances.

She swiped at the tears with the back of her free hand. "Yet you did anyway. Thanks for nothing."

"Don't mention it," the infuriating attorney said without a trace of sarcasm. To the room, he announced, "In case y'all haven't noticed, keeping Hamilton conscious is a heavy load on Finn. Since you insist on this installation, let's get it done. Visit afterward, if you must."

Her father glared at the attorney. Emily felt somewhat vindicated.

Mitchell's hard expression softened, along with his tone. "This is apparently life or death, Sir. And not just yours. I'm sorry."

Lines curved around her Da's mouth. Even ill, his face was more tanned than sallow, evidence he spent long hours in the sun. Gunmetal peppered the stubble on his cheeks and dimpled chin.

He winked at Emily and her belly flopped. Something big was about to happen.

"Emily Bridget?" The reverence in her Da's tone sent chills up her back. "Emily Bridget," he repeated, voice stronger, "it is my duty and privilege as Grand Druid of the Awen Lineage to pass my station on to you, my worthy heir."

There was that name again. Emily's internal alarm clanged and her heart pounded. Who was this Awen? And what was her Da talking about?

"As the last in a long line of druid princesses hailing from Awen, you are my rightful heir and next in line to be Grand Druid."

Sweat beaded on Emily's brow.

"Our line is matristic and matriarchal, meaning leadership resides with, and passes to, the feminine progeny, rather than male. Our grand druids are typically female." Hamilton glanced at the attorney, whose lips were pressed in a stern line. "I am a rare exception."

Her Da pointed his chin at a nodding bear of a man. "Arthur Creeley there, reports directly to the Grand Druid. That will be you."

Emily's vision went fuzzy and the contents of her stomach inched toward her throat.

"Arthur will oversee your training and act on your behalf until you are ready to assume your duties. Then he will continue as your second in command. Do you understand, Emily?"

Hamilton's hand was her only anchor in a world that tipped sideways, a world in which Emily did not understand anything her birth father had uttered.

"No. No, I don't," she all but wailed. "What is a grand druid? And why would you want me to be that?"

Hamilton frowned and locked eyes with his sister before returning his gaze to Emily. "You know nothing of your heritage?"

She shook her head, looking to her aunt for help. Morgan shrugged.

"You know nothing of your powers?" Hamilton Hester demanded, agitated.

At the familiar sting of shame, Emily wagged her head slowly from side to side.

Her father's demeanor hardened. "You are a druid princess and destined to be the leader of the most powerful druid order in the world and you know nothing of what that is? Or what it entails?"

She hung her head, angry at being put on the spot, and being in trouble for something she knew nothing about. And...wait, what?

Her head snapped up. Princess? Druid? What?

Hamilton Hester swore. "What's done is done. There's no undoing it now. Sink or swim, you are a druid princess and only you can lead our order. Failure is not an option. You will have to work harder."

Goosebumps, the universal harbinger of truth, crawled Emily's skin and a shudder passed through her. She stared at the man lying in the bed and swallowed back her ready rejoinder.

She glanced at Finn Foster. Sweat beaded on his scrunched forehead. His eyes were closed. The doctor was obviously suffering. Well, dammit, so was she. Arthur Creeley placed a hand on Emily's back and a surge of energy spread through her.

She found herself saying, "I'll do my best, Da," then hastily added, "but what if I'm no good at being a druid? Much less, what did you call it? A Grand Druid?"

The blue eyes softened and Hamilton squeezed Emily's hand. "The year you were born, a prophecy was uncovered in Norman ruins near the home of our ancestors. Fear not, sweet child. You are heir to Awen's throne. And also, to her powers."

Her stomach churned and the sick feeling worsened. Powers? What powers?

"It is the belief of the Elders, that you, Emily Bridget, are the one to whom the prophecy refers. It is you who will avert Earth's coming disaster."

A wave of nausea washed over her. Wainwright cleared his throat.

Hamilton held up a hand. "Please raise your right hand and repeat after me. I, Emily Bridget Hester."

To a numb and nauseated Emily, it was all mumbo jumbo. But if it would make her Da happy. She held up her hand. "I, Emily Bridget Hester."

"Do accept the position of Grand Druid."

Emily choked out loud. Every eye in the room was fixed upon her and a thousand invisible eyes watched from the ceiling tiles. The weight was palpable.

She couldn't do it. These people needed a hero, but she wasn't it. She was sensitive, not strong. She had proven that when Charlotte ripped Trey Serra from her arms. Emily knew how to run. That was her programming, courtesy of her mother.

Features straining, Hamilton repeated, "Do accept the position of Grand Druid." Sweat dripped from Finn's ashen brow.

"Say it, Emily!" Morgan hissed.

Her voice faltered, but the words came out. "D-do accept the position of Grand Druid."

"I will uphold my position to the best of my ability."

Finn sagged against the bed, but his hand maintained contact with Hamilton's brow.

This time, Arthur Creeley spoke in a buttery voice that belied his bearish stature. "Short version, Ham."

In spite of the fear crushing the breath from her, Emily squeaked, "I will uphold my position to the best of my ability.'

"So help me, goddess."

"So help me, g-goddess."

"I now pronounce you Grand Druid of the Awen Order. May your days be long on this blessed earth and may the line of Awen ne'er be broken."

Hamilton extended an open palm on which Morgan laid an antique ring. An exquisite emerald flashed in the center of a band of etched silver.

Extending it to Emily, Hamilton pronounced, "This is Aóme. I present her to you. May she serve you well, dear daughter."

Taking the proffered ring, Emily slid it on the forefinger of her left hand. It was a little large, so she transferred it to the right where it fit perfectly. A frisson of energy shot through her, invigorating every cell.

She was ready to take on the world and wondered why she had been so afraid. It was just a title. Just a ring. Everything would be fine. Her Da was strong. He wouldn't die.

A vision flashed before her and was quickly gone. One of a verdant glade, with water flowing from the face of a rock wall.

Hamilton barked, "Mitchell Albom Wainwright the Third?"

"Yes." The attorney leaned toward the bed.

"Record these proceedings. Make sure all the legalities are covered, as previously planned and agreed."

Mitchell's voice sounded strained. "I will."

Hamilton stared at him for a long moment, as if reinforcing some previous understanding. Emily thought she saw a flicker of distaste in Hamilton's eyes when the attorney looked away.

"James Arthur Creeley," Hamilton said.

"Yes?" An animalistic power oozed from the big man, despite his soft voice.

She studied the round face. Like his voice, it was gentle, and framed by shaggy, espresso hair that ended above his broad shoulders. A patch of fuzz rode his lower lip, making Arthur resemble an aging rocker. His chocolate eyes peered past Emily to her father.

"Do you declare fealty to your new Grand Druid, Emily Bridget Hester?"

"I do."

Shockwaves passed through Emily, but something kept her knees from buckling. Was it Aóme? She caressed the ring with her thumb, grateful for its presence.

"Do you swear to fulfill your duties as Arch Druid and to support Emily Bridget Hester?"

"I do," Arthur answered. "Sir, Finn's failing. We can do the rest later."

"So, you can." Hamilton reached for Emily's hand and nestled it in his. "Emily Bridget, my precious daughter." His blue eyes misted. "In case I don't make it out of here alive, Wren's Roost and the bulk of my estate goes to you."

Behind her, sharp intakes of breath echoed hers. Apparently, the Fosters hadn't known about this.

Hamilton ignored them and continued, eyes on Emily. "It is the least I can do. I loved your mother, but I'm sure she made your life hell. That I cannot change, but I hope this is some small recompense for the years you were denied your heritage and your gifts."

Hamilton peered at his sister and then back at Emily. "The rest of my family is provided for. Now my daughter is, too."

Emily wept.

"I love you, Emily. I always have and I always will. I only wish I had more time to show you."

She threw her arms around the man she had once adored, the man who loved her still. He had shielded Emily as long as he could, and now lavished upon her that which she craved—a real family and a home of her own.

"Oh, Da. Th-thank you." Her tears flowed freely and her heart opened wide, receiving the love her father channeled.

There was a thud as Finn crumpled to the floor. Her father went still, damp lashes resting on tanned cheeks. She wept, willing him to live.

But he didn't rouse. His lips didn't move, but inside her head Emily heard, "Get me out of this hospital, little wren. Wren's

Roost needs me, as do you." Then even his velvet voice was gone.

She hugged the silent man whose love had opened a wellspring within her. Pressing her face against her Da's chest, she let the ragged tears flow.

Behind her closed eyelids, an image formed. Emily stood upon a hill, crimson hair billowing in a moody wind and arms thrown wide to a heaven that rained fire. For a moment it appeared she would be overcome, then the earth rolled beneath her and the heavens calmed.

Slowly, as if waking from a deep sleep, she became aware of the others working to rouse Finn.

She cradled her father's face in loving hands and gave him the kiss from her dreams—on the forehead, nose, chin, eyes, cheeks, and a butterfly kiss to the lips.

Nothing happened. Emily traced her thumb along his furrowed brow and searched his face for some flicker of life. "Da?"

No answer.

She screamed it inside her head, where he'd spoken moments before. Still nothing.

"I won't give up," Emily whispered. "I will get you home. Rest and recover, and don't even think about dying. I need you—" her voice broke.

Finn roused and shot out of the chair to muscle past Emily. He took Hamilton's hand and scoured the monitors, then announced with relief, "Uncle Ham's vitals are stable."

Everyone cheered, including Mitchell.

"We'll keep him in ICU again tonight and continue our tests tomorrow." Finn turned to Emily and bowed. "Well done, cousin. Let me be the first to offer my congratulations. Along with my allegiance."

A sob slipped out before Emily could bite it back. She cupped her hand around Aóme and tried again. This time her voice barely quivered.

"Thank you, Finn. Da wants to go home."

"He can't yet, Emily. It's too soon."

"But he made me promise to take him to Wren's Roost. So unless his life is in danger, we must."

An Odd Question

Mitch ripped through the gears and peeled rubber leaving Emory's parking deck. The bitch was useless. How Hamilton could even consider naming her as grand druid was beyond Mitch.

It was irresponsible. And extreme. He wasn't the only one who thought so, either. The old man had exceeded his limits this time, putting a trainee in charge. Emily Hester would be the death of them all.

She'd been so lovey-dovey, too. Mitch's skin had crawled. He'd wanted to grab her by the throat and shake her for making Hamilton mad at him. Fucking cunt. If she turned Hamilton against him there would be hell to pay. But the codger would probably be dead soon anyway.

Flicking a button on his steering wheel, Mitch spoke out loud. "Call Mother."

"Calling Mother." The computer was programmed to mimic Latoya Cloud, the sultry-voiced actress for whom Mitch had the hots. After two rings, Rona Barrett Wainwright's face appeared on his instrument panel.

"Mitchell dear, how are you?"

"I'm fine, Mother. How are you?" He could tell his voice sounded strained. Fat wonder. Hopefully, his mother wouldn't notice. Mitch got lucky.

"I'm good. But your father's not feeling well. He threw out his back playing golf today. You know how he gets when he's in pain."

"Yeah," Mitch said, "even more insufferable."

"Mitchell. "That's not nice."

"But true."

"Nonetheless." There was a stretch of silence. "Did you get the Hester girl installed?"

"Um, yeah." Since when did his mother care about Hester family business? And how did she know about Emily? Or the hastily-called meeting?

"Good." She promptly changed the subject. "Tianna called us yesterday."

Mitch made a mental note to pursue her odd question, but for now he let his mother gossip. Anything to take his mind off the hate curdling his stomach.

Swerving to avoid a scruffy kid panhandling a little too close to the road, Mitch checked his rearview mirror. The kid and his gang of ragamuffins scrambled back to the pavement, shaking scrawny fists at the Beemer's hind end.

Mitch chuckled, feeling slightly better.

**

When her son was done venting his troubled spleen, Rona Wainwright replaced the phone in its cradle. Emily Bridget was alive. And in Druid Hills. She caught her reflection in the mirrored cabinet. The oft-reinforced mask had crumbled. Dare she hope?

Her eyes filled with unshed tears and a smile broke through the fog that had defined her existence for too long. Rushing to the secret office in the back of the house, she fumbled for the concealed drawer in her desk and popped it open.

Trembling, she removed a small oaken box and cradled it to her breast as she sank to the chair. She gently placed the box on the desk, then sat frozen. The box had done its job. Maybe Rona should let it be.

She glanced around the only room in the vast mansion that reflected her druid roots. "If not now, then when?"

She stared at the box for another minute, then whispered an incantation, pouring all her love and longing and hope into breaking the seal. The lid sprang open, revealing a perfectly-preserved photograph of the baby she'd let go.

Rona lifted the picture from the velvet-lined case. The emotions she'd buried with the portrait caught in her throat on a sob. Her eyes feasted on the tiny, oval face framed by wisps of scarlet-gold hair. Joy pierced Rona's heart as she gazed at the smiling eyes.

Clutching the photograph of her baby to her chest, she waltzed around the soft rug. Her long-lost daughter was back in Druid Hills, and though Rona had promised to make no claims, and to never reveal the truth, her mother-heart was light, nonetheless.

Druid Library

After Emily had demanded they bring her Da home from Emory, she removed Aóme and slid the ring in her pocket for safekeeping. Not being a druid, she felt unworthy to wear such a precious heirloom. But the tears began pouring and refused to be staunched. Everything else was a blur.

She was aware of Morgan bundling her into her new coat and leading her to the SUV, then helping her into the carriage house. Once inside, her aunt settled her on the sofa in the living room and swaddled her in a woolen throw. Morgan laid a fire in the hearth and disappeared.

Emily stared at the blazing fire, dabbing at her tears with a wad of crumpled tissue. Ralph roused from his cushion to climb in her lap and bump her chest with his head. She hugged him close and let her tears dampen his silky fur.

Morgan swept back in, carrying a cup of steaming liquid.

"Drink this, Hon," the matriarch commanded. "It'll put fire in your belly and warm your bones. It might even help with those waterworks."

The tears leaked from Emily's swollen eyes at a steady, though lessening, pace. She blew her nose before taking a tentative sip and gagged on the bitter brew.

"Urgggh. I'd rather have liquor," she shuddered and pushed the mug back at her aunt. "That's disgusting."

"Yes, it is," Morgan chuckled. "But you will drink it, nonetheless. No mixing it with alcohol, either. I tried that once and you don't want to go there. Trust me. Now drink up. It will help you sleep."

Hearing the magic words, Emily made a face, held her nose, and chugged. Gasping, she thrashed about on the sofa, dislodging Ralph and barely keeping the noxious liquid down.

"God, what is this?" she sputtered. "I damn near barfed."

"Damn-near being the operative words. How much did you get down?"

Emily held the cup for Morgan to inspect.

"One more swallow. A big one."

"You know," Emily sniped over the smelly decoction, "you must be family. I officially hate you now."

Holding her nose, she took another swig and shuddered as the liquid met her protesting taste buds and seared all the way from her throat to her belly. She stomped both feet, quivering and wiggling all over.

Morgan was right about one thing; a fire set up in Emily's solar plexus and radiated outward through the rest of her body. Her hands and feet, cold since she'd stepped from the Atlanta airport, warmed. Her face flushed, her ears burned, and her nose watered.

But the tears ceased and for that she was thankful. A peaceful calm descended upon her. The burn died away. She sighed and hiccupped. Her body relaxed.

Sensing her aunt's scrutiny, Emily looked over at the stately woman. Morgan stood outlined in the amber glow of the hearth, a fire-angel warming her backside. She stared at Emily as if waiting for something. Hope the tabby watched her, too.

"What?" Emily demanded.

"Better?" Morgan's brown eyes glittered.

Emily checked herself to see. "Why, yes," she giggled.

"Good. It's late and I need to get home."

Morgan bent to speak quietly to Hope, then moved toward the door. "Hey, why don't you have dinner with us? It's close and you won't have to be alone."

But that was exactly what Emily wanted, and she said so. She wasn't used to all this family stuff. The day had taken its toll.

"Then, how about I pop that lasagna in the oven for you? Mary's cooking is superb."

111

"No, thank you." Emily rose on slightly wobbly feet to see her aunt out. "I'm not really hungry. I think I'll just rest."

"Emily, you don't have to do this alone. You have a family and a whole community of druids standing with you. We are many, and we are powerful. You will do just fine." Emily wasn't so sure but kept silent.

"Promise you'll call if you need anything? I'm five minutes away. Literally." Morgan's brow creased, in spite of her cheerful tone.

Emily couldn't stand it anymore and had to ask. "Morgan, what the heck is a grand druid? My knowledge of druids is foggy. From fantastical tales, mostly." She thought of the books in her mother's box. They contained druid lore, but Emily didn't get their meaning or relevance.

"I know this is a lot to digest." Morgan shrugged. "The simplified answer to your complicated question is that grand druids are the heads of druid orders. In our case, the Order of Awen."

"And druids? What are they?"

Morgan's brow knit. "Druids are peacemakers, shepherds of the earth. We care for the planet and all she sustains—the trees, the flowers, the birds, bees, and other creatures, including humans. We draw our magical powers from the Earth and that within her dominion—"

"Like the Jedi!" Emily interrupted.

"Kind of. Yes," Morgan chuckled. "We do use our powers to foster peace and harmony on Earth and in the rest of the universe."

"The universe, huh? That sounds pretty lofty."

Morgan ignored the remark. "Follow me."

Emily trailed her to a room tucked in the back of the house. She had explored the carriage house over the last two days but had somehow missed the library, accessible only through the turquoise bedroom.

Stepping inside, Emily drew a sharp breath. It was a wonderland of trinkets, relics, and artifacts. Spinning to take it all in, she glided about the room, indulging her urge to touch everything.

"Are these druid made?"

Morgan nodded.

There were paintings, bronzes, and figurines, along with carvings from every rock imaginable. Most works depicted animals, birds, or trees; the oils lush, the landscapes inviting.

Crystals of every shape and hue glinted in the light of a Tiffany chandelier that commanded the center of the enchanted room. Beyond it, Emily recognized a boulder of rose quartz.

"Ooo look!" The hunk of crystallized earth occupied an entire corner. Only once had Emily seen a crystal this large, enshrined in Bade Baba's temple in upstate New York.

Arms wide, she hugged the pink boulder, awed to find something so magnificent here. Breathing in its energy, she settled on one of the cushions arranged in a semicircle around the quartz.

"Are these here for meditating?" she asked.

"Or just hanging out," Morgan replied, lighting the fire already laid in the fireplace.

Becoming aware of the chill, Emily wrapped sweatered arms around her shoulders and inspected the wall adjacent to the quartz boulder.

An eagle headdress was ringed by bright-colored paintings of animals in their native habitat. A few stood by caves, but every picture boasted a body of water: a pond, spring, waterfall, or ocean. A padded bench invited one to linger.

Emily crossed to a glass-front curio in the opposite corner. The top shelf was full of priceless antiquities, the likes of which she had seen at the Getty Villa in Malibu—voluptuous feminine forms and flinty males with erect penises.

The middle shelf was lined with wooden wands displayed on tufted green velvet, while the lower shelf held larger items of gold and silver, encrusted with gems that glittered in the dragonfly chandelier's glow. Among these were a bronze horn in the shape of a boar's head and a helmet with an eagle's stern visage.

In the far corner, a cherry highboy overflowed with scrolls and charts. Its rich, mahogany veneer was burnished to a sheen around drawers of tiger maple. Adjacent bookcases built in the wall were crammed to capacity.

On the wall between them hung a map of the world. From the shape of the coastlines, the map was old, depicting the oceans before they had risen. Would the Celtic lands she read about be listed?

Resolving to investigate later, Emily joined her aunt by the now-crackling fire. She traced a finger along the tangled vines carved into the ebony mantel and leaned closer to study the design. It was similar to the ones in the other rooms, but with its own distinct pattern.

Above the fireplace hung a large painting she hadn't noticed on entering. Leaning back for a better view, Emily nearly choked. The woman in the portrait could be Emily. The same unruly hair blew about the same oval face.

The locks were longer, like in Emily's dreams, but the fiery tresses were shot through with gold—the same as hers. Arresting green eyes sparkled down at the room and the same lopsided grin Emily saw daily in the mirror rode the woman's lips.

Slack jawed and heart racing, Emily backed away and collapsed into a plump chair. She stared up at the painting, fingers digging into the tufted arms as her last shreds of denial were ripped away.

Raw and exposed, she cowered in the chair. There was no escape. Her ancestry was unmistakable. In the recesses of her mind a door clanged shut, sealing her fate.

"You see it, don't you? We did, too. At the hospital, the moment you walked in. That's why we all acted like idiots. Emily, this is Awen Brigid Hester, your great-grandmother. Gram lived here when you were a baby. This is her carriage house."

Morgan leaned close and added with a twinkle, "Gram was a dead ringer for the Awen. Some say she was the Awen incarnate. Some think you are, too."

A chill crept into the room. Awen. Like in Emily's dreams. "*Ahh-wen*," the voices had cried.

"Holy shit," was all she could say.

"Yeah. Holy shit," Morgan repeated. "Literally."

The last slipped out on a snicker, followed by a snort. Her aunt clamped a hand over her mouth, but the laughter won. The regal woman collapsed in the second armchair, cackling and snorting.

Emily jumped to her feet, not getting the joke. "What's so funny?" she demanded.

"You," Morgan hooted, swiping at tears. "*You*. Holy Shit!"

Had she gone mad? Emily stared.

Morgan dragged the heels of her hands across her face. "I'm sorry, dear. I'm terribly punchy. It's been a long few days and I'm beside myself about your Da." She stood to peer into a nearby mirror and dab at her eyes, then looked through it at Emily.

"What I meant to say is that you, my dear niece, are the real deal."

Emily shook her head. She didn't feel like a real anything. Except a real fraud.

"Now I really must go. But everything you ever wanted to know about druids or druid magic," Morgan spun in a tight circle, arm sweeping the room, "you will find right here. And now that you know about Brigid's Library, you will be allowed entrance. If not, ask Hope. Right, Hope?" The cat had wandered into the library and settled in the seat Morgan had vacated.

"It's been a long time, my furry friend. Welcome home." The cat continued her bath. Morgan didn't notice, having swept from the room chuckling.

Emily stared at the painting for a long beat, then flipped off the light to follow. "Goodnight, Aunt Morgan. And thank you for everything."

Morgan pulled Emily close, rocking her in a warm embrace. After a hard squeeze, she let go and opened the door to a blast of cold air.

Emily watched the SUV drive away, slammed the door against the night, and pressed her brow to its frigid pane. Her head swam and her belly was hungry, whether she liked it or not.

From the kitchen she scrounged a handful of almonds and a small apple. She thought of going for a jog, then dismissed it as too cold, too dark, and too soon after last night's ordeal. On top of that, Emily was too-too exhausted. Too many too's.

Thoughts of her birth father crept into her head. She shoved them aside, not ready to think about Da yet. She focused instead on the bungalow. He'd said it was hers, this grand old house with all its belongings, including the one-of-a-kind antiques.

Emily roamed the rooms, crunching the sweet-tart Fuji while Ralph ran ahead, joining the celebration. At the library, she leaned against the door frame and traced the room with aching eyes. She peered at the painting of her great-grandmother, Awen Brigid Hester.

Butterflies burst into flight in her gut. Emily's double. Awen's double. The butterflies did a loop-de-loop. Hamilton Hester. Grand Druid. Awen. *Ahhh-wen.*

Flipping off the lights, Emily raced through the house, dread pooling in the pit of her stomach. Who was she kidding? She couldn't stay here. She couldn't do this. They were asking too much.

In the red-room, she hauled her suitcase from the closet and threw it on the bed. Without regard for wrinkles, Emily crammed new clothes on top of old. When the teal sweater hit the pile, she faltered.

Her aunt had bought the sweater. And helped pick out the rest. With money from her Da.

Fingering the soft fabrics, Emily gathered an armful of the clothes to her chest and absorbed the scent of family-found. Slowly, the band around her chest loosened until her breath came easier.

Gut queasy and heart still racing, her voice sounded semi-calm when she declared to the room, "There is nowhere to run. Tonight, we are safe. We have a roof over our heads. A comfortable bed. Let's give the rest to God."

Shoving the half-packed suitcase to the floor, Emily climbed into the tall, four-poster bed and pulled the covers over her head. She'd had more than enough drama for one day.

After Hours

When on the prowl, Shalane hid behind an alias. Tonight, she was Magdalena, a tart chica from Spanish Harlem with sassy, brown hair and black, flashing eyes that dared anyone but the invited to come near.

She frowned at the drummette she'd fished from the basket. Fresh from the fryer and piping hot, the chicken wings were crispy the way she liked them. But she'd ordered flats. She always ordered flats. Disgusted, Shalane signaled the waitress.

The young Marilyn Monroe look-alike ignored Shalane to flash a flirtatious grin in the direction of the bar. Shalane had cast enough glances in that direction to know it was packed with a full complement of Pendleton sailors in all their studly glory. Her crotch twitched at the prospect of finding at least one convert in the lot.

But first things first. She snapped her fingers. The Marilyn-wannabe scurried to her side, a bemused smirk riding luscious lips that said she would rather be dealing with the bar boys. Fighting the urge to slap some manners into the pouty girl, Shalane shoved the basket of wings under the girl's nose.

"There are drums in this basket. I ordered flats."

The Marilyn look-alike batted long lashes that needed no mascara and did a perfect imitation of a curtsy. Shalane restrained another urge to smack her.

"All flats," she ordered, with a withering stare. "Get rid of these and bring my order." Shalane tapped the face of her wrist unit. "And bring a glass of merlot on the house."

The girl paled and gasped, "I can't do that."

"But you will. Or call the manager. I ordered twenty minutes ago and will be waiting twenty more. This drink is on you deary, whether you like it or not. And be quick about it. I don't like to be kept waiting." When the waitress hung motionless, Shalane looked down her nose through the gem-encrusted readers she'd begun wearing that year. "Chop, chop. Pace, pace. Tick tock." At the last, she clapped her hands.

It was enough. Marilyn high-tailed it to the kitchen, leaving Shalane chuckling behind the napkin in her fist. It felt good to be wicked.

For the first years of her life she'd been a whipping girl, a misfit, and never-chosen pariah. All because she heard voices and saw dead people. That, plus Shalane knew things. Things that guilty people didn't want others to know. Even in a witches' coven, it was taboo.

Shalane learned at a young age to keep her abilities quiet. It disturbed her parents when she spoke to people they could neither see nor hear. But Camille, Shalane's grandmother, had encouraged her. And, in spite of her parents' wishes, taught Shalane everything about magic—and the Otherworld from which it came. Grandma Camille also shared secrets of the Underworld, warning Shalane to stay away from that realm. Shalane sipped her wine and watched the waitress handle two drunken sailors.

They looked too young to be out of high school, much less toting guns. Each sported a fade-haircut and dress uniform. Both attempted to play grab-ass with the Marilyn-wannabe. The girl sidestepped to snake the money out of one's hand, while backing out of the other's range. All with a smile on her face. The move was a good one.

The wings were perfect the second time around. But Marilyn's mouth-watering cleavage arrived first. The thin tee hinted at erect nipples, cradled by a sheer, pushup-bra. Alarm registered in the girl's eyes when Shalane lifted her gaze from her tits to wink. She stammered when Shalane leaned near to order an Erlanger and squeaked when she bent closer to stroke the erotic point behind the girl's knee. Pink-faced, Marilyn hurried off to get her drink.

That decided it. Shalane would stay till the girl finished her shift. The hotty had fanned the flame the sailors ignited. The warm glow spread as she found her treasure spot beneath the table and dug in discreetly to relieve the unbearable pressure. Not that Shalane cared if anyone saw. Hell, she could buy the joint if she wanted to. She orgasmed twice, then made short order of the wings and the frosty Erlanger.

When she was done eating, she switched back to merlot, a little bit tipsy and a lot horny. It was Shalane's curse. Not even God had been able to curb—much less stop—her insatiable sexual drive.

Shalane settled deeper into the corner booth to nurse her wine. The Marilyn interrupted Shalane's thoughts. "Would you like your check?"

"No. I'm good." Shalane breathed deeply of the girl's scent. "Unless it's time for you to get off. I'd like to buy you a drink."

The girl blushed a delightful shade of pink and shook her head. "No, um, I'm here a while yet."

"Then I am, too." Shalane tipped her glass to the confused girl's receding tush and sipped her grandmother's favorite wine. Swishing the merlot around her tongue, she went back to reminiscing.

**

Nergal broke free from the military briefing and ducked out of the command center to cross the compound to the lab. Like most Draconians, he was a loner and preferred his own company to that of the lowlifes inhabiting Xibalba IX. Nergal had thought transferring back to California might improve the caliber of companions. So far, that had failed to be the case.

He stood at the console to study his protégé. "Display primary target," he grunted, then waited for the main brain to access the Fomorian's.

"Displaying data," the androgynous computer voice replied.

Nergal's eyes narrowed. The woman on the screen looked different. For a moment he thought he'd gotten the wrong feed. Then she spoke and he recognized the sultry lips. They were painted ruby-red and her hair was a rich shade of brown.

Voluptuous breasts overflowed a low-cut peasant blouse pulled down at the shoulders.

Nergal licked his thin lips in anticipation as the target signaled to a blond waitress. He watched their exchange with growing excitement. This woman could be Nergal's shill. Preparing a directive, he sent it to the main brain, knowing that within minutes it would identify the waitress and download any information Nergal might want or need, pertinent or otherwise. Soon the girl's file appeared on the screen.

Patrika Danner Tolbert was eighteen, barely turned, and had worked as a waitress even before her birthday. Enrolled in the Coachella Valley Beauty College, Patrika Tolbert's listed major was Aesthetician, with a minor in Massage. The touchy-feely type. Reading the rest of the file, Nergal searched for a key to unlock the girl's secrets. Born and raised in La Quinta by a single mother who worked two jobs, no mention of a father. No father.

He stopped reading to observe the interaction between the humans. The girl wasn't responding well to the reverend's advances. She was coming on too strong. Sitting down at the console, Nergal tapped the keys. He accessed the Fomorian's direct link, inserted two instructions, and sat back to watch.

This time the Draconian leader wasn't disappointed. The blond returned to the table, where Shalane rested her head on her arm. Crocodile tears dripped from the half-closed eyes. Instantly concerned, Patrika Tolbert squatted beside the woman and leaned close to put her hand on the petite shoulder.

A Rocky Start

The temperature plummeted, carried on a wind that buffeted the house and whined of snow. Emily woke, curled in a ball on the wrong side of the bed. The cats slept back to back, taking up most of the available space.

She reckoned it was a fitting ending to a dream-filled night in which she had slept without peace. But at least her head felt better. She wiggled and rolled over, claiming enough room to lie on her back.

The Awen dream had taken a weird turn and morphed into a surreal parade of animals led by a mouthy raven. Now that she thought about it, Emily was pretty sure they were the same animals whose ghosts she had seen in the park. One by one, they had tromped through Awen's glade, introducing themselves as druid Elders.

Each demanded something of Emily. Art the bear insisted she remember an important prophecy. He'd said it was about her, but try as she might, Emily couldn't. What she did recall, in vivid clarity, was the stone left for her on the shore of Awen's pond by Dobhran the Otter, and the feel of the duke's mouth on her lips.

Clad only in a cotton T-shirt, she steeled herself for the icy blast and shivered when blanket-warm skin met morning air. Shrugging on the robe, she relaxed as the fleece enveloped her body and calmed the chills. She fished for her Uggs, found one and put it on. The other was missing. Annoyance flared. Emily fumbled for the lamp and flicked it on. No boot. Only four sleepy eyes blinking back in protest.

Getting down on both knees, she lifted the bed skirt with puckered distaste. Murky shadows and a trail of dust bunnies

121

greeted her. The annoyance festered. Her druid training started this morning and she still wasn't sure if she wanted to partake. Why couldn't she find her stinking boot? Flopping on her belly, she peered into the darkness, ear smashed against the prickly wool rug in an effort to avoid the cold bedrail.

Near the footboard, Emily detected a variation in grays. She stretched until her fingers brushed the boot and pulled it toward her, dislodging something cold and hard. Recoiling, she hit her head on the frame. Squealing in righteous indignation, Emily heaved her torso out of the confined space and rubbed the goose-egg forming on her crown.

"Damn, damn, damn, damn, DAMN!"

That rousted Ralph. He hit the floor and scurried from the room, used to his master's mercurial moods. Hope, on the other hand, yawned and stretched, circled in place, and flopped to the quilt. She, apparently, was going nowhere. Fat paws mushed the spot Ralph had vacated and the blunt-tipped tail swished the air. Wide amber orbs stared at Emily.

"What?" she snapped, yanking on her boot. Hope folded her feet and tail under in what Emily thought of as Buddha pose and pretended to doze.

Emily snarled at the insufferable cat and fetched a long match from the hearth. She lit it and kneeled at the footboard to peek under the bed, only to be accosted by an acrid puff of smoke when a dust bunny burst into flames. Coughing and retching, she patted out the fire.

Not an auspicious start to her first day.

Rubbing her sore head, Emily scooped up what appeared to be a small, round stone. The polished surface was transparent and as smooth as glass. She cradled it in her palm. The stone warmed and something extraordinary happened—its interior melted. Emily stared as inky inclusions appeared in the liquid. They floated and swirled in no particular pattern, like black snowflakes on a still winter's day.

As she watched, her frustration drained away, taking the anger with it. Puzzled, she held the stone to the light and marveled when the black spots fizzled to nothing. New, snowy inclusions took their place, drifting on the invisible current. A shuddering sigh of release shook Emily's body. The flecks flashed and vanished, leaving the stone clear and quiet.

Emily shook the stone, but it looked again like an ordinary lump of glass. She slid the talisman in her pocket and closed her eyes. The anger was gone. Not even a trace of annoyance remained. Instead she tingled with anticipation, a lightness of being that was almost euphoric.

Remembering Dobhran the Otter, Emily thanked him for the mysterious gift.

She dressed as Hope had previously instructed, layering against the cold. Morgan and Mitch would be here soon, along with her teacher. The otter stone warmed her thigh where it nestled in her pocket beside Aóme.

In the kitchen, she ate some raw cashews and grabbed a Granny Smith apple. The outside lights kicked on. Peering through the peephole, she saw a determined Wainwright climbing the steps, followed by Morgan, Arthur, Becca and Dana, and several others Emily didn't know.

Why so many people? The doorbell trilled and Emily jumped. A loud knock followed—three raps, a pause, and three more. Was it druid code? How would she know?

A sudden urge to escape gripped her. On the other side of the peephole was a small druid army. She shrank away. Hadn't her mother taught her that leaving was always an option? That she could always disappear? That she could always run?

The doorbell trilled and the raps came again. She peered around the cozy cottage. In three short days it had become Emily's home, enveloping her in safety, warmth, and family. Belonging. The realization had her reeling. She had never belonged. Not anywhere. Not that she could remember.

She put a hand against the wall, closed her eyes, and tried to ignore a new flurry of raps and muffled exhortations. The image of her mother appeared behind her eyelids. Obsessed with her own needs, Alexis Mayhall had never lifted a finger for anyone else. It was her downfall. She died a horrible death. An alcoholic alone in her cups.

Shuddering, Emily shut the flashback down. It was time to let go of that wretched legacy. Time to grow up and stop running from her mother and her fears. Something cold and leaden stirred inside her. Primordial and deep, it wrapped in a tight ball at the base of her spine and went back to sleep. Emily fished in her pocket for the heirloom. The silver gleamed. Touching the emerald to her brow and heart in an unconscious act of reverence, she slid the ring on her forefinger. The stone sparkled, a flash of green that lifted her spirits as Awen's amulet worked its magic.

Calm strength replaced the fear. Courage and confidence, two things Emily hadn't felt in ages, surged and filled her being. She inspected her reflection in the hall mirror and fluffed her saucy red hair.

She really did like the color. Seeing her great-grandmother's picture might be the reason. Weird, but she was beginning to like the thought of that, too. Emily tucked Aóme back in her pocket. Until she was worthy. She winked at her image winking back in the mirror and opened the door.

Making It Official

With a stiff nod at Emily, Mitchell Wainwright strode past her to the living room, where he took a position in front of the blazing hearth. The druids assembled around him.

"Coffee anyone?" Emily asked.

Several nodded, including Wainwright. She poured generous cups of the strong, steaming brew and handed them out. The druids thanked her and returned to the living room, chatting quietly amongst themselves. The attorney cleared his throat and they looked up with expectant faces. He motioned Emily to join him at the fireplace and watched as she picked her way across a sea of legs and feet. She reached the hearth, rolled her eyes at him, and faced the group.

"Order," the attorney paused for dramatic effect. "Meet your new Grand Druid, Emily Bridget Hester. Emily, meet your governing body."

A sharp rat-tat-tat peppered the front door, followed by three successive raps. Emily moved to open the door to the latecomer, but Mitchell's arm snaked out and held her in place. She yanked her arm away and rubbed her elbow, glaring at the attorney. He glared back.

Hands on hips in designer jeans, Morgan got in Wainwright's face. "That will be our Priest. You do remember our High Priest, don't you Mitchell?" Ice radiated from Morgan's calm exterior. What was going on?

Allowing the man no time to respond, Morgan ranted, "It's the Priest's duty to oversee events of importance. Yet, for some reason, he wasn't notified. You may be Ham's attorney, but you do not have the right to circumvent our laws. As Head of

Security, I am responsible for the wellbeing of this clan. Our customs will be obeyed. The priest will perform Emily's initiation." The doorbell warbled.

Initiation? Emily had been told today was her first day of training. What the hell?

"Sorry I'm late." Lugh swept through the door opened by a woman she didn't know. "What did I miss?"

Hope materialized from the corner to weave through the legs of the gypsy priest. But his dark eyes devoured Emily.

"Hello, Hope. Welcome back," Lugh crooned, still ogling Emily who reeled in disbelief. The handsome manager from Jocko's Pizza was in her living room. And he was a druid Priest.

"Hello, Lughnasadh," the cat purred. He stooped to lift Hope in his arms, like she was a feather weight instead of a solid forty-pounder. Good-looking in the dark roguish sort of way Emily admired in a man, she tingled at the very thought of him. Now here he was, a druid Priest. Her druid Priest. Holy cannoli.

Hope abandoned his arms and sauntered across the living room, black-ringed tail high and twitching. The druids crowded around the talking tabby, plying her with questions. In typical cat fashion, she ignored them all and waded through the druids to vault to the top of the cherry armoire. Emily hid a smile behind a sleep-starved yawn.

 From her prominent perch, Hope announced, "During Hamilton Hester's reign, the duties of Grand Druid and High Priest coincided. But no longer." She gazed at each druid, ending with the attorney, who squirmed beside Emily in some obvious distress. "In Mr. Wainwright's defense, he knew no better. After all, he is not druid trained."

Emily straightened. Why was she defending him?

"Without this man, Emily Bridget would not be with us today. Mitchell is responsible for bringing her home. For that, we owe him a debt of gratitude. Thank you, Mitchell." From atop the cupboard, Hope dipped her head ever so slightly to Wainwright.

The others followed suit, adding reluctant thanks. He nodded around the room with a tight smile, managing to keep his chin aloft. He didn't deign to look at Emily, though her own thanks were sincere.

Hope harrumphed loudly. She turned to the handsome newcomer and purred, "Lughnasadh MacBrayer, meet your new Grand Druid, Emily Bridget Hester."

Emily extended a shy hand to acknowledge Lugh's well-wishes and had to tear her gaze from his lopsided grin to focus on Hope.

"Lugh has trained for the priesthood," the cat was saying, "working with Hamilton Hester and the Eastern Order in preparation for this day."

Emily was having a hard time concentrating. The man was too virile, too rugged to be a Priest. Clad in jeans and leather jacket, he oozed pheromones that made Emily's tummy churn in a most delicious way. A yowl from Hope interrupted her musings.

"We will attend to Emily Bridget's initiation, but first I have vital news from the animal Elders." That got everyone's attention. "A Darkness broods beneath our feet. A force that will soon be upon us, whether we're ready or not. There is a veil beyond which the Elders cannot see. But the head of the Awen nation is failing. Haste is critical in getting our new Grand Druid up to speed."

The somber announcement landed on Emily like a bucket of ice. Six months earlier, she had tried to convince her boss of the same thing. That, and losing Trey to the cyclone, had gotten her fired. Morgan and Da had spoken of imminent danger. Now, Hope confirmed Emily's fears.

In a French accent smattered with Southern, Hope declared, "I, for one, am not willing to let that happen. Are any of you?" As a unit, the druids' heads wagged. All but the attorney, who was looking a tad green. Peering down upon them, Hope continued, "On behalf of the Elders, I am here to take charge of—and accelerate—Emily's training."

Hope's tone brooked no argument, but the moment was broken when she twisted away to lick her shoulder. Gasps and hallelujahs filled the air, along with the fragrant scent of fruit wood burning. Beside Emily, the lawyer twitched. A sideways glance at his red, contorted face told her Mitch was in the throes of some intense, inner battle.

A gurgling croak escaped his tight lips. "Excuse me. But who the hell are you?"

"Silence!" Hope roared in a booming voice too large for her body. The room stilled. "Hold your tongue, young mouse, or I shall tie it for you."

In the flickering light of the morning fire, the wild-eyed attorney shrank. Fright flickered across his handsome features before the lawyer mask clicked into place. Hatred poured from him in waves. To escape the vitriol, Emily stepped to the armoire and bowed in deference to Hope.

"I am honored, Hope the Wise, and gladly accept your kind assistance. It is most welcome, I assure you." To the others she announced, "The animal Elders visited my dreams last night. Each offered magical aid. I am ashamed to admit that I tried to run, but that bought me nothing but a wakeful night. Each Elder persisted until I was forced to listen."

Chuckles arose around the room. Apparently, the other druids had tangled with them, too.

"You probably don't know this, but I am a trained disaster specialist." Emily waited to let that sink in. Mitchell cleared his throat, a habit she had come to despise. She ignored him and continued, "What Hope says is true. I have evidence that supports the Elders' claims."

The stubborn attorney muscled in front of her, ignoring Hope's previous warning. "Look, Hamilton Hester brought me into this Order. It is my intention to follow *his* instructions." The icy demeanor dared the druids to defy him.

Clearly unimpressed, Hope stretched and yawned.

Wainwright paced the floor, a lawyer gearing up for opening remarks, commanding the eyes of judge and jurors. His next words dripped with disdain, "Nowhere in Hamilton's command to me, nor in the hierarchical structure of this Order, does it recognize or even mention the authority of talking cats or animal Elders."

A collective gasp went up from the druids. Hope's head was buried to mid-thigh, licking her already impeccable fur. Emily resisted an urge to giggle, wondering if the cat did it to disarm her opponents. Hope straightened to stare at the attorney, the tip of her pink tongue caught between her incisors. With an air of practiced tolerance, the Elder said, "Are you finished, young mouse?"

Apparently not. Mitchell opened his mouth to speak, but nothing came out. Not a squeak, not a word, nada. Hope leapt from the armoire to the back of Arthur Creeley's chair and down to the floor where she padded toward the apoplectic attorney. Wainwright winced but stood his ground, sullen lips pressed together, veins pulsing in his temples.

Emily had a fleeting vision of the attorney clutching his head and falling to the floor, dying from a burst aneurysm like some actor in an old movie. But before anything of the sort could happen, Hope sidled up to him and whispered something only he could hear. His black brows beetled and a deep shade of vermillion suffused tanned cheeks. Mitchell Wainwright did not keel over. Instead he shriveled like a stomped violet, zombie-stare plastered to his black, shiny shoes.

An angry stain spread to Mitchell's throat, stirring Emily's sympathy. As Hope had said, in spite of the man's despicable, no-good rottenness, he was responsible for bringing her to Wren's Roost. And for that she was thankful.

Hope's fat tail swished as she made the next pronouncement. "Mr. Wainwright, you will continue as the Order's attorney. But that is all." She turned on the wilted lawyer. "I recommend you stick to what you know, young mouse. Leave the rest to the druids."

The attorney paled, but his gaze didn't leave his patent-leather shoes.

**

The Komodo dragon awoke and tested the air. An excitement long dormant rippled through him. Something was happening.

He slid from his man-made bed and shuffled outside the artificial cave in Zoo Atlanta. Stretching hoary bones, Tienu yawned and looked to the sky. Dawn approached, that magical time when light beat back the dark and for a few fleeting moments, the veil between the worlds thinned.

The dragon swung his head from side to side, surveying the small structure that had served as his home for the last years. He took his fill of tepid water and devoured the bland dinner he'd left sitting the night before. Purple rimmed the brightening sky. Birds whistled a waking song. Animals called to one another in low, morning voices, knowing zoo handlers would soon appear bearing food.

Draig Tienu plodded up the rise and draped his puny body on the fake promontory. He let his world-weary lids sag and sank into the Otherworld. Soon enough, the erstwhile fire dragon's suspicions were confirmed. Draig Talav was awake and nearby. Ooschu was crossing the Gulf of California bound for a wormhole east. The fourth Keeper, Draig a-Ur, was beyond Tienu's ken.

But it was the dragon master who drew his attention.

The Awen was back. And in close proximity. Soon Tienu would be returned to his own body. Or so he hoped.

**

For Emily, the initiation was anticlimactic. Robes were passed around for the group to don. Like the other garments, hers was crafted of soft, spun silk, white and ankle-length. The druids marched in single file with Hope in the lead, followed by Emily, Lugh, Arthur, and the rest, in order of rank. Wainwright brought up the rear, impassive mask abandoned for a disgust he didn't bother hiding.

The clearing was a good hundred yards across and ringed by birches, like the ones guarding the fountain in the park. With Emily in the center, self-conscious and spooked, the group formed a loose circle around her. Lugh led the brief ritual, similar to the one her Da had performed from his hospital bed.

When instructed, Emily held her right hand in the air and repeated the words. But rather than Lugh's sultry, southern tones, Emily heard her Da's tenor, brimming with love. A tear trickled down her cheek, followed by another. When the ceremony was over, the druids gathered close, congratulating

Emily and welcoming her to the Awen Order. Each declared fealty to their new Grand Druid.

All except Wainwright, who stood off to the side, face averted. As usual, he disapproved of Emily, though she'd done nothing to deserve his disdain. Except exist, she reasoned. He treated everyone that way.

After a while, the druids meandered toward Wren's Roost and Emily was left alone with Hope. The Elder reiterated the instructions conferred earlier; Emily was to remain in the clearing through the day and night, spending time in prayer and meditation, with no food or drink except a flask of water.

It sounded like, and turned out to be, something of a vision quest. But early that night, starved of sleep and unable to keep her eyes from closing, Emily curled on the grass and fell asleep. Nothing else happened until the wee hours of morning when in the vault of the heavens, the constellations rotated into place.

The Elders appeared, ghostly outlines filling the clearing. One by one, they heaped blessings on their new Awen, each animal promising protection and aid against the Darkness and the troubled times ahead. As dawn approached and the veil between the worlds thinned, the spirit animals slipped back into the Otherworld.

In parting, each whispered the same counsel, "Arise, Priestess. Without you, all is lost."

The Awen stirred, but Emily slept on, unaware.

Able to fly unhindered between worlds, the owl, Callaich Oidche, and Bran the Raven remained perched in separate birches, hooting and weaving spells until the crack of dawn when Emily awoke. She rose with a wide, sleep-soggy yawn and rubbed the night from her eyes. Peering about the clearing, she wondered if she was supposed to feel any different. If so, she didn't.

Disappointed, Emily trudged from the clearing to her four-poster bed, barely noticing the birds keeping pace overhead.

Conquest

The Marilyn lookalike sprawled across Shalane's hotel bed, legs entangled with hers. The girl had never been with a woman and was resistant at first but had given in once Shalane feigned tears. She studied the girl whose name, as it turned out, was Patrika.

"Sweet, delectable Patty," she murmured and stroked the girl's slender thigh. It trembled beneath her touch. A fat tear rolled down the girl's cheek. "What is it sweetie?" Shalane brushed it away with her thumb, solicitous now that her lust was slaked.

The voluptuous lips moved but no sound came out. She tried again and squeaked, "Why did you do this to me?" She cleared her throat and her voice was stronger. "I was a good girl and now I'm not. I'm a whore. A lesbian whore." The last whooshed out in anguish.

Shalane cackled, not hiding her amusement. The girl pulled away, aghast. "There, there sweet Patty," Shalane coaxed in a low voice. "You're not either of those things. You are a woman, awakened to the world of sexual prowess. You enjoyed it, didn't you? You sure seemed to." The girl nodded, eyes squeezed tight.

In the hypnotic voice Shalane used to address the masses, she cooed, "Sweetie, sex, like love, is given to us by God. We were meant to have both and enjoy them."

"But you're a woman and lying with a woman is a sin," the girl cried.

"Who told you that?"

Patty bolted upright. "The bible! It says so. My church says so." Her now-wide eyes held an accusatory glare. "My family will disown me. They'll never speak to me again."

132

"Then they're not a very good family and you're well rid of them." Shalane thought of her own parents and how they'd abandoned her. She touched the girl's cheek and said contemplatively, "You can come with me. I'll be your family."

The girl sobbed and fell into Shalane's arms. She stroked her hair, making shushing noises and drying the tears. Patty's innocence had awakened something new and terrible inside Shalane—an overwhelming need to protect. Gathering the girl close, she rocked her, whispering, "Come with me, Patty. Let me take care of you, be your family. Just say the word and I'll make it so." The sobs eased to snorts and sniffles. A new light sparkled in the girl's tearful eyes. Shalane's heart leapt; Patty was considering the offer.

"Are you rich?" The question caught Shalane by surprise.

"As the Pope," she chuckled.

Patrika Tolbert eyed her with speculation. "You can get me out of this hell hole?"

Shalane nodded.

"Then I'll go. But only if you'll give me a good home and whatever else I might think of. Do that and I'll come with you."

Satisfaction tickled Shalane's lips. The vixen was very much a child, in spite of outward appearances. She would be easy to mold and bend to Shalane's will, where Ebby Panera had not. In a vague sort of way, Patty reminded Shalane of Ebby. But only a little. It was that innocence thing. If it worked out, Shalane would teach Patty everything. Well, not everything. She would not be teaching Patty the death-fuck.

The Wyrd

"Excellent," Hope purred from her perch atop the quartz boulder.

Emily's bruised ego soaked up the platitude, in desperate need of positive reinforcement. The Interrogation, or so Emily had dubbed it, was taking place in the library and had lasted for the better part of two hours. Other than a begged-for bathroom break, Emily's trainer had been relentless.

"So, to recap," Hope said, "you meditate. You are trained in both jujitsu and aikido. You sometimes sense things before they happen. You have an affinity with animals and birds, and they with you. Same with broken people. They gravitate to you.

"You are happier near the ocean or water, but not in it. Strange phenomena take place in your presence. You have been told by healers and shamans that you have supernatural powers yet you insist you have no knowledge or control of these powers." The cat's amber eyes gleamed. "Did I miss anything?"

Chuckling, Emily rose from her cross-legged position and grabbed the quartz boulder to keep from pitching sideways. Her foot was asleep.

"Probably, but I think you got the meat of my answers."

She tapped her toes against the floor. The lump of nothing registered a slight tingling. Letting go to hop backward on the good foot, she collapsed in the plump chair. Lavender wafted into the air, left behind from Mary's cleaning spree.

Emily slung her leg over the stuffed arm and bent double to rotate her numb foot with her hands, kneading the feeling back into her toes and instep. Hope bristled, her ears pinned back.

"Emily Bridget, please. Sit up and pay attention. This is serious business."

134

Doing as instructed, Emily wondered for the umpteenth time why she let the bossy cat order her around. Hope padded to the hearth and turned her tail to it.

"I will give you the good news first." Dreading the bad news, Emily twirled her waking foot in the air. "It appears your mother wasn't as remiss as we had thought."

Gulping, Emily sat up straighter. "What do you mean?"

"You have been trained in martial arts with an emphasis on self-defense. Your intuition has been encouraged and developed, as were your independence and love for all things living. Your affinity with the animal world is strong. Plants lean toward you. Spirits speak to you, though you dismiss their words as wanderings of your own mind."

It had never occurred to Emily to think of her mother's inattention as an asset. And it disturbed her to think that the thoughts in her head might not always be her own.

"To set the record straight," Emily said, "plants and critters are *my* thing. Animals ran from Mama. And plants died in the car on the way home from the nursery rather than submit to her torture."

Hope snorted. "Nevertheless, you are not as hopeless as we had feared."

In spite of the obvious insult, Emily's mood lifted. She wasn't as useless as they had believed. Anticipation rushed in. A new adventure. She leaned forward.

"So, now what?"

"Now, we begin." Hope's amber eyes danced. "Each day you will start with philosophy and history lessons from me or one of my designees. Then an hour or two with Arthur Creeley studying divination and learning how to recognize the signs you receive. And how to get in touch with, and embrace, your powers.

"After that, spells and curses taught by Finn Foster and his sisters, Becca and Dana. Somewhere in there, Lughnasadh MacBrayer and whomever he designates will test and hone your combat skills."

A buzz went through Emily at the prospect of a hand-to-hand tussle with the man who looked more pirate than priest.

"The headmaster, David Daniels, will instruct you on druid hierarchy, and along with your Aunt Morgan, familiarize you with the depth and breadth of the druid ranks and how they interact with agencies here in the United States and abroad."

Shocked, Emily blurted, "We're international? The government knows about druids?"

Hope blinked somber eyes. "Of course."

"Huh. If we're so powerful and widespread, why doesn't the general public know about druids? Before I came to Atlanta, I'd barely even heard of them, except for the books I found in Mama's stuff."

As the words left Emily's mouth, she felt a sinking sensation. She'd meant to keep her mother's box a secret, though it was probably better to get it out in the open. Maybe it would help.

Hope leapt to attention. "Alexis had druid artifacts?"

Emily nodded, wary.

"May I take a look? Some may be items that came up missing about the time Alexis ran off with you."

With a reluctance she didn't quite understand, Emily led Hope to the red bedroom. Collecting her suitcase, she spread the druid items on the bed. All except for the manuscript. That, Emily left concealed in the false bottom. An excited Hope pawed through the books and trinkets. When she was done, she looked up at Emily expectantly.

"Is this all?"

Emily shrugged. "Yes."

Her insides lurched at the lie. The cat stared, and for a moment, she thought Hope was reading her mind.

"Well, this is something." Hope leapt to the floor. "Let me know if you remember anything else." The cat padded from the room.

Relieved, Emily repacked the suitcase and stowed it in the closet, rejoining Hope and Ralph in the library.

"What about my question?" Her internal skeptic still balked at the idea of a secret subculture hiding beneath the public's nose. For millennia. An organization with a peace-keeping mission and the power to influence world events. "Why don't people know about druids?"

"It's a clever cover-up, really. Once druids were defeated and supposedly wiped from the face of the earth, they were relegated to legend. Like Arthur and the Knights of the Round Table. Who, by the way, relied heavily on a druid priest named Merlin."

"But there are tomes written about the Arthurian legend," Emily noted. "Plus, witches, werewolves, and vampires, too. The world's literature teems with dwarves and elves and fairies and the like. Why not druids?"

The cat's hackles rose. "Peacemakers need no books or airplay for validation. Written documents fall into the wrong hands. The druid way has always been to pass our rituals and Earth-magic from priest to acolyte. It is fortunate for the world that a few, like Awen, survived to continue the druid lineage and traditions."

Emily thought of the ancient, hand-penned tome hidden in the bottom of her suitcase. Why was she so reluctant to share?

"But how did that handful grow into a secret, worldwide subculture?" she asked.

"By integrating into the very society we protect, Dru-y-en. Hiding in plain sight. Today, just as in the ancient world, druids are teachers and poets, musicians and entertainers, wordsmiths and artists, statesmen and warriors, lawyers and politicians. Our culture remains alive and vital by staying secret." Hope turned a circle and plopped on the rug in front of the crackling fire.

"Fine," Emily huffed, though she still wasn't sure her question had been answered.

Hope blinked. "Myths and legends are rooted in history, little wren. History that others choose to forget—or hide. Any other questions?"

There was that other thing. "Do I have to learn all these druid gods? Who they are and what they do? Or can I just insert 'God' for whatever god's name I come across in the literature?"

"If you must." The Cat Elder looked amused. "Or you can imagine each as an aspect of the one God, just as every organism making up the Wyrd is an aspect of the one God. You. Me. The deep blue sea."

"The word?"

"Wyrd, not word," Hope corrected. "Capital double-u, wye, ar, dee. The Wyrd is the core of druid belief. It is the essential pattern of life, the crystalline web that makes up the Universe. Druidry is based on these ancient laws, the natural truths that govern all lives and the web within which we live—the Wyrd." Waxing philosophical, Hope tucked all four legs and tail under her bulk.

"Think of Life, all life, as Energy with a capital E. As a scientist you understand this, Emily Bridget. Every element vibrates at its own frequency; each rock, leaf, drop of water, puff of wind, lightning sizzle, and creatures large and small. Each has its own unique vibration."

Emily nodded.

"Now imagine the elemental energies of nature and life as a vast, crystalline web that pulsates light—eternally active threads of pure Energy, each also vibrating at a different frequency, creating the patterns of Nature. The patterns of Self. As we change, the web changes, too."

"Yes, I get that." The concept had been proven by science.

Hope purred, "The web and the ever-changing patterns of its interwoven processes are known as the Wyrd."

"Not word?" Emily interrupted. "Like 'in the beginning was the word, and the word was with God, and the word was God'?"

When she was younger, her mother had taken her to Sunday school at whatever Methodist church they happened to be near. Drawn to the teachings, Emily still attended from time to time.

"Exactly!" Hope stood and circled the rug. "Only again, different spelling. Wyrd with a wye, not oh. The Anglo-Norman derivation of Wyrd means both 'law' *and* 'earth'."

"Ahhh." Emily was beginning to see where Hope was headed.

"Because we are an essential component of the Wyrd," the Elder continued, "druids craft our lives and spells to honor the whole. We are individual, but interwoven, threads. You. Me. Our people.

"It is imperative that we are responsible for our actions *and* our craft. Every transformation we make, everything we do, affects the entire web. Which brings us to today's lesson."

"Isn't that what we've been doing?" Emily pouted, ready to be done.

"Yes, but this is the lesson part. The first essential law of druid magic is:

'Harm none,
do as you will,
for the good of all,
insofar as you may see.'"

"Kind of a 'do unto others as you would have them do unto you'?"

"Exactly. *And* the more experienced a druid, the more profound the effects she has, and can have, on the crystalline web."

"What about the darkness?" Emily pondered. "Is that also part of the web? Or Wyrd? Is the darkness of God?"

Hope's mouth stretched wide in a feline smile. "That has been a topic of debate for time immortal, Emily Bridget. The druid belief is—yes. What is dark to us is not to the darkness.

"Even darkness that has no discernable 'good' plays a part in the Wyrd. Things like war, hate, greed, and the like pervert the spirit but are not of the spirit. The Wyrd is composed of the light *and* the spaces in between. Do you understand?"

"Yes, I think so," Emily nodded. "Just as humans are inherently good, so also is that which might appear to be bad."

Hope lifted her head and wailed, a long, eerie caterwaul that sent chills up Emily's spine.

"What?" she asked. Had she done something wrong?

Hope bowed. "You, Emily Bridget—and those like you—are the reason the light shall prevail. Why the light shall always prevail. You have a pure heart and can fathom nothing less in others.

"That belief, that purity, is key. It holds the power to transform and the power to deflect darkness. To disarm it, turn it off. It also has the power to seek out good and turn that *on*. Awen had this power. Now it has passed to you."

Hope's declaration triggered a sudden, paralyzing fear in Emily. She cowered in the armchair, mind and heart galloping down a frightful path littered with death and destruction. She tucked her knees under her chin.

"B-but what if I fail? If my past is any indication, I will mess this up. The world will explode and everyone—you, me, my new family—will all die. It's too much. I can't do this."

In a stern tone, Hope commanded, "Emily, look at me."

Underarms clammy, Emily obeyed.

The Elder's tone softened, but remained firm. "I am here for you. The druids are here. When the time comes, the Awen will be here. She'll awaken inside you and then you will be ready. Plus, there are others."

Others? What others? Before Emily could ask, the doorbell trilled, followed by three raps, then three more.

Druid in Training

After the philosophy lesson with Hope, Emily had time to snatch a quick sandwich. Arthur arrived soon after to introduce Emily to divination. The Arch Druid towered over her, with a physique reminiscent of Artaois the bear god, for whom he was aptly named. In contrast, Arthur's voice was like velvet and he spoke in a calm, even tone that put Emily at ease.

In spite of her lack of formal training, Emily soon learned that she was fairly adept at rudimentary divination. The hints and prods she got from the Universe, those flashes of intuition that told her to take her raincoat, not to follow a particular route, or leave Venice Beach posthaste, all were signs telling her what to do. Or not do.

If she attuned to these signs, she could pay heed and choose her actions accordingly. To Emily's mind, divination was nothing more than intuition and she said so.

"Exactly," Arthur cheered. "Intuition equals divination. The magic comes in extending the senses to people and situations unrelated to the diviner's Self. By placement of intent, you can shape and filter the information you receive. Like channels on an old-fashioned radio or television. You 'tune-in' to a question or situation and ask, preferably out loud, "What next? Or what does this mean?"

"But isn't that just asking and receiving? Like in prayer?"

"Exactly!" Arthur's face shone. Hope sauntered into the library. "Hope, you're right. She's a natural. There won't be much to teach this one, other than technique. And how to manage and direct what she already knows, while applying her skills to a larger arena."

Hope's satisfied purr filled the room.

**

Lugh rapped on the door of the carriage house. To his surprise, Arthur opened it, letting himself out. Lugh grinned at his bowling buddy and bumped knuckles with a fist the size of a grizzly's. Arthur grabbed him up in a bro hug that nearly lifted Lugh off the stoop. Letting go, he waved to the warm interior. "She's all yours."

"If only," Lugh mumbled, and stepped through the door.

**

Emily returned from the bathroom and paused, dazzled by the sight of Lugh MacBrayer standing in her library. Their eyes met and Emily's brain froze. The room suddenly felt very small. And very warm.

Thrusting a hand out in greeting, the priest murmured a polite, "How do you do?"

Emily recovered sufficiently to reciprocate. He took her hand gently, but instead of a warm shake, Lugh deftly flipped her to her derriere without warning or provocation. She landed on the rug with an indelicate thud, grunting in a most unladylike manner. She scrambled to her feet, anticipating another assault, and backed away in defensive posture.

"No fair!" she grumbled, rubbing her tush. "I wasn't ready."

Whereby, Lugh bowed, a smile playing on amused lips. "There will be no warning from our enemies, Miz Hester."

The drawl, while attractive, infuriated Emily. Lunging at her combat teacher with the intent of showing him a thing or two, she ended up on her backside again. For a moment, she sputtered, breath knocked out, then she twisted upright and crouched in a defensive stance, sucking air.

Nonchalant, Lugh turned his back and held his hands to the fire.

"That's it?" she gasped, seeing red. "Is that all you've got?"

"Hardly," the druid priest glanced over his shoulder. "Just testing your mettle, seeing what you're made of."

"And?" Emily ground through her gritted teeth.

Lugh turned to face her, dark eyes hard.

"You're too soft, Miz Hester. Too trusting." The eyes narrowed. "If we don't change that soon, we are all going to die."

But wait. Hadn't Hope said——?

Contradiction or not, she had no time to argue. Lugh's foot slammed into her chest.

**

Emily soaked in hot water spiked with Epsom salts and lavender oil, hoping it would calm her jangled nerves. Her muscles ached from the trouncing she had received at the hand of Lugh MacBrayer. Her ego suffered too, despite having excelled at all the rest of her lessons. Emily lathered her shoulders and indulged in a private pity party.

Turns out, the man she'd been romanticizing was really more pirate than priest. He'd attacked without warning and shown no mercy. Worse, he had declared her too soft, too trusting. Which was doubly confusing, considering Hope had professed Emily's pure heart as her greatest asset only hours earlier.

Which was it? Saving grace? Or the world's downfall?

She stepped from the tub, exhausted from no sleep and the sheer volume of data thrust upon her that day. She toweled dry, dressed, and stoked the red-room fire. When it crackled and blazed, Emily climbed into bed, damp hair curling around her face.

Weather Witching

The eye pain had eased from rip-roaring to a manageable ache. Shalane nudged the clouds again, intent on seeing San Francisco's usually-hidden vista. The veil receded and both the Golden Gate and Oakland Bay bridges appeared.

"Ahhh," she purred, "there you are."

Outside the bay window, morning sun glistened on dew-kissed flowers bobbing in a capricious, offshore breeze. Tiny butterflies like pale moonlight skipped from bloom to bloom. Ruby-throated hummingbirds pillaged gloxinias overflowing the suite's window box. On the post of a nearby lamp, a multi-hued windsock flapped and danced. Shalane was glad she had insisted on flying to San Francisco instead of making the interminable trip by bus.

She poured a cup of freshly-brewed coffee and sank into a cushioned settee. She folded her legs in lotus pose and savored the rich brew. Her gaze wandered the still-emerging cityscape. In the distance, Mount Diablo stood guard over the bay, a rare sight for visitors to San Fran. Luckily, Shalane had an in with the weather gods. She sighed all the way to her toes.

It was at times like these that Shalane most missed her grandmother. A master weather witch, Camille had made learning fun. And special.

Shoving the memory aside, she considered her new concubine. She was itching to teach Patty a thing or two, but the girl slept like a mummy. Too bad it wasn't Emily in there in Shalane's bed. Ten days had passed since news of that one. But who the hell was counting?

Relinquishing her coffee to the end table, Shalane closed her eyes and breathed in the earthy essence of the city, letting it fill the inner space that longed for her grandmother.

She grounded for meditation, sending roots into the earth and staying vigilant for signs of danger. Buoyed by a flow of iridescent energy, Shalane relaxed. No frightful apparitions lurked here today. Nothing dared approach Shalane the High Priestess.

Roots touching Mother Earth, she gently pushed off for the surface, erupting through the brittle outer crust, spirit soaring high into the sky and out through the universe until her tendrils made contact with Divine.

There, Shalane paused for an ecstatic moment, letting the golden light fill her with love. Then down the cord she descended to her earthly body, bringing the light of heaven back to merge with that of Earth.

Turning her attention to the pain behind her eye, Shalane examined its texture and quality. Rough and jagged around the edges, the diffuse crystal had needle-like tips, each making Shalane's life a living hell as the mass rotated through its axis. The crystal throbbed, fueled by a force determined to incapacitate Shalane.

She dove into the mass and peered out through its surface. Each point was a prism, each prism an alternate reality, mocking Shalane with the brilliant suns of a thousand earths, each growing larger as she hurtled toward them through space and time.

Shalane's energy body morphed; she was not human but a gargantuan with wings as long as she was tall and as wide as the sky. She tumbled from the heavens, locked in battle with another like her. Glimpses of knowledge flew past, painful darts that avoided capture.

Wrenching out of the other's grasp, Shalane reached for the shiniest, sharpest barb and understanding dawned. The other was Ebby. They were best friends—both mighty creatures of God.

But dissent had broken out in the heavens. They had quarreled. Chosen sides. Opposite sides. Both believed they served the light. One was deceived. It had to be Ebby.

A sickening suspicion arose within Shalane as she careened through the void. Was it she who'd chosen wrong?

Then she was on the settee in the Twin Peaks chalet. Random feelings caromed off others that rebounded and hit home. The alternating bouts of attraction and animosity Shalane felt toward Ebby were not new, but ancient. Shalane was ancient.

Were they angels? Celestial beings? Come to earth to continue the fight? Shalane's hand shook as she reached for her cooling coffee. Were they expelled from heaven? Or some planet shattered to smithereens on the last high note of the celestial choir?

The almost-memory faded. Left behind were the feelings, especially the righteousness Shalane had taken as her shroud. She was God's warrior, the bespoken of Archangel Michael. She couldn't be evil. It was Ebby who had chosen incorrectly. Just one more reason her lovely nemesis should be punished.

Closing her eyes, Shalane reached energetically for Ebby's Elemental. It was faint but there, swirling in a mist of murky green. She rose from the sofa and hurried outside to face Mount Diablo, ignoring the early-morning passersby.

Arms in a wide vee, Shalane reached for the sky. Power from the heavens poured down. Her energetic Self grew wider and taller. Grinning maniacally, Shalane shot past the treetops and continued rising, above and beyond the clouds.

From this vantage point, she looked to the north and spied a weak storm front. She gathered it between her massive hands and swirled it with the Elemental into the shape of a cyclone.

Spinning three times, Shalane released the whirling dervish, hurling it like a bowling ball down the alley for a strike, then stood to admire her handiwork. The tempest skimmed the mountains outside Vegas and tumbled across the country toward Atlanta, gathering strength as it skipped along its drunken course.

Not satisfied yet, Shalane crossed the continent in one long stride. She reached into the Gulf of Mexico to fan the air, then watched with delight as the wind gathered upon itself. When it drew enough moisture and energy from the equator-warmed waters, she flung the second Elemental toward Ebby.

Cackling with glee, Shalane rubbed her hands together. Combined, the two storms would pack one hell of a punch.

**

A ding interrupted Nergal's scrutiny of Shalane Carpenter's recordings. Across the screen scrolled the data he had requested on Ebby Panera.

Born in Pasadena, California to mother Alexis Brown Cabot and father Jonah Cobb Cabot in June of 2012. Mother divorced father and moved repeatedly with daughter, changing names over the years. Both parents deceased, no siblings. The Panera woman's last known address, Five-Eleven Ocean Blvd, Orange, California.

Nergal tapped the keyboard, sifting through the sparse ancillary information. Ebby Panera had worked for the U.S. Disaster Recovery Agency until her discharge last year. No information was available on her past that date.

Not satisfied, Nergal instructed the computer to dig deeper.

Answers in the Wind

Emily exited the house at a trot, anxious to escape the interminable lessons. Halfway down the block, she realized her brain was busy categorizing information from the last two weeks and had to chuckle. Her brain must do what her brain must do, even when she aimed to derail its machinations.

Determined to quiet the whizzing processor, she increased her pace and focused on the late-afternoon ambiance of Druid Hills. An abundance of rain had graced the south since Emily's arrival. With the advent of warmer weather, the landscape had transformed in a prodigious display of greenery and flowers.

Catching a delightful scent, she spied a patch of wild azaleas blooming at the edge of a wooded lot. On her first encounter with the native shrub, Emily had mistaken the frilly flowers for honeysuckle. Their delicious aroma enveloped her for a moment, prompting a grin that sent endorphins all the way to her toes. She had to admit—spring in Atlanta was utterly enchanting.

A raven croaked in a nearby pine reminding Emily of her first night in Georgia. Many times she had retraced her steps in daylight hours, but she'd never come across the ramshackle houses or the grove with the shimmering fountain.

She *had* become intimate with the parks outlining the fifteen hundred acres of Druid Hills. Designed by Frederick Law Olmsted and his progeny in the early twentieth century, the series of linear parks threaded through several neighborhoods and boasted shrubs and flowers native to the South.

Old-growth oak interspersed with birch, beech and elm trees formed a tender green canopy over slender streets. Driveways threaded behind late-Victorian homes and bungalows carved into the rambling, ofttimes steep, hillsides.

Lavender thrift tumbled over terraced rock walls. Even the added landscaping was mostly native. But what were their names and healing properties?

"Animals, plants, and trees, oh my!" Emily groaned out loud.

So much to learn and so little time. Wondering again whether she was up to the task, Emily bounded up the trail skimming Deepdene Park and fought the urge to make like a tree and leave.

Make like a tree and leave? She stopped in her tracks. That was something her mother would say. Well, to hell with that. And all of her mother's clichés. Trees also grow roots.

She was staying in Druid Hills with the Hester family. *Her* family. So, what if they were slightly demented? Emily fit right in. They might want her to save the world, but at least they believed in her.

Turning back toward Wren's Roost, she said aloud, "I'm staying, by God, and that is that." It was the smart thing to do. The world was disintegrating. She'd seen the evidence. Overpopulation. Crumbling infrastructures. Collapse of the bee colonies.

Everything was poisoned—air, food, and water. Weather events and rising seas had claimed places Emily had vacationed as a kid. The world was on a collision course with total disaster. And the rats were running the ship.

Attesting to the mass insanity, cars clogged all four lanes of Moreland Avenue, a main artery for metro Atlanta. It was gratifying that many of the vehicles were hybrids and cold-fusion. A few even boasted photonic drives. But the race to reduce carbon dioxide levels was too little, too late. She jogged in placed at the traffic light.

Thunder rumbled in the distance, drawing Emily's gaze. Ominous clouds gathered in the south. The signal changed and she set off at a lope, crossing the thoroughfare headed for home.

When she rounded the corner on Wren's Lane, Emily was running flat-out, arms pumping, knees in the air. In her head, she repeated in time to her stride, "This is home, I am staying. This is home, I am staying."

At Wren's Roost's driveway she slowed and gasped for breath. She had decided her reward for two long weeks of nose-to-the-grindstone would be Jocko's pizza. Then, she would drive to the hospital to visit her comatose Da. Tomorrow they were supposed to release him to come home.

Thunder rumbled and a rising wind sighed through the trees. Behind her, black clouds gobbled the sky.

**

Emily backed the electric Scorpion from her father's garage and pressed the steering wheel remote to close the door. The convertible coupe was sexy and sporty in a luscious, pearl-green package. Mitchell had been reluctant to part with the keys to her Da's favorite car but had relented, nonetheless.

With rain imminent, Emily left the top up but opened the windows to the cool breeze. Lightning sparked. A gust of wind carried the sweetness of Carolina jasmine from the yellow trumpets flowing over the fence along the turnaround. A vision-cum-body-memory tiptoed to the edge of Emily's senses and twisted with the scent.

A woman cradled baby Emily. They both had the same shocking-red hair. With practiced gentleness, the woman kissed her forehead, nose and chin, then blew butterfly kisses on her eyes, cheeks, and lips, making her erupt into giggles. Stomping the brakes, Emily skidded to a stop.

Her Bebe. Great-grandmother Brigid. Omigod. Emily closed her eyes and was back there again, safe and loved and adored.

A crack of thunder brought her back as a gust of wind rocked the Scorpion. It swirled away through the woods, inciting leaves to life. Their voices rose on the gale and fell again, twanging Emily's nerves. Goosebumps prickled along the nape of her neck and her senses buzzed with the frenzy.

A bolt of multi-forked brilliance yanked Emily's attention to the storm. Boomers rolled across a firmament bruised black. The hair on her arms stood to attention as ozone-flavored electricity rinsed the air. Against the tumult of trees thrashing in the mad wind, unembodied voices echoed from the forest to join the

150

cacophony. They gathered in volume, uniting to shout in an ancient language something Emily didn't understand, though she sensed she should.

"In English," she yelled out the window.

A jolt of energy shot from her tailbone up her spine. It exploded against the base of Emily's skull and bloomed along her scalp. From there it danced across Emily's shoulders, spreading to her chest and arms, then down her torso and legs, before exiting both feet. Her body convulsed in a wracking shiver that left Emily questioning whether lightning had hit her, though she knew it hadn't. What in living hell had just happened to her?

Her belly growled, distracting her from the sensation and pulling her back to the moment.

She eyed the approaching system. Could she make it to Jocko's before the deluge? It was only a mile. Emily shuddered at the thought of being caught in a nasty storm, but she wanted, no she needed, pizza. Plus, she had to know why Lugh continued to give her the cold shoulder, in spite of his obvious interest. Unless you could count kicking Emily's ass repeatedly interest. Not once had she managed to stay upright during their sessions, much less pin the priest, despite having floored every other opponent he'd sent her way.

Thunder boomed, forcing her to answer the question that had shaped Emily's life—should she go, or should she stay?

"Goooo!" The voices roared in unison.

She glanced at her reflection in the rearview mirror. Was she hearing things? Or finally paying attention?

"Goooo." There it was again.

This time she was certain. Chills propelled her to jam her foot down on the accelerator. The svelte Scorpion fishtailed and peeled through the neighborhood, racing the storm. She pressed the buttons to raise the windows and turned on Magnolia to brake for the light, gasping as the full-frontal view appeared.

The southern sky was as ominous as any Emily had ever seen. A clearly-defined shelf of gray roiled beneath voluptuous white clouds. Lightning danced along the shelf's underbelly. Thunder rolled in its wake.

High winds and hail, possibly a twister, were in store for Atlanta. She was ill equipped to deal with any of that right now. But in spite of her fear, every cell of her being leapt in excitement when she pointed the Scorpion into the storm.

The sweetness of adrenaline coursed through her as old instincts sprang to life. Then the projector clicked on in the back of Emily's brain and Trey Serra tumbled through the air in slow motion, snatched from her arms by Cyclone Charlotte. Ever lurking, ever ready, the panic attacked and threatened to drive everything else from her mind.

The light turned green and she gunned the Scorpion, racing for shelter, safety, and food. Holding onto her sanity by a thin thread, she pushed back at the terror. The next red light gave it purchase. Thunder boomed, so close Emily screamed. She rocked in the seat, gulping air and trying to calm the panic that had hijacked her senses, curdling her insides and branding itself into her cells until there was nothing left but the metallic, all-consuming fear.

When the light finally changed, she shrieked at the car in front of her, "What are you waiting for? An engraved invitation?" Frustrated and panicked, Emily popped the clutch and kept the Scorpion's nose glued to the chrome rear-end of the Town Car. Glancing up at the black sky, she searched her repertoire for a druid spell that might hold back the onslaught. Just a few more minutes. That's all she needed.

Not remembering any, much less one for weather, Emily resorted to a prayer she'd learned as a child and still used whenever troubled. Out loud she recited, "The Lord is my shepherd, I shall not want."

Fat, but isolated, raindrops collided with the windshield. One more traffic light and she would be at Jocko's.

"He maketh me to lie down in green pastures—"

Emily bit off a scream when a plastic bag blew across the windshield, blinding her for an instant. The drops came harder and closer together. She wheeled into the parking lot and slammed the brakes to avoid hitting a family with small children. Waving them across, Emily watched them dash through the parking lot, getting drenched in spite of raincoats and umbrellas.

"He leadeth me beside the still waters, and restoreth my soul."

She parked as close to the door as possible and frowned at the design flaw she had noticed on her first visit; the parking lot was more than twenty yards from Jocko's door and not an inch of it was covered. Emily killed the engine and spoke loudly to hear her words over the torrent pummeling the hemp canvas roof.

"He leadeth me on the path of righteousness for His name sake."

Lightning flared and thunder rolled, a prolonged rumble that shook the car. This storm was a monster, writhing and beautiful, that gobbled up every patch of light in the southern sky. Reaching in her pocket to touch Aóme, Emily thought of her fathers, both heavenly and on earth, and spoke with conviction. "Yea though I walk through the valley of the shadow of death, I shall fear no evil, for thou art with me."

A calm descended, within and without. The storm had stalled. Sinister clouds held the rain at bay, enshrouding the world in an eerie, yellowish-green glow. In the lull, the dissonance of blaring horns and screeching tires was a stark reminder that drivers still jockeyed to negotiate traffic and escape the churning tempest. It was now or never.

Emily stretched her raincoat around her purse, tugged the hood over her head, and shoved the door open. The negative pressure pushed against her as she crawled from the car and turned toward the entrance. Aghast, she stopped midstride.

Another storm, as large as the first, was brewing to the north. Electricity rippled through the ebony layer cushioning the approaching thunderheads. Emily shivered. Rarely had a Nor'easter made landfall this far south or inland.

And it was on a collision course with the tempest that had stalled.

Tension, amped-up and zinging, rippled in the air as thunder crackled overhead, riding the wind the storms created and perpetuated. Emily bounced on excited but terrified toes as her storm-chasing Self fought the fear. Twisting, she ogled the squall to the south and pirouetted to gawk at the nor'easter. A gust of wind slapped her from behind, literally shoving her forward.

The southern front was on the move again, riled by the mass hurtling toward it. Needing no further motivation, Emily ran toward the door while willing the storms to hold off a little longer. She resumed her prayer.

"Thy rod and thy staff, they comfort me. Thou preparest a table before me in the presence of mine enemies—"

A scream pierced the raging din. Emily clutched her purse and paused to search for the source. Seeing no one in trouble, she raced for safety. The traffic sounds faded, lost again in the howl of the wind that buffeted from all directions. Craning her neck for one last look at the monster storms, she shoved through Jocko's door and wrangled it shut as a gust of wind armed with fat raindrops and pea-sized hail pelted the window and rattled the panes.

"Thou annointest my head with oil, my cup runneth over." Giving in to an inner urge, Emily fished Aóme from her jeans pocket, slid the ring on her finger, and raised her fist to the clashing storms. "Surely goodness and mercy shall follow me all the days of my life and I shall dwell in the house of the Lord." Ad-libbing, she added, "Rebuke these storms, oh Jehovah, I pray. Protect Jocko's and keep us all alive and safe. And so it is, and shall be. AMEN!"

Feeling slightly better, Emily turned to go inside, but the inner door held tight. She pushed again. Nothing. Surely they hadn't closed the place. Panic licked at her innards and she shoved hard. The vacuum seal broke and the door flew open, spilling Emily into the relative calm of Jocko's Pizza. Embarrassed, she teetered but kept her balance, throwing back the hood to shake out damp curls.

When she saw several patrons eyeing her with concern, heat sprang to Emily's cheeks. It was obvious they had been watching her through the plate glass windows. A few nodded. Others waved, accepting her into their sanctuary, as relieved as Emily that she had made it inside before the storm broke. But the cherries rode high in her cheeks.

A Hunk, A Hunk, A Storm

Awaitress stood near Jocko's entrance and waited for Emily with a plastic menu clutched to the chest of her hot-pink tee. The logo sported a pizza with a slice missing and the slogan "Best Pizza Around". Between that and the yeasty, tomato-y smell of the restaurant, Emily's mouth was watering.

Lucille, according to the name tag, motioned for her to take a seat. She thanked her and chose a booth as far from the windows as possible, then slid in on the side facing the kitchen and away from the storms. Lucille relinquished the menu, took Emily's drink order, and checked on the occupants of the next booth before heading to the kitchen.

Fidgeting in her seat, Emily searched in vain for Lugh MacBrayer. Above the bar on a large screen, WXAA was broadcasting live from Georgia Stadium. Rain pelted a slickered weatherwoman. Not wanting to watch, Emily opened the menu. But her rebellious gaze crept back up.

She wished it hadn't. The reporter clung to a lamp post, bombarded by rain and gale-force winds. Scanning the restaurant, she saw several more screens tuned to different stations. All covered the storms. Or storm. The two had merged into one colossal squall.

Outside, rain lashed the thick windows, blurring the street and traffic beyond. A young couple stood to peer out, as if trying to decide whether to go or to stay. Lightning flashed, too close for comfort, and they leapt backwards in unison. A sharp, cracking boom shook the windows. The storm was literally on top of them.

Leave it to Emily to choose a restaurant with glass walls—a detail she'd overlooked first time around. Lucille arrived with root beer, fear tightening the lines around her eyes. The server stared out the window, then turned to Emily.

"I hope we don't lose power again." Her nasally Midwestern twang pegged her as a fellow transplant. "Between the roving blackouts and the storm outages, it's been one heckuva spring. We'd be out of business if it weren't for our generators." She nodded toward the window. "Yaah, and it's getting worse."

Emily would rather not have any of that information. She groaned and rolled her eyes. In spite of her resolve, she peeked at the window. The rain was banding in waves of nearly horizontal sheets. She hadn't seen anything like it since Fiji.

Out on North Decatur Road, the overhead signals flashed red and yellow, gyrating wildly in the whirling wind. Cars, barely discernable through the downpour, battled bumper-to-bumper traffic. The young couple sat back down, obviously deciding it wasn't safe to leave.

Thunder crashed, so near and so loud that the waitress jumped, and Emily squealed. Aftershocks rumbled through the restaurant, a low-pitched roll that shook the floor underfoot.

Shuddering, Emily wrapped her arms around her own shoulders, glad she hadn't stayed home alone. Ralph would be hiding in a closet or beneath the bed. With luck, Hope was huddled beside him. She ordered a slice of the Italian Special and handed the menu back to Lucille.

Her stomach grumbled, loud enough to hear over the noise. Where was Lugh, dammit? Had she picked his day off? In the middle of a god-awful storm? Based on his frequent absence from Emily's training sessions, she would have bet he lived here.

As if by magic, the druid priest exited the kitchen through swinging doors. A rush of relief and anticipation weakened Emily's knees. She was glad she was sitting. After a glance at the storm, he ducked behind the bar for an exchange with the bartender, who slipped to the back. Lugh filled a drink order, his worried gaze returning to the windows.

He was average height, maybe five-ten in boots, and he possessed a rugged appeal that turned Emily to goo. She figured that was why she couldn't best him in hand-to-hand. Trembling with nerves, she leaned over her tumbler to sip sugary soda through the plastic straw.

Glass shattered in the kitchen on a sharp crash of thunder. Emily bit back another squeal. The storms were hitting and hitting hard. Like Lugh MacBrayer. He stuck his head into the kitchen, anchoring an elbow on each of the swinging doors.

When he leaned in further, Emily grinned. The druid had a nice butt. The further he leaned, the wider her smirk. Until he let go of the doors and looked straight at her. Busted, she blushed and dropped the leer. Surprised satisfaction flickered in Lugh's eyes before his gaze shifted to the rain-lashed windows.

Lightning flashed in the nearly dark sky and he scoured the restaurant as if counting heads. He nodded pensively and gave Emily a half-hearted smile. Grinning, she threw him a four-finger waggle and was rewarded when an endearing grin lit his face.

With another nod in her direction, the manager slipped through the swinging doors. A shiver much like the one Emily had experienced in the car ran up her back and through her body. This time she restrained the urge to shake like a dog. Just in case anyone was watching.

A loud siren wailed, not more than a block away. Lugh burst from the kitchen, face drawn. The low wail progressed to ear-splitting proportions before calming and growing louder again. The outer door slammed open and shattered. Wind-driven rain and siren blare shrieked through the shards.

Lugh sprang to action, turning the "CLOSED" sign around and locking the interior door. Sheets of debris-laden rain with tree limbs and leaves blew into the exposed foyer, dragging the newly-turned sign into the melee. A lawn chair cartwheeled down the sidewalk and ricocheted off cars before disappearing, gripped in the clutches of rotating winds.

Tires squealed, metal crunched, and glass shattered as cars collided. A series of crashes rent the air as more vehicles plunged into the first. The siren caterwauled—cycling over, and over again. Clamping the heels of her hands over her sensitive ears, Emily groaned to no one in particular, "Make it stop."

The sight of Lugh with his mouth open, staring at the TV, made Emily crane her neck. Splayed across the screen was a radar image of the storm covering the entire state of Georgia. The next frame was worse—a bird's eye view of funnel clouds forming around Atlanta. And according to the map, one was on top of them. Holy cow.

Not again.

Her fear was reflected in every face in the restaurant. Raw adrenaline coursed through Emily's already-charged system. Her disaster training kicked in. She leapt from the booth and motioned toward the back. "Get away from the windows," she shouted in her most commanding voice.

"To the basement," Lugh yelled, "Through the kitchen."

Emily herded the patrons in that direction. Zigzagged lightning reflected off the mirror behind the bar. The room went dark and an explosive boom muffled Lugh's exhortations. A young girl screamed, echoing Emily's soundless one. The lights sputtered and died. Customers milled in the dining room like cattle.

Lugh waved toward the swinging doors and shouted over the madness, "That way! Hurry!"

Emily steered the people in that direction. The backup generator kicked on, bathing the restaurant in a dim yellow glow. A round of cheers went up from customers and staff. Emily's stomach growled so loud she heard it over the hubbub.

Reaching the kitchen, she stepped aside to let a couple with two terrified kids go ahead of her. Lugh slid past them, shouting orders to the cooks and servers about turning off ovens and clearing away knives and sharp utensils. One of them hefted containers of water onto an old-fashioned dumb waiter, another gathered candles and fresh provisions. Emily hoped they wouldn't be down there long enough to need them.

The kitchen was full of frightened customers. Lucille and another waitress waved them downstairs, while Lugh disappeared into the dining room. Had he gone to rescue the money from the till? More likely to search for stragglers. Emily eyed the manic patrons jostling through the cellar door. She would take her chances with the storm.

The wind overpowered the siren, which still persisted, its pitch more urgent. She spied Lugh in the corner of the middle dining room, speaking to an elderly gentleman. Lugh motioned her over.

"Would you help Mr. Peterson?" She nodded and he yelled to the white-haired gent, "I'll find your nephew. Ms. Hester will take you to the back."

The roar took on a shrieking edge. The walls shook and the windows rattled.

"Hurry!" Emily shrilled and swept Mr. Peterson to the kitchen, as gently as possible in the circumstances. She delivered the elderly patron to the end of the dwindling line and a server's capable hands, then ran to find Lugh steering a young man across the dining room.

"Go," he commanded, pointing to the kitchen.

Metal screeched on the roof overhead. Emily waited a beat, then shoved through the swinging doors. A waitress waved frantically from inside the cellar.

The screech changed to an ominous sucking noise—the roof being dragged from the building.

Druid Cellar

The men burst through the kitchen doors. Together, the three of them tumbled into the cellar, almost knocking the waitress down the steps. Lugh slammed the steel door, securing it with the deadbolt. He sagged against it as the young man helped his uncle downstairs.

Emily let her eyes adjust to the dim light. She hated basements. Nasty things lived underground in the dark, of this she was certain. But at least the awful noise had stopped. The steel and concrete blocked the sound.

"Ladies first," Lugh gestured to the stairs.

Acutely aware of him behind her on the narrow landing, Emily felt for and found the handrail. Steeling her nerves, she started down, shivering when Lugh's breath feathered her hair.

The room under Jocko's was remarkably large, its walls and drop ceiling lined with recessed lighting that gave the illusion of daylight. But Emily was uneasy. She was in a cellar, no matter how pleasant.

Employees were busy unstacking chairs around tables that dotted the room. Wide-eyed children cowered behind adults with cell phones to their ears, most grumbling of no service.

The smell of pizza wafted to her and Emily's hunger returned with a vengeance. She quickly pinpointed the source—a table in the far back corner. Behind it, Lugh shoveled steaming slices onto paper plates.

She made a beeline for him and took the plate he offered with a smile. Thanking him, she promptly bit in and sank into a chair at the adjoining table.

"Mmm. Good pie," she mumbled around the piping-hot mouthful. That earned her a proud smile and nod from Lugh.

Between the dark lock of hair that tumbled over one brow, and the smile that transformed his enigmatic face, Emily was undone. "You own this place, don't you?"

A twinkle sprang into the dark eyes. "Why, yes, I do. Welcome to Jocko's Pizza."

Emily smiled and glanced at the other patrons. "Why is no one eating?"

Shrugging, Lugh announced to the room in general, "Hot pizza on the house, come and get it."

Chairs scraped as people shoved away from the tables. The elderly man and his nephew, plus the family Emily had almost run over in the parking lot, moved to form a line. An older, affluent couple and a group of Emory students of varying shapes, sizes, and nationalities shuffled to join them. The rest remained seated.

When the patrons were fed, the kitchen and wait staff grabbed their own plates and huddled at a table in the back. Lucille made the rounds, filling glasses to the brim with crunchy ice. Another server poured soda, tea, and water.

Lugh slid into the chair opposite Emily's and studied her with a curious expression.

"What?" she asked, around a mouthful of pizza, her internal hotty alarm clanging.

"You're different than I imagined when I first met you here with Mitchell."

Emily stopped chewing. Frissons danced up and down her spine. "How so?"

He studied her face, then gave the rest of her a once-over. "For one thing, the deer in the headlights look is gone."

Emily chuckled. "I'd just gotten in from L.A. and was pretty shell-shocked. What's the other thing?"

He leaned in so that his nose grazed her hair and his lips were millimeters from her neck. Lugh inhaled slowly, as if sampling her scent. Sensual, searching, and oddly familiar, the move caught Emily unaware. Goosebumps danced along the nape of her neck as a memory of a roaring fire stirred, then Lugh pulled away and it faded.

"God, you smell good," he damn-near sighed. "And that other thing? You're even sexier than I'd thought."

Before Emily could choke out a response, Lugh chucked her under the chin and walked away. Attraction warred with confusion. At Wren's Roost, Lugh consistently kicked her ass, showing no mercy. Yet today he'd done nothing but flirt.

Emily watched him mingle and work the room, noting his quick smile and solicitous manner as he spoke with the other displaced customers. Charisma and charm rode him well.

Her heart beat faster when she thought of the way Lugh had breathed in her scent, as if to inhale her. It was intoxicating, like nothing Emily had ever experienced. The man was a dichotomy. One she would enjoy unraveling. Assuming he wasn't married. Or otherwise taken. But surely he wouldn't flirt so brazenly if he was?

She munched her pizza and studied the crowd around the surprisingly-cozy room. The adults sat at tables, eating and chatting amongst themselves. Most looked comfortable and reconciled to spending time in the cellar of Jocko's. From the corner, music played, cycling through oldies from their grandparents' era.

Lugh approached a group of children with playing cards and coloring books. Eager for a distraction, the younger kids fell upon the coloring books, while the older ones commandeered the cards.

Emily was no expert on children, but these were well-behaved given the circumstances. She thought of Brian and wondered if Lugh's nephew was safe.

When he neared, she asked, "Is Brian at school?"

He turned with a solemn smile. "You've met my nephew?"

She nodded and Lugh gave her an odd look. "My cell reception sucks like everyone else's, but I reached him on the landline before that went down. He got home just before the storm hit."

Emily frowned, imagining the worst.

"It's okay," he assured. "Brian was heading into the basement. I'm sure he's down there playing some video game."

Her sphincter relaxed. "Thank God for that."

162

"Thank God for that," Lugh echoed. "And no, I'm not married."

Emily's head jerked up. "Huh?" she gasped, voice shrill. Mortified, she lowered it a couple of octaves. "Why do you say that?" Lugh's smirk widened. Her cheeks grew warm.

"You know."

"Okay, first? No, I don't. And second? I don't want to." There. That told him.

"Well," Lugh huffed, looking wounded for about two seconds before the wolf grin appeared. Damn he was cute.

"What?" she sulked.

"You. Me." He pointed at her, then to himself. "Dinner. Friday night."

"No." She shook her head. "I don't think so." Then she stuffed the last bite of pizza in her mouth.

As much as she enjoyed flirting with Lugh, he was the high priest of her druid order. And Emily was supposed to be the grand druid. She was pretty sure that would be frowned upon.

"My treat," Lugh cajoled.

She chewed furiously, head bobbing back and forth, and eyebrows glued in the 'no-hell-no' position.

"Have you had a chance to see Atlanta? Let me show you around. If there's anything left of her after this."

His voice dropped and caught on the last sentence, melting Emily's resolve. The hitch resonated, echoing the sadness that had colored her life. Especially since losing Trey.

Too perceptive, Lugh asked, "What is it?"

"Nothing." She glanced away to hide the quick tears. "Where would we go if I did say yes?"

His tone promised worlds. "Your pick. Anywhere your heart desires."

Emily knew she shouldn't. But she wanted to. And why not? What was that old saying? Better to ask forgiveness than permission?

"How about Zoo Atlanta? I'd love to meet the famous Willie D. He and I are twins."

"Are you now?" Lugh teased. "Got a bit of silverback gorilla in you, Miz Hester?"

Emily chuckled. "No, silly. We were born on the same day."

A peculiar light flashed in the druid's eyes. "So that would make you twenty-nine, going on thirty. Huh. You and Willie D," Lugh said with an odd smile.

"Yeah. Me and Willie D."

"Then Zoo Atlanta it is. Assuming, of course, it's still there after today."

Lugh shoved away from the table. "I can't take it anymore. I've got to know what's happening up there." He ran a hand through the unruly black hair. "I'll be back."

But he didn't leave, instead leaning his hands on the table.

"Since we're going to the zoo, let's make it Saturday morning. Nine o'clock? Pick you up at Wren's Roost?"

Emily snagged a refill from a passing waiter. Swigging the soda, she suppressed a burp and gazed up at Lugh with googly eyes. Patient, he waited for an answer.

Finally, she muttered, "Okay. Nine o'clock. Saturday morning. But I'll meet you here."

Lugh opened his mouth to protest.

Emily swallowed, unwavering. "My terms."

"Then, here, it is." Lugh saluted and clicked his heels. "Now I must check in with APD and find out if there will be a 'here' then."

**

Less than an hour after the siren first sounded, Lugh received the all-clear from the police department. Accompanied by two of his men, he climbed the stairs to assess the damage. From his initial scan, the kitchen—Jocko's heart—appeared intact. That was a huge blessing.

He stuck his head through the swinging doors and gasped. The front wall and part of the roof were missing. Rain poured in, soaking the patio and the front half of the restaurant. He put Xerxes and Kyle to work moving the furniture out of the rain and punched a number on his cell. Trent Phillips answered in one ring.

"Trent, Lugh MacBrayer. You guys okay over there?" He listened to the reply. "Glad to hear it. We weren't so lucky at Jocko's. The storm ripped the roof off the front and the windows are shattered. Could you possibly bring a crew over and close 'er up? Enough to keep the rain and looters out?" Lugh gulped and held his breath.

The druid builder yelled, "Blessed be! The storm missed Jocko's!" to someone on his end. Of Lugh, Trent asked, "Is the kitchen okay?"

His concern brought a lump to Lugh's throat. "Kitchen's fine. Did you say the storm *missed* Jocko's?"

"Kitchen's fine," Trent reported, then said to Lugh, "Hell yeah, man! We just heard on the news that the whole block was wiped out. I can't imagine life without your pizza. Oh, look! There you are on television. Sheesh, Lugh. Is everyone okay? Christ a'mighty."

"What? What do you see?" Lugh rushed to the exposed front and gasped. Where the coffee house had been was a pile of rubble. Flashing lights from emergency vehicles threw garish shadows on the wanton destruction. Workers dressed in Fire Department gear swarmed the sidewalks and street.

Paramedics labored to extricate passengers from vehicles and dig patrons from cellars of once-thriving businesses. They loaded the injured onto stretchers, then in ambulances and fire trucks. One took off, siren blasting, toward Emory Hospital. All in a steady, slogging rain.

"Shit, Trent," Lugh muttered. "Christ a'mighty is right. It looks like Armageddon out there."

"Yeah," Trent agreed. "Thank God Jocko's made it. Is everyone okay? Any injuries or," the gulp was loud enough for Lugh to hear, "any casualties?"

"No, thank God." Lugh hadn't realized just how lucky they were. "We made it to the basement. Everyone's fine. Jocko's isn't." He was grateful the bulk of his building was intact, especially since the others weren't. But he couldn't keep the disappointment from his voice.

"I know, buddy. We'll get her up and running as quickly as possible. You hang tight. I'll be there with a crew as soon as I can. They're reporting downed power lines and trees blocking some streets, but I'm leaving now." Emotion thickened the builder's voice. "We'll get her buttoned up for you, I promise, Lu-Mac."

"Thank you, Trent. Be safe out there." Lugh stared at the damage.

The whole of Jocko's front was demolished. The sign Lugh had paid an arm and a leg for last year hung precariously close to the sidewalk. Shards of glass covered everything, inside and out. The rain poured in, unrelenting.

Luckily, the bar and deeper sections had been spared for the most part. Lugh ducked behind the counter to access the panel for the overhead screens and waited for images to appear around the room. Powered by the generator, all but two flickered on. Encouraged to know the building still had some life, he instructed his guys to spread plastic tablecloths over what couldn't be moved.

Lugh picked his way outside to take a look at the damage. Fire trucks and police cruisers had parked haphazardly on the curb and sidewalk. Stepping into the melee, he turned a slow circle to take in the devastation.

A battered Jocko's stood at the top of the small rise, but everything else was gone. The Coffee House. The Peruvian Barbecue. The twenty-four-hour pharmacy, the grocery, Post Office, convenience store, the filling station. All were razed, nothing left but a few block walls and exposed plumbing and wires. Police strobes flashed, throwing an eerie glow over the scene.

Lugh shook his now-wet head, barely believing his eyes. Everything but his restaurant was gone. How could that be? He watched a familiar cruiser jump the curb to park on the last available patch of sidewalk.

Taurus Gowan climbed out with his partner Pete Peschi, a retired middle-linebacker from the majors. The officers' expressions mirrored Lugh's.

He unlocked the inner door and retreated beneath the intact part of the roof to wave them in. They plodded through the entrance, solemn heads shaking in unison as they removed dripping hats.

"Taurus. Pete," Lugh nodded to each.

"Lugh." They returned somber nods. Peschi stepped up to shake Lugh's hand.

Taurus did the same. "Is everyone safe?"

Lugh nodded.

"We're looking for Emily Hester. She's not at Wren's Roost and we've been unable to locate her. Hamilton's car is in your lot. Please tell us she's here and safe."

"She is." Lugh hitched his thumb toward the back, "Miz Hester came in just before the storm hit. She's in the cellar, with the rest." Taurus whipped out his radio and relayed the message that the priest and grand druid were alive and well.

When he clicked off, Lugh asked, "What happened, exactly?"

"Three tornadoes," Peschi bellowed over a wailing siren. "All converged into one, big-ass twister that walloped Emory Hill. Someone up there's looking out for you, Lu-Mac."

"I'd say," Taurus nodded, eyes big. "The usual enchantments didn't hold at the Health Food Co-op. Those girls should have been protected. But it's a pile of rubble, same as the non-druid stores."

A knife twisted in Lugh's guts. He'd been friends with Jo and Stef since grade school. "Was anyone hurt?" The knife carved through him and angry impotence made his hands shake. "Is there anything I can do to help?"

Pete answered, "No, they're all fine. Just shaken, like you. And determined to rebuild. News is mostly good from the businesses, thanks to the old storm cellars. But the folks in their cars and the homeless were hit hard. Too many were caught outside."

Lugh rubbed his chin to calm the tremors. "And I thought we had it bad. We heard the roof rip from the building on our way down cellar. We barely got everyone out in time."

Taurus eyed the rain pouring in the gaping hole and shook his head. "Jocko's will be attractive to looters. We'll make sure she's well patrolled tonight."

"Trent's on his way. He promised to button her up. But I appreciate you keeping an eye on Jocko's. How did the rest of the order fare?"

"All most folks got was a bit of wind damage—broken windows, downed trees, and the like. Yours is the only place with a hole and the Co-op's the only one demolished." Peschi exchanged looks with Taurus. "A few injuries, nothing major. No fatalities that we know of, though plenty of civilians died. What about your nephew?"

"He made it home from school before the storm hit. Hold on, let me check in." Lugh whipped his cell out and punched Brian's number. After a brief exchange, he hung up, calmer.

"He says he thinks the only damage is to the old sycamore out back." The officers nodded, relieved. Lugh edged toward the kitchen. "Is it okay if I let Emily and the other forty customers out of my cellar?"

Taurus settled the plastic-encased hat on his head. "The winds and hail have passed, and Jocko's side exit is clear. The cars in your lot survived, though goddess knows how."

One more thing for Lugh to be grateful for. "Thanks, fellas." His voice went husky. "I'll let them know. Thank you both for what you do out there. And for looking after Jocko's."

"Are you kidding?" Peschi said, "I grew up eating here. This town wouldn't be the same without Jocko's Pizza. We've got you covered, Lu-Mac. No worries. Okay?" Lugh nodded.

He let go of a pent-up sigh when the officers left. Peschi was right. A lot of people had grown up eating here. Jocko's was an institution. He ignored the ache in his gut and gave the all-clear to the two cooks hovering nearby. "Go on home to your families, guys. And thank you for getting the stuff out of the rain. We'll clean up the rest tomorrow."

Grateful "thank yous" and "see you thens" were Lugh's answer.

He cut through the kitchen and prickles danced on the back of his neck. He twisted to search for his mother's ghost. She hovered in front of the swinging doors, a sassy apron cinching her ample waist. Smiling, she waved in that way she'd had that put everyone at ease.

Across the room, his father stood before the pizza oven, round middle dusted in flour and secret sauce, a twinkle in his merry eyes. Lugh's stomach lurched. Seldom did his deceased parents pop in just to visit. They usually brought bad news.

"Don't worry, Lughnasadh." His mom sparkled. "Chin up, Son. You have forgotten that what seems bad is ofttimes good. This storm has reached the Otherworld." She glanced over at the love of her life, who winked as she whispered conspiratorially, "The dragons are stirring. Draigs Talav and Ooschu now roam unfettered. And after this bit of magic," she waved her hands over her vaporous head, "Tienu and a-Ur will be up and about, too."

The hairs on Lugh's arms stood up and waved. Her ghost pointed an ethereal finger at the basement, then vanished to reappear beside him in a cool breeze.

"The dragons are searching for Emily, Lugh. They need her for something—most likely to defend the world. It was she who saved Jocko's. Keep her close. She needs your strength and protection. And you hers. But to fall in love with her would be most unwise." She brushed his cheek with a hand that went right through him. Her eyes grew large with warning. "Emily would be your downfall, Lugh. Awful things have I seen on the wind."

She slowly faded and disappeared, no doubt whisking his father on some Otherworld adventure. But her voice floated to him, thin and fading, "And remember this—the four answer to her, only her."

"Goodbye," Lugh whispered, his throat tight.

He considered his mother's warning about Emily and shook his head. It was too late. He'd already fallen. Disappointment wafted through him and the hairs danced on the backs of his arms. He'd finally found his somebody and wouldn't ya know she'd be the one he couldn't have. He muscled the cellar door open.

"Great," he mumbled as he headed down the stairs. "Like things weren't bad enough already, now we have dragons and magical tornadoes. And my balls will be blue forever."

New Student

S halane paused in the middle of an early dinner to stare at the television. The weather bombs had converged on a restaurant where Ebby Panera had been eating. Now her image filled the screen. Part of Shalane was thrilled that Ebby was unscathed. She hadn't meant to hurt her, just scare the pants off her.

And it should have worked. Devastation and pandemonium surrounded her old student. But Ebby's eyes glittered. And not with fear. A handsome man stood beside her with a protective hand on her shoulder. Who was he? And what was he to Ebby?

Pondering these questions, Shalane put Patrika to work clearing the table, then moseyed to the living room to prepare for lessons, a job that included shooing Cecil off to a movie. Soon Patty joined her for her first magic lesson. The girl had been vocal about her doubts but had promised to give it a try.

"Ready?" Shalane asked. Lips a petulant moue, Patty shrugged. "The first step in meditation is to sit in a comfortable position, with your back straight." Patty rearranged her legs on the sofa to mirror Shalane's cross-legged lotus.

"Now," Shalane continued, "just follow my instructions. If your mind wanders, bring it back to my voice. Ready?"

For the hundredth time, the girl asked, "But what if I can't?"

"Then we'll try again. But believe me, Patrika, there is nothing to it. Just follow my instructions and do as I say. You'll be a pro in no time."

Pout skeptical, Patty reached for a pillow and tucked it under her knee.

Patience not her forte, Shalane clenched her teeth. When all movement ceased, she tried again. "Ready?"

To her relief, the girl nodded.

"Close your eyes and listen to the sound of my voice. Let all else fade away. Nothing matters but my words. All else is noise, let it go." Shalane opened her eyes to see if Patty's were closed. They were. "Now take a deep breath in, hold it for a count of four, then exhale."

She spoke slowly, pausing between instructions. "Another breath. Exhale. On your next breath, pretend you are sending imaginary roots from the base of your spine into the earth. Let them penetrate easily and effortlessly, cutting through the rock like butter."

The girl sniffed.

Shalane ignored her and continued, "Keep your attention on the sound of my voice. Breathe in, hold, breathe out, hold. Breathe in, hold, breathe out, hold. Imagine your roots are going deeper into Mother Earth. When you reach the bottom, let your root tips grip the bedrock and anchor in." She waited for the girl to do as instructed.

**

Nergal watched from his perch as the Reylian descended with the girl, moving fast. He doused his light and took a position directly below Patrika. She reached the bottom, moments after Shalane ascended.

Nergal touched Patty's leg, connecting with her consciousness long enough to make the energetic transfer. He left his body and traveled to the surface of AboveEarth with the girl. When Patrika opened her eyes, Nergal found himself seated next to the smug Reylian.

A jolt of righteous glee sizzled through him. It was foreign, this feeling, but thrilling, too. The reptilian closed Patty's eyes and tried to focus on the priest's words.

"…when you reach Father God, thank him, then slowly return to earth, to your body, bringing his divine essence back with you…"

"This is drivel," Nergal thought.

"…now imagine in front of you a grand staircase leading up to the sky, higher and higher, until way up in the far reaches you see a castle gleaming in the sunlight at the very top of the stairs..."

**

Nergal hung around until the human fell asleep. He then returned to his own world, keeping an invisible thread attached so he could come and go.

The day had been productive. Nergal had learned, among other things, that the source of the reverend's power was coupling with a being she called Archangel Michael. The revelation caused Nergal some consternation. In his world, the entity was known as the Destroyer. He would have to be careful, which went against Nergal's natural instinct to charge ahead. Instead, he would need stealth and secrecy. Meanwhile, he would learn Shalane's magic. Then, when the time came to take AboveEarth, he would have an edge over the other generals and factions.

Accessing the Onyx Gate, Nergal caught a chute to the main level and crossed to the officer's hall, ignoring the riff-raff that parted for him to pass. He would eat and return to his own quarters before it was time to provide an update on the project. The latest development regarding Nergal's brainchild he would keep to himself. For now.

Air Dragon

The next day dawned chilly and bright. Emily woke to the insistent trill of the doorbell. Beside her on the bedtable, her iBlast vibrated. She picked it up and squinted at the screen. What did Wainwright want at this hour? She climbed from bed into the fuzzy robe and let the call go to voicemail. The assault on her doorbell continued, interspersed with loud knocks.

Tugging on her Uggs, Emily made for the front door. Through the peephole, she eyed her Aunt Morgan, cheeks rosy and dressed to the nines. What the hell? Removing the deadbolt, she stepped aside to let Morgan bustle in.

"Brr-er-ER! It's c-cold out there," the tall woman proclaimed, wringing her leather-gloved hands. "Got coffee?"

Nodding, Emily bumped the thermostat up a few notches and shuffled to the kitchen, where she barely avoided tripping over a meowing Ralph. Morgan followed, chattering about the storm and what a miracle it was that Emily and Jocko's Pizza were spared when the rest of Emory Hill was decimated.

Emily started the tea and coffee brewing and opened a can of food for Ralph. Done, she propped her backside against the counter to study her still jabbering aunt.

"What's up?" she asked, interrupting Morgan mid-sentence.

Her aunt sputtered, eyes widening. "Emily, I came as soon as I heard. Mitchell Wainwright and some of the druids are claiming you summoned that storm last night."

Emily clutched the robe to her chest and stared, heart in her throat. For the love of all that was holy.

"Now, I know it's not true," Morgan hurried on, "I mean, you don't yet have the power to summon a storm, and even if you did, you wouldn't. But Mitchell and several of your father's detractors are on the way here."

The thought of fleeing crossed Emily's mind; these people were batshit crazy. Then the teakettle whistled and instead of running, she poured water over the leaves. Excusing herself, she hurried to the bedroom to dress.

When she returned, Morgan sat at the dining room table, sipping a cup of rich-smelling coffee. Emily plopped in a chair beside her to wait.

**

One hour later, the group was still divided. Mitchell Wainwright, Olga Phagan, Frenchy Payne, and Jessie Burress believed Emily had conjured—or at least had a hand in—the Superstorm and refused to be satisfied until Morgan agreed to mount a full investigation. Lugh MacBrayer, Arthur Creeley, and Don Foster had shown up in Emily's defense.

"All right, all right," an exasperated Morgan relented. "We will start an investigation. But I will tell you now, Mr. Wainwright, this is NOT endearing you to us."

Mitchell's brows raised so high they nearly merged with his bangs. "I am merely trying to protect the order. What do we really know about this interloper anyway?" His steel eyes burned with so much hatred, Emily gasped.

Lugh stood and pounded his fist on the table, rattling the cups against their saucers. "I don't care what you think, Mitch. Emily is our grand druid and she saved us last night. If it hadn't been for her, Jocko's would have been flattened along with the rest of the block." Touched by his fervor, Emily fell in love a little more.

Mitchell rose, haughty in his self-righteousness. "Are you willing to risk the order's safety on that?"

"Absolutely!" Lugh shouted.

"Boys!" Morgan stood and banged a spoon against her cup. "The claim will be investigated. Now, stop arguing." She glared at everyone around the table. The matriarch was formidable when riled. Emily made a mental note not to get on her bad side.

Arthur stood and the others rose, too. "I motion we table this discussion pending Morgan's findings. All in favor?"

All hands raised except Mitchell's. He shoved back from the table, seething, and shot out the front door without a word. The remaining detractors mumbled goodbyes, more sheepish than defiant, and followed their leader.

The energy in the room calmed considerably. Lugh, Morgan, and the others departed, advising Emily not to pay attention to Wainwright. But the damage was done. Her already-flagging confidence was dragging the ground. She needed to get out of the house.

Agreeing that was a good idea, Hope gave her a new assignment. Awareness Training. In the guise of a treasure hunt.

Emily laced her running shoes and grabbed her coat, a bottle of water, and the keys to the cold-fusion Marauder. Minutes later, she was tapping the address for Oakland Cemetery in the Global Positioning System. While the nav computed the drive, Emily pondered the confrontation. In spite of her belief that her prayer-spell had protected both her and Jocko's Pizza, she had a sneaking suspicion she may have attracted the storms. It wouldn't be the first time. But she had no idea why, or how.

Oakland Cemetery had been spared by the twisters. Considering the large, fragile tent city stretching up and down the adjacent block, it was a darn good thing. A permanent soup kitchen and a mobile clinic stood in one corner of the public lot. People thronged the area, waiting. Aching for each one, Emily made a mental note to talk to Morgan about getting involved. With her Da's riches, surely they could do a lot toward helping these people's plight. But for the grace of God, she could've been one of them.

Heart still aching, she parked near the entrance and jogged up the gentle rise. Inside the stone and iron gate, she slowed to a walk to get her bearings and take in the vista. The only sign of yesterday's epic storm was the wet grass and an occasional puddle. Delighted anticipation filled her, emptying her mind of the attorney's accusations. Oakland Cemetery was no mere graveyard, but a historical park filled with plots and monuments spreading in all directions into the distance.

Traffic noise faded and Emily was back in another time, in an Atlanta rebuilt upon the ashes of a war, one fought between brothers and cousins. Chill bumps danced along the backs of her arms as she whirled in every direction like a dervish spinning, a wide grin splitting her face. Here, in Atlanta's oldest cemetery, throbbed the heart and soul of the phoenix city.

Finding her feet on a narrow cement lane built for horse-drawn buggies, Emily scanned the cemetery for the three "treasures" she'd been tasked to find. But the gravestones dated back to the eighteen-hundreds and the inscriptions were worn by the sands of time, some barely discernable. All manner of growing things graced the symmetrical plots, many in the early stages of bloom.

Mature, slick-leaved magnolias capped salmon wild quince and tulips of varied hues. A row of yellow daffodils danced in the breeze, a perfect contrast to the carpet of lavender phlox blanketing the nearest grave. Ivy wound around an etched urn and trailed over the low brick wall. A whiff of rosemary tickled her nose.

Following the aroma to the low terrace over which it tumbled, Emily ran her fingers along the base of a stalk to its feathery tip to release the pungent odor. Opening her fist, she inhaled the spicy scent and for a moment was back in Southern California, where the drought-resistant herb was a landscape staple. Homesick tendrils squeezed her heart as she breathed in its fragrance and let the memory wash through her.

A rising wind misted her with what could've been ocean spray. Startled, she looked up and spied a fat robin fluttering in the leaves of a liquid amber tree. Or sweet gum, as they were called in Georgia. Thus anointed, Emily scooted out of the way, wiping her damp cheek with the sleeve of her hoodie.

A single jogger passed Emily by, then a trio with a Lab on a leash. A sign announced the Visitor's Center was in the opposite direction. She followed the arrow, ooo-ing and ahh-ing at statues and altars, reading names and epitaphs and snapping photos of the exquisite artwork with her iBlast. Above the narrow, grave-lined lanes, oaks provided shade and guarded the dead, along with sourwoods and sweet gum trees, resplendent in varying shades of spring green. Under these, purple-blossomed redbuds brushed against dogwoods still bare.

The path opened to a manicured lawn lined with swaying maples. Whirly-birding seeds formed a reddish mat on the ground underneath. Behind them in the distance, the Equitable Building spiked black against a billowy sky, the white cumuli hinting of another storm. Her throat tightened.

To quell the rush of nerves, Emily studied the monolith. Atlanta's first high-rise, it still bore its original name a century and a half later, a feat in this day and age. She searched the cityscape for a glimpse of the Candler Building, but its whimsical lines were hidden by the trees. Seeking north, Emily rotated twenty degrees and stumbled into a black, cast-iron bench.

"Ow!" she grumbled, rubbing her shin. "Why didn't they paint the damn thing red?"

The iron had been shaped into branches and leaves, and an intertwined-snake motif adorned the legs. Wondering if it was druid-made, she plopped down to enjoy the vista, but from this vantage point the buildings disappeared.

Emily closed her eyes to listen to the drone of bees pillaging the nectar of some blossomed feast. A raucous crow cawed overhead. Someone laughed, a clear, melodious tinkle, and a dog barked.

A shiver crawled up the back of Emily's neck. Behind her, she could hear the clatter of what she hoped was a wooden chime and not the rattle of dead bones in the wind.

**

The air dragon blinked in the afternoon sun. Or tried to. a-Ur had been encased in stone for so long he had forgotten how. Something had awakened him.

At first it tickled, an itch a-Ur couldn't scratch. Or even pinpoint. But it intensified until his entire being swelled with the irritation. A flame long-dead erupted in a-Ur's belly, calling him back to the world.

**

Emily was still empty-handed after scouring the entire west side of Oakland Cemetery. She had found no reference or likeness to honey bees or blackbirds, though plenty cavorted in the trees. Also in abundance were crosses, urns, willows,

177

epitaphs, doves, olive branches, bible verses and the like, but Hope's "treasures"— including anything related to the peacemakers passage—were nowhere to be found.

Now it was well past lunchtime and she was frustrated and hungry. Not a good combination for anyone, much less a hypoglycemic. Chugging half the water in her bottle, her third refill, Emily sank to a stone bench. From this angle, she had an unobstructed view of the high point of the cemetery. She had dubbed it Mausoleum Row. Opening the map she'd purchased from the Visitor's Center, Emily scanned it again, hoping to trigger a spark. The map stared back, withholding its secrets. Her irritation mounted.

"Dammit, this is ridiculous!" she blurted out, then looked around, embarrassed. No one lurked nearby. Hot tears of frustration gathered. After the morning and afternoon, she had come up with nothing. Nothing, except doubts and fears. It was a stupid child's game, for God's sake. One Emily should be able to win.

A tear trickled down each cheek. She sat, miserable and defeated. Her thoughts strayed to yesterday's storm. Then to previous disasters, especially the ones after her mother's death. The Hum incidents, starting with Peru and ending two weeks ago here in Buckhead. The earthquake in Vietnam, tremors in Chile and the Andes. The Manhattan Beach storm surge. The mini-tsunami in Seattle. Cyclone Charlotte. And back to yesterday's humdinger.

Was she to blame? Had they happened because of her? Maybe. Wainwright's accusations had forced Emily to look at the disasters in a different context.

The trees shimmered in the afternoon breeze, filling the alley with a dead-bone clatter. She stared in the distance at an old brick-mill cum fort at the edge of the cemetery. Her doubts weighed heavy upon her. For a moment she let the tears flow. None but the dead would see.

What if Wainwright and the others were right? What if Emily had created those disasters, even unconsciously? The thought pierced like an arrow. Was she responsible for Trey's death? Their boss certainly thought so. He'd even fired her.

What about the people killed yesterday? And the ones who lost everything, businesses and livelihoods shattered and scattered to the four corners by tornadoes?

Emily sobbed and hiccupped. No way had she done that. No way.

**

The force grew in strength, fanning the flame inside Draig a-Ur. It engulfed him and beat against the inner walls of his stone prison. The Awen. She was back.

Awakened power surged through a-Ur. With a mighty crack, his cocoon shattered into a thousand pieces, shards exploding into the sky. The air dragon tottered on limbs unused to holding his weight. He blinked marble dust from his newly-naked eyes. The fire receded to his belly.

The sight of the Awen shocked him to full awareness. The youthful druid was seated on a bench, tears streaming down a too-young face, in obvious distress. The dragon blew a breath of welcome in troubled greeting.

**

Emily dashed the tears away. She'd had a badly-needed cry, now it was time to get serious and find Hope's treasures. She rose from the bench and faced south to search the mausoleums. Leaves tumbled toward her on a gust of warm wind and she froze. In front of her was a dragon. A real one.

Sweat broke cold as the leaves skittered past her down the alleyway. The dragon's wings were slightly lifted, and it perched on a brick wall, the one delineating the druid section.

That hadn't been there before. Of course, Hope's treasures would be hidden. Emily hadn't thought of that. She remained rooted, heart pounding, adrenaline pumping, not sure what to do. The beast blinked and Emily stared into eyes of the purest silver.

A flash of recognition ran between them, surprising Emily. In a twinkling, the dragon's powerful hindquarters cleared the wall and its nearly-translucent wings propelled it into the sky. Drawn to the place it had vacated, Emily watched it rise in sure, strong

179

strokes. But a powerful downdraft swirled in the dragon's wake, dragging Emily into the center of its vortex.

Panicked, she grabbed hold of a gnarled elm towering beside the trail. She wrapped her arms around it so tight that the horny bark cut into her cheek. Her scarlet hair whipped wild in the wind, biting her face and mouth. It was Trey all over, only he wasn't here to protect her.

"Trey," she sobbed, clinging to the elm. Wracking sobs burst from the place where Emily kept the grief locked. The maelstrom gathered and swirled around her, tearing at her from all sides. Then sorrowful anger took grief's place and hardened into cold fury at a God who'd failed them both.

"How could you?" she screamed. The wind tore the words from her sun-blistered lips and scattered them to the heavens to disappear with the dragon. But the elm held firm, giving Emily strength. Remembering Aóme, she wiggled the ring onto her finger, raised her trembling fist to the swirling winds and bellowed, "You! Can't! Have! Me!"

Abruptly, the fury calmed to a whisper, a puff against Emily's bark-tattooed cheek.

Shaken, she let go of the ridged trunk and saw a squiggly marking etched on the bark. She leaned closer to examine what appeared to be an outline of her body. A low laugh rumbled in the recesses of her mind. Then the etching faded, along with the eerie laughter.

Enough was enough. Emily fled to the Marauder, legs growing stronger with each stride. As did her resolve. She was sick and tired of feeling helpless. It was time to ask for help.

**

a-Ur rose on his spiraling updraft, lifting higher with each beat of his wings. Something was wrong with the Awen. It colored her thoughts, keeping them hidden. Rather than recognition, she had reeked of fear.

Confused, a-Ur had taken flight and then the draft took him, displacing all thoughts save those of the velvety air currents stroking scales that reflected the dragon's surroundings. Higher and higher a-Ur soared until the lift petered out, dropping him back toward the horizon.

But the terrain was all wrong. Where there had once been hillocks and countryside, hard surfaces and soaring structures rose from the earth like massive boxes, one atop the other for miles. Gone were fen and meadow, deer and bear. Gone were his lovely moor and the mountain at the edge of the sea. Even the sea had gone missing. What magic had wrought these changes?

Searching his memory for an explanation, the air dragon found none. Could he have been whisked to this strange place without his knowledge? That would account for the missing ocean. But he'd never seen a land like this. And that was saying a lot; a-Ur had been around since before the humans and lizard men.

He spied a low, rambling castle in the middle of teeming chaos and landed on the dome. Below the minarets and sweeping archways, the humans scurried. Some were on foot, but most whizzed by in shiny honking metal contraptions that belched and fouled the air.

All were oblivious to Draig a-Ur. Only the Awen was resistant to the memory curse. Now the Awen had forgotten him, too. A rare tear slid down a-Ur's horny cheek. He shoved away from the parapet and a blinking light caught his eye.

"FOX THEATER" shouted the glittering runes.

Puzzled, the dragon rose into the befouled air. He gazed beyond the borders of the new city to green forests and pastures and smaller edifices. Ribbons clogged with the noxious boxes connected the city to a greening countryside. Out there, a dragon could find food. But first, a-Ur needed information.

Moral Support

Jocko's Pizza was closed for repairs. And noisy. Carpenters and electricians worked side by side amidst the whine of electric tools and pounding hammers. Emily sat near the back, in the booth with the initials carved in the varnish. Her spaghetti was delicious, cooked to perfection, the sauce every bit as tasty as that of Lugh's pizza. Maybe better—Lugh himself had prepared and delivered it to her table.

While she ate, Emily rehearsed her news in her head, eager to unload it on a more experienced druid. She had chosen Lugh because he was always in her thoughts. But so what? He was more than a pretty face. He was a priest, even if a new one. That was the highest rank in the druid order.

Other than grand druid. Plus, Lugh was considered a warrior. One Emily had yet to beat in combat. But more, she trusted him, even though he had a habit of ignoring her. He consistently stood against Wainwright in her favor, too.

Lugh returned to the table and Emily summoned her nerve. "I have something I need to tell you. Do you have a minute?" His black brows beetled, and Emily feared he would say no. "Please? I need help. And besides, you owe me."

He slid onto the opposite bench, rested his elbows on the table, and propped his chin on his clasped hands. "In that case I'm all ears. But first remind me why I owe you?"

Emily batted mascaraed lashes. "Um. Because I saved Jocko's from annihilation yesterday?"

Lugh burst out laughing and tipped his head. "That you did, Miz Hester. Which is why the owner of said establishment defended you against Mister the Third and his hench-people this morning. And is cooking and waiting on you hand and foot, even though Jocko's is closed and in the middle of major repairs. And why your meals are on the house. Like *forever*."

Emily laughed. "That's not necessary, Lugh."

"Oh, but it is. Spill. What's up?"

Nervous now, she fidgeted in her seat and glanced at the priest from behind lowered lids. Would he think her crazy? Emily took a steadying breath and straightened. "I came straight here from the cemetery. Oakland Cemetery."

His black eyes blinked.

"After y'all left this morning, Hope sent me there on a treasure hunt. I didn't find any of the things on her list, but I *did* see a dragon." Emily held her breath.

The priest sat up and dropped his hands in his lap. "You mean the marble dragon above the gate in the Druid section? By Mausoleum Row?"

"Yes! There!" Emily exclaimed, excited he knew the place. "Only the dragon wasn't marble. It was real and it looked straight at me, like it wanted me to do or say something."

A sharp intake of breath preceded Lugh's careful response. "Are you sure? The statue is extremely lifelike."

"Absolutely sure. Only it was smaller than I thought a dragon would be, maybe the size of a young kangaroo. It had horns, and freaky-long nails, and see-through wings, and its scales reflected the stuff around it. At first, he just sat there on the wall. Then he took off, straight up, in a vertical ascent." At Lugh's incredulous stare, Emily added, "I promise. I kid you not."

The druid leaned across the booth and spoke slowly, as if choosing his words, "I believe you saw a dragon. But if it was real, you wouldn't remember. You couldn't," he pressed.

"What do you mean?"

"Dragons carry a built-in forgetfulness curse. It is how they survive without detection."

Emily's jaw fell open. "Seriously? Dragons are real?" she squeaked. "They live here?" Something shifted inside her.

"Yeah, they do. Or did. Who knows if they're still around? Like I said, everyone forgets, so no one knows. Not for sure. But if they actually do, dragons protect us, not hurt us."

"Protect us? From what? Or whom?"

"Ourselves mostly. And each other."

Emily let that sink in. "And they're small? Like the one I saw?"

"They can be. Some are the size of Godzilla." Lugh opened his arms wide in measurement and leaned close again. "What did you do?"

"I cowered like a cur and watched it fly away." Remembering, Emily shuddered. "Then I got sucked into its backwash, which was almost as scary as the dragon itself."

Lugh's expression was blank.

Emily sighed. "The upward spiral of the dragon's wings created a whirlwind. I got sucked in. Literally."

Understanding dawned and the blank eyes grew wide. "Holy shit, Em. What'd you do?"

Be still my heart. He'd called her Em. "I grabbed a tree and held on for dear life." She touched her cheek where the faint indentation of the bark still lingered.

"And the dragon? What happened to it?" Lugh's tone was still skeptical

Defensive, she shrugged. "I don't know. He disappeared before the wind stopped blowing." That's all she'd meant to say. The rest slid out. "But when I let go of the tree, I heard laughter. Not out-loud laughter, in-my-head laughter. And I saw an outline of my body on the bark. At least until it disappeared."

Emily leaned against the back of the booth, knowing how crazy she sounded. Her cheeks blazed.

In spite of his obvious incredulity, Lugh remained solicitous, if not a hundred-percent convinced. Encouraged, she swallowed and laid her hand on his. "I know I sound looney tunes. But I swear to you. There is a very real dragon on the loose in Atlanta."

A black-haired teen burst through the swinging doors and hurried toward the table. Emily grinned. It was Lugh's nephew, Brian. And he looked enough like Lugh to be his son.

"Brian," she crowed. "It's good to see you again. How's your back?"

"Fine," he sniffed. "How's your boob?" Lugh's eyes narrowed.

Emily laughed. "It's okay. Thank you again for showing me the way home my first night in Atlanta."

Lugh looked from Emily to Brian.

"I told you about it," Brian said defensively. "I was walking Cu, remember?" His uncle's glare didn't waver. "The lady that saved my life?"

Lugh's frown changed to a surprised smile. "That was you?"

Emily nodded.

"You did not tell me it was Emily Hester. *That* I would've remembered." He winked at Emily and smirked. "But what was that thing about your boob?" She could feel the heat rise in her neck and color her face.

"W-we fell when I tackled him. Cu tangled us up in his leash. Brian tried to stand and fell on me. Elbow-first." She put a hand to her breast.

"Ouch," Lugh said.

"Ouch indeed. But no harm, no foul. We both made it home safely and that's what counts."

"Uncle Lugh," the teen interrupted, running a restless hand through shaggy black hair that gleamed with cobalt highlights and fell in natural curls around a narrow face. "Stan needs you in the kitchen." He glanced at Emily and winked, ever so slightly.

Lugh's smile was tight. "I'll be there in two shakes."

Brian sniffed and nodded at Emily, "See ya."

"See ya," Emily said as he sauntered back to the kitchen with a speculative look over one shoulder.

Lugh leaned close. "Sorry for the interruption. But, back to the dragon. Have you told anyone else?"

Emily shook her head. "No, I came straight here."

"Let me do some checking. Or better yet..." There was a gleam in his eyes. "Would you be willing to go back to the cemetery?"

"With you? Sure. When were you thinking?"

"It'll be dark in an hour." Lugh stroked his chin as if hatching a plot. "If you're done eating, we could go now. They don't need me here and it shouldn't take long. We can drop Brian home on the way."

Though Emily dreaded going back to the cemetery, a thrill went through her at the prospect of going there with Lugh. "Sure. And I can drop Da's car at Wren's Roost, so we don't have to do it later."

"Perfect. Stay right here, I'll be back in a few." Lugh scooped up her dishes and headed for the kitchen, then stopped and turned around. "Are we still on for our trip to Zoo Atlanta?" He pointed at her, then at himself. "You and me? And Willie D?"

"Oh crap, I forgot." She slapped her hand on the table. "Finn called. Da finally comes home tomorrow. Could we make it next week?"

**

a-Ur traced a data feed to the Georgia Institute of Technology and extracted the information he needed—a millennium's worth according to an enormous sign with fluctuating, flashing runes that told a-Ur he was in a land called Atlanta. Last time he had looked at a map, there was no such place. Of course, a lot would change in a thousand years.

The up-link provided a summary of global history, enough to flesh out a-Ur's memories and bring him current on human events. But not to answer his most burning questions. Like why the Awen had no memory of a-Ur. Why he couldn't remember the last thousand years. And why a-Ur had ended up in a foreign land encased in stone guarding a cemetery. A cemetery, of all things.

Buildings, interstates, highways, and roads spread before Draig a-Ur. He circled Atlanta, keeping his wing strokes gentle so as not to affect the weather. Wind brought clouds, clouds brought rain. And while a-Ur could use a good soaking—it had been way too long since he'd had one and he longed to be rid of the marble dust—now was not the time. Plus, with limited visibility, a-Ur could easily become entangled in the wires strung everywhere by the crazed humans.

a-Ur shook his head. The static from their cell and radio towers, mixed with the microwaves and the signals bouncing from hundreds of thousands of flea-like satellites, tickled his ears and set his teeth on edge. Luckily, his dragon scales acted as an interstellar filter, protecting a-Ur from the worst of the damaging rays.

Intuition told him he was near a dragon line, or ley line as they were apparently called today. He could follow it to the nearest vortex and catch a wormhole back to the Isle of Beli. The countryside along the way would provide for a-Ur's appetite. Already he had doubled in size, though he'd had to eat a human to get there. A vile creature intent on beating another to death in a back alley. Like most dragons, a-Ur avoided human flesh, preferring four-legged animals with less fat and more meat. But he needed the energy from food to get to Tara.

In Tara, the dragons' gathering place, a-Ur would get the answers he needed. Though Beli was no longer listed on the world map, Britain and Wales remained.

A deep sense of urgency impelled a-Ur to veer southeast. Time was running out. He wasn't sure how or why he knew this, but the world would soon end. And only the Awen could prevent the catastrophe. a-Ur was supposed to help, but the whys and wherefores lay hidden from the air dragon's usual crystalline sight.

**

"It's gone." Lugh had wanted to believe, had tried to believe, or at least to withhold judgment, but until this very moment, he had failed. The dragon had vanished, just as Emily said. Marble dust surrounded the spot the statue had occupied, guarding the druids of Oakland Cemetery for at least two freaking centuries.

Lugh shook his head. The dragon was gone. Vanished. Caput. Nothing left but dust and shards. Troubled, he laid his hand on the bare brick where the dragon statue had crouched for the entirety of Lugh's life. It felt strangely warm in the cool evening air.

Several plots away, Emily inspected the Ravinski headstone. The delight on her face did something to Lugh's stomach, something he'd never felt. Before he could decipher it, she glanced up and shot him one of those killer grins and his belly flip-flopped. Emily waved.

"I found Hope's treasure. Well, one of them. Now I know where to find the rest." She pointed her chin toward the empty ledge. "So, what's your take on that?"

"Well," Lugh said as she sashayed back to stand beside him. "You're right. It's gone. Only powerful magic could have turned that statue into a real dragon."

"Unless it was real all along, encased in marble and lying dormant until it was needed. Or called. Or until it had an opportunity to escape." She gripped Lugh's arm and looked around, frightened in the gathering gloom. "You don't think the Darkness released it, do you?" Feeling the need to protect her, he wrapped an arm around Emily and drew her close.

"No doll, I don't." A golden glow settled on the cemetery, bathing the world in that eerie light that precedes the dusk. "We should get going, though. I'm not keen on cemeteries, especially after dark. And especially not this one. There's evil afoot in the older sections."

Lugh gestured in the direction of the car. "Spells were cast here long ago to hide and protect this part of the cemetery, along with any visiting druids. That dragon was part of the protection, which means," Lugh lowered his voice to a near whisper, "the balance has been disturbed."

Emily shivered against him.

"To restore the balance, the breach must be mended. How is your spell work, Emily?"

"So-so," she admitted, shame-faced. "I could use some help. Doing magic is apparently not my forte."

Lugh tucked a curl behind her ear and studied her strained features. His feelings for her warred with his mother's cryptic warning.

"Maybe because magic is not something we do, Emily. Magic is what we are. *Who* we are. Magic isn't about knowing something; it's about using your imagination to create things."

He was rewarded by the flicker of a spark in the novice's eyes.

"Before any spell, you must get in touch with the magic of who you are. Something like this." He faced the wall, ready to talk Emily through the steps.

"I take a deep breath and silently sync the earth in my body to that beneath my feet; the water coursing through me to Earth's rivers, lakes and oceans; the fire charging my nervous system to that in Earth's molten core; and the air that fills my lungs with that which brushes against my face. Grounded and connected, I raise my arms overhead in a vee to open to the universal power, and speak the words with command:

> "Dragon of quicksilver, dragon of gold,
> Ye who protect these druids of old,
> Return to your post with the greatest of haste
> Defend their essence, their honor, their place.
> For the druids alive, keep watch and alarm,
> That we visit our loved ones without any harm.
> And so it is for now and the rest of time,
> Or until you are released from your duty fine."

Lugh turned slightly to watch Emily's rapt expression as the marble dust lifted from the earth, drawing shards and larger chunks and everything that was left of the once-guardian into a fluid mass that swirled in the air above the wall. It then coalesced into the shape of a winged dragon and hardened to a silvery marble. Emily ooo'd and ahh'd, impressed.

He admired his handiwork in the light of the early moon. Then darkness overtook the waning light and he spun toward the exit.

"Let's go!" he urged, grabbing Emily's arm. Then Lugh half-dragged, half-chased the Hester princess to his car.

Awen's Handbook

Hope paced back and forth in front of the smoldering fireplace. Her fur stood on end and her fat tail twitched. Emily and Lugh had relayed their dragon tales, first Emily's encounter and then Lugh's spell to repair the statue. But the news upset Hope. Emily had never seen her so agitated.

The cat stopped pacing to face Emily. "Zee dragon deedn't say anyzing? 'e just flew away? Wizout a word?" Hope's accent had thickened so that Emily could barely understand, but she nodded.

"Zees is important. Deed zees dragon geev you eeny sign at all?"

When Emily started to shake her head no, Hope stopped her.

"Tzeenk, Emily. You are good at zees. You read people and zeengs well. Zere was somezing, zere must've been. Some 'int zat zee dragon recognized you, or some clue as to 'ees inteentions? Zeenk!"

Emily closed her eyes and replayed the scene, looking past her fear. There had been a moment. The dragon had blinked enormous, silver eyes and there was a flash of something. Sadness? Disappointment?

"a-Ur," Hope purred.

"What?"

The Elder settled on her haunches in front of Emily. The accent softened. "You saw sadness and disappointment."

"Hey, you read my mind! I thought that was off limits!"

"Oops." The wildcat didn't look sorry at all. Instead she ogled Emily, tail thumping on the thick rug, until a speculative gleam crept into her luminous eyes.

"What?" Emily grumped, feeling violated.

"Awen's handbook. I have looked high and low in Brigid's library, but the manuscript eludes me."

The nape of Emily's neck tingled. "What is Awen's handbook?"

"A manuscript that has been passed from one reigning Awen to the next since the beginning of the eleventh century. Because you weren't available to receive it, Awen's diary remained with Brigid until she passed. Your great-grandmother preferred the carriage house, so I assumed she'd hid the manuscript here. But where?" Hope stared at Emily intently.

Lugh spoke for the first time since relaying his part in the cemetery. "What would the handbook tell us?"

"Everything, my young priest. Awen's diary is her handwritten collection of magic spells, the ones that were wielded by the most learned and powerful druid priests and priestesses. It is the only known compilation of its sort, and but a handful know of its existence. I am one. Now you two make three."

Goose bumps danced along Emily's shoulders. The papyrus manuscript belonged to Awen. And her mother stole it.

The cat paced the floor. "Awen's diary tells the new Awen— Emily—what to do about a-Ur and the other dragons. Where they gather. How to call them."

"Dragons plural?" Emily squeaked.

"Dragons plural," Hope affirmed.

Lugh's head bobbed, as if he knew all about dragons. "Hope, tell her about the curse." He glanced Emily's way and she scrunched her nose.

"It is the dragons' job to look after Earth and all her beings. But they are bound by a forgetfulness curse that immediately wipes clean the memory of anyone or anything coming in contact with a dragon. All except the Awen. Which is why you, Emily Bridget, remember seeing a-Ur in the cemetery."

"But I'm not Awen," she protested, uncomfortable with the moniker.

Lugh intervened. "Maybe not. But the weather and the dragons don't know that, Emily. You stopped that storm from destroying Jocko's. And you brought back Hope." He gestured at the cat. "I believe it was you who woke a-Ur. I'd say you are more Awen than you think."

But as much as she would love to be, Emily wasn't a powerful priestess. She was mostly inept and full of fear.

A guilty look crossed Lugh's face. "Hey, Hope. If Awen's diary is supposed to be secret, why tell me?"

The cat stopped grooming her thick fur to gaze at him with somber eyes. "Lughnasadh MacBrayer, you are a powerful druid priest and wise for your years. The secret of Awen's diary and the spells therein can be trusted to you. I tell you because Emily Bridget needs your help."

Lugh gasped, startling woman and cat.

"What is it?" Emily asked.

"That's what Ma said!" They stared and waited for an explanation. "After the tornado, Ma's spirit appeared to me. She said that you saved Jocko's, Emily. And that everything now depends on you. She said you need my strength and protection. And told me to stay close to you."

Emily stared. Lugh had discussed her with his dead mother?

"She and Pa ran across the dragons in the Otherworld. Draigs Talav and Ooschu are restless and the others are waking. I believe those were the names." Lugh pounded his forehead with his palm. "She did mention a-Ur! And another named...Tienu."

Hope's ringed tail twitched back and forth. "Yes, those are the four Keepers. Talav is an earth dragon, Tienu a fire drake. a-Ur, whom Emily saw, is an air dragon. Then there's Ooschu, the water dragon."

Four dragons. Emily gulped. And she was supposed to be able to talk to them. To call them. Command them. In her mind's eye, a misty clearing formed. It was surrounded by craggy mountains and filled with dragons of all shapes and sizes. Emily clutched at the memory as it fled.

"And another thing," Lugh interjected. "My mother suggested the tornadoes were produced by magic."

"You didn't see fit to share that in our confab with Mitchell and his lynch squad this morning?" Emily huffed.

"As Mitchell's charges were ludicrous, it was hardly necessary. But I did pass the information along to Morgan. She and her team are following up and will let us know if they uncover any traces of magic. But this talk of dragons has me wondering. Could they be responsible for the storm?"

"I think not," Hope said. "They are wild and unpredictable and have a complete disregard for rules other than their own, but the dragon-race swore long ago to protect the earth and its humans. No, Lugh. If that storm was produced by magic, a dragon wasn't the perpetrator."

Satisfied, Lugh nodded. "Ma said the four answer to Emily. Her alone. Do you think she was referring to the Dragon Keepers?"

"I suspect she was. Which is why we need Awen's handbook. The dragons could help us defeat the coming Darkness."

Warmth surged through Emily's body. All was not lost. She rose from the armchair and cleared her throat. "I know where it is."

The cat and pirate-priest stared.

Hope recovered first. "You've seen Awen's manuscript? Where?"

"Wait here." Emily hurried to the red bedroom. She slipped through the door and locked it behind her. Collecting the manuscript from its most recent hiding place between the mattress and box springs, Emily returned to the living room with the heavy tome clasped to her chest.

"Awen's handbook!" Hope yowled. "Where did you find it?"

Emily laid the papyrus manuscript on the coffee table and sat on the aubergine sofa. "Oh, it found me."

Hope rubbed against her leg, meowing up a storm.

"Wow." Lugh sat beside Emily and lightly traced the carving on the thin, wood cover—a lightning bolt striking an oak tree with three stars overhead in an arc.

Hope stood on hind legs, front paws resting on the coffee table and nose sniffing the binder. Looking up, she urged, "Go ahead. Open it. Let's see what Awen has to say about the dragons."

Emily lifted the front cover with reverence. The inside page was sprinkled with hand-drawn stars depicting constellations. The facing page was covered in small, spidery figures. The same squiggly lines, along with diagrams and pictures, filled the entirety of the thick handbook.

The language was foreign and though Emily had leafed through the papyrus pages almost daily since she'd found it in her mother's box, she was no closer to understanding the glyphs and runic figures.

"What does it say?" she asked the purring Elder.

"Say?" Hope looked up, surprised. "Beats me. Cats don't read. Can't you?"

Emily shook her head. "No, not this."

Lugh shrugged and leaned back. "Looks like ogham to me. It's a secret, ritualistic language no longer in use. As far as I know, no one can actually read ogham. I learned the letters as a boy, but that's the extent of my knowledge. I can't make words, much less sentences."

"Great. So, we're still screwed," Emily groaned.

Hope meowed and looked thoughtful. "We will find a way. Perhaps a language scholar could interpret the words."

"I can search the internet," Emily offered. "You never know what you might find online. How do you spell it?"

"Oh-gee-aitch-a-em," Lugh said.

Hope wagged her shaggy head. "It's doubtful you'll find anything, but you can start there. I will consult the Elders. Lugh, you can check with the priests, especially in Europe. There must be an older druid there who can help."

Lugh nodded acquiescence.

"In the meantime," Hope cautioned, "keep this between us. Be discreet in your searches. It's imperative Awen's handbook and the dragons remain secret."

**

Mitch hurried from the courthouse in Carroll County. His client's case had been delayed until Monday. He was halfway to the car when a call came through from a Los Angeles prefix. A nasally voice inquired as to the whereabouts of one Emily

194

Bridget Hester. Mitch stopped in his tracks, wheeling to make sure he was alone in the parking lot.

"Ma'am," he said in a quiet tone, "I don't know who you are, why you think I have information related to this person, or would give it to you if I did, but you've wasted a phone call and my time. Good day."

Mitch pressed the button to sever the connection and stared at the phone. What in the world had possessed him? What had made him so nervous? The phone vibrated in his hand and Mitch damn near dropped it. Same number as before.

Making a decision, he answered, "Mitchell Wainwright, how may I help you?"

"You can help by giving a message to Ms. Hester. Tell her Shalane Carpenter will be at the Fox Theater in Atlanta on April 17th. Two front-row tickets and VIP passes will be held in her name at Will Call, courtesy of Reverend Carpenter."

When the woman finished, Mitch parlayed, "If, by chance, I did happen to know a person by that name, and if, by chance, I were to agree to do as you ask, what benefit would be in it for me?"

"Mr. Wainwright, the reverend will make it worth your while, I assure you. Will you deliver her message?"

Unexpected Opposition

Nergal gaped at the images on the holoscreen, stunned by the new development. Shibboleth, the legendary warlord from Gamma Reux, had summoned him to Irkalla like a common drudge. Having ruled the southern hemisphere since the great migration—in name only for the last millennium—Shibboleth had set his sights on AboveEarth.

Over Nergal's dead body.

The meeting was to take place in two earth-weeks' time in Irkalla, beneath the streets of New York City. They were to discuss Nergal's role in Shibboleth's campaign. Anger surged through him, hardening Nergal's resolve. He would go to Irkalla, but only to set matters straight.

Striding from his office in Xibalba IX, Nergal instructed his aide to gather the northern hemisphere commanders. He'd clashed with the warlord in the past and knew the importance of presenting a united front.

It galled him to leave his work with the reverend, but Shalane and the magic lessons would keep for a few days. As would Nergal's search for the mysterious Ebby Panera. He'd be damned if he would let Shibboleth steal his thunder. Not this time.

Ham Comes Home

I t had taken longer than expected, but Emily was finally keeping her promise and Da was coming home. It was a fine, spring day, replete with azure skies and mild temperatures. Even better, Mitchell Wainwright was out of town and wouldn't be around to ruin the occasion.

The east coast Hesters were gathering en masse to greet their patriarch. Curious, considering Hamilton was in a coma and wouldn't know. But the cars arrived anyway, delivering relatives large and small. The ones Emily met for the first time acted polite and solicitous. But as a lot, they remained distant.

Elise Hester Johnson was the one exception. An odd bird of indeterminable age, Elise latched on to Emily as soon as they met. A slip of a woman, Elise had coiffed hair the color of pine straw and picked her way through the Hester pack as if loath to come in contact with another's body parts.

The relatives that knew Emily greeted her with welcome. Maria and Sirona nearly bowled her over, wrapping little arms around her legs, one on each side. Eyes adoring, they begged for stories of California until their cousin Sean swooped them up, offering piggyback rides in the yard. To the accompaniment of giggles and squeals, Sean herded the girls outside with the other children. Elise went along to watch.

Finally alone, Emily seized the opportunity to browse living quarters as grand as any she had ever seen. While the carriage house was impressive, the main house was even more so, its rambling structure easily three times the size. Eager to touch everything, Emily's hands traced the lines of exquisite lace doilies, lustrous wood, and cool marble.

There was a presence here. A hallowed atmosphere. Like God himself was in residence. Emily found this profoundly comforting—and encouraging. From the sound of things, they would need His help. She wouldn't be here now without it.

The reverence lingered as Emily wandered into the formal dining room, where twelve-foot ceilings framed hardwood floors that glistened like burnished honey. The dark furniture and crystal chandelier transported Emily to another age, one in which she was barefoot and lower to the floor.

From the opposing archway, Morgan swept into the room with a time-worn couple in tow. Halting in front of Emily, she introduced Simon and Mary Cobb, the pair responsible for the day to day upkeep of Wren's Roost through three generations. Emily took Mary's and then Simon's hand, squeezing gently.

"Thank you for taking such good care of me and Ralph. It's great to finally meet you." She had begun thinking of the elusive pair as fairies—fresh fruit, cat food, toilet paper, and other necessities magically appeared.

Simon's ears reddened. He was thin and stooped, with silver hair combed across a shiny pate and in need of a trim around the nostrils and ears. The twinkle in his smile belied the groundskeeper's shuffle. Mary beamed. She threw wiry arms around Emily and burst into tears, hugging her close. Tears sprang to Emily's eyes as forgotten feelings flooded though her—she was loved, wanted, and even adored.

If Simon Cobb said little, his wife made up for it. She took Emily on a tour of the house, delivering a steady stream of commentary in a leathery but melodious voice. Emily delighted as memories were recounted and Mary imparted anecdotes from Emily's childhood.

When the old housekeeper lifted a ring of thin sticks with runic carvings and bragged of young Emily's proficiency in reciting the alphabet—both English and ogham—she couldn't believe her good fortune. But the extent of Mary's knowledge was limited to rudimentary symbols and those now forgotten.

Disappointed, Emily focused on Mary's tale of an Amsterdam ancestor who had come to America to make his fortune. Within days of arriving, he fell madly in love with

Mary's Iroquois grandmother, wooed her, and won her heart. Mary's jet hair, ruddy skin, and aquiline nose confirmed her heritage.

They wove through the bedrooms and Mary prattled about piggyback rides and hide-and-seek games with Emily's brother. At the mention of Sean, Mary's long face clouded and her breathless ebullience faded.

"What is it, Mary?" Emily probed. "Sean Jr mentioned something about my brother being murdered. Do you believe that, too?"

"Pshaw, no, deary," Mary wagged her wizened head. "Sean had been depressed most of his life. Murder? No. More likely the depression and the meds drove him to end it."

"An overdose?"

"Yes." Mary's face crumbled.

Emily could tell there was more, but she let it go when the doorbell rang, and Mary excused herself to answer. Not up to meeting any more relatives at the moment, Emily wandered the house and discovered a sitting room filled with framed portraits and photographs.

Many were of Hamilton and Alexis, some from their wedding. From the photos, the lavish druid ceremony had been heavily attended. Her mother glowed and her Da looked ecstatic.

So, they were happy once. Pre-Emily.

She spied a picture of her teenaged mother and lifted the frame. Alexis was dressed in a ceremonial robe and wielded a slightly-bent wand. Emily stared at the photo, wagging her head back and forth.

"You didn't know your mother was a druid?" Emily jumped, not expecting Morgan's familiar voice. Wheeling, she clutched the frame to her chest and shook her head.

After a moment of silence and a long, searching stare, Morgan flounced into a corner chair and announced matter-of-factly, "Well, she was. And quite an accomplished one, too. Though after you came along, I wondered if Alexis hadn't gone mental."

Choking on her own saliva, Emily sputtered, "What do you mean?" The aroma of Kyotiri wafted to her as Morgan fluffed her hair.

"Alexis was convinced, though it was highly illogical, that marrying my brother would grant her a claim to the Hester throne. When you came along, she finally understood she would never be grand druid or anything close.

"It broke her, I think. One day I saw her eyeing you with such anger, it frightened me. I mean, how could a mother feel that way? Especially about her own child? I had little ones of my own and I still can't imagine."

Emily's heart squeezed. Her mother had despised her. Here was confirmation.

She replaced the frame and faced her aunt. "I can't imagine it either."

Morgan took her hand and held it tight. "Alexis came unglued at your confirmation, Emily. She had to be sedated for days. After that, she denounced her druid roots and turned her back on the old ways. She drank heavily and refused to nurse you or even hold you in her arms. Hamilton cared for you the best he could."

Emily listened to the harsh words, knowing them for truth. She snatched a Kleenex from a nearby box and blew her nose. "Poor Da," she mumbled.

"Poor you," Morgan snorted. "But you're right. Your mother took to partying and staying out until all hours of the night, having one affair after the other. She made sure your father knew about them, too, breaking his heart. Yet my brother loves her still."

Sorrow creased Morgan's brow. "He's a prime example of not being able to help who we love. When Alexis ran away with you, Ham was beside himself. We all were. He hired a private investigator and even when the authorities gave up, your Da didn't. He never stopped searching for twenty-six years." Morgan's gaze held hers.

Emily slid into a small rocker facing her teary-eyed aunt. "Thank you, Aunt Morgan. Your explanation helps. Mama was never nice to me, at least not on purpose. When she drank, she was downright mean. At least now I know why." Emily clenched her jaw, resolving to put her mother in the past where she belonged. "Can I ask you a question?"

Her aunt nodded and dabbed her eyes with a tissue.

"Why me as grand druid? Why not you?"

Morgan cleared her throat and gave Emily a steadying stare. "I'm pretty sure you know the answer to that. But I will tell you again because it bears repeating. Emily, you are the direct female descendent of Awen, the druid high priestess, and William the Conqueror. Their union, one thousand years ago, set into play a series of events that have culminated in the here and now. With you."

"But why not you? You are a direct female descendant, too. And much more qualified. Or Becca or Dana? Why me? I'm no hero. Believe me, the druids would be better off with someone else."

"Dru-y-en." Morgan leaned forward. "It is important you understand this, once and for all. You are the Awen. The signs are incontrovertible. You were born during the new moon, on Midsummer's Day, only months before the world was prophesied to end. You bear the sign of the oak, strong and enduring as the sun, yet you are also a moon daughter, fluid and ethereal. The Elders declared it at your birth. *You* are the Awen."

Emily started to argue, but Morgan stood and bowed slightly. "You, Emily Hester, are prophesied to save our world. Not I, Morgan Foster. You." A whooping siren punctuated the "you," commanding their attention.

"Hamilton," her aunt chirped and dashed from the room.

Emily followed on suddenly reluctant legs. The air left her lungs and she gripped the door jamb, overcome by a cold and familiar darkness. What was she doing? Her mother was right. No way was she worthy of being a part of this important family. She held on tight until the panic wave passed, leaving her off-balance and shaken.

When she opened her eyes, Mary Cobb stood before her. "You okay, Emmy?" Mary clutched Emily's wrist.

Grateful for the support, Emily meant to nod. But her head wagged slowly back and forth. Mary's scrawny arms opened and she melted into them, seeking the comfort she remembered from her childhood. Strong arms drew Emily close, their strength as heartening as the woman's next words.

"There, there Miss Emmy. Me and Simon have some tricks left up our sleeves. We're gonna take care of you. And your daddy. You'll see." The housekeeper held her at arm's length. A crooked grin split the weathered face.

Something about the smile made Emily believe. When she beamed back at Mary, her fear was gone. In its place was a ball of something warm and fuzzy. Love. Holding on to the feeling, Emily hurried to join Morgan and Don outside on the front landing.

Maria and Sirona were on their best behavior, with Dana between them, arms around the girls. Sirona twisted to clamp on to Morgan's leg and chattered about her Uncle Hamilton.

Randall, Mosely, Jules and the other distant cousins whose names Emily couldn't remember stood behind the more immediate family. Off to one side, Elise fingered a dogwood blossom, newly opened in time to greet the owner of Wren's Roost. A hush fell upon them as the paramedics wheeled Hamilton's gurney across the flagstone drive. They parted as the crew hefted it up the brick steps to the front door.

At Dr. Finn's insistence, Ham's bedroom had been converted to a hospital room for around-the-clock care. It was the condition under which Finn had allowed Ham to come home, and only after the hospital had run every imaginable test. Even then, Finn released his still-comatose patient under protest.

Once the paramedics settled Hamilton in bed, the family filed in one by one, then left the same way they came. Most told Emily they were praying for his quick return to health. A few expressed happiness she was back at Wren's Roost. And one had the bad manners to say it was too bad Emily hadn't gotten to meet her Da. Which was true, and Emily had thought it herself, but still.

When the family was gone, Emily climbed the stairs to her father's room. Hope was curled by Hamilton's side, one long, striped arm stretched across his waist.

**

Mitch strode up the grand brick entrance to Wren's Roost and used the emergency key to open the massive front door. He swept through the house, managing to evade both Mary and Simon Cobb before bursting into his father's bedroom.

Emily Hester leapt from a chair by the bed. "What the hell? You're supposed to be gone!"

The remark rolled off Mitch's back but when he saw the cat, he wavered. He hadn't expected the cat. The tabby stood and stretched in a slow, sardonic motion designed to irk him, before sniffing the air and jumping to the floor, where it sat in the doorway at attention. Amber eyes accused.

Turning his back to Emily and the cat, Mitch observed the rise and fall of the old man's chest. That and the beeping machines were the only signs Hamilton Hester was alive. Mitch stepped closer and lifted Hamilton's cool hand.

How small and insignificant the hand felt, not the overpowering force Mitch had known. Letting it fall, he pondered the revelation. Gone was the inferiority Mitch had felt when in the same room with his unprofessed father.

Silently rejoicing, he rounded on the woman who had no idea he was her half-brother. "Are you all settled in?" Mitch asked, not caring one way or the other. Emily nodded, but didn't speak. Apparently, she felt no compunction to be nice to him either. Fine that. "Good to know." He leaned forward to stick the knife in. "I came by to deliver a message from Reverend Shalane Carpenter."

Mitch paused for a reaction.

When none came, he continued, "She will be performing at The Fox Theater in a couple of weeks and is leaving free, front-row tickets for you at Will Call." When Emily planted her hands on her hips and cocked one brow, Mitch jabbed, "A friend of yours?"

That scored a snarl. "I sincerely doubt it. I'm pretty sure any friend of mine would call me directly, not waste time sending messages through a second-rate attorney."

That did it. Something in Mitch snapped and he struck out at Emily.

But he had underestimated his enemy. Emily blocked the punch and bent his arm behind him with such force Mitch crashed to his knees. Pain shot from his shoulder down his arm. She shoved him backward into the bed. Mitch stumbled and barely avoided landing on Hamilton, yelping when his hurt arm broke his fall.

Fear overtook the churning hatred. Mitch backed away, rubbing his arm. No way was he sparring with a mad woman. There was more than one way to skin a cat. He hissed loudly at the striped one by the door then slipped past it and down the hall.

**

"Brava, my dear girl, brava! You put young Wainwright in his place. He'll think twice about tangling with you again. I knew you had it in you! Brava!" Hope leapt to the bed. "But who is this Carpenter woman, and why did his news make you so angry?"

Emily groaned, not wanting to talk about it. "She was the shaman in California I told you about. I studied with her until I figured out she was a controlling, narcissistic sociopath. Then I went to great lengths to separate myself from her and make sure she could never find me again. Since coming here, my face has been plastered all over the news. It was only a matter of time."

Emily shuddered at the thought of having to tangle with Shalane again.

A speculative gleam sharpened Hope's regard. "You give this woman too much power. Will you go to this show and face her?"

Emily snorted. "Not on your life. That bitch can rot in hell before I go anywhere near her *or* her so-called performance. That woman is bad news. Trust me."

Patty's Odd Behavior

S halane paced the room, ranting and threatening, not for the first time, to send Patrika Tolbert home. Over the last couple of weeks, the girl's behavior had changed dramatically. And not for the better.

Patty's defense? She couldn't help it. One minute the girl would be her usual cuddly self. The next, she would snarl and attack, striking out at Shalane over philosophy she didn't agree with or actions Patty felt were not right.

Which was absurd, considering the girl had no idea about either.

The doctor thought Patty's hormones might be whacked out, but the tests came back negative. Now Patrika had pitched a bitch about Ebby Panera, screeching at Shalane in the middle of a phone call with Mitchell Wainwright.

On top of that, the sexy-sounding attorney had delivered news that Ebby, or Emily as she called herself now, had declined the tickets. Now Shalane would have to devise a new plan. What she did not need was another of Patrika Tolbert's temper tantrums.

"You get zero say in my love life," Shalane snapped. "I see whom I want, when I want. You," she poked a freshly-manicured finger in Patty's sternum, "are here at *my* behest. Remember that and keep your sulks to yourself. You hear me, young lady?"

The girl's lower lip trembled, but she nodded. She liked being kept, liked having everything she needed and more. She was even learning magic, free of charge. "I'm s-sorry," Patty hiccupped. "I don't mean to mess up. I can't help it. Words pop in my head and out of my mouth before I can stop them. I'll try harder, I promise."

It would have to do for now. They had booked an appointment with a world-class specialist at the Emory Clinic in Atlanta. If that didn't help, Shalane would make good on her threats and send the girl home.

**

Nergal stroked his nubby horns and studied the screen. He was making little headway with the human Shalane. And time was growing short. Soon he must leave Xibalba IX for the meeting in Irkalla. To circumvent any plot Shibboleth might be hatching, Nergal had decided to reveal his project at the called gathering. But he had run into a snag.

He thought his idea to control Shalane through the shill was a good one. In some ways, it was. Through her, Nergal had determined the witch might actually be his descendant. She was stubborn, cold, vicious, and cutthroat.

And like Nergal, she was inappropriate when it came to sex, consistently outperforming her grandmother Camille. Nergal had also learned a handful of spells, but simple magic that would do little for his bid for AboveEarth.

His trial with the shill, while disappointing, had served a larger purpose. Nergal had learned that in order to control the priest, he would have to link with her directly. Meaning, they must end her connection with the Fomorian.

But the transition could kill his most valuable asset. Nergal stroked his chin scales and considered the loss. He didn't like the odds and needed time to effect the change.

He would wait until his return from Shibboleth's meeting. Just in case.

On Cu's Cue

Emily hurried along the trail to the cave, the last stop in Hope's treasure hunt. The apocalypse thing was wearing thin, but obviously still effective. On a normal day, Emily wouldn't go near a cave, much less into one. Especially not alone.

Whether she could muster the courage to venture inside was another matter. But the trinket, the last and most valuable on Hope's list—a druid collar made of solid gold—was hidden nearby.

She had been all over Atlanta looking for items and still found the treasure hunt silly. But the Elder insisted it was crucial to her druid training and would teach Emily to pay attention. To follow the threads presented by life.

The woods opened on a small clearing and Emily froze. There, in the middle of her path, was Brian's dog. The one she had encountered her first night in Atlanta. Its back was to Emily and it stared out across a sunlit pond. Brian was nowhere to be seen. On the far side of the lake was the yawning mouth of what would be her destination.

Cu sniffed the air and ignored her, easing Emily's fear. A breeze ruffled the surface of the pond, lapping ripples against the cave. Hope's instructions had been to find the glade by the pool that springs from the heart of the world. This must be the place. But what was Cu doing here?

Emily stayed still, taking her cue from the wheat-colored colossus. After their encounter in the park, she had searched the web and found it was an Irish wolfhound, the tallest of all dogs.

Bred for hunting wolves, it was fast enough to catch an alpha and strong enough to rip it to shreds. Coo was easily three feet at the shoulders and could take a hunk out of Emily's face, should he be so inclined. Lucky for her, she'd met him before.

The wolfhound's long, elegant snout swiveled in Emily's direction. It snorted and looked away to gaze at the cave again, as calm today as it was manic the other.

From a willow on the opposite bank, a mockingbird trilled, a series of notes strung together in a lilting aria that filled the glade. Beneath its perch, mosses and reedy grasses veiled the rocks surrounding the cave.

A cave Emily had been directed to enter. Alone.

A rush of panic jellied her legs. To steady her nerves, she studied the pony-sized dog. It had a distinguished bearing that commanded respect, even awe. She could imagine him as a duke or an earl with an expensive druid torc adorning the long, royal neck.

A torc? Of gold? Holy shit!

Consulting the slip of paper clutched in her fist, Emily read what was already committed to memory: a collar of pure gold, two inches wide with a rope inlay banding the middle. As calmly as possible, she eyeballed the torc. The collar that was supposed to be hidden in the cave glittered instead around the dog's neck.

She flashed to that night she'd gotten lost. Hope and the wolfhound had appeared the same day. Were they in cahoots? Had the Elder meant for Emily to find the dog? Was it part of the whole treasure hunt thingy?

The wolfhound sprang to life. It whipped around and sniffed at Emily, wiry body wagging and hairy tail thumping, sending the aroma of crushed violets in the air. Emily squealed, backpedaling. The dog stood tall, its graceful snout parted in a sardonic grin. The collar looked at home on its regal neck. She hoped she wouldn't have to wrangle it from the beast.

"Nice doggy. Nice collar. Did Hope ask you to bring it to me?"

Every part of the dog wagged.

Emily found this encouraging. She tried again. "You're Cu, right?"

"Yes." The voice sounded in her head, in an accent similar to Hope's.

"So, you talk, too." That struck her as funny. She snickered, then giggled. Heat rose in her body as she tried to contain the bubbling laughter, but it burst from Emily like pressurized lava.

So certain had she been that she would be crawling through a dark, vermin-infested cave searching for a priceless collar, she'd been barely shy of panic all day. Over a stupid treasure hunt. The dog was the kicker. Emily's laughter peeled through the glade.

"I'm glad you find me amusing," the dog muttered with an air of genteel patience. "Try Cu, capital cee, letter u. Cu."

"Oh, oh, oh—" Hilarity burst through the hand Emily clamped over her mouth. Trying not to laugh was making it worse. "I'm sorry," she managed, in between giggle fits. "It's…not you…it's just—"

She collapsed on the soft verge, laughing hysterically into the grass.

"It's me!" she finally managed and struggled to pull it together. Tears bubbled up to join the laughter. "I'm supposed to…go in that cave." She raised her arm to point. "I'm supposed to…find a collar. Only…you're wearing it. Or one like it."

The hundred-plus pound dog sidled closer on feet that could grace a claw-foot tub. Wavy hair covered a lean face and body and the long, graceful legs. Emily watched Cu through teary eyes, but she wasn't afraid.

"Yes, but it didn't take much coaxing. I retrieved the old torc from the cave for you. Now come, little one. We've no time for magic collars or for tears. Sir Hamilton needs me."

"Sir Hamilton?" Emily sniffled, wiping at tears with her sleeve. "You mean Hamilton Hester? My father?"

"Yes, yes! He awaits. Take me to him!"

"Of course," Emily consented, springing to her feet. Then wondered why. The dog had brushed away her fears as easily as she swept the must from her shins. Once again, all was not as it appeared at Wren's Roost.

The wolfhound charged up the path toward the house. Emily followed at a jog. Cu knew her Da. Had Hamilton somehow communicated with the dog? Maybe through Hope?

The dog sniffed the underbrush and lifted a hind leg to pee.

"Nice!" she snarked, just managing to avoid his stream.

209

"When you gotta go, you gotta go." Scratching off with his hind legs in a show of doggy dominance, Cu trotted toward the house. The forest fell silent. Siesta time.

Slowly, softly, the leaves began to rustle in the trees overhead, the wind passing on its way east. The bushes fluttered as they traversed the last few yards and exited the woods. Wren's Roost rose before them in all its Tudor glory. Cu stopped to sniff the air.

"What now?"

"We go in. To Hamilton."

"Why do you think my father needs you?"

The dog looked baffled. "Because he does. He's been calling for days. I only just managed to get away. Please," Cu pleaded, "the master needs me. Won't you take me to him?"

As farfetched as the wolfhound's story sounded, Emily detected no lie. Her father was in a coma and hadn't communicated with her since that day in the hospital. What if Hamilton had been able to reach the dog?

"Follow me."

Hamilton and the Wolfhound

H is body languished in a coma, but Hamilton's spirit sensed his daughter's approach. She'd brought the wolfhound. Her voice had served as his anchor in the Otherworld, where Ham had been stripped of all senses except loss.

Now light pierced the eerie twilight as Cu's wagging tail swirled the mist. Hamilton's excitement mounted. Soon he would leave the body that had lasted longer than humanly possible.

"Da?" His daughter's presence called.

"Sunshine," he projected psychically, and felt Emily's pleasure as the sentiment landed and absorbed the fear oozing from her.

"Da! You're here!" He couldn't feel her touch, but he knew she took his hand. "I thought you were gone. You haven't spoken to me since that night in the hospital."

Unable to do more, Hamilton whispered in the silence of their minds, "My spirit has wandered, but I am here, little wren." He left out the fact that the Otherworld was ghastly. And that he'd begun to wonder if he would make it out in time.

"I brought you a visitor." His daughter's tone was reproving. "An unexpected one. Though you probably knew he was coming."

"Yes, I had hoped."

Hamilton sensed the hound's long snout touch his body, but felt nothing. Cu whined long and low, ending on a high-pitched yelp that pierced the silence and Hamilton's heart.

"Cu, my good and faithful servant," he whispered. "You're here."

"Aye, master," Cu barked. "I am here. Speak your command that I might serve you once more."

"Old friend," Hamilton whispered, "my vehicle is broken and dying. Without alternate transport, my spirit will follow. Would you allow an old man passage?"

Cu wriggled, a joyous yip escaping his doggy lips. "Aye, Sir. I am delighted to welcome an old friend. Tarry not. Your end is near. Do it now." The wolfhound thrust his wet nose against Ham's cheek. When the dog made contact, Hamilton slipped from the dying body into Cu's vibrant one.

Neither of them felt more than a tickle.

**

Emily listened to the exchange between her Da and the dog, conflict knotting her stomach. This never happen in the rule-riddled world in which Emily had lived before coming to Wren's Roost. The emotion radiating between man and beast was so sweet and so pure it filled her heart to bursting and tears streamed unchecked down her cheeks. Before her eyes, the wolfhound transformed, taking on the air of a king. Emily stifled the urge to curtsy.

The dog's lips moved, and sound came out. She heard her Da's voice, not in her head, but with her ears. "Hello, Sunshine."

The melodious voice carried a hint of amusement, its clear Southern drawl a close approximation of her Da's. So close it gave Emily goose bumps.

"Da?" The trepidation and need to believe vibrated in her voice. "Is that you?"

"Yes," the dog chuckled. "It is I."

Throwing her arms around the long neck, Emily hugged Cu so tight he yipped. She let go and was nearly bowled over by exuberant face-licking. Giggling, she squirmed away.

"Well, what do you expect?" Cu sat, tail wagging. "I'm your Da in a dog's body. Now, where to?"

"Where to?" Emily repeated, not comprehending.

"I've been in bed for weeks. I need to stretch my legs." The sentence ended on a doggy whine. "How 'bout I give you a tour of the estate?" Like Emily hadn't tromped all over it searching for Hope's treasures.

"What about Cu? Won't his owner be worried?"

"I'm a passenger, not the owner of this body, dear. Cu and I will return to his house later. And tomorrow we'll be back here bright and early. We've got a lot of ground to cover and years of catching up to do."

Emily eyed the chunk of gold around Cu's neck. "Maybe we should leave the torc here." Cu dipped his head to let her remove the precious collar. "Where should we put it for safekeeping?"

Cu led her to an alcove she hadn't entered before. A door opened to a library similar to the one in the carriage house. In the center was a huge desk piled with books and papers. Sliding into the oxblood-leather chair, Emily opened a side drawer and placed the golden torc on a pile of manila folders. Cu circled the room, touching his nose to one thing after another.

They returned to Hamilton's bedroom and Emily studied the form that had been her father. The chest barely rose and fell. "What about your, umm, body?" she croaked around the lump in her throat.

"It's failing, Emily." No emotion registered in Hamilton's voice. "When it does, the others will mourn. But you will know better." He blinked at her with Cu's big dog eyes and added furtively, "I believe that someone wants me dead. Let them think they have succeeded."

"What?" she gasped. "You think someone…what? Who, Da? And how? We must go to the police."

"No," he said adamantly, shaking Cu's head. "I have no proof, only suspicions. And I could be wrong. Let's not give the Order a reason to doubt you, a ghrá. Especially if I'm mistaken."

Emily looked at him askance, not sure whether she could ignore his allegation. Or its implications. Would the same person want her dead, too? The thought made her tremble. She wrung her hands and tried again. "Shouldn't we at least tell Morgan? Or Lugh MacBrayer? Someone should look into this, Da."

Cu ambled toward the door, tail high. "No, Dru-y-en. As your father and druid superior, I'm ordering you to let it go. When the time comes, we'll deal with it. But for now, let me give you that tour."

Conflicted, Emily followed Cu's wagging behind out the door and down the hall. "Well, at least I know where my stubbornness comes from."

The long, regal face looked back and quipped, "Yeah. I'm afraid you got a double dose of that. Your mama was the world's worst."

Snort-laughing, Emily followed him down the steps. "Amen to that."

**

After an amble around the estate, Hamilton left Emily at the carriage house and took Cu home. The walk from Wren's Roost was only a few blocks, but he sprinkled every mailbox along the way and half as many fences. The residence at Twelve Twenty-One Audrey Lane sat back from the street at the end of a long and gently sloping driveway. Newly-greened trees shielded the lot from the road.

Thinning sod, bare in places, could use a trim. Blackberries and wayward private hedges flourished in the islands, overrunning native azaleas and rhododendrons. Poison oak grew in dense mounds, its thick ropes snaking up soaring pecans whose canopy would provide shade in the hot summer months. What a shame they'd let it run down.

The house languished in similar disrepair. Old and elegant, the build was early-1940's and was smaller than most homes in Druid Hills. Probably the carriage house of a larger property. Hamilton strained to recall the estate house that had once stood here, but nothing came to mind. Did being in Cu's body limit the capacity of his brain?

Cu stopped walking and growled. "Excuse me?"

Hamilton chuckled. "Sorry, my friend. I meant you no slight. Carry on."

Brian and the Talking Dog

Loud snores filled the den—Cu sawing logs in his oversized bed. Jonathan Brian Walker MacBrayer, known to his family and friends as Brian, poked the dog with a bare toe. "Roll over, Cu. You're snoring."

The dog mumbled, "I don't snore," and went back to it.

Brian gulped. "He doesn't snore. The dog says he doesn't snore. UNCLE LUGH!!!" he screamed, tearing down the hall toward his uncle's bedroom. "The freaking dog talked! Omigod! The dog! SHIT!" Brian peered over one shoulder, grateful Cu wasn't behind him. Even knowing it was a bad idea, he pounded on the locked door. "Uncle Lugh! Open up!"

Just home from a long workday, Lugh had yelled at Brian only fifteen minutes earlier for being up late playing video games. Mid-knock, the door opened on his uncle in a terry robe, hair dripping from the shower.

"What? Brian, what?" It was the long-suffering tone Brian hated.

"The…um, uh, oh never mind." He backed down the hall. Dealing with his uncle at this exact moment might just be worse than a talking dog.

"Go to bed!" Lugh yelled and slammed the door so hard the floor vibrated.

Brian thought of his father. Would he have shouted? At least his uncle wanted him. Not that he'd been given a choice. But neither had Brian, who had come prepared to spend a weekend in Atlanta with his dad's family. Turned out, Lugh was the extent of the MacBrayer clan. And one weekend had multiplied to two months, two weeks, and three—almost four—days.

But yikes. The crazy dog had talked.

215

Brian's mind raced. Cu had shown up in the middle of a snowstorm. Uncle Lugh was at work and Brian hadn't had the heart to make the dog stay outside. When his uncle found him cozied on top of an old blanket in front of the fireplace that night, he had hit the roof.

Peeking in the den, Brian spied the dog asleep on his back and stifled a giggle. Cu's skinny legs were high in the air, his big feet drooping. Brian tiptoed past the twitching dog whose loud snores had calmed to gentle snuffles. When no one had claimed the wolfhound, Uncle Lugh had caved and let him stay. Other than a hamster, Cu was Brian's first pet. But who lost a giant dog and didn't notice? Or claim it? Lugh had said considering the food the wolfhound ate and the huge piles of poo, probably half of Atlanta.

Poking through the remains of several nights' take-out, Brian settled on pepperoni pizza. He unwrapped it, plated it, and tucked it in the microwave in no time flat. It dinged and Brian grabbed the plate, yelping when it was hotter than he'd expected. He tossed the plate to the counter and stuck his scalded fingers in his mouth to the knuckle. The plate landed clattering and the pizza slid part-way off.

A strange voice demanded, "What's going on in here?"

Brian wheeled to face the intruder, not much relieved to find it was Cu. Snatching a bag of carrots from the freezer, he wrapped his stinging fingers around the soothing cold. Determined to get to the bottom of this nonsense, he sputtered, "You did not just talk to me."

The dog cocked its head. "I most certainly did. What was that racket? Can't a fellow get some sleep?" The wolfhound shook its head, ears flopping.

"Dogs can't talk." Brian's knees knocked a little. "You are not talking. I am imagining things. My mother says I have an overactive imagination."

"You do, Brian. That's one of your better traits. Don't let anyone tell you different, not even your mother. One of the greatest men of the last century said, 'Imagination is more important than knowledge.' That was Albert Einstein, in case you didn't know. A druid, like you."

216

Brian heard the words and saw the dog's lips move but comprehended nothing. How could this be?

"I *am* going crazy. You really are talking." He retrieved a slice of pizza with his good hand and stuffed it in his mouth, mumbling past it. "Why talk now and not before?"

The dog remained silent and watched him chew.

"Cat got your tongue?" Brian snickered, and almost choked on the pizza. The dog let him hack.

"Gonna make it there, son?"

When the coughing passed, Brian wiped his runny nose on his sleeve.

"Eeeeuuww," the dog exclaimed.

Brian sneered, "At least it's not my butt."

"You have a point there. Nevertheless, use a Kleenex please. You can help it—I can't. Now, did you want an answer to that question?"

Brian nodded, stuffed the slice in his mouth and chewed.

"I met a friend. A very old friend," the dog said, like that explained things.

Brian put the table between them and nabbed another slice. He bit in and moaned. His uncle's recipe was killer, better than the store's patented sauce. The dog's eyes followed his every move.

"So, what's your name?" Brian asked, munching.

The dog stared. "You get to ask a question of a talking dog and you ask one to which you already know the answer?"

"I didn't. And I don't. I've had Cu for nearly a month, and never once has he spoken or told me what to do. You snore. You sleep on your back. You're bossy. Who are you and what have you done with my dog?"

Lugh shuffled into the kitchen in worn leather slippers, damp hair curling around his neck. Blue-plaid pajama bottoms and a rumpled white tee had replaced the terry robe, but not the sour look. "Who you talking to?"

Brian glanced at the dog, waggled his Smartphone in the air and lied, "No one. I was watching a show on VideoCloud."

"Is that right?" Cu said and flopped to his belly looking from man to boy. "I thought we were having a conversation."

Something about me being bossy and demanding. Oh. And I snore. Anything else?"

Brian's belly hit the floor.

Lugh wheeled toward the dog, shock wrinkling his dark brow. Cu lay still, tail waving slowly. Confused, Brian watched his uncle sink to one knee, so close to Cu they were nose to nose.

"Hamilton? Sir? Is that you?" Lugh's voice was so low, Brian had to strain to hear. The dog chuckled. Chuckled! And then licked his uncle's face. Brian's jaw dropped open. Lugh didn't even like the dog. But when he stood, the dog reared and put its paws on Lugh's shoulders and looked him square in the eye.

"Lugh MacBrayer, to you I owe my deepest gratitude." The wolfhound licked his uncle's face and then dropped to all fours. "Where did you find my old friend Cu?"

He had no idea what was going on, but Brian interjected, "Bonsai!"

Lugh shrugged. "He showed up on my doorstep about a month ago."

"And Brian?" The dog pointed its nose in his direction.

With an apologetic look, his uncle answered, "About a month before that. His mom dropped him off for a weekend visit, then called from the airport. She actually went to Bali for a job." Lugh wrung his hands. "Hamilton, Arthur phoned the restaurant an hour ago and said you had died. Is that true?"

Brian froze. A dead man had possessed his dog?

"My body expired, yes," the tone was curt. "Thanks to Cu, I am still alive. But you know that, Lughnasadh. I wouldn't be here having a conversation through canine lips if I had remained in the Otherworld."

Straightening, Lugh looked across the table at Brian, then back at the dog. "That changes everything, Sir. What would you like us to do now?"

"I would like to take your nephew to Wren's Roost for druid training. Like my daughter, Brian has apparently been kept ignorant of our ways. He didn't even get my Einstein reference."

What now? Brian hiccupped. The pizza wasn't sitting well all of a sudden.

"Yes, Sir. You know that when Brian was a toddler, my sister-in-law Cybele left Jake and moved back to Utah—"

"Wait. What?" Brian put the half-eaten slice on the plate. "She said he left us!"

Lugh glanced at Brian and his expression softened. "No, Bri, it was the other way around. It broke Jake's heart. Then when Jake was recruited by the Axiom Corporation, he left the states. We haven't heard from him since."

Brian swiped at a fat tear before it ran down his cheek. He hadn't minded so much being dumped on his uncle. It was warmer here and more civilized than back home. Plus, Brian knew his mother would eventually come back for him.

But she had lied about his father. Never once had she hinted that she was the one to do the leaving. His world brightened, and the dead man in his dog couldn't spoil the hope growing in Brian's heart.

His father hadn't left him, after all.

**

At one in the morning, Brian was still wide awake. He stared at the Demons and Dragons game on the screen. He was losing to his buddy Lars in Utah and decided to pack it in for the night.

Signing off, he opened a new window and typed "man in body of dog." The browser came back with over forty million hits, including instructional videos and how-to's. Most links were for novels about shape shifters, werewolves and the like.

Brian clicked on the EuroPedia-link for shape shifter. Most references, it said, were recorded in mythological and fantastical literature—poetry, books, movies, and video games. Brian snorted. Fat help, that. Clicking on other links, he found nothing of use. He played with keyword combinations, yielding little more.

Disgusted, he closed the tablet and climbed between his sheets, clapping his hands to turn off the light. But his mind ran on, trying to make sense of a dog possessed by a bossy dead man.

The outside security light bathed his room in fluorescent purples. Brian rolled away from the lurid light and pulled the covers over his head. Silently, he recited the prayer his father had taught him when he was little.

"Stretch thine arms, oh Goddess bright, across this place I sleep tonight, that I may know your watchful eye, and shield protect both me and mine."

In his imagination, an angel bright and beautiful but terrible, too, put her arms around him and his uncle's house. The angel drew them into her powerful embrace and tucked them under her left wing, holding her shield at the ready with her right.

Letting go a long and shuddering breath, Brian slipped into a restless sleep where Jake MacBrayer took pains to teach his son the fine art of shape-shifting. Only Brian didn't like it inside his pet hamster. And swore he would never do that again.

Nergal in New York

When his eyelid twitched for the umpteenth time, Nergal let go a string of silent profanities. The random spasms had begun that morning and troubled the Draco. He was unfamiliar with such worldly flaws.

Last night he had arrived late to Irkalla—the underbelly of New York City. Below the caverns of Grand Central Station, Nergal stepped from the chute and was whisked unceremoniously to the great hall by one of the ugliest troglodytes he had ever seen. There Nergal was questioned by the warlord, Shibboleth.

Normally Nergal would rage at such circumstances, or be coolly oblivious. At the moment, he was neither, too aware of the sickness that plundered his gut.

When his brow vibrated again, he slapped it, barely registering the blow. The Dracos nearest him moved away. Nergal had fought larger, viler opponents in the past, and come out on top. But something about Shibboleth curdled his blood.

The warlord was strong, even in Nergal's home territory. Intel told him Shibboleth's spies were everywhere. A contingent of his men crowded the great hall of Irkalla, making a show of force in front of Nergal and the Northern generals.

The warlord commanded the dais, surrounded by a host of his burly Dracos. Nergal studied him, astounded not only by Shibboleth's far reach but by the ancient Draco's youthful appearance.

Not to mention his enduring capacity for revenge. The warlord had no love for humans and even less for Nergal, who had long ago bedded one of Shibboleth's daughter spawn.

Had Nergal known the female's lineage, the coupling would never have taken place. It was his policy not to mix politics with recreation—he had surpassed too many dead predecessors to let some tail interfere. But that dalliance nearly cost him his position on the World Council.

Generals and attachés from around the globe packed the cavernous room. Nergal noted most were Dracos, though a few were Pindejahs or Jahkquadis that had wormed their way through the ranks.

With a start, he realized the room had gone quiet and Shibboleth no longer spoke. Nergal looked up. The warlord was striding toward Nergal, beady eyes glittering in anticipation, two of his henchmen close on his heels.

Nergal gulped and got ready for the attack. If it was a fight Shibboleth wanted, a fight he would get. The warrior halted in front of Nergal and gestured with one hand, bidding him rise. Nergal did, chest puffed out. Shibboleth raked him up and down with a hard stare. The goons held rank.

To the hall the leader announced derisively, "This one thinks he should be ruler of AboveEarth."

The room exploded with laughter. Nergal glanced down to hide the hatred that flashed and threatened to burn. "Anyone here think Nergal would make a good leader?" The commander held up a hand as if voting "yea." Not one of the generals dared respond.

Rage licked at Nergal's insides. He held it close. He must bide his time. It wouldn't do to start a fight in front of his peers. There was a war to win. He kept his eyes on the floor and refused to engage. Shibboleth spun on his heel and returned to the stage with his goons.

The warlord resumed his tales of long-ago adventures across the galaxies. And though Nergal's mind was busy plotting Shibboleth's demise, from that moment on, he kept his eyes on the dais and Shibboleth.

Brian Joins the Fray

Several days had passed without rain in Atlanta and each got progressively warmer. Emily perched on the rocks by what she'd dubbed Crane Lake, basking in the sun while Hope droned on.

"As you know, powerful spells veil Wren's Roost from all eyes except those who know its whereabouts. Official maps and surveys list the estate as a smidge over sixteen acres. In reality, it is much larger, as are the other druid holdings. All total, there are twelve hundred acres of spell-protected land in Druid Hills, and millions more across the United States. Not to speak of worldwide."

Again, Emily was shocked. The world knew nothing of druids, or unknown lands hidden by magic spells. Druids must be powerful indeed.

"The enchantments protect the land, including Wren's Roost, and draw power from the earth, its trees and flora, and its many bodies of water. For example, this underground spring provides special magic, having once held healing properties like those of Luftshorne. The fire of the sun and the air we breathe weave the magic together and hold it in place.

"Luftshorne?" Emily breathed, entranced. She'd heard the name somewhere before.

"The healing waters in Awen's glade," the Elder answered. "But that's a story for another time. Close your eyes. Feel the energy."

She opened her senses to the energy. It sizzled and pinged around her. This, Emily was familiar with, though she'd never been able to identify the source. She had learned instead to ignore it, after once consulting a doctor who called tinnitus.

"You mean that's not just my ears ringing?" she asked. "I hear that all the time. Where's it coming from?"

"The earth. Its water. The air. The sun." The Elder peered across the pond. "Do you know anything about ley lines?"

"I've heard of them. What are they?"

Repositioning her bulk, Hope tucked her feet and tail beneath her in Buddha pose. "The Earth is encased in an energetic grid similar to a skin. In olden days, the connecting lines were called dragon lines because the dragons used them as highways. Today they are known as ley lines. It is possible these pathways could help us locate Draig a-Ur and the other dragons."

Emily's ears pricked up. No one had mentioned dragons out loud since the day Emily saw a-Ur in the cemetery. The day she had revealed Awen's manuscript to Hope and Lugh.

"You need to understand these geocentric forces and become familiar with Earth's energy grid. There is a globe in the library depicting every ley line and connecting vortex. I want you to study that grid. Memorize every pathway and its related vortices."

Emily half rose and Hope interjected, "But first, I want you to be still and close your eyes. Get acquainted with the energy." Hope sprang from the grass and pounced on an unsuspecting Ralph, then scampered off into the woods with Ralph in hot pursuit.

Chuckling, Emily settled into a more comfortable position. She quieted her mind and directed it toward the power pulsing around her, allowing it in. After a while, the energy throbbed with such force Emily felt it as a physical vibration.

She took a deep inhalation and called to the elements, inviting them to calm. The thrumming softened and a realization bubbled from the depths of her being. She felt this energy all the time. And heard it, too. Her body was a giant tuning fork. Maybe now, having identified its source, the agitation would be easier to handle.

An explosion of disturbed geese charging into the water sent Emily vaulting into warrior pose. And staring into the eyes of a grinning, wriggling wolfhound.

"Cu! Da! You're here!" she squealed, throwing her arms around the yipping giant. What Emily saw behind him made her let go. Lugh's teenaged nephew wavered on the path like a frightened cobra.

Cu swiped a tongue at her cheek and crooned in Hamilton Hester's voice, "Afternoon, Dru-y-en. Remember Brian MacBrayer?"

Emily nodded to the teen. "Yes. Hi, Brian."

He held out his hand, then snatched it away, a scowl darkening his swarthy features. He stared at Emily like she might turn him to stone.

"What is it?"

"I knew I'd seen your face before. I just figured it out. You're that woman in the picture! You look j-just like her! How old *are* you, anyway?"

"What picture?" she and her Da chorused.

Brian backed toward the path.

"Wait!" Hamilton commanded. Brian swayed in place, eyes like twin baseballs.

"What picture?" Emily asked again.

Brian took another step back.

"Sit!" the dog barked. Emily snickered at the irony.

"No one's going to hurt you," her Da said. "I told you before. We are your people. We're different, too. Well, obviously I'm different." His quick laugh was melodious, at odds with his appearance.

Still looking spooked, Brian dropped to a nearby boulder and tucked his gangly knees under his strong, sharp chin. His dark eyes locked on the dog.

"Emily is my daughter," Hamilton pointed with Cu's nose. "She's different too—druid born. Like you." Brian scowled and stared toward the pond, posture stiff and erect.

"Like Emily, all you need is training. Her mother took her when she was little, same as Cybele did with you."

Brian bolted this time, face flaming.

Drawing to Cu's full height, Hamilton blocked his escape. "You promised to do this, Brian. Where are you going?"

Fists balled, Brian snapped, "Don't talk about my mother."

Her Da teased, "Ooo, touchy, are we?"

Brian's wild eyes flit from the dog to Emily, to the path and back, as if calculating the odds on making it should he run.

Emily stepped between them. "At least you're starting early. I'm nearly thirty. How old are you?"

The kid scratched the back of his head. "Almost fourteen."

"See. You'll run circles around me."

A lightning smile softened the boy's face, momentarily lifting the melancholy. As if startled by it, Brian scowled and shoved his hands into the pockets of his jeans.

"I said I'd let Cu out and I said I'd come here. Nothing more." He turned to leave. "I have schoolwork to do. I'm going home."

Hamilton proclaimed, "No, son. You're not."

Surprised at her father's fierceness, Emily tried again, "Brian, won't you tell me who you think I look like?"

He spun and stalked back to face her, hands on hips, head cocked to one side, fascination warring with defiance. Without the sulk, the teen was quite handsome. His black eyes searched Emily's face.

"We had a picture when I was little." He jabbed a finger in her direction. "The woman looked just like you." Then he pointed at Cu. "And the dog looked like you."

Cu's tail swished.

"They looked happy," Brian blurted. "I used to pretend I hung out with them in the forest. There was a cat, too. A really big one, with black strips and whiskers as long as the day." The smile flashed again before Brian clamped it down.

The dog yelped. "Where did you hear that?"

The boy's face clouded. "What?"

"That thing you said about the whiskers." Hamilton's tone was sharp. Why was he being so overbearing? It was obvious the picture was of Awen. Why Cu and Hope were in it was another story. But still.

"My father," Brian said. "He used to make up stories about them."

"Where is the painting now?"

The boy hung his head. "I don't know. That was a long time ago. I haven't seen it since my dad…I mean, since we left. But I swear. I'm telling the truth."

He looked at Emily. "That's why I freaked out. It was weird enough when Cu showed up. Uncle Lugh said it was a coincidence, but now I'm not sure."

"Look," Hamilton softened, "I have a proposal. If you agree to train with Emily, I will tell you about the painting. But not until I declare you both ready. Do we have a deal?"

Brian looked from the dog to Emily, then beyond her to the lake. Ruffled by the light breeze, its surface mirrored blue sky and puffy clouds. No one spoke.

Still gazing at the lake, the boy broke the silence. "Okay, I will. Uncle Lugh wants me to, and it might be fun. But I have school and chores. So, don't be surprised if I'm not here much."

"Here first, chores second," Hamilton rejoined.

The boy protested, "But my homework!"

"My daughter will help with that if need be."

Emily balked. Hamilton glared at her and then turned back to the kid. "From the looks of your uncle's place, nothing is being done there already. That changes today. As part of your training, you will do what Lugh asks. Anything else needs doing? You will do that, too—without being asked. Druids are not garden slugs. We pay our way. That goes for you too, young lady." Hamilton rounded on Emily.

"Hey, what did I do?" she protested.

"Nothing. That's the problem." She crumbled like an accordion. But Hamilton was just warming up. "It's time to buckle down. We have to turn you into a grand druid and time is short. The Darkness is coming, and it will not wait for you to get ready. And you must, Emily Bridget. Or we might as well kiss this earth goodbye."

The lump in Emily's throat was so big she could choke. Her Da had been harsh for the first time. She was surprised it hurt so much.

"Okay," was all she could manage to say.

"A ghrá," Hamilton softened. "You always were sensitive, even as a child. I'm sorry to be firm, but I must. This is important." It was hard to read the dog's expression, but Hamilton's tone meant business.

Exasperated, Emily rubbed her face in her hands. "Well, we'd better get started then. What do you think, Brian?" She extended her hand to the rangy boy. "Be my partner in crime?"

There was a moment of hesitation when Emily thought Brian would say no again. But he grinned his uncle's grin and took her hand. "Partner in crime, yes. As long as you're not a ghost."

Humiliation

Nergal had been delayed in Irkalla much longer than expected and was anxious to get back to Xibalba IX and his work with the human. Shibboleth had pushed him to the back of the agenda, no doubt to steal his thunder and to throw him off balance. Nergal ignored the current speaker and practiced his speech in his head. It was important he show no sign of weakness.

Many of the generals had submitted schemes to the High Council, none workable. The general from Naraka, the Bangladeshi UnderEarth, was currently suggesting shooting fire bombs from every portal between the worlds. When the humans were dead and the fires ceased raging, the Reptilians would assume command.

Someone pointed out early in the Narakan's presentation that the Reptilians wished to harvest AboveEarth resources, and the explosions and fires would destroy these assets. Despite that, the Narakan idiot had been allowed to continue ad nauseam. He finally finished and clomped to his seat in the back of the room.

Nergal rolled his eyeballs. The logic, or the lack thereof, was beyond him. The general had not even addressed the main problem – breaching the membrane between worlds.

But it was finally Nergal's turn.

The emcee stepped to the podium and announced him to the assembly. Nergal listened to the sonorous listing of his accomplishments, chest swelling with pride. He strutted to the front of the auditorium, basking in the applause. Today, Nergal would seal his place in the invasion and his claim to the rulership of AboveEarth.

Reaching the platform, he strolled across it to stand in the middle of the dais facing the crowd. Acutely aware of the disapproving glares from Shibboleth and his henchmen boring into his back, Nergal studied the faces in the auditorium. The majority of the room clapped and nodded. The rest, particularly the delegation from Gamma Reux, scowled or looked elsewhere to avoid eye contact.

Expecting as much, Nergal memorized his dissenters' faces. He would win them over later, with brute force if necessary. The thought gave Nergal a sizzle of anticipation. He tapped a portable device and Shalane's face appeared on one half of the giant screen, the shill's on the other.

Angry murmurs rose around the room and behind him. Inwardly Nergal smiled, though he kept his demeanor passive. The generals were responding as he had anticipated. He stared at the screen until the room quieted. "Warriors," he pointed to the images, "this is how we will take AboveEarth."

The room exploded in pandemonium. Generals yelled and shouted, some in protest, others in agreement. All demanded an explanation. Shibboleth and the henchmen behind Nergal objected the loudest.

Nergal tapped the mic. "Let me explain."

Silence was slow to descend, but when it finally prevailed, Nergal continued. "The human on the left is Shalane Carpenter, an internationally-known televangelist. To her right is her associate, Patrika Tolbert."

A sea of mostly Reptilian faces peered at the screen. A quick glance told him Shibboleth and his goons watched, too. "I have discovered a way to influence the humans' behavior." Unshod feet shuffled and stamped as the curious generals waited.

"During a practice they call 'meditation,' humans send energetic 'roots' into UnderEarth. All that is required to link with a human is to connect with this energetic root." The room erupted again but Nergal powered through.

"The connection is fed to the Main Brain where all memories, thoughts, and actions of the human are recorded and displayed on the screen. We influence the human by inserting instructions via this connection."

230

The naysayers roared and Nergal paused until the others shouted them down.

"We have been testing for months and these are the first humans to be linked successfully. Our primary target is connected to a Fomorian under my command. I relay instructions to the human through the Fomorian, which is effective, but cumbersome. I personally linked with this woman." Nergal pointed to the human, Patrika. "Through her, I am able to exert control over the priest."

Well, pressure really. Control had been elusive thus far. Nergal would keep that to himself, though.

From the dais, Shibboleth harrumphed for attention. "Why do you not link directly with the target? Why have you entrusted this to some inferior creature?"

Nergal raised his hand to call for order. "In early testing, we found that while the first link is strong and effective, it can be injurious and even fatal to the one making the connection.

"Lesser beings were used for this task while we improved the technique. Likewise, multiple links tend to damage or kill the human host. This one is an exact match for our profile. It may become necessary to test her limits."

Shibboleth sat down reluctantly and waved Nergal to continue.

"We have identified key influential figures around AboveEarth." Nergal toggled through frames depicting various human targets. "Each controls a significant human following. Once we get these leaders under Reptilian control, we will incite the humans to annihilate one another. Then, lofty sirs, an intact AboveEarth will belong to the Dracos."

This time the room exploded with jubilation to the tune of catcalls, whistles, and foot-stomping applause. Nergal rejoiced in the adulation. He had known it was a good plan, better than anything they had dreamed up in a thousand years.

There was a crash behind him and Nergal wheeled. Shibboleth's chair spun upside down on the dais. His henchmen glowered, in attack posture. Shibboleth clomped to the center of the stage, his glare daring Nergal to speak. There was a smattering of half-hearted applause.

"Thank you, General." Shibboleth sounded far from grateful. He stroked the prominent ridge of horns that flared from his forehead to the back of his cranium, eyeing the crowd. Nergal wondered whether he should exit the stage or take a bow.

"Thank you for that marvelous idea," Shibboleth continued. "But I have one question." Nergal's sphincter tightened. "Once the humans destroy one other, how do we break the barrier? We still can't live on AboveEarth—our agreement with the federation binds us to UnderEarth." Shibboleth's tone hardened. "How do you plan to get around that, Nergal?"

"Good question, Sir. We have yet to work that out but are getting closer." Nergal held his breath. What happened now was crucial, the difference between him winning or losing it all.

Shibboleth's expression telegraphed his black thoughts. Nergal could tell he had not expected a viable solution from him, nor did the warlord want one. He wished merely to be rid of Nergal. And the sooner, the better.

"Be gone foul-tongue." Shibboleth roared, true now to his face. "Come back when you've something better to offer."

The hall quieted, save the shifting of generals in chairs, uneasy at the thought of being similarly skewered. A few clapped, but most waited to see what would happen next. When Shibboleth sat down in the chair his henchmen had righted, the room exploded.

Traitors. Refusing to show emotion or any other sign of weakness, Nergal squelched the urge to swallow. He moved to exit the stage amidst a cacophony of boos, hisses, and grunts. As he passed, one of Shibboleth's bodyguards drew a red-clawed forefinger across his throat.

That clinched it. Nergal gulped down the lump clogging his airway. Head held high, he ignored the red-nailed henchman and clomped down the stairs. Not one of the generals met Nergal's gaze as he traversed the aisle to take his seat.

When the emcee stood to announce the next speaker, Nergal studied the goon that had threatened him. Even for a Draco, the Reptilian was large. He wore a half-helmet, wristlets of leather, and a vest fashioned from an arthropod's carapace—some vanquished foe, most likely. The claws on all four of the Draco's

232

limbs were painted blood-red. Nergal found the practice disgusting and prohibited it in Xibalba IX.

Perhaps sensing Nergal's malevolent perusal, the muscle-bound Draco eyed him with contempt and mimed being hung by a noose, complete with bulging eyes and lolling tongue.

Rage reddened Nergal's vision, but he kept his fists clenched in his lap and looked away. He'd have to watch his back. And the best way to do that was to get out of Irkalla. He would be leader of all Earth, no matter the opposition. Nergal considered his limited options and made a decision.

When the meetings adjourned, he would reroute to the UnderEarth base nearest the reverend's current location. Nergal's scientist, Ishkur, would handle the delicate extrication process between the Fomorian and the human, and join Nergal with the necessary equipment.

It was time to ramp up the experiments. Even if it meant injuring his prized target.

Premonition

Lugh slammed the phone in its cradle. Jocko's was finally up and running after the tornado damage, but that was his third call-in today, making the current down-and-out count two waitresses and one short-order chef. And it was only eleven oh five.

On waking that morning, Lugh had known it wouldn't be a good day—nothing he could put his finger on, but the hairs on his arms vibrated and that was enough. Now rain lashed the windows and the temperature dropped. The lunch rush had started, and Jocko's needed help something fierce.

Punching Suzy's number, Lugh got her voicemail and left an urgent message, then hung up and called the next on the list. Topher answered, on his way to class. And so it went. Even the always-available Zaleem couldn't help, at home babysitting four "snot-nosed siblings," as he so graphically lamented. The doorbell jingled and a party of six bustled in shaking off…was that snow?

Shit. How could it be snowing? Outside, the white stuff fell in thick clumps and had already formed a blanket on the wet concrete. Dread crawled up Lugh's neck. March winter storms made him nervous. One had claimed his parents.

While the newcomers found a table, Lugh switched the overhead to The Weather Station. Earlier this morning, there had been no mention of snow. Or freezing temps. Now NOAA was predicting blizzard conditions for the entire southeast.

The hairs on Lugh's arms stood and danced. He lifted a handful of menus and hurried to greet guests and take drink orders with a patience he didn't feel and an almost genuine smile.

The bell jingled on a group of four, laughing and in high spirits. Lugh passed his ticket to the bartender and searched the dining room for Talli. His lone waitress was nowhere in sight. With a heavy sigh, he grabbed four menus.

Directing a young brunette to the bathroom, Lugh scribbled beverage orders and dropped the ticket at the bar. Hefting the tray of drinks for the six-top, he delivered them to the table and answered questions about the menu. Talli appeared and Lugh nodded her to the four-top.

When the bell jingled again, his stomach lurched and sweat broke out on his brow. Jocko's was headed toward a full house and he was desperately short on staff. He glanced up at an empty doorway. He scribbled the order and rushed to the kitchen.

"Did someone just come in?" he asked Talli as they passed.

The waitress nodded toward the garden room. Emily Hester. Of all the rotten luck. She would show up today of all days. His smile was tight as she closed the distance.

"A little birdie told me you could use some help." Emily beamed, genuine and open.

Lugh stopped in his tracks, the six-top's order forgotten in his hand. "That was one wise bird. Ever waitressed?" He prayed the answer would be yes.

"I worked my way through college waiting tables. Give me a pad and an apron and I'm yours for the next two hours. I'm warning you, though, it's been a while. I'm a little rusty."

"Sweetheart, you're a lifesaver. Follow me."

Lugh showed Emily where to hang her coat and stow her purse, then handed her an apron, pad, and pen. He ignored the spot where his mother had warned him about her.

"You and Talli are in charge of seating, taking orders, and delivering the food. I'll keep the drinks filled, bus, and handle any overflow. Ready to rumble?"

Emily nodded.

"Then let's do this." Lugh shoved through the swinging doors.

The restaurant was already half full and customers piled through the front door, wiping feet on a rug dotted with melting snow. Emily grabbed a fistful of menus and hurried to greet them.

**

The lunch rush was over as early as it had begun. In spite of the nasty weather—snow drifted several feet up the building and blew sideways outside—Jocko's limited staff had fed two hundred and twenty-two people including take-out orders. They'd sold more than double the normal amount of coffee and hot-tea drinks.

Only a few guests lingered, conversing and ignoring the growing threat outside. Talli bussed the vacated tables. Emily dropped checks and collected tabs from the remainder.

Lugh watched his new grand druid make her way across the restaurant. She swept the room with a gaze that took in every detail and gave patrons an opportunity to catch her eye. Not just her tables, either. All of them. Only the best did that.

She glanced up and he grinned, busted. But damn, the woman was good. On her walk to the kitchen, Emily pranced a little.

"Like my moves, dahlin'?" she said it in a mock southern accent, punctuated by a lilting laugh.

"Honey, you can bust yo' moves in my dining room any time." Lugh chuckled with admiration.

She shook her head. "In your dreams."

"I'm serious," Lugh pursued. "You're not working. It would do you good to get out of that mausoleum and hang out with people now and then. You know, once a week, twice a week, whenever I have a call-in."

"I'd love to say 'yes' but you know I can't. Hope would have a hissy." She chuckled. "No pun intended. We're packing twenty-six years of lessons into weeks. Months if I'm lucky."

"You have a point," he admitted, though reluctant. "But you're here now, so I had to try." He opened the cash register and fished out a crisp fifty-dollar bill, ran it under his nose to savor the money smell, and handed it to Emily.

Her fine eyebrows shot up registering shock. "For two hours? Really? Servers make a lot more now than I remember."

"No, actually, they don't," Lugh grinned wryly. "Put that away or Talli will be hitting me up for a raise."

"Ahh. A bribe then." Emily tapped the fifty-dollar bill on her nose while he looked around for Talli. She was in the back corner but walked toward them lugging a full bus tub.

"One I will take back in a heartbeat if you don't stop waving it around. Here she comes," Lugh growled. "Put that away."

Emily folded the bill twice and palmed it. Talli closed the distance.

"Thanks." He relaxed.

"Hey Talli, I bused that last table for you and look!" Emily held the folded fifty in the air.

Lugh's heart sank.

Talli squeed and danced to reach for it. "Which table?" Emily pointed. "Wow. I wouldn't have pegged those guys for big tippers." Talli started to slide the fifty in her apron pocket, but then hesitated and held it out to Emily.

"You earned this more than I did. If it hadn't been for you, I would have made squat today. Nobody tips when the service is lousy."

Lugh watched the interaction, warmed by Emily's generous spirit and falling for her a little more.

His savior for the day shook her head, hair escaping its confining band to curl in ringlets around her exertion-pinked face. "It's yours, Talli. You worked your buns off. You deserve it. Keep it."

Talli hesitated, then tucked the bill in her apron and hugged the surprised redhead. "Thanks. It will come in handy, believe you me. I'm a single mom of two and short on bills."

With a nod, Talli made a beeline for the kitchen, lugging the bus tub with her. There was a spring in her step that hadn't been there before. Emily Hester had that effect on people. Especially Lugh. But she had given away his fifty.

"Really?" Lugh mock-glared, preferring to hide his gooey side.

"Really." Emily glared right back. "It was a bit unfair to Talli. Plus, Brian was worried and I wanted to help. I didn't do it to get paid."

"Not even minimum wage?" he joked.

She pulled a wad of bills from her apron pocket. "I'm pretty sure this covers that. Take me to dinner if you insist on paying. Hanging out with cats, a kid, and a testy dog has me jonesing for adult conversation."

Lugh dismissed his mother's warning again. What harm could dinner do?

"How about this weekend? After we get through this blizzard? We still haven't made it to Zoo Atlanta." The doorbell jingled and they both looked up.

The druid cop Taurus Gowan, sans partner, shook the snow off his plastic-shrouded police cap. He dusted it from his overcoat and surveyed the almost empty dining room with a seasoned eye.

When Taurus spied Lugh and Emily behind the bar, he nodded and headed their way. She waved and ducked into the kitchen, leaving Lugh alone at the counter.

"Taurus," he acknowledged the aptly named officer whose neck was as thick as Lugh's thigh. He'd grown up with the guy and still wouldn't want to get on his bad side.

"Lugh." Tense, Taurus leaned against the bar and murmured in a low voice, "Mitchell sent me to spread the word. Arthur has called an emergency meeting and you know what that means. You gotta close the place down unless someone else can run 'er for ya. No one can miss, least of all you, Mitch says." The burly officer's expression said he didn't envy Lugh.

"Taurus, I have no time for false alarms."

The officer groaned. "Nor do I. But I'm afraid this isn't. Arthur and Morgan agree there's some outside force at play here. A few hours ago, this wasn't a blip on the radar. Now WNN is calling it a once in a lifetime weather bomb. The barometric pressure dropped forty points in under an hour."

The cop massaged the stubble on his chin and the underbelly of his throat.

"A tiny non-system," Taurus drawled, mimicking an announcer. "A wisp of a nothing stalled over the Gulf of Mexico turned into a vicious, cyclonic cell." He dropped the farce and his voice turned serious. "Just before that, a Canadian cold front changed directions and barreled down the center of the country toward Atlanta. Both are heading straight for us. Coincidence?"

Lugh shook his head.

"None of the other druids think so either. Even the weather dudes are scratching their heads. It looks like trouble may've found us, my friend."

Lugh glanced at the screen above Taurus's head. The sound was muted, but a reporter stood in front of Atlanta International Airport. The caption showed several runways closed. A list of delayed and cancelled flights scrolled across the screen. More were flashing iffy.

He cocked his head at Taurus. "And what do you think?"

The cop leaned closer, his meaty hands planted flat on the counter. "I think something's up. Don't you feel it?"

Looking down at his own clenched fists, Lugh nodded. He did feel it. In his bones and in the hair vibrating on the backs of his arms. He caught an echo of his fear in the cop's eyes, then the flicker was gone.

"Yes," he agreed. Unclenching one hand, he laid it on Taurus's. "Something is fishy for sure. And it looks like the storm will get worse." He opened the register to close out. "What time and where?"

"Two hours. Wren's Roost, main house." Taurus looked out at the blowing snow, then up at the television screen. "Or as soon as possible. Be careful out there." Concern carved valleys across his wide forehead.

"We will. Brian will be with me. Emily is in the kitchen, so I'll make sure she gets the word."

"I'm sure Mitchell's ahead of you on that, but please do." Taurus tipped his hat and turned to go, solemn to the core.

"Have you eaten?" Lugh called after the hunched cop.

"No, but no time. More stops to make. Mrs. Mary will have something, I'm sure. Oh!" The policeman turned back. "I almost forgot. Bring clothes. We may be there till this thing blows over. They didn't say, but if it lasts more than a couple of days, we'll be celebrating the equinox indoors."

Lugh stuffed the day's receipts in a money bag. No sense in keeping Jocko's open in a blizzard. "Got it. Two hours."

Emily emerged from the kitchen, bundled in a thin coat. "I got a text from Mitchell. Time to get home."

"Yeah, he's in bossy mode again. Taurus came by to tell me about the meeting. You okay driving in this?" He glanced at the street clogged with traffic. The blowing snow piled around the fountain.

"Piece of cake." She grinned and pulled her hood over her curls.

"Serious?" He wasn't sure he believed her.

"Oh yeah. You worry about you, Cupcake." Emily poked him in the chest. "I'll be fine." She dodged the light punch he threw at her shoulder and hightailed it to the door. "But you'd better hurry before the roads get too bad." With that, the redhead was out the door and slogging through the blustering snow.

Lugh eyeballed his new laminated-glass ceiling, grateful for Trent's expert repair job. When the last employee clocked out, he reinforced the protection spell around his beloved restaurant and locked the front door. The wind shrieked and pummeled him as he braved the growing blizzard.

Time to Gloat

S halane perched on the edge of the sofa and surfed the channels for news of her latest Elemental. She had forgotten how much fun tampering with the weather could be. It brought misery and madness to all it touched. Being in the God business, she felt it part of her job description to create conditions that brought the masses to Him.

Human beings were tough nuts. They needed a crisis to bring them to their knees. To break them, to get them to admit their way wasn't working, was no easy thing. To ask for help? Even harder. As long as folks believed they could run their own sorry lives, they would continue trying.

So far, only a few stations mentioned the news. Not a peep on the local Nashville stations. K-Tide in Birmingham and WNN out of Atlanta were covering it live. She clicked back to WNN and laughed out loud. The reporter was bundled like an Eskimo. Nothing showed but her eyes, nose, and mouth. Sixty mile-per-hour winds slammed snow into the woman.

Fool reporters. They'd do anything for a story.

Shalane turned up the volume and popped a frozen pocket pie in the microwave. She grabbed a Dos Equiis from the fridge and took a swallow.

"…meteorologists are calling the phenomenon a weather bomb. These only occur when rapidly dropping pressures meet a moisture-packed jet stream. In this case, a she-devil of a cold front ripping down from Canada is smacking up against rain-pregnant clouds roaring in from the Gulf.

"The last time the United States experienced a storm like this was January 2028, when a low-pressure system moved up from the Gulf and met with two others, one from the Southwest and one from Canada, to create the worst snowstorm the Midwest has seen."

The microwave pinged and Shalane dove to retrieve the piping-hot pastry.

"Think hurricane-force winds driving snow and voila, you have a Superbomb. With barometric pressures tanking and gusts up to one hundred ten miles an hour, this storm is breaking wind-speed records all over the southland…"

A loud buzzing interrupted the broadcast, signaling a special bulletin. The same scratchy transmission they had used since Shalane was a kid announced in a crackling voice, "The National Weather Service has issued a severe winter storm warning for the Southeastern United States from Eastern Louisiana to South Carolina."

Shalane ate the pastry in three bites and backed the volume to normal. She flounced on the sofa, sipping beer to chase away the fake pepperoni taste.

"Expect blizzard and white-out conditions, including high drifts. An all-craft alert has been issued for waterways from Eastern Louisiana to South Carolina. All coastal and inland vessels should seek shelter.

"The barometric pressure is nine hundred and sixty-four millibars or twenty-eight point four seven inches of mercury and falling. If you are in the path of the Superstorm, seek shelter immediately. This is the National Weather Service. Please stay tuned for further updates."

Shalane jumped up to do a shuffle-stepped jig, holding her beer in the air and dancing around it. Cecil walked in and caught her up in his arms.

"Care for a partner?" he spun her with the beer.

"Always." She laughed and cocked her head to see around him. He danced her away from the television and bent her backwards to plant a wet kiss on her lips.

"Down big boy," she said in a sultry voice, her head a foot from the floor. "Mama's nursing a storm."

Cecil stood Shalane up and sank to the sofa, pulling her down with him. On screen, footage from Montgomery, Alabama showed an eighteen-car pile-up. It had closed a snow-covered overpass.

"...road conditions are treacherous. Please stay inside. Only travel if absolutely necessary. Dress in layers and drink plenty of water. Stay hydrated. On your screen is a list of local shelters with websites and phone numbers."

An anchor's voice cut in, "Thank you, Anne. That was Anne Banks, ladies and gentlemen, reporting live from the Georgia Dome where March Madness was due to get underway in a few short hours.

"We have just been informed that Game One between Kentucky and Indiana has been postponed until tomorrow. Stay tuned to WNN for game times and breaking news on the 2042 Super Southern Snowbomb."

Shalane fished for the remote under a squirming Cecil and ran the channels. WKNR aired footage of a fifteen-foot storm surge powering its way through Bayou La Batre on Mobile Bay in Alabama. On the crest of the surge rode a gaggle of shrimp and fishing boats sweeping inland on the rising water. Families caught unawares clung to rooftops as the water rose.

"You didn't?" Reproof darkened Cecil's features.

Shalane had been on the verge of bragging about her handiwork. His horror stopped her. Cecil didn't understand, and never had when it came this stuff. His heart was too soft.

Like Ebby's.

"Nooo," she lied without guilt. Taking his plump hand, Shalane turned it over to kiss the soft palm and changed the subject. "Dinner, my dear?"

"Dinner would be good. In or out?" Cecil asked and nibbled her cheek.

"You choose darling." She patted her husband's hand and turned her attention to the news anchor who had just admitted the storm had caught the National Weather Service by surprise.

Shalane suppressed a giggle. In her mind's eye she saw newsrooms of meteorologists all over the country getting their asses chewed for failing to predict the Super Southern Snowbomb of 2042.

"You look amused, dear. Care to share?"

"Oh, nothing." Shalane wagged her head. "It's just hard to believe none of them saw this coming."

"Yeah. And this might put a hitch in our travel plans. We head to Atlanta tomorrow morning."

Shalane gulped. Shit. She hadn't thought about that.

Snowed In

In spite of what she'd told Lugh, by the time Emily made it to Wren's Roost in the blowing snow, she was a nervous wreck. She was happy she had taken the Marauder. The all-wheel drive vehicle had maneuvered her past lighter and less stalwart cars abandoned along the short but treacherous route home from Jocko's Pizza.

That she and the others had made it was a major accomplishment. No one had been prepared for a blizzard in Atlanta, especially not in March. Yet outside the thick snow blew sideways and hadn't let up for hours.

Like Mitchell Fucking Wainwright. No sooner had Emily burst into the main house covered in snow than the attorney had accused her of conjuring the blizzard. She had just fought her way from the carriage house, clinging to the wall in a forty mile-per-hour wind, and Emily was in no mood for Mitchell's theatrics. She ignored him and flounced into the other room peeling off her overcoat and handing it to a tut-tutting Mary Cobb.

Once again, Lugh and Morgan pooh-pooh'd his allegations, forcing Mitchell and the others to stand down. For the rest of the interminable afternoon, Wainwright took pot shots at her every chance he could. The dangerous gleam in his icy blue eyes made Emily uncomfortable. The man was trouble. And it was as apparent as ever he had it in for her.

A chill went through Emily that had nothing to do with the storm outside. What if Mitchell was the one who'd caused her father's death? If so, it made sense that he would be after her next. But why would he want either of them dead?

Pondering this question, she escaped the crowded living room and snuck upstairs to settle into a comfortable chair in her father's private quarters. To say the day had been enlightening would be an understatement.

She'd found Morgan bossy, Dana insufferable, and Becca alternately delightful and annoying. The only one that hadn't worn a hole in Emily's nerves was fourteen-year-old Brian. Go figure.

The afternoon and evening had been full of politics and maneuvering, posturing and bragging. Accusations and thinly-veiled threats were thrown around. Not just by Mitchell, but by several distant family members.

Every one of them had an agenda, each intent on pushing it down the others' throats. Hamilton Hester remained quiet, disguised as Cu. Only once, when Emily was on the verge of losing her cool, did her Da speak in her head.

To her surprise and slight annoyance, Lugh was popular with the Hester clan. Especially Dana, who followed him around like a puppy dog. Between a touch of jealousy and Mitchell's condescension, Emily welcomed the seclusion of her Da's bedroom.

She leaned her head on the chair back and rubbed her aching temples. The rare headache had begun on arrival at Wren's Roost. She longed to retire to the quiet of her carriage house. But first she had to get through dinner with Mitchell and the other crazies.

**

Scooping the last spoonful of chili from his bowl, Brian shoved it in his mouth. Mrs. Mary's chili was the best he had ever eaten, topped with a layer of cornbread rather than crackers.

At first, he had turned up his nose, but the combo was totally bonsai. He looked around at his uncle and at Emily Hester's family. It was his first-time meeting most of them, though he recognized several from Jocko's.

Brian's gaze landed on Mitchell Wainwright. There was something about the man he didn't like. Probably the way he treated folks. Like Mitchell was a king and they were his servants. When the attorney laughed, Brian's jaw dropped.

Instead of a mean ol' sourpuss, the man looked nice. If he would just lighten up, Mitch might be all right.

Emily shoved away from the table. "It's been a long, hard day. I, for one, am ready to retire. Need help clearing up, Mrs. Mary?"

The woman bustled over and took Emily's plate and utensils. "Lordy no, honey. You'd just be in the way." Mary Cobb glanced at her husband who shuffled in on cue. "Simon will help me, won't you dear?"

The wiry man pushed his glasses up the bridge of his long nose, nodded and cleared dishes from the table.

Brian stood, intent on saying what he'd rehearsed in his head all during dinner. "Emily, we should stay in the carriage house with you tonight. You can't go out in the blizzard by yourself. I saw a vid at school where people got blinded and all turned around. They froze to death three feet from their front door."

A look of horror scrunched Emily's face. "No one's getting lost or frozen. Hush your mouth."

"But we will stay with you, won't we Uncle Lugh?" he wheedled, bouncing up and down on his toes. From the corner, Cu barked and thumped his tail against the hardwood floor.

A thoughtful Mitchell looked from Brian to Emily, then from the fawning Dana to Lugh, before returning his gaze to Brian. "Excellent idea, young man. Any objections?" he asked Lugh, who hesitated. "I believe there are enough beds for all three of you, in case you were worried."

Brian watched for his uncle's reaction. The attorney had been needling him all afternoon.

But Lugh's face was unreadable as he pushed back his chair to stand. "Now why would I mind spending the night with a beautiful redhead?" Emily made a choking noise. Mitchell's eyes narrowed and he turned a bit green.

Brian suppressed a snicker.

"You're right, Brian, it is a good idea." To Emily, Lugh said, "Brian and I will accompany you to the carriage house. And if it's okay with you, we'll bunk there tonight."

Her face turned red. "I am perfectly fine by myself, thank you."

Don Foster spoke up. "No one's questioning that, Emily. But if this storm is an omen of things to come, none of us should be alone tonight. Especially you."

Morgan and her daughters nodded in agreement. Sirona chirped, "I'll go, I'll go. I'll stay with Emiwy!"

"No sweetie," Morgan said. "You stay here with me and Poppo."

"No! Don't wanna! I wanna go with Emiwy," the little girl pouted.

Mary Cobb chirped from the doorway, "Anyone want some chocolate cake?" She held it up for all to see.

"Oh, Lord," Emily groaned, holding her belly. "I couldn't eat another bite."

"Me, me! I want some," Brian cheered, his mouth watering. "I love chocolate cake. It's my favorite!" When he saw Emily's face fall, he asked politely, "But could we take it with us?"

"We can do better than that," Mary beamed. "I left a whole cake in Emily's kitchen, in a keeper on the counter. If I remember correctly, chocolate is your favorite too, Miss Emily?"

"Yes, it is. Thank you, Mary."

Brian did a jiggle dance. A whole cake to themselves, just the three of them. Well four, but Cu didn't count. Dogs don't eat cake. Or chocolate. Of course, not long ago, he also believed they didn't talk.

"That settles it," Lugh said with finality. "Let's go, you two."

Brian ducked out of the dining room. Maria had taken a shine to him and he didn't want her fussing. Nor did he want to answer any more of her stupid questions.

He shucked on his winter gear and waited by the coat closet, daydreaming about chocolate cake. Soon his uncle and Emily joined him. He lifted the curtain and stared out the hall window while they bundled in overcoats and scarves. A solid white wall of blowing snow was all he could see.

"How are we gonna do this?" Brian asked, worried. The adults joined him at the window while Cu barked from the end of the hallway.

"There's a low wall connecting the houses," Emily said. "I used it as a guide to get here earlier. The trees provide some shelter." That cheered Brian up.

Cu barked and tap danced.

Lugh pointed to the wolfhound. "I think Cu wants us to use the underground."

As if by magic, Mary Cobb appeared with Simon by her side. "Lordy, you are not going out in this weather," Mary declared. "The wind is gusting seventy miles-an-hour, and it's at least two hundred yards to the carriage house. Even if you made it, you would catch your death of pneumonia. No sirree. You kids follow Simon."

Shrugging, Emily turned and trailed Simon and Cu up the grand staircase. Lugh slung his duffel bag over one shoulder and walked behind her. Far enough back to enjoy the view, Brian noticed. He sniggered and grabbed his backpack.

Soon they huddled in the hall around a closed door. "The access is in here, in Mister Hamilton's closet," the grizzled Simon said.

"Bonsai brilliant!" Brian interjected.

Giving him the stink eye, Lugh said, "Lead on."

Mary held the door. Cu barked twice and trotted to the opposite side of the room. Simon crossed and opened another door that Cu wiggled through. A light came on and the old man disappeared after the wolfhound. They all entered a room too big to be a closet, but clothes hung on hangers and shoes and hats occupied one whole wall. In the corner, Cu pawed at a colorful rug.

Simon pulled the rug back to reveal a trapdoor in the floor. He pressed a latch and the door slid away. There, below them, was a lighted stairwell leading under the house. Cu scrambled down the steps, toenails clicking. Simon stood to the side and waited for them to gather around the opening.

"Mister Hamilton will take you the rest of the way," Mary said.

"You know?" Emily and Lugh asked in unison.

The housekeeper smiled in her calm, gentle way. "Simon and I have been with Mister Hamilton his whole life. Of course, we know. Now don't worry, children. Your secret is safe. And so are you."

Mary patted Emily's cheek and motioned them to the stairs. "Go on now. Ham's eager. He'll be able to relax in the carriage house, away from prying eyes. Let us know when you're settled. And call if you need anything at all."

**

As they descended, the heebie jeebies crawled up Emily's back and wrapped tiny fingers around her throat. She kept her eyes on Brian's tousled head bobbing in front of her and tried to remain calm. But the deeper they went, the thicker Emily's dread grew.

Fighting the urge to knock Lugh out of the way and run back up the stairs, she enumerated silently those things about the situation that could be deemed positive. She was at Wren's Roost. With Lugh and his very cool nephew. And Da, though he shared the body of a scary dog. And, thank God, it didn't smell like a basement.

In fact, the closer they got to the bottom, the lighter and airier it became. Recessed lighting lined the ceiling and reflected off mirrored surfaces, giving the illusion of daylight. Emily's fear gave way to relief and then admiration. She had never seen anything like this. Cu waited at the bottom, his impatient whine mixing with excited yips.

When they joined him on the landing, her Da said, "Okay, follow me." But they were not in a corridor, as Emily had thought. Instead they were in a room almost identical to the one upstairs, down to the masculine décor.

"What is this place?" she asked with wonder.

Pride laced Hamilton's voice when he answered, "Our home away from home."

At Emily's baffled look, he skittered across the room, talking over his shaggy shoulder. "Beneath Wren's Roost is an entire house, similar in layout, though not as grand. It was built years ago, along with the other warrens throughout Druid Hills."

"Warrens?" Brian asked. "I thought rabbits lived in warrens."

"Very good, Brian. That is where the name originated."

They reached what must have been the end of the house and entered a hall about ten feet wide. In spite of the daylight effect, for which Emily was grateful, anxiety pinged her insides. By the time they came to a flight of stairs at the end of another very long hallway, her whole body vibrated.

Hamilton and Brian scrambled up first. Emily followed, with Lugh close behind.

"Brian, can you reach that latch?" Hamilton asked.

The door swung upward and glorious relief flooded Emily's system. The cats greeted them with worried meows that gave way to loud and hungry ones. Retrieving a can of Fancy Fixings from a kitchen cabinet, Emily divided it into two dishes. Lugh disappeared to the living room to start a fire.

Brian stood staring at the cats.

"What sweetie?" Emily asked in that special tone adults reserve for kids and animals.

"That cat." He hitched his chin in Hope's direction. "It's the one in the picture. Your dad's gotta tell us tonight, Emmy, or I'm gonna bust from not knowing."

She, too, was anxious to hear her father's explanation about the painting of the woman who looked like her. "We'll get to the bottom of it, I promise," she assured. "Want to help your uncle with that fire?" Brian stood suspended, like he wanted to say something, then threw his hands in the air and shuffled from the kitchen.

Hanging her coat and scarf on a peg behind the door, Emily wondered why Mitchell had insisted the MacBrayers stay in the carriage house. Yes, there was room—besides Emily's, there was a queen bed in the turquoise room and two large sofas. But it was odd, and she was more than a little nervous knowing the handsome priest would be sleeping in the next room. Cu bounded into the kitchen, slid across the shiny floor, and made a beeline for the cat dishes.

"Eh-eh," Emily scolded, using her body to block the big dog. He cocked his head to one side, long tongue lolling in anticipation spoiled. She had to laugh.

"Oh, alright. Got anything else?"

"All kinds of people food, but nothing for a dog. Baked chicken, perhaps?"

"Nah," Hamilton shook Cu's mighty head, so that his jowls flapped. "It's a dog thing. You know—cat food." He licked his lips and looked wistfully at the bowls.

"Promise you'll leave it be, Da."

Cu did the jowl-flapping thing again and gazed at Emily with doleful eyes.

She tapped her foot, arms crossed. "Well?"

"Oh, whatever," Cu huffed, and shambled back to the living room. Emily followed.

She showed the guys to the turquoise room, then went to her own to get the fire going. It had been a long day, but overall, a good one. In spite of the freak blizzard. And being accused by Mitchell and his cronies of its creation. She had earned points helping Lugh at the restaurant and spent the rest of the day getting to know her new family and order members.

The heat from the fire crept into her bones. She thought of Morgan and her nasty tea. On a day like today, it might almost be good. But in the kitchen was a bottle of aged cognac she'd had her eyes on since day one. Emily rarely drank, but brandy was something she indulged on occasion.

From the other room came Da's stern voice and Brian's high-pitched whine. Emily had known them only a short while, yet their voices lifted her spirits. A door slammed. Emily hurried to retrieve the brandy, plus two snifters and a shallow, glass bowl.

On the living room rug, Brian was curled on his side petting a purring Hope. Lugh was on the hearth with Ralph. All four looked up, a tad guilty, when Emily entered the room.

"Where's Da?" Lugh gestured toward the storm door, eyebrows vanishing behind shaggy bangs. The dog was barely visible through the gusting snow. "Is that wise?" Emily asked.

"Beats me," Lugh shrugged. "You try to tell him anything."

"HA! Good point," she chuckled. "Brian, I have cocoa. Would you like some hot chocolate?"

The angry eyes softened, and he bobbled his head yes.

"Something wrong?" she checked.

"Him," Brian mumbled, jabbing a finger toward the door. "He won't talk about the picture. It's not fair. I'm not a kid."

There was a light in Lugh's eyes as he reached for the brandy and snifters Emily held. "No?" he teased.

Brian heaved a loud sigh. "No. Apparently, I'm a druid. And I want to know why the people in that old picture are here in this house."

"What picture?" Lugh asked.

"OH, GRRRR," Brian growled. He stood and presented his backside to them, hands held out to the fire.

Lugh uncorked the brandy. Emily wagged her brows and warned, "Only a bit, please. Me and alcohol don't mix well." The druid's slow smile had her already-tense tummy doing backflips. But she was supposed to be the grand druid. And he was her high priest.

To put distance between them, she tabled the goblet he handed her and crossed to the door. Opening it a crack, she yelled over the roar of the storm, "Da! Come in!"

The dog twisted its snow-capped head, long tongue flicking at blowing flakes. "Nothing like a thick pile of snow to make you want to roll around," Hamilton yelled over the storm.

"Don't you dare!" she hollered. "Come in and settle a bet for us." She winked at Brian, who winked back.

The dog hesitated, then shook off his snow coat to nip through the door. Inside, he shook again, sending wet globs of snow flying. Emily scuttled sideways, squealing when a fat wad caught her in the temple. Brian giggled. When she did a looney dance to brush it off, the kid laughed out loud.

All eyes in the room went to the thin boy who rarely broke a smile.

"What?" Brian planted his fists on boney hips, pout firmly in place. "Sir, you promised. Why does Emily look like that woman in the picture? And why are Cu and Hope dead ringers for the dog and cat? You promised," he whined, stomping his feet.

Cu bumped Brian's chest with affection and settled on his haunches.

"You're right." Ham was rewarded by Brian's arms encircling his long neck in an exuberant hug. When Brian let go, the dog sidled up to Lugh and nosed the snifter dangling in his hand. "You do know that's my cognac you're drinking, eh son? The least you could do is pour me some."

Emily leapt to retrieve the bowl from the table. "Here, Da. I thought you might be in the mood to partake, though you know Cu shouldn't."

"Hell girl, we'll all die from something. Might as well be good brandy."

Emily winced. Cu's dreamy eyes glittered.

"There, there a ghrá, a little brandy won't hurt me—or Cu. How 'bout you break out Miz Mary's cake and whip up that hot chocolate you promised the boy?"

At Emily's sharp inhale, Hamilton chuckled. "Oh, yes, a ghrá. I sometimes hear things I'm not supposed to. Now fetch that cocoa and when you're back, I'll tell you all about Brian's painting."

Emily hurried to the kitchen, shaking her head.

Back to the Beginning

Hamilton herded his small audience to Brigid's library. Lugh built a fire, stoking the blaze until it crackled. Hope settled on a pillow by the hearth, Emily and Brian claimed the armchairs, and Ralph stayed behind in the living room. Outside, the snow beat against the tall windows, driven to a fury by a wailing wind.

A series of druid raps sounded from the hallway, startling Emily from the depths of her chair. Cu barked and skittered from the room, nails clicking on the shiny floor. She followed in time to see a picture frame emerge from the underground staircase, balanced precariously in Simon Cobb's wiry arms. Lugh rushed to relieve Simon's burden.

"Simon, my good and faithful servant," Hamilton gushed, "Thank you for bringing the portrait, my friend."

Mumbling acknowledgement, Simon nodded his respects to Emily and the MacBrayers before disappearing back down the stairwell.

"To the library." Hamilton lead the way in Cu's body. Lugh followed with the painting. Brian shoved to the front.

"Can I see it, Uncle Lugh?"

"Patience, boy," Ham growled. Brian huffed and stomped to the fireplace. "Up there," Hamilton commanded, pointing Cu's nose to the mantel. Emily hurried to move the antique clock and other curios, while Brian helped heft the heavy frame, tilting it to rest beside the portrait of Awen. Standing back for a better view, Emily's insides leapt.

"Wow," she whispered, overcome by awe.

In the center of a glade surrounded by dense forest, Awen stood. Her face was lifted to the heavens, flaming hair curling

airborne behind her. A Scottish wildcat stood on one side, an
Irish wolfhound on the other. Her right hand rested on a jeweled
wand and her regal robes whipped in the wind. The golden torc
Emily had first seen on Cu graced Awen's slender neck.

"That's it," Brian crowed. "That's the picture!"

"Indeed, it is," agreed her Da, flopping on the wool rug near
Hope's pillow. "Now gather round and I'll tell you the story of
Awen and her companions." The window panes rattled.

Emily lifted a curtain and peeked out at the solid swirl of
white. Shivering, she let go to reclaim her chair. Lugh half sat,
half propped on the arm. Ralph meandered in and curled on the
hearth. When all were settled, Hamilton sat at attention and
cleared his throat.

"Brian, this woman is our ancestor, Awen. She lived a
thousand years ago and was heir to a small realm ruled by her
mother and father in the south of Briton. Peace and prosperity
smiled on their kingdom until roving armies killed her parents
and burned the castle and nearby village to the ground."

Grief tore at Emily's heart. She retrieved the brandy snifter
and buried her nose against the cool rim, inhaling deeply of its
bracing bouquet.

"Young Awen escaped with an older acolyte and they
embarked on an arduous journey to northern France in the
company of other surviving druids. But they soon discovered
that the long arm of persecution reached Normandy, too.

Not satisfied with merely conquering the land and its people,
the Pope sought to control their souls. Druid shrines, standing
since the dawn of time, were torn down and churches built upon
them. The practice of druidry was forbidden by law and carried
the penalty of a public and very painful death."

Heart near to breaking, Emily bolted a mouthful of cognac to
stifle a sob. Hamilton threw a concerned glance in her direction
and continued.

"Druid priests, bards, and acolytes, after ministering to the
people for thousands of years, were forced to adopt the ways of
the new church or see their communities burnt out of existence.
Many were slaughtered, including Felisté, the acolyte who alone
knew Awen's origins."

The grief knife twisted. Emily gulped more brandy, welcoming the burn down the back of her throat. Anything to distract her from the emotions ripping her to shreds.

"The remaining druids abandoned the old ways to escape the bloodthirsty persecution. No longer allowed to honor the Earth or her elements, they gave in and worshipped the one God thrust upon them by the clergy.

Soon, the old ways were forgotten. The pagans, as druids were branded by the Church, were wiped out. Or so they thought. Awen and a few isolated druids remained secreted in the neighboring realms."

An intense loneliness beset Emily and mixed with the grief, creating a palpable ache.

"Awen survived by hiding in an enchanted forest and living off the land. As the years passed, the world became ever more hostile."

"Is this going somewhere?" Brian interrupted.

Hamilton growled and cast a stern glare in the teen's direction. "One evening in a blinding snowstorm much like this, a dog appeared on Awen's doorstep. It was a great shaggy beast with long, spindly legs and a ravenous appetite. It filled its belly from Awen's provisions, then curled on her hearth to sleep."

"Cu!" Brian chortled, bouncing in his chair.

Emily laughed, grateful for a respite from the intense feelings.

"That night in her dreams, Awen was visited by her parents, the queen disguised as a Scottish wildcat and her father in the guise of the wolfhound. The two informed Awen she would be called upon to intervene in the fate of the world. But first, the animal Elders would complete her studies."

Hamilton stopped to bite at a hindquarter, then straightened again. "As you've already guessed, the dog's name was Cu. The cat's name was simply Cat."

Goosebumps crawled over Emily's body, though she'd known what was coming.

Brian snickered, "Man, you're old."

"Hardee-har-har. If I remember correctly, you were the one begging me to tell this story. Now hush and listen."

The boy leaned back in his chair, his face twisted in a scowl.

"Where was I?" Hamilton asked. "Oh, yeah. The dream. Awen woke to find the storm still raging and an enormous tabby, our Hope," he inclined his head toward the unusually quiet feline, "outside the door, half frozen in the snow."

"Poor Hope," Brian murmured and stroked the cat's fur. "That's how I found Cu."

"Inside and thawed, the cat reiterated what Awen's parents had said. As the sole surviving heir of the Mountain Lord and the Lady of the Lake, it was Awen's destiny to save Earth from destruction." A howling gust of wind banged against the windows and they all jumped. Emily chuckled, but the sense of foreboding remained.

"The Elders completed Awen's training within the year. Soon after, she rescued the young Duke of Normandy from sure death." Emily's heart leapt. "Their alliance changed the fate of the world."

"William went on to claim England and his reign ushered in a new age. The rest, as they say, is history." Her Da peered at each of them through Cu's brown eyes. "Any questions?"

"Well, yeah," Brian whined. Emily had plenty but raised the snifter to her lips as a strange exhilaration coursed through her. "You didn't answer the question. Why does Emily look like Awen? And why are Cu and Hope here? They're pretty darn healthy to be a thousand years old. Shouldn't they be mummies or zombies or something?"

Emily snorted and barely kept from spraying brandy on the rug. Trust a teenager.

Hamilton chuckled. "Emily inherited Awen's looks, as well as her powers. Though she's yet to embrace them." He glanced at Emily and she felt the sting of shame. "The animals are harder to explain, but suffice it to say that when Awen reincarnates, so do they."

"So, the animals are here because of Emily? Or Awen?" Lugh asked. He crossed to the window and pulled the curtains back to reveal the same near-solid wall of snow. The storm hadn't eased one iota.

"That is correct," Ham said.

"When she appears, they appear?" Brian asked.

"Exactly. And when the Awen passes, so do Cu and Hope."

Emily set her glass on the end table as the enormity of that sank in. She stood for a closer look at the painting and wobbled a bit.

Grabbing the mantel, she held on and asked, "What is this cane Awen is holding?" It was decorated with jewels and held in front of her like a walking stick. Or a queen's scepter.

"That is the Wand of Awen, fashioned by her hand at the bidding of the Elders. It is what she used to control the Keepers and command the Elements," her Da said.

Lugh dropped the curtain and joined Emily in front of the painting. "Keepers? A powerful wand? Why have I never heard of this?" He sounded annoyed.

"Because it was Emily Bridget's to discover as the new Awen."

Brian muscled in. "So, what happened to this magic wand?"

The dog barked. "It was here at Wren's Roost. Then it wasn't. I thought your mother had taken it, but Alexis denied any wrongdoing. Did you ever see it amongst her things?"

"There was a walking stick." Emily had often wondered why her mother kept it. Alexis had never hiked a day in her life. "But it was plain. There weren't any jewels."

"No, there wouldn't be. The stones were removed long ago. Aóme was fashioned from one of the gems and passed down from each Awen ancestor to the next. But the others, who knows?

"I have never seen them. It is said that each stone had a special power of its own. And together they are said to give the One who wields them the power to rule the world. Most believe that to be legend." Hamilton grimaced, showing Cu's canines.

"And the wand?" Lugh asked.

Hamilton sighed. "Security searched high and low, but the wand was never recovered. When Alexis left with you, I knew I had been deceived." Hamilton turned to Emily. "Whatever became of that walking stick?"

She grinned. "I still have it."

The others gasped. "You have it?" The dog and cat exchanged a look.

"In my bedroom, yes."

"Well, I'll be blessed." Cu's body wiggled in Hamilton's excitement.

Hope yowled. "Awen's wand might ensure victory over this insidious Darkness we know so little about. Where is it, Emily Bridget?"

"I'll go get it." She hurried to retrieve the wand from its hiding place and then returned to the library. The others crowded around to touch it with reverence. Fishing the otter stone from her pocket, Emily unfurled her hand.

"Is this one of the missing jewels?"

Cu sniffed the talisman and gazed up at her. "No, little wren. I do not think so. Did your mother give it to you?"

Emily hesitated. "No. I found it under my bed in the red room."

Cu's tail thumped against the woolen rug. "Here in the carriage house? My, my." The wolfhound looked at the tabby who was busy grooming her thick fur. "Did you have anything to do with this, Hope?"

The Elder stopped bathing. "No. Not I."

"Then how did it come to be under Emily's bed? It couldn't have escaped Miz Mary all these years."

"Maybe it did. I found it the morning of my initiation." Outside, something smacked against the side of the house and the wind moaned, high and long.

"Maybe," Hamilton conceded. "But I do not believe this to be a wandstone."

"I think you are right, Ham." Lugh peered at the painting and pointed to the wand. "This top stone looks like it may be a diamond, and this must be Aóme. The other two appear to be a ruby and a blue sapphire. So no, Emily. That is not a wandstone."

"Should we try to find them?" Emily asked. "If they've been missing for as long as Da says, where would we even start?"

"It'd be a fool's errand," Lugh said, "But Mitch specializes in this stuff. He found Emily. We could ask him to find the jewels."

Lugh had a good point. As much as she didn't want to, Emily agreed.

"No!" Hamilton growled, shaking his head so that his jowls flapped. The others were flabbergasted. Lugh recovered first.

"No, we shouldn't look for the gems? Or no, we shouldn't ask Mitch? He was the one who found Emily when no one else could. It makes sense to involve him. Plus, it would get him out of our hair."

Emily cheered, "Yes! I'm all for that."

"No. Not Mitchell," Hamilton remained adamant. "As you said, it's a fool's errand. The stones were probably made into jewelry or ended up in a museum somewhere. With no way to identify them as Awen's wandstones, it'd be a dead-end and a huge waste of time. But I also don't trust Mitchell. I didn't before I fell ill, and even less now."

His regal head lifted, and a piercing gaze pinned each of them in turn. "I haven't said it before, but I believe Mitchell Wainwright to be responsible for my death."

Emily gasped. So, it was Mitchell. The others looked as shocked as she felt.

"So no, I don't trust Mitchell Wainwright. And the rest of you shouldn't either."

"Sir, that is a serious accusation." Lugh's face was ashen. "Do you have proof? I know Mitch is an asshole, but he has never given reason to doubt his loyalty to you or the Order." The windowpanes rattled on another strong gust.

"No, no proof, just things that don't add up. Or rather, that do. Check for yourself. But trust me, Mitchell had opportunity, means, and motive. He covets the title of Grand Druid, Emmy, and would wrest it from you any way he can. He poisoned me and will do worse to you. Let's not give him that opportunity."

Emily's stomach churned. "That would explain why he has it in for me." She glanced at a silent Lugh and could tell he was having a hard time assimilating the news. As the uneasy silence spun out, Hamilton settled on Cu's haunches in front of the fire.

Lugh capitulated. "If you're right, goddess help us. But we should put Morgan to work investigating your claim."

"And we will," Emily agreed. "Should I be the one to tell Morgan?"

"No, I'll do it," Lugh said. "First thing tomorrow morning. But first, I want to know about the Keepers. Hamilton, do you mean the dragons?"

"I don't know," Hamilton said. "I know nothing of Keepers. Or dragons. That information came from Cu."

"And the Elements?" Emily asked.

"Cu again. But I suspect he meant controlling them. Creating and calming storms, that sort of thing."

Hope finally joined the conversation. "Yes, Lughnasadh, the Keepers are dragons whose destinies and lives are bound to that of Earth. They are Earth's sworn protectors. And ours."

To Emily, Hope said, "The Elements are literally just that. Air. Water. Fire. Earth. Awen's wand focuses the energy of each, allowing Awen—now you—to control and command the dragons *and* the weather. Plus, the earth and her waters."

"Control the dragons and weather," Emily repeated as the significance hit her. "So even if we find the dragons and miraculously learn ogham to decipher and master Awen's spells, without her fully-jeweled wand, her handbook is of no use?"

"What handbook?" chorused Brian and Ham.

Hope hissed, loud and long. "Foolish girl. Mind your tongue!"

Emily flushed. Fat good she was at being the Awen. She had already forgotten to keep the manuscript secret.

To Hamilton, Hope said, "It is a tool that will allow Emily Bridget to access Awen's spells. You are forbidden to know, much less to speak of this. To anyone. That goes for you both." Hope glared at Hamilton, then Brian, who promptly changed the subject.

"So...you and Cu just materialize out of thin air? Doesn't that bother anyone besides me?" Everyone laughed, Hope included.

"Something like that," Hamilton chuckled. "I don't know if anyone really knows. But from what Cu showed me, both he and Hope are the real deal. Both are capable of wielding magic when by the side of their mistress."

"Which is now, Emily," the priest added.

"Ya," Hope meowed. "Emily Bridget, once she accepts and embraces the Awen's powers." Emily gulped. The wind howled as Hope's words sank in. The cat leapt to the back of her chair. "So, Lugh will talk to Morgan in the morning. It's too late to do anything tonight.

"But Hamilton, if your suspicions are correct—and you have infallible instincts—Wainwright must be taken out of the equation. And kept away from Emily at all costs. We shall leave that to our security chief. But it sounds like the gems are lost for better or worse."

With the details decided, the party went back to the living room. While Lugh stoked and banked the fire, Brian sat on one end of the aubergine sofa and Emily curled on the other.

Her eyelids drooped, heavy from the effects of the potent cognac, and in no time at all, she fell into a restless sleep. In her dream, Lugh MacBrayer covered her in thick throws and with his nephew Brian in tow, retired to the turquoise bedroom.

Awen Rising

Awen blinked the Otherworld from her eyes and struggled awake. It'd been a long, deep slumber, but someone or something, had called. She looked about the dark room. A fire smoldered, providing scant light. The surroundings were familiar. The wind howled and a shutter banged against the structure. Startled, Awen rose and hurried to the window.

It was the dark of night. A solid wall of blowing snow blotted out all else. Awen watched for a moment, dread growing in the pit of her stomach. Something unnatural and malign was afoot. She dropped the curtain and searched the dim room for Cu, her faithful hound.

He laid in front of the fire, chin on his paws as if asleep, but open brown eyes followed her every move. She slid cold feet into wool-lined boots and called the hound to her. Cu greeted her exuberantly as she wrapped her arms around him and buried her face in his wiry hair. At a loud meow, Awen greeted another old friend. She opened one arm to circle Hope's bulk and pulled the cat to them.

Letting go of her old friends, Awen searched the room for a cloak or a robe. Finding nothing of the sort, she tied a small blanket around her neck and turned it, so the opening faced backwards. Resolved to put an end to the malevolent blizzard, she faced the door.

Cu's shaggy forehead bumped Awen's shoulder. Hope's bristled back arched and her puffed tail pointed down to the floor.

"Ready, you two?" Awen asked out loud. She heard their affirmatives in her head, and cautioned, "Stay close. This storm is evil." Then, wrenching the door open, she stepped outside and braced against the oppressive wind. The porch afforded scant shelter.

She clung to the door handle, stung by the onslaught of tiny ice crystals that bombarded her in sheets. The weight of the negative pressure bore down upon them as the animals moved into place beside her, snug up against each of her legs. Awen let go of the handle and the door slammed shut.

She readied herself quickly and spoke the spell. The wind shredded her words, reducing them to nothing. The blanket flapped violently against her back.

Trusting the animals to anchor her, Awen sent imaginary roots into the earth and threw her arms high to the heavens. The Elders held strong, and when she spoke this time, their combined magic entwined with Awen's to ripple in waves through the atmosphere.

The wind calmed perceptibly and within moments, stilled. No longer tormented, the snowflakes meandered to the thickly-blanketed ground, then ceased falling altogether. Victorious, Cu threw back his head and barked three times. Hope's yowls joined the celebration.

Shivering, they all piled through the door into the warmth of the house. Awen removed the wet blanket and spread it on the hearth. Adding wood to the fire, she huddled between the animals. Cu's locks sizzled and Hope worked overtime to restore her soaked coat to its normal state. Before long, the fire dried the worst of the dampness.

Groggy headed and drained from the ordeal, Awen rose from the hearth and settled on the sofa, pulling the soft blankets around her. Hope climbed on top, between her feet. Cu circled the rug, sighed and plopped down, resting his head on Awen's belly. Before long, his gentle snores lulled her to sleep.

**

Emily tried to roll over and realized she wasn't in the four-poster bed. Smacking super-dry lips, she groaned at the taste of stale cognac. Cu's head pinned her midsection. One of the cats held her feet in place.

The last thing Emily remembered after the powwow in the library was returning to the living room with Lugh and Brian. She must have conked out right after that; she didn't even remember them going to bed. The mantel clock was hidden from view. She had no idea how long she'd slept. Emily groaned. She knew better than to drink.

Stomach heaving, she wiggled from under the throws, disturbing both animals. She gripped the sofa with one hand and her forehead with the other as she stood cautiously. Sick-saliva pooled in the back of her throat. She ran, barely reaching the red bathroom before hurling her guts.

When the retching finally subsided, she mopped her face with a damp cloth and pressed her thumbs to her throbbing temples. A vision gathered in Emily's mind. She was outside the carriage house in the blinding blizzard, arms in the air and a blanket tied around her throat. Cu and Hope pressed against either of her legs in gale-force winds. The words of a spell tumbled from her lips. Unfamiliar and foreign, they rose into the night and calmed the elements.

Turning the exotic words over her thick tongue, Emily shivered and wrapped her arms around her shoulders. It would wait until tomorrow. No way was she going outside tonight in this frozen mess. No way.

She stumbled to the bedroom, ignoring the guilt, and climbed into the four-poster bed. Emily brushed a mass of ringlets from her face, barely noticing they were damp. Sleep drew her under, where the lilting words of the simple spell filled her dreams.

A Deadly Drunk

Nergal shoved through a nearly invisible door in the sheer rock wall and glanced around the sorry excuse of a saloon. The scum of the UnderEarth drank here and appeared to be engaged in a variety of nefarious deeds and illicit dealings.

In a corner, Cephalopods played Rumpacajac, rolling three cubes resembling human dice. A pile of paper bills and coins were stacked on the table. On a miniscule platform that passed for a stage, an erotic dancer gyrated to electronic music piped from hidden speakers. A male slug shoved money in the dancer's booty trap, copping a feel with slimy tentacles.

Nergal had been in worse places.

Muscling through the crowd, he delivered a well-placed elbow to a Fomorian's chest and a forearm to the head of a Zynog, getting a much-needed jolt of satisfaction when the first victim groaned and the second pitched sideways, stunned. The Fomorian scrambled to the other end of the bar and the ruffians cleared a zone around Nergal. The Zynog lay sprawled on the sticky, booze-soaked floor, out for the count.

"Furroot. Large," Nergal spat at the barmaid, who resembled a giant weasel.

Whatever the species, and there was no telling in Irkalla, the barkeep scurried to fill a beaker with the brown, carbonated beverage. The drink of choice for all self-respecting Draconians, furroot was best sipped and consumed in small quantities. It tasted like fermented troglodyte piss and kicked like a Valdesiane Horned Ass.

The barmaid plopped Nergal's drink on the counter alongside a handheld register. "Ten quisha."

Nergal cringed. The voice was as shrill as he would have expected, had he given it a thought. Tapping his code into the register, he was rewarded with a melodious purr from the device when it accepted Nergal's payment and opened a tab. The weasel nodded an obsequious thanks and left him to wait on another customer.

Swirling the bubbling liquid, Nergal stared into his glass and let the misery wash over him. Shibboleth the Draconian Warlord had blocked Nergal at every turn and the meeting he had expected to last two days max had dragged on for over two earth-weeks. He'd made it through the proceedings thus far without being slain, at least. And, though tenuous, Nergal's honor as a Draco warrior and leader remained somewhat intact.

Of course, it was only a matter of time. His iron nerves were stretched to the limit, and that rotting commander had dealt Nergal and his plan for overtaking AboveEarth potentially irreparable damage. If Shibboleth had his way, Nergal would be the laughing stock of the entire UnderEarth contingent.

Still, in spite of Shibboleth's fearsome opposition, Nergal believed he could prevail in his mission. He had trained all his life for this. But his confidence was shaken, and he was beginning to wonder if his plan was too small and had too many holes.

Chugging the contents of the glass, Nergal squirmed when fire blazed from his throat to his belly. It occurred to the Draco that he hadn't eaten since the night before. He'd been late waking and sessions had gone straight through lunch. The burn warmed Nergal's gut and set his body on fire. The tension stringing him in knots eased and he relaxed for the first time since his arrival in Irkalla.

Edge smoothed, Nergal searched the dingy room for hostiles. Everyone, or thing, was minding its own business, caught up in whatever despicable acts were being perpetrated in the shady den.

Breathing easier, Nergal flagged the server and ordered another furroot. The skinny eyebrows went up, but the barmaid wisely chose to keep her mouth shut, scurrying to draw another from the tap. Nergal drank that and ordered a third.

Extracting his communicator from its thigh sheath, he punched in the coordinates for the reverend's feed. The Reylian-humanoid appeared to be in a market with the shill. But Nergal could only watch so he ended the feed, frustrated. Shibboleth had yanked Nergal's mainframe privileges until the proceedings ended, along with that of the rest of his North American contingent.

Nergal did learn that Shalane and company were enroute to Atlanta. He thought of the abode he maintained near Agartha, beneath the seedier suburbs of that Georgia city. Nergal could use a good mud bath. For that, red Georgia clay had no equal.

Shoving the device in its holder, Nergal slammed the third glass of furroot. When it hit bottom, his head reeled. He grabbed the counter to keep from falling. The rush passed and Nergal stood, knocking his stool backwards. Stumbling over it, he teetered in mid-air, then crashed toward the still prone Zynog.

**

Inanna watched her mark from the relative safety of a corner table, in no hurry to make a move. Over the last nine hundred or so years, she had thought often of Nergal and what had ended up being the single most defining moment of her life. She had often wondered what she would do when she saw him again.

It wasn't that he had been Inanna's first—she had initiated the coupling and enjoyed the sex. But her actions had sealed Inanna's fate with Shibboleth, the ruler of all.

Had she known her litter father felt so strongly about the young cadet, a muscle-bound reptilian of the vilest sort, she might have reconsidered. But Inanna was reared in a compound and had no contact with Shibboleth. It was there she met Nergal, on the other side of the world in a much different kind of bar. An upscale cantina that catered only to reptiles.

Catching a lungful of smoke, Inanna coughed and sputtered. She fought the urge to slap the offending cheroot out of a passing Balthot's rubbery mouth. It wouldn't do to make a ruckus and reveal her presence. Not until Inanna was ready.

Through the smoky haze, she watched the rugged Draco down another drink. He swayed on the barstool and Inanna resisted the urge to step in. It was important she not mess this up.

She ordered another Piz, a fizzy drink made from fermented mushrooms and gingerroot. As bad as her life had been since bedding the Draco, if Inanna didn't follow instructions exactly as relayed, her litter father would make it worse.

"Shibboleth," Inanna spat under her breath. She had been shocked at his anger all those years ago. She'd thought he would be happy she had chosen such a decorated and virile specimen. Instead, Shibboleth was furious and ordered her to stop seeing the cadet. Or else.

Angered, Inanna had refused and saw Nergal whenever she damn well pleased, even when Shibboleth threatened to cut her off. Then one day Shibboleth made good on his threats.

Fingering the scar that bisected one brow, Inanna's insides churned as she remembered her father's ire and the thug Shibboleth had sent to deal with her. Locked out of her abode, accounts wiped out, cards nullified, Inanna had taken to the streets, fending for herself in the cesspools of UnderEarth.

Haunted by roaming bounty hunters carrying holographic images, she had burrowed deeper underground, rubbing shoulders with the scum of the alien world. Or more accurately, the spawn of that scum.

Her mark slammed his beaker on the counter, drawing Inanna's attention. Nergal stood and stumbled over his own barstool. In one sinuous motion, a pair of Cerulean guards stepped in to break the general's fall.

Electricity shivved through her when Nergal looked Inanna's way, but the lizard was schnockered, his eyes unseeing. When he tottered toward the latrine, Inanna slid from her seat to follow.

**

Nergal came to with a start. He searched his booze addled brain for clues as to his whereabouts. Remembering, he groaned and untangled his legs and tail from those of the female lizard. Gaining his feet, he staggered to the loo. Legs spread wide, he leaned spiked forearms and horned head against the rough clay wall and let go his bladder.

The torrent gushed into the trough and the pressure eased. Memories of the day streamed through his head. It had ended on a high note, thanks to Inanna. Nergal squeezed out the last drops of foul-smelling urine, grimacing at the razor-sharp pain; the wench had ridden him raw.

Slinking back to the bed where she lay comatose, Nergal chuckled. The bitch thought he hadn't recognized her. He might have been tanked up on furroot, but not enough to miss the royal tattoo placed discreetly on one inner ankle. Inanna—Shibboleth's spawn—was a fracking good lay, but she was also the cause of Nergal's problems with the warlord.

Eyeing his old paramour, he fastened his belt and shoved his weapons in their holsters. He ransacked Inanna's room, finding a stack of credits taped to the bottom of a chair and a cache of weapons hidden behind a false wall in the closet.

He shouldered what he could carry and made sure the wench was unconscious, then crept to the door. The draught he had slipped her would keep her under a while longer.

Nergal would be far from Irkalla by the time she woke. He'd decided not to return to Shibboleth's war party. Instead, he would go to Agartha and link up with the reverend. There, he would quietly gather his army and contemplate his next move.

Half drunk and nursing a raging hangover, Nergal scanned the dim corridor for watchful eyes, then hurried to the nearest transit chute. A deserted car rumbled to a stop and its doors slid open.

He boarded, settling his arsenal beside him on a grimy bench. Extracting his communicator, Nergal cursed and slapped it against his leg. Damn thing was dead. Either that or there was no reception at this level.

The rickety car picked up speed. Clattering over the tracks, it rocked and swayed through the bowels of UnderEarth with Nergal its lone passenger. He was just nodding off when the lights in the unit sputtered and died, then blinked on again.

The car lurched to a halt in the middle of nowhere. The onboard computer whirred and sputtered a lame excuse about a maintenance stop, but Nergal could see no station.

Before he could do more than grumble, he and his munitions were flying through the air, ejected from the car. Reacting quickly, Nergal landed upright, but his weapons flew helter-skelter and disappeared into the dark. The reek was disgusting. And if the filth was any indication, neither the passage nor the car had been serviced in centuries.

Where in UnderEarth had he landed? Eyes yet to adjust, Nergal felt for his weapons in the muck and tried not to imagine what was causing the stench. Then something slammed him hard from behind, catapulting him forward. He landed spread-eagled on the slimy floor, pain radiating from his kidneys up his back and down both legs.

He scrambled to all fours, shrieking when a concussive device detonated, shredding the side of his face and cartwheeling him through the rancid air to crash against the schist wall.

Roaring with rage more than pain, Nergal leapt to his torn feet. He charged the unseen attacker, intent on pulverizing whatever Draco had the gall to challenge a General of the Reptilian Forces.

But there was only thick, fetid air. Drunk and disoriented, Nergal thrashed about, jabbing at first one fleeting shadow and then another. A well-placed kick connected with Nergal's torso and he flew backwards, crashing into the opposite wall.

Clambering to his knees in the slippery slime, he grunted when another blow connected with his chin. His head whipped back against the solid schist with a loud crack and an ice pick of exquisite pain pierced Nergal's skull.

He roared and clutched his head with his hands, legs betraying him as he crashed to the ground and curled in a defensive ball against the unending onslaught of kicks and punches.

Pride forgotten, Nergal writhed there on that nasty ground, howling in agony. Blows landed on every exposed centimeter of his already-bruised body until all he could comprehend was pain.

Then that, too, was gone.

**

He had no idea how much later, but Nergal woke on a heap of decaying bodies in the corner of a deserted way station. By all accounts, he should be dead. According to the sign, he was near Virginia City. He had a vague suspicion that was somewhere beneath the Appalachian Mountains. Far from where Nergal had started.

He lay unmoving for a very long time, in and out of consciousness, until the pain in his head reached fever pitch and convinced Nergal he must be alive. Pain wouldn't follow him into death.

Millimeter by excruciating millimeter, he crawled off the heap of maggot-infested flesh, across the glass and debris-strewn floor, and out an opening that used to be a door.

Finding a spigot with running water, Nergal drank his fill and bathed his wounds as best he could. Then he dragged himself behind a waste recycler and passed out.

Grand Druid

Cu's barks woke Emily from a deep, untroubled sleep. In her ear, he chanted, "Emily Bridget, you did it! You stopped the blizzard!"

Groaning, she rolled her head his way and was greeted with an exuberant tongue bath. She squealed and yanked the comforter between them, then wiggled out of bed on the opposite side.

Cu beat her there. "Did you hear me? You did it!"

Her head pounded, drowning out her Da's ridiculous assertion.

"Not so loud," she pleaded, holding her head between her hands.

"But you stopped the blizzard!" her Da insisted. "Last night. Don't you remember?"

"Um. No."

She had a momentary inkling of the vision from last night, but it was a wisp of a thing and quickly gone, leaving no recollection of the actual deed. Head down, she shuffled to the bathroom in search of an aspirin. Damn cognac.

Hamilton followed close on her heels. "Well, you did. I was there with Cu and Hope. They helped. I watched."

The vision danced through Emily's head, stronger this time, and the words of a spell ricocheted around her brain. She gaped at the wolfhound, aspirin bottle in hand.

"Are you shitting me?"

"No. I shit you not. You can ask Hope. But now that you mention it, I could take a dump. Wanna let me out?"

He trotted from the room and Emily hurried to dress, pondering his revelation. How great would it be if what he'd said were true? But try as she might, the only memory Emily could muster was the brief vision and the strange words that still played in her head.

Fighting the keen edge of disappointment, she brewed a cup of tea and carried it to the lanai. The sun drilled crystalline splinters of light into Emily's corneas. She clapped a hand over both eyes, then slowly peeled away one finger after another as they adjusted.

The world sparkled, transformed by the blanket of snow that glittered diamonds from every surface. The trees and bushes bowed low, dressed in coats of wondrous white.

The blizzard had indeed ceased. Could she really be responsible?

Grinning, Emily opened the door for a whining, dancing Cu. Hope materialized and ran out behind him as he plowed a path through the fluffy snow.

Ralph stretched on his pillow by the hearth, content to stay inside where it was warm. Emily knelt to hug the purring cat, then threw logs on top of last night's embers.

By the time the fire caught, Lugh had joined Emily in the living room. And by the time the fire blazed, Brian was awake and running to the storm door to let the animals in.

Hamilton shook off the snow and to Emily's chagrin, proceeded to regale them with the story of how Emily got off the couch in the middle of the night and marched outside to calm the raging storm. Hope added details here and there.

But though Emily felt a growing sense of déjà vu, probably ignited by the vision, she had no physical memory of being out in the blizzard, much less casting a spell.

While the animals talked, Emily pondered the glimpses she'd had into Awen's mind. Could it work the other way, as well? Did Awen have the ability to take control of Emily's body? Had *Awen* done that spell?

The thought sent a shudder from Emily's head to her toes. If her body was being commandeered by someone else, shouldn't Emily remember?

**

The companions slogged through the dense melting snow to the main house. The druids were already gathered in the great hall, anticipating Mary Cobb's call to breakfast.

That, and Emily's arrival, as she soon learned.

To her dismay, news of her purported feat had reached the house ahead of them. As the druids greeted Emily en masse with congratulatory fervor, dread lodged against her spine until she shook in her Uggs. They all believed her a magical whiz, but she was nothing of the sort.

True to his usual pattern, Mitchell Wainwright spewed bile. He accused Emily of blatant witchcraft and ending a storm she had created herself. But the others were fed up with his endless accusations.

Even Olga Phagan and Mitchell's fellow detractors moved away from the attorney. Olga came over to shake Emily's hand and offer sincere congratulations for her newly-found powers.

Around the great hall the druids murmured amongst themselves, remarking on the suitability of their new grand druid. Emily's defeat of the storm was cause for celebration— but it was the awakening of Awen's power, they all agreed, about which the druids were most excited.

Emily shivered. If that had truly happened, why couldn't she remember?

At breakfast, someone posited it was time for Emily to assume her leadership role. Any druid capable of performing such advanced magic was gifted indeed.

Another wondered if the new grand druid was strong enough to defeat the coming Darkness.

Knowing she was an enormous fraud, Emily wondered the same thing.

**

Breakfast at Wren's Roost was a noisy affair. The Hester family and the visiting druids overflowed the formal dining room. Mitch ate quickly, chaffing to escape.

He was not pleased with Emily Hester's rise to power. It was all he could do to restrain himself when Lugh's nephew regaled them with yet another asinine story of her magical prowess. But when he bragged about how she stopped the tornado, then the blizzard, Mitch couldn't stand it any longer.

"Bullshit," he snarled. "Emily Hester is a witch, taught by the not-so-reverent Shalane Carpenter."

The Hester heir glowered at him.

"You studied with the sorceress, didn't you Miz Hester?"

"I studied with the shaman for a short time, yes. But I only learned simple spells. No weather witching. Get a grip, counselor."

"I *am* getting a grip—on why you insist on undermining our Order." He stood and leaned in her direction, ready to tear her a new asshole.

Lugh MacBrayer slammed his palms on the dining room table and growled in his coldest voice. "That's enough, Mitch! You will apologize to our grand druid and get the hell out of Wren's Roost."

Glancing at his one-time friend, Mitch sneered at Emily, "Admit you created those storms. And that you used dark magic to end them in the hopes of gaining our trust. Isn't that right, *Miz Hester?*"

The witch sputtered, eyes wide.

Lugh's chair crashed to the floor as he leapt at Mitch.

Mitch stepped back, surprised. He hadn't seen Lugh this angry since he'd stolen his girl in high school. Lugh stuck his sharp chin in Mitch's face. His dark eyes were cold with an uncharacteristic glint of disgust. When his arm shot up, Mitch flinched backwards, relieved when he jabbed his finger toward the door.

"YOU HAVE GONE TOO FAR! GET OUT!" Lugh thundered.

Shocked at his vehemence, Mitch glanced around the table, looking for support. Every face glared. Not one of them believed him. Hot indignation bubbled inside Mitch and ate at his composure. Screw them all.

He took a moment to dab at his mouth with a cloth napkin from the buffet and nodded at Mary Cobb, who stood in the corner holding a butcher knife like she would use it on him.

"It's okay, Miz Mary. I'm leaving."

To the room at large Mitch announced, "But mark my words. This woman is a witch and she will continue to bring nothing but heartache and ruin to this family and Order."

Done with the lot of them, he turned to leave, only to be blocked by the interloping bitch. Her face was calm, her manner even as she said in a wintry tone, "Where do you think you're going, counselor?"

A chill went up Mitch's spine. He'd heard that menacing note somewhere before.

"I'm going home. I've had enough of this shit. You may be fooling them, but you have no sway over me. You are nothing but a pretty face."

Gasps went up around the table. Mitch studied Emily's turned-up nose with its tiny groove and her wild lion's mane of coppery hair.

"No, come to think of it, you're not even that pretty."

He wheeled toward the door and went flying through the air, tripped by her out-flung leg. His arms stretched to break his fall, but he skidded nose-first on the hardwood floor.

Groaning, Mitch rose to his knees, blood spurting onto his crisp oxford shirt. Pissed to the max, he pinched his nostrils and peered up at Emily, whose expression took his breath.

She stood over him like an avenging angel, fists clenched and ready to strike. Remembering her ample martial arts skills, he scrambled up and backed away, grabbing the cloth napkin to stay the blood.

The grandmother clock over his head ticked loudly, the only sound until Hope and the wolfhound materialized out of nowhere. They crossed the room, nails clicking on the burnished floor.

Mitch stiffened when Hope purred, "I think it's time for you to leave, young mouse."

But Emily snarled, "Not until I'm done with him." His head snapped up when she went on to say, "Lugh? Arthur? Am I or am I not, the Grand Druid of the Awen Order?"

Arthur bobbed his burly head.

A smirk broke out on Lugh's face. His black eyes gleamed. "Yes, Emily, you *are* the grand druid."

Mitch felt his blood freeze.

The redhead moved closer and he backed to the wall, out of her reach.

"And since my Da hired this snake of an attorney in his capacity as grand druid, then I also have the authority to fire him. Isn't that right?"

Mitch glanced around the room, stomach plummeting as grins broke out on several faces.

"You wouldn't," he gasped and tossed the napkin on the buffet. The bleeding had stopped.

"Go get 'em, Em," Lugh's nephew hollered.

Mitch glared and the impudent kid leered back. Around the table, other druids nodded and grinned, obviously enjoying Mitch's discomfiture. Even Olga sneered. Damn them all. Damn every one of them.

Emily crowded as close as Lugh had earlier. Mitch held his ground this time.

"What are you gonna do?" he bellowed to the room. "Let this upstart of a witch get rid of your only voice of reason?"

Lugh gurgled, "Ohhh yes. Do us all a favor, Emily. Fire the bastard."

Livid that his old friend would suggest such a thing, Mitch lunged at Lugh, only to be tripped by Emily again. This time, he caught himself.

"You bitch!" he squawked and charged at her, grabbing a handful of unruly hair.

Chaos erupted as the druids around the table reacted. Before they could interfere, Emily seized him by the throat with one surprisingly-strong hand. She squeezed hard, cutting off his air.

The amount of pain surprised Mitch. He let go of her hair and clawed at her fingers, but her chokehold tightened and he went down on his knees. Flecks appeared before his eyes and his body went slack.

She let go with a backwards shove just as he would have passed out. Mitch landed on his ass, gasping for air. The witch leaned over him.

"Mitchell Albom Wainwright the Third," she intoned in a singsong voice, "you are hereby relieved of all duties to which you were previously contracted by my father, Hamilton Hester, or by any other member of this Order.

"You will leave Wren's Roost and never come back. I forbid you to speak of, or reveal anything related to, druids or the Awen Order. If you violate these terms, you will be prosecuted to the full extent of druid, state, and federal law."

Everyone in the room clapped and cheered.

"Fuck you all!" Mitch screeched. Barely suppressing the urge to retch, he scuttled away, hands to his throat.

"Taurus? Pete?" Emily said quietly, "Would you please escort Mr. Wainwright from Wren's Roost? Then I'd like you to go to his office and remove the Order's records from his possession."

"What? I—no!" Mitch howled. The two officers rounded the table.

"You heard the boss, Mitchell. Get your things. We're going for a ride." Pete pointed toward the door.

"Fuck you!" Mitch shouted. He could tell his face was flaming. It felt like he might explode in a ball of fire. "Fuck *all* of you. You will rue the day you let this bitch into the Order. Mark my words."

He stormed from the dining room to collect his overnighter and strode to the front door. The two cops nodded. He ignored them and slammed the door in their faces, but one of them caught it as they exited behind him.

"We'll follow you to the office," Taurus said, descending the front steps. "Don't try any shenanigans either, Mitchell. We know where you work *and* where you live."

Mitch glowered and they went to fetch the cruiser.

Outside, the snow drift had melted considerably. The wet stuff seeped into the tops of Mitch's ankle boots, making him even more miserable. At the sight of his BMW blanketed in white, he damn-near cried. Anger gnawed at his insides. He used his coat sleeve to brush the snow from the driver's door and yanked it open, then climbed in, teeth chattering.

The vapor of his breath filled the interior. He started the engine and climbed out to retrieve his foul-weather kit and cleared away the worst of the snow. Looking up at the imposing lines of Wren's Roost, Mitch gave it the finger, climbed in the

BMW, and drove slowly down the driveway. Snow crunched beneath the all-season tires.

The cruiser pulled onto the street behind him and the perfect revenge came to Mitch.

"Call Shalane Carpenter's cell phone," he instructed the BMW's computer and winked at his image in the rearview mirror.

**

Alone in the quiet of the carriage house, Emily pondered Mitchell Wainwright's accusation. Today was the second time he had mentioned Shalane. Had her stalker somehow gotten to the attorney? Had they formed some alliance against Emily?

A knock on the door startled her. Three short raps, silence, then three more. She leapt to peer through the peephole, heart thudding.

Lugh MacBrayer loomed on her doorstep, larger than life. What did the priest want? She fluffed her hair in the foyer mirror and opened the door, unable to keep the smile from her face. "Well hello, you."

But something was wrong. Lugh stepped inside and as Emily turned the deadbolt, he rounded on her, face glowing accusatory red.

"What in the hell was Mitchell talking about? Who is Shalane Carpenter and what is she to you?"

Not liking his tone, Emily turned her back and made for the kitchen. "Can I get you something to drink?" she tossed over her shoulder in a nonchalant tone.

"I asked you a question!" Lugh growled and grabbed her arm, twirling her to face him.

Emily reflexively shifted her weight, seized a hairy forearm, and flipped the warrior deftly to his derriere right in the middle of her front hall.

The shocked priest scrambled to all fours.

Emily rubbed her arm and said, chin in air, "You hurt me."

Then she pranced down the hall toward the kitchen. She had finally bested her combat teacher. Finally, finally, *finally*.

Behind her, Lugh grunted, "Talk to me, Em. Is what Mitch said true? Did this Carpenter woman teach you witchcraft?"

Though his voice held a touch of anguish, the implication rankled. Plus, he'd made no mention of her first takedown.

Emily turned in the doorway to face the priest. "Yes."

Lugh's face fell. She laid a hand on his shoulder and gave him what she knew he really needed.

"But not like Mitchell said. He made that shit up about the weather."

Puzzlement wrinkled the dark brow. Lugh rubbed the back of his head and consulted the clock above the stove.

"It's not even noon, but I find myself needing a drink. Did I see beer in your refrigerator?"

Emily chuckled. "It's five-o-clock somewhere."

Retrieving two long-necked bottles, she handed one to him, twisted the top off the other, and tilted it to clink against his.

"Nice move back there, by the way." Lugh gestured toward the hall. "Bottoms up."

Emily beamed at the belated acknowledgement and murmured, "Cheers." She took a tiny sip of the peach-flavored lager, unwilling to repeat the morning's hangover. "Come in and sit. I'll tell you about the shaman."

They moseyed to the living room and perched on the edge of the aubergine sofa. The fire Emily had stoked earlier blazed. Ralph napped beside it on the hearth.

Setting her full bottle on the end table, Emily drew a fortifying breath and faced the druid priest.

"Last year, a friend introduced me to a shaman named Shalane Carpenter. I didn't know at the time that she was also an evangelist, but that makes what happened even more bizarre.

"Shalane told me in a reading that I am a 'powerful being.' Others had told me this before, but I didn't feel powerful. I still don't." She pulled a Kleenex from her pocket and shredded it systematically.

"Shalane said she could teach me. Help me find my power. I was curious and decided to train with her. Then things got weird. She became more and more controlling and obsessed. So, I did what I do best. I quit." Emily peeked sideways at Lugh to gauge his reaction.

"Sounds to me like that was the right move. Knowing when to quit is not a bad thing, Emily."

The compliment landed. It felt good to come clean. She hurried to get the rest out.

"Then the stalking began. Shalane called me, texted, emailed, begged, offered free lessons, promised not to ride me so hard, anything if I would come back. But her actions only confirmed my apprehension." Remembering all Shalane's crazy stunts, Emily shuddered.

"I was spooked, Lugh. I moved to another city, let my hair go native, and even changed my name to get away from that woman."

Lugh set his beer on the table. "And now she's found you. I'm sorry, Emily."

He took her hand and leaned closer, black eyes gleaming. "I want you to know that as long as I'm around, Shalane Carpenter will not bother you. I promise."

The words melted Emily's defenses.

A shock of wavy hair fell across Lugh's forehead and he brushed it back. His tone hardened. "But how would Mitch know about Shalane?"

Defensive again, Emily stood and warmed her backside by the fire. The priest was pushing all her buttons today.

"I didn't tell him, if that's what you're implying."

Lugh glared and tapped a foot on the floor. She knew she hadn't answered his question.

"Remember the day Finn brought Da home?"

Lugh nodded.

"After everyone left, Mitchell stopped by Wren's Roost to inform me that Shalane Carpenter had called his office looking for me."

At Lugh's startled expression, she added, "It was bound to happen—we've been all over the national news. Anyhow, he said Shalane was performing at the Fox Theater in April and would leave two tickets for me at Will-Call."

"Are you going?" he asked, brows high.

"Hell no! I've had enough of Shalane Carpenter and people like her for ten lifetimes, thank you."

The lines around Lugh's eyes relaxed. "So, you don't do witch magic?"

Emily chuckled. "No, not really. Only what you guys have taught me."

"So not much," Lugh snickered.

"Hey! I resemble that remark!" Emily laughed at her own joke and plopped on the sofa to punch his arm. The jab landed harder than she meant.

"Ow!" he yelped and grabbed her hands. In a move she hadn't anticipated, Lugh hauled her across his lap and tucked her arms under his. She couldn't escape without a struggle. A dangerous glint shone in the pirate-priest's eyes.

A nervous titter bubbled from her lips and then Lugh's mouth was on hers, crushing her laughter into a thousand jittery pieces. Need filled those jet-black eyes when he finally pulled away—the same aching hunger that swirled inside Emily. Her breath hitched and all rational thought went out the window. She touched her lips to his.

He deepened the kiss, shaping her body to his lean, muscular frame. Emily nearly swooned. She wrapped her arms around Lugh's waist and held on tight as he kissed her like she'd always wanted to be kissed. All warm and melty, his tongue exploring hers gently, his hands cradling her face.

A memory stirred and Emily was in Awen's glade, tasting the forbidden kiss of a young duke. Only she wasn't herself, and the fear of getting lost in another grew until it was so overwhelming, Emily ended the kiss and put several-feet's distance between them.

"What is it?" Lugh croaked, blinking dusky eyes.

Feeling silly, Emily muttered, "Déjà vu. Or a brownout or something. I had the odd sensation of being somewhere else, as someone else, and with someone else. In another time, too."

Lugh angled his hard body toward Emily, intrigue animating the dark features. "Really? Who were we? And where?"

She hesitated, not sure she wanted to share that particular information. He took her hand and gently squeezed. Emily caved.

"Promise you won't laugh?" He nodded, eyes wide. "You were the Duke of Normandy and I was Awen. We were in her glade. In Falaise."

"Were we making out?" Lugh smirked, and closed the distance between them.

With a chuckle, she relaxed against him and entwined her fingers with his long, warm ones. His eyes were pools of playful kindness, but there was something else too. A reluctance, maybe.

"As a matter of fact, we were," she teased, wondering if his hesitancy had anything to do with hers.

"Like this?"

Lugh leaned closer and kissed Emily thoroughly, quieting both their qualms. She melted into the pirate-priest's arms, giving herself to the kiss. When a commotion arose at the front door, she surfaced from the embrace in a half trance.

"Don't answer it," Lugh groaned, drawing her to him.

The bell trilled again. Impatient fists pummeled the door. With a groan of her own, Emily disentangled herself to stand. The bell rang again and again as she leaned in for another soulful kiss.

"Believe me, I'd rather not." She dragged herself from his embrace. "But it doesn't sound like they're going away."

Peeking at her reflection in the hall mirror, Emily smoothed her tousled hair, mind racing. What was she thinking? Lugh was her priest, for Godsakes. She still hadn't checked with anyone, but she knew intuitively their intimacy would be frowned upon.

She took several deep breaths to calm her pounding heart, then peered through the peephole. Brian, Cu, and Hope stood on the porch facing the door. Brian leaned close and knocked again.

"Emily, is Uncle Lugh in there? Can we come in?"

Wagging her head in disappointment, Emily sighed and opened the door.

Elementals

The next afternoon, the sun shone brightly on the garden outside the library window. Remarkably, the blossoms suffered minimal damage in the heavy snow they had endured. The temperature was rising, and Emily itched to go for a run. Instead, she was inside studying.

She eyed the ominous cover illustration of the book Hope had insisted she read—a writhing earth with lava spilling from its ruptured bowels and a ball of darkness swirling nearby. On the inside page was the familiar epigram by Albert Einstein: Imagination is More Important than Knowledge.

Emily huffed, still not getting Einstein's meaning. She brushed her unruly hair out of her eyes and the thin hardback book fell open to page ninety-seven. It read:

> "In essence, Elementals are thoughtforms. We create them in our astral temples and bring them to life by working with the elements—air, water, earth, and fire—usually with a specific purpose in mind. Elementals are powerful manifestations of the creator's will and are fashioned for various reasons, including individual protection, truth-finding, gathering and relaying information, cleansing the atmosphere, as a magic companion, to protect against natural disasters..."

Emily stopped reading. To protect against natural disasters? A sick feeling welled inside her. If an Elemental could be created for good, it could also be perverted for evil.

Shalane Carpenter's red face, contorted in anger, swam into her vision. The day Emily had confronted her, Shalane had swelled like a pufferfish and spouted venomous slurs faster than Emily could dodge them. Including something about weather bombs. Could it be that simple?

She reeled as the realization sank in. The weather woes had started soon after Emily quit her lessons with Shalane. The witch had created the storms, including the ones that had killed Emily's fiancé and all the others. With a freaking Elemental.

Guilt flooded through her, followed by an anger so pure and hot that it set her afire. Slamming the book shut, Emily stood, determined to try her hand at casting her first solo counter-curse. She would be damned if she'd let Shalane hurt anyone else on account of her—especially those she loved.

In the center of Brigid's library, between the semi-circle of cushions and the pink quartz boulder, Emily closed her eyes, gulped three breaths, and spread her arms overhead in a wide vee. Exhaling, she chanted,

"Water, Earth, Air, and Fire,
Combine forces to remove and retire,
All Elementals, curses, hexes and evil eyes,
Directed toward me, at any time.
Protect me and mine from future attacks,
And send all such attempts hurtling back.
So it is and shall be, forevermore.
Thank you, my dear and precious Lord."

The oppressive mantle of guilt melted away and a lightness infused Emily's being. Her shoulders relaxed. She lowered her arms and took a deep breath of peaceful calm.

Laughing out loud, Emily hurried to tell Hope the news.

Travel Plans

At two o'clock sharp, a series of druid raps summoned Emily to the front door. The snow that had been so thick yesterday was mostly melted. Morgan engulfed Emily in her usual bear hug. Emily squeezed back, amazed she no longer detested the ritual.

"Howdy, Aunt Morgan. You're looking vibrant today."

Morgan's outfit was impressive with a royal purple blouse of watered silk paired with mustard-brown slacks. A long red scarf, sassy red boots, and a clunky red bracelet tied the ensemble together.

"Why thank you, hon. I've got business in Atlanta when we're done here. Where's Lugh?"

Emily averted her eyes to hide the flash of shame. Could Morgan know she'd almost had sex with their priest? "He called and said he's on his way and that if you're in a hurry, we could start without him. Their lunch rush went late."

She led her aunt to the sun porch, where Ralph blinked sleepy eyes. Hope claimed Morgan's attention by leaping to the floor to wind through her legs meowing. Lifting the oversized cat, Morgan hugged her to her chest and rubbed her cheek on the thick fur before letting Hope down.

"Remind me to get Alexis's book out of the car before I leave, would you dear? I was on the phone and forgot to bring it in." She was referring to the ledger Emily had volunteered, the one cataloguing their aliases and whereabouts through the years.

There was another series of raps and Emily hurried to let in the druid priest. Shyness seized her as she opened the door. Lugh wore his usual Jocko's attire—khaki slacks and a white, button-down oxford shirt. Cu shoved past him and licked Emily's face before tearing down the hall to the kitchen.

"No cat food!" she shouted after him then glanced up at Lugh. He was looking at her like he wasn't sure if he wanted to scoop her up and eat her or shove her out of the way. Emily shared the priest's uncertainty.

"Hello, Em." His drawl ignited that delicious feeling in Emily's tummy.

She tried to ignore her body's response, but her words came out slightly breathless. "Come on in. Morgan and Hope are on the porch. Can I get you something to drink?"

"Water would be great. I'm parched. I haven't had anything since before lunch."

Leaving him to find his way, Emily filled three water glasses and returned to find Morgan and the priest in an animated conversation. Lugh chugged his water and Morgan set hers on the coffee table.

"I've only a few minutes," the matriarch said, "but I wanted to thank you for your mother's ledger. You had quite the nomadic life, didn't you, Dru-y-en?"

Emily nodded. "That's one way to put it."

"Well, you're here now. No more running." Morgan took a sip of water. "I blocked Mitchell Wainwright from all order communications. I also opened an investigation into your allegation that he murdered my—" Morgan's voice broke and she cleared her throat. "We can't formally charge him, you know. Not until we find some evidence."

Cu yapped like a loon and stuck his head in Morgan's lap. She ruffled his hair absentmindedly. "According to his secretary, Mitchell skipped town. He hopped the first flight to Rome after you fired him and hasn't checked in with her since."

"Bully for him," Emily said, with a pang of relief. "Good riddance."

"Agreed." A sheepish tone crept into Morgan's voice. "To be honest I never paid Mitchell much mind. I knew Hamilton had turned most of our legal stuff over to the Wainwright firm, but legal was Ham's responsibility, not mine. I've seen more of Mitchell Wainwright in the past six weeks than I did in the two years before that. And from what I have seen, you might be on to something."

Morgan patted Cu's shoulder and glanced at her watch. "I'd better grab that ledger and get going." She moved toward the door and Cu blocked her path, barking furiously. "Well, I'll be. What is it, dear?"

The wolfhound reared on hind legs and hooked hairy front paws on the silk-draped shoulders. When he proceeded to lick Morgan's perfectly made-up face, she gasped and giggled like a school girl. "Get down, you!"

Cu retreated to all fours and followed Morgan from the room. When she returned with the ledger, he trailed behind her and flopped to the floor..

Morgan said her goodbyes and Emily walked with her to the SUV.

"Aunt Morgan, can I ask you something personal?" The matriarch turned, hand on the door handle.

"Of course, little wren."

"Is it, um—" Emily hesitated, not wanting to ask for fear the answer would be "no".

Worry creased Morgan's brow. "What is it, sweetie? Is everything okay?"

"Yeah." Emily rubbed her face in her hands. "It's j-just," she stuttered, then took a deep breath and blurted, "is it against Order policy to date another druid?"

Morgan chuckled. "You mean our priest?"

The heat rushed to Emily's face. "Is it that noticeable?"

"Yes, honey, it is." Morgan smiled knowingly.

Emily eyed the concrete driveway, mortified. She could feel the adrenaline coursing through her body as butterflies plundered her belly. "And would that be okay? Or is it expressly forbidden?"

Morgan took her hand and squeezed, compassion and kindness softening her regal features. "It is absolutely okay. Most of us druids end up with other druids. It's the way of things. Does our priest feel the same? Sometimes I think so, but others, I can't tell."

"Me too!" Emily cried. "And it's driving me crazy. He asked me out a long time ago. But he's flip-flopped so many times since then, I have no clue what he thinks. Or wants. Thank you,

Aunt Morgan. At least I know it's not taboo." The butterflies flew to Emily's throat. "But if it's not that holding him back, what is?"

"Beats me, sugar." Morgan opened the door. "But I can tell you that Lugh MacBrayer is a complicated man. And he's been through a lot over the last several years. I'd say go easy on him, give him some time. And some space. If it's meant to be, there's nothing either of you can do to keep it from happening. And if it's not, same thing." She climbed in the vehicle.

Waving goodbye, Emily walked to the house. It wasn't exactly an answer, but it was something. At least she didn't have to feel guilty if she kissed the pirate-priest.

Back on the porch, she pounced on her Da. "Why can't we tell Morgan about you? She's pretty broken up. It would help if you could tell her about Mitchell yourself."

"Sweetheart, the fewer who know I'm alive, the better. I'd prefer to stay dead for a while longer, if you don't mind." Emily winced.

Lugh changed the subject. "I hate to tell you, but I have more bad news. I had a lead on the Callaich in Wales who was rumored to be proficient in ogham—"

Hope hissed, "Not now, Lughnasadh."

"Is she a no-go?" Emily asked, disappointed.

"Emily. Hush." Hope cocked her head at Hamilton.

Lugh sighed and threw his hands in the air. "What's he gonna do, Hope? He's a dog for godssakes." Cu whined and thumped his tail. "Besides, Cu already knows this stuff." Lugh turned to Emily.

"I was told the Callaich lives off-grid with no phone or internet. And that's assuming she's still alive. My source didn't have a name, so finding her will likely prove impossible."

"I have friends in Wales," Hamilton offered. "With a little help from one of you, I could ask if they've heard of this Callaich. What else do you know about her?"

"Only that she lived in the most rugged part of Wales. On the northern coast near Snowdon Mountain. And she's old, nineties or more."

"Any family?" Emily asked.

Lugh shrugged.

Hope roused. "The dragons' dwelling place is on the Isle of Beli. In Dinas Affaraon as it was known then, or Emrys, the City of Higher Powers. It, too, is in Northern Wales. Somewhere in the highest mountains of Snowdonia."

Emily buzzed with excitement. "So, you're saying that both this Callaich and the dragon-keep are in Northern Wales? Why don't we go there? We can look for the dragons *and* the old crone."

But Lugh balked. "No way! It's too dangerous and we need our grand druid here."

"I can finish my training on the road," Emily pled. She'd been grounded forever and sorely missed the travel.

But Lugh was adamant and refused to agree to a trip to Wales. Instead he declared he was needed at Jocko's and rushed out the door leaving Cu behind, like a man pursued by demons. They stared after him.

Hamilton cleared Cu's throat. "Well. I guess that's that. At least for now. I'll work on Lugh again tonight. From what I've gleaned, someone needs to find that Callaich, assuming she's still alive. *And* the dragons. Although, it sounds like the dragons may save us the trouble by finding Emily first."

With that, he went outside with Hope and Ralph, leaving Emily alone with her thoughts.

The Calm Before

Shalane listened absently as her husband raved about a fast-food restaurant. Cecil and the boys had dropped Patty at the airport on their way to preview the fabulous Fox Theater, their weekend venue

"You'll get a kick out of the Varsity, Shay-Shay. It's the world's largest drive-in, complete with car hops on roller skates and dogs walking—their slang for hotdogs to go."

"Uh huh," she replied, not really listening. If things went right, she would be seeing Ebby tomorrow, and that was all she could think about.

"Hey honey, sounds like you're in the middle of something. I'll catch up with you later," Cecil offered.

"Uh-huh. I am. See ya later." Shalane ended the call and heaved a sigh of relief. She had a rare afternoon to herself. The Emory appointments were cancelled and Patty was on her way to California for a week or two.

Shalane had booked a half-day at the Villa Rica Spa for a deep-tissue massage, far-infrared sauna, mani/pedi combo, and a Brazilian wax job. Afterward, the stylist would trim Shalane's hair so that she looked her best for Ebby.

The only thing left was to cancel that Elemental. The last thing they needed was bad weather cancelling Shalane's performances. She exited the parked bus and faced east toward Atlanta. The snow that had hindered their trip yesterday, had all but melted.

Shalane drew a deep breath, raised her arms overhead, and commanded Ebby's Elemental to appear. Nothing happened. Sucking in air, she connected with Archangel Michael and tried again. But where darkness should be, there was only light— swirling, sparkling, effervescent light.

Confounded, Shalane dropped her arms. She looked around to make sure no one was watching, turned a circle three times, and walked its perimeter three times. Standing in the middle, she raised her arms, focused her will, and commanded the Elemental to appear.

Still nothing. Temper pecked at Shalane's nerves. She dusted her hands and turned to climb the stairs into the bus, but was suddenly overcome by a strong urge to be anywhere but there. She stood quietly hoping it would pass. When it didn't, she accessed the internet on her wrist unit. Querying hotels, Shalane found a charming inn a few blocks from the spa. The anxiety grew as she packed her overnight bag.

Shalane nabbed her vape pen and took a couple of hits, but the anxiety grew. Her hand trembled. She took another hit. The windows rattled and the bus shivered.

She cracked the door to peek out. The wind had kicked up, whipping trees and slamming little eddies of current against the aluminum shell. Had she miscalculated her target? Her cell phone jangled and she leapt to answer.

Mitchell Wainwright launched into a rant about Ebby, aka Emily Hester, then gave Shalane what he'd refused to give her before: Ebby's address.

She hung up, crowing, "Woohoo! Gotcha!"

If she hurried, she had enough time to get to Druid Hills and back. Shalane grabbed her purse and jacket. If finding Ebby took too long, she could meet Cecil and the crew for rehearsal at the Fox Theater. She scooped up her packed overnight bag, in case.

As she pulled from the parking lot, the wind swirled angrily around the rental car. Black clouds gathered and dumped sheets of rain, partially obscuring the road.

Awen Brownouts

S halane's rental car crept along the tree-lined street. The navigation screen showed her in the correct location and insisted Shalane had reached her destination. Puzzled, she searched in vain for the address Mitchell Wainwright had given her.

There was no house, only a thickly-wooded lot that appeared to belong to the mansion next door. She made a U-turn at the intersection to make another pass. Should she drive down the gravel alley? Her danger-meter was saying no.

The GPS advised, "Your destination is on the left. Twenty-one-twenty-one Wren's Way."

"No, it's not," Shalane moaned.

A petite figure emerged from the woods at a slow jog. Shalane's heart thumped and she inhaled sharply. It was Ebby Panera. Gold-tinged scarlet curls escaped the hood that framed her oval face and a half-smile twitched on lips that moved. Was she talking to herself? Or was there a Bluetooth hidden in that mop of hair?

Shalane's hand went to the horn, but she didn't blow it. Ebby was halfway down the block and running fast. Shalane stayed back to avoid detection, debating whether to confront Ebby now, or hang around until she came home. She'd prefer having her say in private, not on the street where anyone and everyone could see or hear. But she couldn't resist following.

Turning right at the intersection, Shalane kept a block between them. Not that Ebby would suspect it was Shalane, but she didn't want to spook her. At a main intersection, the light turned red and Ebby sped away. Shalane gripped the steering wheel and tapped her free foot against the floorboard. The crosswalk signal counted down. The hoodie disappeared around the corner.

**

Emily loped along the avenue, daydreaming about Lugh MacBrayer. Unable and unwilling to censor her thoughts, she replayed the tryst they almost shared in the library. Lugh had been a bit cold since then, but tomorrow was their trip to Zoo Atlanta. Their first date. Assuming he still wanted to go. The way he had run out of the carriage house, she wasn't so sure. She'd find out during her combat lesson this evening.

Sprinting across Moreland Avenue, Emily slowed to jog through Oak Grove Park. She didn't have time to do the whole loop today, but the first of the Olmsted gardens stretched two miles through Deepdene Park and ended at Fernbank Forest.

**

When the light changed, Shalane punched the gas pedal. She searched frantically and caught a glimpse of the navy hoodie and copper hair. Ebby had crossed the street and was entering a clump of woods in the median.

"Damn, damn, DAMN!" Shalane shouted, pounding the steering wheel.

**

She had barely entered the snow-dotted woods when Emily came upon a family bathing in a swollen Peachtree Creek. She threw up a hand and gratitude rushed through her at having escaped a similar fate. Unashamed, the group waved back. Compared to these folks, Emily had it good. Hell, compared to her own plight six weeks ago, she had it good. And now, thanks to Hope's book assignment, Shalane Carpenter and her Elementals were a thing of the past. As was Mitchell Wainwright.

Emily attacked the next hill and an unwelcome sensation crept upon her. For a moment, she was Awen, running barefoot through the forest near her hut, pursued by something large and unknown. Fighting panic, Emily focused on her breathing. The glimpses of Awen's memories were becoming more frequent.

She likened them to the drinking blackouts to which she was prone. Only these she remembered—if in a vague and spacy sort of way—like someone else had done the deed using her body. It had happened a couple of times during magic lessons. "She" performed complex spells with confidence and flair. But afterward, the details were fuzzy, and Emily had a sneaking suspicion that when called upon to do the incantation again, she wouldn't know how.

These, plus the incident with the blizzard, had led Emily to conclude that Awen had indeed awakened inside her. And was acting through her. As crazy as it sounded, and as uncomfortable as it made Emily feel, nothing else made sense. Still, she hadn't mentioned the incidents to anyone—not even Da, or Lugh, or Brian MacBrayer.

She thought wistfully of the teen who had improved so much over the last several weeks. The Elders had insisted on transferring him to the after-school sessions at the Acolyte Academy. At the same time, they had advanced Emily to more difficult spells. But without Brian's natural abilities and competitive spirit egging her on, Emily found it harder to concentrate. Or care.

**

The light changed and the car leapt forward. Shalane followed the busy road that skirted the woods, hoping to catch Ebby on the other side. But the forest kept going. And going.

Eventually, the trees gave way to a green lawn strewn with patches of melting snow. Benches and a small playground were mostly deserted.

Shalane pulled the car into an empty space and hoped Ebby hadn't doubled back. She eyed the lean-to's lining the edge of the forest.

Teens threw a Frisbee back and forth, but no Ebby. Shalane glanced at the clock on the dash. She needed to get back. But not without talking to Ebby first. She was too close.

When Ebby emerged from the woods, hood thrown back and arms and legs pumping, Shalane sat at attention, heart racing.

"There you are, my pretty," she smirked, rubbing her hands together in anticipation. She opened the door, leapt out of the car, and scooted across the street, oblivious to the blare of car horns and squealing brakes. She kept her gaze on Ebby circling the perimeter of the clearing.

"Ebby Panera!" she yelled at the petite figure as it reentered the woods on the other side of the island. "Goddamn it all to fucking hell!"

Running back to the car, Shalane turned left at the next light and drove back to the place Emily had first entered the woods. When there was nowhere to park, Shalane pulled into a long, uphill driveway and parked near the street. Tossing her "Minister" placard on the dash, she hurried to the entrance. Ebby would have to come this way to get home.

**

Emily crossed the merry stream on a plank footbridge painted to blend with the scenery. To her right, a mature snowy egret perched atop a vacant bench eyeing a bronze statue of a leaping fish. An owl hooted in a nearby oak, then took flight and sailed down the trail in front of Emily before disappearing into the forest.

"Callaich Oiche," she spoke the owl's name aloud, relishing the foreign feel on her tongue. Callaich also meant hag, crone, or wise woman. Which brought her thoughts back to Lugh MacBrayer.

Why was the priest being evasive? And why had the suggestion of going to Wales freaked him out? Was it because he didn't want to go with Emily?

Her stomach churned and she decided not to think about that. Instead, she pondered the Einstein quote she had encountered yet again in the book on Elementals. How could imagination be more important than knowledge?

She rounded the curve to the last straight-away and saw someone sitting on a bench beside the path. She lifted her hand to wave. The person stood and blocked her path. A woman with blond, flyaway hair. Her stalker, Shalane Carpenter.

Heart racing, Emily skidded to a stop. "What the hell?"

Shalane smiled and took a step toward her. Emily considered knocking her down and running home. She held her ground instead. It was time to put an end to her running days. It was time to stand and fight. She clenched her fists and Shalane laughed.

"What? Gonna beat me up, Ebby?"

"My name is Emily. What do you want? Why are you here?"

"I have a show in Atlanta. Remember, Ebby? I reserved front-row seats for you."

"HA! Like I'd go. What do you want, Shalane? Why are you stalking me?"

"Stalking you?" Shalane crooned. "Why, Ebby dear, I'm shocked. Most people enjoy being pursued." Then her tone turned nasty, "Of course, you're not most people, are you, Ebby? Oh, no. You're an heiress now."

Emily's body trembled, though from fright or anger she wasn't sure. She was a little of both.

"What do you want?" she asked, this time with force. The anger was winning. She took a menacing step toward Shalane. "Get out of my way or I'll move you myself."

Shalane flicked her wrist and a vine wrapped around Emily's feet. She bent to unwind it and Shalane came down on her back with an elbow. Grunting, Emily reached up to grab a handful of thin hair and yanked hard. Shalane shrieked and clawed at her, scratching Emily's cheek and drawing blood. Emily searched her memory for a spell that would disable Shalane without injuring her, but her mind was blank. They stood, facing one another, Emily breathing heavily and Shalane with a smirk Emily was itching to slap off her face.

"You're mine," the shaman growled, rubbing her head.

"Like hell," Emily retorted. "Just what do you want from me, Shalane?"

"You don't know?" Shalane laughed. "I saw it in a vision. You and me. We have been together since before coming to Earth. We are meant to be. I'm madly in love with you, Ebby Panera—Emily Hester—whatever your name. I want you to be mine. Mine until the end of time, as you have been since the beginning. That's what I want. Nothing more, nothing less."

Emily stared at Shalane, horrified. "You can't be serious?"

"As a heart attack. Shall I give you one to prove my point?" Shalane raised her hand as if to perform another spell.

Frightened for her life, Emily whipped her Taser out, jammed it against Shalane's throat, and pulled the trigger. The shaman convulsed and dropped to the ground shaking, then laid still, eyes closed. Emily nudged her with a sneaker. Shalane didn't move. Or wake up. For an unsettling moment Emily thought she might be dead. But that only happened in rare circumstances. And the gun was set to stun, not injure. She bent to check Shalane's pulse.

The woods disappeared. Emily saw in her mind's eye an amorphous blob, flashing lights, then a monster. Her first impression was of Voldemort, the dark wizard from the Harry Potter series. Only its face was scaled, like a snake or lizard, and his eyes glowed an evil red.

Shocked, Emily let go of Shalane's arm and the vision disappeared. But a suspicion came to her; was the snake creature part of the underground threat about which the Elders had warned? The source of the Armageddon warnings?

Trembling, Emily warily touched Shalane's wrist again. This time nothing happened. Her pulse was strong, but racing. Emily looked around, surprised there'd been no passersby to interrupt the confrontation.

But now what? She couldn't leave Shalane on the trail, passed out and alone. The shaman might be a mean, controlling bitch but if something happened, Emily would feel responsible. She thought of calling nine-one-one and heading home, but there was still that alone-on-the-trail thing. She thought about calling Lugh, but there was that avoiding-her thing. Plus, the damsel-in-distress thing.

An incident came to Emily's mind. She was at Shalane's home office and Shalane was giving her the lowdown on light versus dark magic. The doorbell had interrupted, and Shalane left the room. There'd been a heated scuffle and Emily had run to the living room to find a man sprawled on his back in the foyer. Shalane stood over him, mouthing a spell. The man had jumped up with no memory of why he was there.

Emily racked her brain for the exact word Shalane had used. Obliviate? No. Obscuro? No. Obfuscate? Yes! That was it.

Would it work on Shalane? If not, the witch would likely call the police. And given her ability to manipulate people, especially men, Emily would be painted the bad guy. And likely get locked up. She shuddered at the thought of prison.

Trey had told her the Taser wasn't traceable when he'd given it to her. But she couldn't leave Shalane alone on the trail. The shaman stirred. It was now or never. Emily closed her eyes and took a deep breath, anchored into the earth and connected with the other elements. She felt that funny feeling and Awen emerged. Only this time, Emily was there beside her.

Focusing her attention, Emily said clearly, "Obfuscate Ebby Panera."

The shaman groaned and rolled over to her stomach. Emily backed away quietly and hid behind a large boulder a few yards from Shalane. Peering around it, she watched the shaman slowly stand, brush off her thighs and derriere, and look around vaguely.

The spell had worked. Hallelujah.

From behind the boulder, Emily slipped into a stand of pines. She covered her hair and tucked her curls inside the hoodie, then hightailed it down the path as noiselessly as possible. At the light on Moreland Avenue, she slipped past a dog walker and her three dogs and hunkered low to wait for the signal. Thus shielded, Emily glanced over her shoulder. Shalane was nowhere in sight.

The light changed and Emily sprinted through the intersection, heart racing when she saw a police car idling in the line of traffic. Suddenly she thought of Taurus McGowan and Pete Peschi, the druid officers. They would know what to do. Praying hard, she put a couple more blocks between her and Shalane, then stopped to make the call. Pete answered on the first ring.

"Pete, this is Emily Hester." She sucked in air as she waited for his salutation, then threw herself on his mercy. "Remember Shalane Carpenter, the witch Mitchell was talking about?"

"Yes'm," Pete drawled.

"After stalking me for months, she just found me and ambushed me in Oak Grove Park."

There was a quick intake of breath. "Are you okay, Miz Hester?"

"Yes. But I think I messed up," she admitted. "When Shalane attacked me near the Moreland Avenue entrance, I panicked. I tasered her, then I did a spell to wipe her memory. I'm pretty sure it worked, Pete. But if not, I'm afraid she will go to the police. Or that something might happen to her if she's forgotten her way. Could you and Taurus—"

"Absolutely, ma'am. We're not far from there. You get on back to Wren's Roost. Taurus and I will take care of Shalane Carpenter. What does she look like?" The incredible tension in Emily's chest lessened as she gave Pete the description.

"Thank you, Pete. Thank you so much. Is there anything I should do?"

"Just go on home and don't speak of this to anyone. We've got you covered, boss."

"Will you let me know the outcome?"

"Absolutely, boss."

Emily hung up and breathed a sigh of relief. Sliding her cell in her pocket, she jogged toward Wren's Roost with a grin on her face. He'd called her boss.

"B-ahhhh-sssss," she enunciated aloud. "I like the sound of that. And the feel." There was a spring in Emily's step as she crossed a quiet intersection and threw up a hand at a passing jogger.

Boss. Her grin widened. Pete and Taurus would come through and Shalane would no longer be a threat. Or a concern. No more weather disasters. No more terroristic stalking. Remembering Shalane's unexpected declaration of love, Emily shuddered. She had said they'd been together since…what had she said? Since before Earth? What the eff?

A strong brownout washed over Emily. She stumbled on the sidewalk and stopped running to bend double. This time she was an angelic entity falling through space, massive wings beating furiously as she evaded the attack of one equally matched. Through space, Emily spiraled head-over-heels, out of control, wings limp by her sides. Then Shalane appeared again, oozing anger.

Calling for God's help, Emily used her powerful hindquarters to break away from her friend-turned-foe. Twisting, she blasted the colossus with one long fiery breath. The hold loosened and Emily dove, ripping free of the iron grip to somersault through space into oblivion.

Then the vision faded, leaving Emily baffled and shaky. Was that the before-Earth Shalane had been talking about? Slowly, she looked up. She was within a hundred yards of Wren's Roost. Dismissing the eerie vision, Emily trotted the rest of the way to the carriage house.

Fifteen minutes later, she was stepping into the shower when her iBlast buzzed. It was Pete. She turned off the water to answer.

"Miz Hester," Pete drawled, "I wanted to let you know that we found Miz Carpenter right where you said, sitting on a boulder. Your memory spell worked."

"Excellent!" Emily crowed. "But how can you be sure?"

"When we asked after her, she said she was fine—just sunning herself. Then she looked at her watch and jumped up and ran, saying she was gonna be late for some show. We watched until she drove away, but I don't think you need to worry about Miz Carpenter, boss. If you'd like, we could tail her for you. We're off duty in thirty."

"No, no. That's not necessary. But thank you for offering. With any luck at all, we've seen the last of Shalane Carpenter." Emily hung up and climbed into the shower to let the hot water stream over her head and body.

Pete had called her boss again. Emily grinned, chest swelling with pride. She liked that. And the fact that Shalane had no memory of Ebby Panera. But even better? Emily was beginning to have a feel for Awen. She had performed the memory spell herself, but she'd been aware of Awen's presence beside her.

"Take that, Mama!" Emily gloated, rinsing her hair. "I'm not as pathetic as you made me believe."

Then she sobered, remembering the lizard-man. What was it? And what did it have to do with Shalane?

She toweled dry. It was almost time for her combat lesson with Lugh MacBrayer. Emily would tell him her news and they could decide what to do next.

**

As it turned out, Lugh didn't show up. Nor did he call. Or answer when Emily called him. Disappointed and on edge, she climbed into bed early, tugged her laptop from its case, and settled it on her lap. She had barely opened it in the six weeks she'd been in Atlanta, except to research druids, wolfhounds, and other peculiar things. And to take a glimpse at her files on the Hum.

She accessed the browser and typed "lizard man". Thousands of references appeared in the results.

"Well, I'll be." Emily pulled at a lock of intensely-red hair, wrapped it around an index finger, and nibbled at the golden ends. Deeper and deeper into the web she went, reading page after page about the Reptilians, as they were more-commonly called.

Most of the sites could be characterized as conspiracy theories, but a few were written by scientists and ex-military personnel. Or those claiming to have been kidnapped by the Dracos, as they were also known.

Some of the sites claimed these Dracos had cross-bred with humans in order to infiltrate the governments of the world. Emily couldn't help snickering. Could lizards even mate with humans? Just how would that work?

Several claimed the Reptilians were descended from the Nephilim, which could be traced back to the Anunnaki. One said the Anunnaki had been aided by the Grays and opposed by the Pleidians, who passed down their spiritual beliefs and spawned ancient movements like Zoroastrianism, European Paganism, and Hindu Vedantism.

"Wait just a minute," Emily said in disbelief. "European Paganism? That would have to include druidry. Is this saying that the druid religion came from outer space? And from those who'd opposed the Dracos' ancestors? What the hell?" As fascinated as she was repelled, Emily kept reading.

The site went on to say that after linking the Reptilians to the Illuminati Cabal, the Andromeda Council had all but destroyed the reptiles in the early twenty-first century by targeting their underground compounds with high and low-frequency sonic beams. Despite that, over the last several years, reports of sightings and abductions had risen sharply.

What the hell? Emily leaned against the headboard and stared up at the crystal chandelier. Illuminati Cabal? Andromeda Council? What a load of crap. But deep inside her, doubt stirred. What if it wasn't?

She let her mind empty and her gaze go soft, then reached for the vision she'd had when she touched Shalane. It had only lasted the briefest of instants and had shocked her such that she couldn't be sure. But she'd had a vague impression of a shapeless blob, flashing lights, and a distinct face that looked almost human. It and the chest were covered in scales, and where a nose should be were slits. But the eyes—

A shudder racked Emily's body. The eyes had glowed an evil red.

She studied the screen. The creature in the picture looked very much like the one in Emily's vision. Only it was smaller and a distinct, almost iridescent green, where the one in her vision was more olivine and beige. And this one's eyes were black. The onscreen dude was eerily creepy, but not nearly as intimidating as the one in her vision.

Emily closed the laptop. Weariness settled deep in her bones. Shalane Carpenter had found her again. Would the memory spell hold? Would it keep her shielded from the shaman? She certainly hoped so. And what about the lizard man? Sighing, Emily looked at her cell for the hundredth time in the last two hours. Still nothing from Lugh MacBrayer.

Restless and needing to process, she put the laptop away and climbed out of bed to search for Hope. The Elder hadn't been around all afternoon. Emily pattered to the living room barefoot, glad it was warm enough not to bother with a robe. She searched every room for the big cat, then exited the lanai to the back gardens. Out here it was balmy, though a cool breeze blew gently from the west.

"Ho-ope. Here kitty, kitty."

Ralph scampered up behind her, meowing. Emily bent to tickle his head.

"What are you doing out here, Bubbe? Did you sneak out behind me? Where's our friend Hope?"

Ralph meowed and rubbed against her, purring.

"Say you don't know, either?" She lifted him in her arms with a grunt. "My, my, I think you've gained a pound." Snuggling her face into his fur, she carried him to the porch, then made one last attempt to find Hope.

Back in bed, she switched off the lamp and smoothed the covers. But in her dreams, the moon was nearing full and played hide and seek with an ominous cloud shaped like Lord Voldemort. The dreams wove in and out of a restless sleep in which Emily tossed and turned, rolling from side to side so often and emphatically that she almost fell out of bed.

At two a.m., Emily sat up straight and turned on the light. She checked her cell and resisted the urge to call Lugh, remembering her dignity. In desperation, she climbed out of bed to pour a finger of Da's brandy in a juice glass. Holding her nose, she chugged it down sputtering and gagging, then trudged to the red room, determined to get at least a few hours of sleep before her date with Lugh. Assuming he bothered to show up.

Emily sucked in air through her nose until her lungs reached their maximum excursion, then held it for four seconds. Letting it out to a count of eight, she held it four seconds, then started the process again, hoping against hope it would lull her to sleep.

Fire Dragon

The Komodo dragon registered the rumbling deep in the earth beneath Zoo Atlanta. The commotion had started a while back, too far down to be detected by humans or their fancy instruments. But dragons were attuned to such things.

In the wee hours of morning the rumble had changed, rising in pitch and intensity. That meant Draig Tienu's earthen counterpart, Draig Talav, had broken through the mantle and was making for Earth's surface to contact Awen. With a little finagling on Tienu's part, she would emerge near the magma shelf and bring the molten rock with her. If so, he wouldn't need the Awen to free him from the lizard's body. The fire would do it for him. He only hoped his scheme didn't land him in more trouble with the dragon master.

Heat seeped from below the surface, warming the fire drake's belly and dispelling the chill that had plagued him since winter. Barely-visible steam escaped a nearby vent, tickling Tienu's nostrils.

Talav and the Awen were coming. Tienu's time was near.

Zoo Atlanta

The day dawned flat and bright, with the sun hiding behind a layer of voluminous clouds that hugged the horizon. Annoyance warred with Emily's excitement. She was supposed to be going to the zoo with Lugh MacBrayer. Only he'd missed their combat lesson the night before and hadn't bothered to call, even after Emily left a message saying she needed to talk.

She was dying to tell him about the lizard men. And about her run-in with Shalane, though Pete had said not to.

But if Lugh didn't show, Emily had decided she would share her news with Hope, then go to the zoo alone. She'd been too thrilled at the prospect of meeting Willie D, her sort-of twin, not to go. Then she would call and talk to Lugh when she got home. If he still didn't answer, she'd call Morgan. Or Arthur.

Emily inspected her outfit in the full-length mirror. She'd paired skinny black jeans with comfortable ankle boots and a form-flattering kiwi turtleneck. It may or may not make it to sixty-five degrees, but Atlanta's spring winds were damp and capricious. To top the ensemble, she grabbed her red raincoat from its peg by the door. Along with the car keys. Just in case.

By nine fifteen, Emily was vacillating between worry and anger. Lugh was usually punctual. What could have happened to make the priest stand her up two days in a row? Anxiety nibbled at her gut. She started to call his cell phone, then hesitated. She would give him a few more minutes. Damned if she needed a man anyway. Emily was perfectly capable of going to the zoo by herself. She'd been solo most of her life, hadn't she?

Her cell phone vibrated, and Emily's heart lurched. Noting the four-oh-four area code, she answered quickly.

"Emily?"

It was Lugh. Thank God. Anger spiked now that she knew he was okay. "Where are you?" she demanded.

"Um, leaving the house. Damn," he swore under his breath, then yelled, "IN THE TRUCK!" so loud she had to rip the phone away from her ear. Putting it back, she heard, "…I'm really sorry. We'll be there in five minutes."

"We?" she squeaked. Her answer was the beep-beep-beep of the disconnect signal.

**

Lugh ended the call and glared at the pair in his back seat. His nephew, Brian, had been cruising for a bruising since getting out of bed. Hamilton Hester, as the wolfhound Cu, had been even worse, insisting without compromise that he accompany Lugh and Emily to the zoo.

Exhausted from arguing most of the morning, Lugh had finally conceded, hoping Emily could talk some sense into her father. Lugh thought it unwise to take a pony-sized dog anywhere near the zoo. But more to the point, it was supposed to be their first date.

Climbing in the Land Rover, he adjusted his seat, grateful to be out of the biting wind. He frowned in the rearview mirror and tried one last time. "Sir, won't you reconsider and stay here? Or at Wren's Roost with Brian and Hope?"

The stubborn man-dog shook his hairy head. "No sirree. I have a bad feeling about this, and since you insist on ignoring my better judgment, I am going with you. If anything happens, I will be there to help. If nothing does, then no big. Right?"

Lugh rolled his eyes and concentrated on the road. Until a few weeks ago, Hamilton Hester had been a man commanding an empire. It stood to reason that he would want to orchestrate things. But Lugh wasn't used to anyone telling him what to do, not since his parents had died.

"There's Emily," Brian chirped as they pulled up the driveway.

The change in the teen was most welcome—their new grand druid had been a positive influence on Lugh's nephew. The redhead stood on the front porch, ogling his backseat passengers. Her gaze shifted and met Lugh's. He waggled his fingers and shrugged, which brought a half smile to Emily's lips. She nodded and wiggled her own.

Lugh relaxed and grinned. She wasn't mad. Thank the goddess. An ear-splitting explosion erupted from Cu, followed by a series of shrill whimpers. Lugh threw the truck in park and leapt out, happy to escape with his eardrums intact.

"Good morning," he circled the Land Rover grinning. Emily smiled back. His stride faltered when his guts did that crazy, melty thing.

"G'morning," she mumbled, gathering her stuff from the chair. "What happened to you last night?"

"Last night? I was at Jocko's." She cocked both eyebrows and it suddenly hit him. "Oh shit! I missed our lesson. I totally forgot."

She took a step and literally pitched forward into Lugh's arms. Fire coursed through him as her body met his. She hung suspended, purse pressed against his chest, his hands cupping her elbows.

Unable to resist her uptilted nose with its smattering of freckles, Lugh kissed it and watched the expressions flit across Emily's face. He fought the nagging desire to whisk her to the bedroom, and lowered her to the ground.

She curtsied ever-so-slightly and blushed scarlet, pixie face matching her wayward hair. "Thank you. I caught my toe on something."

"My pleasure, ma'am." Lugh tipped his Braves cap and motioned toward the Land Rover apologetically. "I couldn't shake those two."

"You invited your nephew, your dog, and my father on our date?" The question dripped with sarcasm. Lucky for Lugh, it was the good-natured kind.

"No. I did not invite them on our date. Your dad has a bad feeling and insisted on coming. I protested. I did," Lugh added when her eyebrows arched. "But as you can see, I lost." He opened the front passenger door. Cu's hairy mug hung between the seats, yipping a frantic greeting.

Brian joined in, crackling with pent-up energy, "Hey Emily, we're going to the zoo with you!" He bounced beside the wiggling dog, ignoring Lugh's patent stink-eye.

Emily ruffled Cu's head and climbed in the Land Rover, swiveling to address the tagalongs. "What is this I hear about you guys crashing our date?"

"Date? Uncle Lugh didn't tell us it was a date."

Suppressing a grin, Lugh circled to the driver's door in time to see Cu poke his muzzle in Brian's face. "What else would it be?"

To which Brian rolled his eyes and shrugged.

"Something is about to happen, little wren," the man-dog said. "I don't know what, or when, or how—or even where. But my danger meter is off the scale. I'd prefer you stay at Wren's Roost, protected by magic. But Lughnasadh refuses. So, my child, I am going to the zoo with you, whether you like it or not."

"You won't mind staying in the car?" Emily asked.

There was another canine outburst. "Hell, yes, I mind. I could do as little good in the car as at home."

Brian brandished his Smartphone between them. "It says here they allow service animals at the zoo."

"But none of us are disabled and Cu is not a service dog, nor does he have a harness." Emily looked to Lugh for support and the druid priest nodded.

"I can pretend I'm blind," Brian interjected, "and you can lead me around, Cu."

"Um, no," Lugh scowled at his nephew in the mirror. "You will *not* be faking a disability. That's just wrong, Brian. Don't you know that?" The boy had the grace to hang his head.

"Yes sir. But this is an emergency."

"No, it's not. And that still wouldn't make faking blindness okay. We can, however, tell the zoo personnel that Cu is an emotional support animal. We get them now and again at Jocko's. Even yappy little Chihuahuas. Zoo management won't question that. Besides, it's true. Cu is coming along for emotional support."

"That works," Emily agreed reluctantly, though she was opposed to the whole thing. "Do we still need a harness?"

Lugh reached for his seatbelt. "Not really, but it'd be a good idea to get one anyway. Buckle up. We're off to Zoo Atlanta, via Pace Hardware."

Hakuna Matata

The front gate attendant at Zoo Atlanta parked Brian and his group beside the fence and went to find a manager. She had never seen a support dog like Cu the Irish wolfhound. Brian's eyes darted about, taking in everything. It was his first trip to the zoo since he was little. And first time ever to Zoo Atlanta. As far as he could remember, anyway.

Brian leaned against the iron fence to watch a woman disguised as a pink flamingo strut across the inner plaza. A cluster of children formed a loose, moving circle around the big bird. She stopped to let a brave child pet the delicate, pink head.

Cu nuzzled Brian's shoulder. He threw his arms around the beast's neck. An official-looking black woman with hair the color of ripe oranges hurried over. Cu perked up, wagging his tail. Brian held tight to the leash, worried he would get them in trouble.

"Hello," the woman said with a smile. Her gentle burr put Brian at ease. "My name is Yvonne. Welcome to Zoo Atlanta. What a beautiful support animal. Minnie tells me you need a pass for him."

**

The late-morning sun peeked through the clouds to shine on a whispering canopy of oaks and poplar trees. Still-emerging leaves shimmered in various shades of spring-green to mix with the deep emerald bamboo bordering the paths of Zoo Atlanta. Emily eyed the thick canes. Many had reached a diameter of six inches, rivaling those of the South American rainforests.

They had visited elephants and giraffes, a warthog and two zebras, all in simulated-natural habitats. Now they laughed at a rhino wallowing in sticky mud. It rolled to its back, snorting and kicking its hooves in the air with wild abandon. Emily read its placard aloud and they all stopped laughing. Felix the Black Rhino was the last of his kind. Anywhere.

Swallowing hard, she zoomed her phone camera in for a close-up. The rhino gave a shake of its head, dislodging a fat splat of mud. She snapped the picture and Felix turned to strike another pose.

"What a ham," she laughed around the lump in her throat.

Lugh chuckled and took a picture of his own. "I wish Felix had a female in the barn. You know, to keep the species going." Emily wished so, too—in spite of the sign. The rhino snorted and cavorted in the mud, unconcerned about incomprehensible things like extinction.

An Asian family, chattering in their native language, ambled up to read the interpretive sign. Emily waved at the little girl, whose waist-long hair echoed black-saucer eyes. The girl waved back. A middle-aged man shouldering an expensive camera bag stepped between them. He removed a flashy digital camera and a tripod, setting up to shoot the rhino as if Emily and the others were in his way, instead of the other way around.

Annoyed by the man's hubris, she let Lugh take her hand and pull her toward the path. Pleasant jolts of electricity ran up her arm. Did he feel it, too? She looked sideways from under her lashes. A smile played on his rakish lips. Yeah, Lugh felt it.

She was still worried the wolfhound would cause them trouble, but at the moment, Emily was daydreaming about melting into Lugh's arms. She breathed a long sigh and contented herself with holding hands. His was the perfect size, enveloping hers. She squeezed and he responded with a gentle, reassuring pressure.

They moseyed behind Hamilton-as-Cu, who led Brian toward Mandhari Ya Simba, the lion overlook. The wind had calmed and with the sun out, it was turning into a fine, California kind of day. Emily basked in the moment, chatting with Lugh about nothing in particular.

Their two companions had their noses pressed against the glass enclosure, watching the lions nap. A mature male lazed on its back, giant paws twitching in the air. When it rolled indolently to one side, still sleeping, Brian laughed and pointed. Lugh snaked his free arm around Brian's shoulders for a brief hug. Cu barked, sharp and loud.

On the other side of the thick, sheet-glass partition, the lion's tail whipped against the grass. The massive head turned, and the tawny eyes opened to blink lazily at Cu, who barked again—three short, staccato bursts ending on a high note. The lion scrambled to its feet, all vestiges of sleep gone. He threw back his head and roared like the MGM lion of filmdom. Emily grabbed her phone camera. Lugh turned away to answer a text.

But Cu was on a mission. The wolfhound lurched, dragging the leash from Brian's hand. The boy pounced and missed, no match for the hundred-plus-pound dog once it got the jump.

"What happened?" Lugh asked when Emily gasped.

She pointed. Cu's neck strained across a split-rail fence, winning a tug-of-war against Brian. Bystanders hurried down the path toward the spectacle. Mortified, Emily followed Lugh, who rushed to the boy's aid.

"Da, what are you doing?" She put a hand on Cu's head as the alpha lion padded across the compound. When the big cat came to a halt below them, Cu relented. He gave Emily a silly dog grin, then yipped and pranced in place like a puppy.

"What is it, Da? We have an audience." She stroked the long, bobbing neck and brushed the shaggy hair out of Cu's eyes.

Hamilton's voice rang in Emily's head. "A ghrá, this is my friend, Leo Prime."

The lion let out a majestic roar and took two steps closer to snuff the ground and the air between them. Cu barked and slung his neck across the fence. The big cat reciprocated, stretching its neck until the animals' noses were yards apart. Goose bumps rippled up and down Emily's spine. Lugh and Brian eyed the animals, slack jawed. An expanding group of onlookers shouted comments and snapped pictures of the two animals.

Emily leaned close to Cu to whisper, "Da, please. There's a crowd and you promised not to draw attention." She glanced

315

over one shoulder. "Of course, that ship has sailed. Can we go? Please?"

"Why sure, darling." Cu barked twice at the lion and backed away. The lion's answer boomed, stirring something primal in Emily.

"Cool!" Brian said, gaining control over the dog. "I need a pee break." He pointed at a nearby pavilion. "Okay if we go over there?"

Emily nodded and looked to his uncle for affirmation. Lugh stood, shaking his head with a vague expression clouding his handsome face. Emily waved a hand in front of his eyes and snapped her fingers. He blinked and focused, a new light glowing in his eyes.

Noticing the retreating figures of his nephew and dog, he asked, "Where are they going?"

"To the bathroom."

Lugh pointed to the enclosure. "But they're missing it, look!"

Emily's gaze followed his finger and shock shimmered through her. The hairs on her body stood to attention. Two lionesses had joined the patriarch, and a young male had climbed from its perch on the promontory and hurried toward the fence. The lions looked up at them, as if plotting a coup. Emily shuddered, grateful for the sheer walls and fence that contained the big cats.

Brian reversed course and galloped back with Cu, crowing, "Whoa! Look at the lions! What are they doing?"

"Gawking at her." Cu shoved between them to stare at Emily. The guys stared, too.

Unsure of what they meant, Emily looked from one to the other. "What?"

"It's you," the priest whispered with reverence. "The lions are looking at you."

Fire leapt to Emily's cheeks. Leo Prime roared. The young male and lionesses answered, jostling one another for a better view. A feeling she couldn't identify raised a lump in Emily's chest that spread to her throat. Swallowing released it and something in her shifted, igniting a glow of understanding.

She could barely mouth the whisper, "Do they think I'm Awen?" She was acutely aware of the noisy crowd pressing from behind and grateful for the wolfhound and MacBrayer men. They surrounded her, keeping them at bay. For the moment, anyway.

Leo Prime dropped to sphinx pose. "All hail Awen, Queen of the Druids," his gruff voice boomed in Emily's head.

"All hail Awen," the pride roared, dropping into place beside Leo.

The crowd erupted. The trees sprang to life in a rustling clatter. Emily's legs wobbled. Her stomach churned queasy. Tiny spots swam before her eyes. Fingering the talisman in one jeans pocket and Aóme in the other, Emily slid the ring on her forefinger and fisted the Otter Stone. The usual, subtle changes swept through her, calming her insides and fortifying her limbs. Hamilton-as-Cu nodded approval and nudged Emily forward.

She stepped to the enclosure and leaned over the fence, holding Aóme out for the lions to see. "Hail Cath Sith and Leo Prime. I am honored, but my name is Emily." She spoke in her head, as had the lions.

The patriarch sprang to his feet. "Name matters not. To us, you are Queen Awen."

A small mob approached from the cat pavilion, moving fast. "Look! The lions!"

"Let's go," Lugh and Cu barked in unison. Emily's sentiments exactly.

"My deepest thanks." She bowed to the lions and slipped through the throng with the others. Roars and snarls pealed from the pride. The mob joined the already-assembled crowd, milling where Emily and her friends had vacated. Of the lions, only the patriarch remained by the fence. He lifted his head and roared several times in succession.

Throwing her hand in the air to acknowledge his well-wishes, Emily waited as Leo Prime sashayed from the fence, giving the clamoring crowd a view of his regal behind. Lugh slipped his hand into Emily's and squeezed, then led her away from the noisy bystanders.

Falling into step behind his nephew and dog, and her father's hitchhiking-spirit, they quietly retreated from the lion exhibit.

**

Pit stop accomplished, the guys joined Emily and Cu by the path leading to the African Rain Forest. A directional sign declared the habitat home to the largest population of lowland gorillas living in captivity. Emily had a soft spot for gorillas, including a stuffed toy named Jeb given to her by the man she had thought was her father. The well-worn Jeb still lived with Emily, despite her many moves over the years.

Scratching the top of the wolfhound's head, she rose from the bench and handed the leash to Brian. "Ready to see the gorillas?" She slid Aóme from her finger to her pocket.

Brian snickered, "Yes, I am," and scratched at his side, mimicking an ape.

Lugh popped him with his Braves cap and reseated it on his head. With the sweep of one arm, he pointed in the direction of the rainforest. "To the gorillas."

But a pair of giggling girls about Brian's age exited the bathroom. Spying Cu, they approached, cooing. The chocolate-eyed cutie gushed, "What kind of dog is *that*?" Tight midnight curls framed the upturned face.

Struck gaga, Brian looked from the girls to Cu and back again.

"He's an Irish wolfhound," Emily answered, fearing Brian would give them away.

"You can pet him if you want," the teen found his voice and massaged the shaggy face. When the girls hung back, he coaxed, "Go ahead. He won't hurt you. He likes girls. I mean…" he quickly backtracked. "Cu likes people."

The tall girl held her hand out, palm up, for Cu to sniff. Thin and striking, her straight, black hair swung back and forth when she tossed her head and squared bangs fell into her almond eyes. The teens surrounded the wiggling dog.

To Lugh, Emily mouthed, "Gorillas?"

He nodded, tipped his hat, and in his sexy, southern drawl said, "Ladies, y'all enjoy your day at the zoo. We'll be moving on."

The teens' faces fell. Cu barked.

"Bye." Brian waved shyly.

"Bye," the girls tittered, watching them retreat.

Emily glanced over her shoulder. The two girls stood together whispering. Probably making plans to follow. The bamboo rustled in a gentle breeze. Making an executive decision, she grabbed Lugh's arm, bobbed her head toward the approaching girls and whispered her desire to change directions.

The dark eyes blinked understanding. Lugh touched Cu's harness and reversed directions. A puzzled Brian followed without comment, waving to the girls as they passed. Around the curve, they came upon a pair of large gray birds with stork-like legs and brown wings. Their necks were long and shiny, with vermiculated feathers like a rooster's neck.

Lugh read the placard in a loud voice, "Aha! It's Kori Bustard of the bustard family,"

Sneaking a look, Emily let go an audible sigh of relief. The path was clear.

"What's up?" Brian bounced on his toes. "I thought we were going to see the gorillas."

Hamilton-as-Cu wiggled between them. "My daughter is worried about those girls. She's afraid I'll get us thrown out of the zoo. Aren't you?" he demanded, thrusting his nose in Emily's face.

"So, sue me," she hissed. "Why am I the only one who cares? You shouldn't even be—"

"Ca-caa-ca, ca-caa-ca," the nearest bustard shrilled. The tall bird had moseyed to the fence. Its neck feathers ruffled and fanned out in a magnificent display of vibrating plumage. "Ca-caa-ca, ca-caa-ca," the bustard shrieked. It fluttered its neck and flapped its wings in what Emily guessed might be a courting display. Not to be outdone, the other bustard answered, joining the first to shriek and ruffle its iridescent neck feathers.

Brian covered his ears. Lugh grabbed his phone to record the brown and gray birds in action. An out-of-shape family huffed toward the enclosure from the other direction, exclaiming over both Cu and the birds. Emily's heart pounded. It had been a really bad idea to bring the wolfhound.

"Ca-caa-ca, ca-caa-ca," the birds shrilled in unison. Pony-dog forgotten, the family crowded the fence. The calls intensified, "Ca-CAA-ca, ca-CAA-ca," then morphed into an unfamiliar accent that rang in Emily's head. "Hail the queen. Hail Awen, Queen of the Druids." Then the bustards bowed. To Emily.

"Shit, shit, shit." Word traveled fast.

"Ca-CAA-ca, ca-CAA-ca."

The family stared at Emily now. A group of visitors in matching orange tees bustled up to surround them. Not sure what to do, Emily edged closer to the fence hoping to calm the vociferous birds. The orange-people milled, talking loudly over the bustards' goings on.

Standing tall to her right, Lugh signaled Brian and Cu to stand behind and to Emily's left, effectively blocking the spectators.

Speaking a silent prayer of protection, Emily slipped a hand into her pocket to don Aóme and presented Awen's ring to the birds.

The bustards quieted and lowered their long, greenish beaks to the ground. Knees bending backwards in salute, the birds cried as one, "Hail Awen, Queen of All."

Placing her hand over her heart, Emily responded, "Hail to you, great birds of the mother continent."

"Look!" a girl screamed. Emily turned. The young girls had doubled back and were shoving their way through the mob.

Lugh grabbed Emily's arm and tugged. "Time to go."

She was in full agreement. Nodding to the still bowing birds, Emily thanked them and retreated with Lugh, the wolfhound, and Brian.

Hamilton-as-Cu took them on a side path that wound through a bamboo forest and back toward the gorilla compound.

Once they were safely out of sight, Emily stopped and glared at the dog. "This is all your fault, Da. I wanted a quiet day at the zoo with Lugh. But noooo. You had to tag along and now look at us. We're a four-ring circus in the middle of a very public venue." Cu hung his head in mock contrition. "And what's with this 'Hail Awen' crap? Is that your doing, too?"

Emily fought for control, angry with herself more than at her Da. She was the one who had agreed to his shenanigans. Now she'd lost her temper. In front of Lugh.

"Dammit, dammit, dammit!" She turned away to regain her composure, hating the helplessness the anger evoked. A breeze shimmered through the bamboo.

"Let it go, Dru-y-en," the delicate leaves sighed. Emily eyed the fluttering foliage, annoyed by its unsolicited advice.

"Hey, look! It's a baby gorilla!" Unperturbed by Emily's outburst, Brian ran ahead, pulling the target of her ire along with him.

She resisted the urge to yell after the wolfhound's retreating hind-end and grunted loudly instead. This day wasn't turning out the way she had envisioned. Lugh stood beside her, watching.

"What?" she grumbled.

A study in priestly patience, he extended a hand. "Shall we?"

"Fine," she snapped. But she ignored his hand and followed their uninvited guests down the trail.

**

Lugh hurried after Emily, not sure what to say to make her feel better. He'd just caught up when she stopped so abruptly several people nearly ran them over. Nodding apologetically, he pulled her to the shade.

Emily's lips turned down and hurt twisted her brow. "You know, I still don't get why you didn't show up for our combat lesson. Or call. Or return *my* call. What if I'd really needed you?"

Lugh's gut lurched.

"I really forgot," he said sheepishly. "And I had an epic phone fail. I'm sorry, Em."

"You lost your phone? Seriously?"

He shook his head. "Lost, no. Misplaced, yes. That's what happens when you have a messy teenager and a slob of a dog. Speaking of which…"

"Dog ate my phone?" Emily snickered. And not very nicely. She planted both hands on her hips and waited.

Lugh laughed uncomfortably. He'd never seen that glint in her eyes before. "Nope. Just…"

He didn't know how to say what he knew she needed to hear. But the glint hardened and sparks flew. "I'm, uh, just..." he sputtered.

The truth was, he'd been terrified of his attraction to her. Especially in light of his mother's mysterious warning. But worse, the idea of searching for the dragons had reawakened his fear that a dragon-hunt was responsible for his brother Jake's disappearance.

The sparks turned chilly. "You're just what?"

Lugh knew he was on thin ice. He couldn't avoid it any longer. Time to fess up.

"Well, shit. I guess I'll just say it outright. My mom spooked me, Em. She warned me not to fall in love with you."

The corners of Emily's mouth turned down again and her shoulders slumped inward.

"I didn't say I listened," he hurried to add, but the damage was done. The trees fluttered in a gust of wind and a sigh rippled through the zoo. Emily pivoted toward the Rain Forest.

"Fine then." Her tone was icy. "Probably best we keep it casual."

Lugh caught her by the arm. She jerked away, then waved off a concerned couple who'd paused.

Emily's face settled into a study in serenity. "Just drop it. I'll be fine. No problem."

Lugh did a double take. How'd she do that? He stared and couldn't help when his lip curled in a sneer. "Just so you know, you suck at receiving confessions."

That caught her by surprise. Her jaw dropped and her eyes widened. Then the mask slipped back into place.

"You're the priest," she said quietly. Crossing her arms over her chest, she propped against the split-rail fence.

"Yeah. Well. Big fat deal." He shoved his hands into his pockets. Talking to Emily when she was like this was like trying to talk to someone else he knew. Lugh's stomach twisted, then dropped to his toes. Holy shit. Mitchell Wainwright.

"What did you say your birthdate is?"

"June 21, 2012, same as Willie D. Why do you ask?"

"Because I know someone else with that same birthdate."

322

"There are lots of someones, I'd imagine."

"Yeah, but this someone is…" Lugh paused. He might not be the right one to break it to Emily, but he was tired of keeping secrets. "Mitchell Wainwright, dammit."

The Hester heir gasped and put her hand to her mouth. Agony and awareness flickered on her face and her eyes shifted faraway.

"There's a picture on his office wall. Of him. As a young boy. In Da's arms. Holding a mess of fish." She sagged into the fence and the blood drained from her face. "He's my brother, isn't he? Oh god, are we twins?"

For some reason it sounded worse when Emily said it. Lugh shuddered.

The wind shivered through the trees, louder and longer. The sun disappeared and a chill fell on the land. People scurried past, on their way to see the gorillas. The odor of eggs wafted to him and Lugh looked up, expecting to see someone eating a sandwich.

"If it's any consolation," though he knew it probably wasn't, "Mitch used to be one of the good guys."

Shock shimmered in her eyes. "Used to be? What happened?"

"I do not know," Lugh lamented. "But whatever it was, it was big. During the summer of his junior year, Mitch devolved from stand-up guy and my best friend to the self-righteous, overbearing prick he is now."

Lugh glanced at the time on his phone. "We'd better catch up with Brian and Cu. No telling what kind of trouble they're getting into."

Emily let go of the fence. The sun escaped the clouds, making her hair glow like a halo.

"Just so you know," she scrunched her nose up at him and shoved the stray curls out of her face, "we're not done with this conversation. If you want me to believe I have a twin brother who's the biggest ass-hat I've met in years, I need to know more. And I want to hear what your dead mother said."

Lugh winced and took her hand. This time, she let him.

As they walked the last fifty yards to the gorilla compound, Emily looked up at him slyly. "Plus, I have news of my own. But not until we're home alone. Deal?"

"Deal." He bumped her hip with his. "Are we okay?"

A shyness crept into Emily's smile. "Yeah. It's just…"

"I know." Lugh stopped to tuck a curl behind her ear and pulled her to him.

"Hey, no PDA's!" She pushed him away and stole a furtive glance around.

He grazed her chin with his knuckle. "After this, I will take you anywhere you want. Just you and me. I promise."

Her smile was on the side of wry as she peered up at the quivering bamboo. The silver-bellied leaves flailed in the breeze. An older couple strolled past, holding hands and sharing an animated exchange about the gorillas.

Pointing to herself, then Lugh, Emily sighed. "What if this is not meant to be? The zoo was supposed to be my anywhere. Look how it's turned out."

Lugh rolled his eyes and leaned in close. "You got me on that. But we're not ruling this out." His finger mimicked her previous motion. "This, we are doing again. Alone. And often." She pulled away with a pout.

"Then let's not tell them where we're going next time."

A gaggle of people passed in each direction, arriving in a hurry and leaving with awe-struck smiles.

Lugh held out his hand. "Works for me. Shall we?"

Emily looked beyond the canopy, where cumulus clouds skimmed playfully over the sun. She let go a pent-up breath and intoned in a low voice, "Dear God, God-dess, please make the four of us inconspicuous." Then she slipped her hand into Lugh's and they strolled the last few yards side by side.

Last Chance

Talav hurried through the dark, granite tunnels beneath the zoo. A change in air pressure hinted of Tienu's side shaft. Talav turned to follow the narrowing course until the ceiling loomed as close as the floor. She sat back on her haunches in the tight space to catch her breath and gather her wits. She needed them to get through to the thick-headed Awen, whose energy signature was stronger and closer than ever. It was now or never.

With a mighty heave, Talav slapped her tail back and forth, up and down, assaulting the walls. Tienu told her they would be thinner here. Soon, the ceiling rained dirt and gravel. She continued her gyrations, twisting and bucking, snorting and bellowing, throwing her whole body into her efforts. The earth groaned and trembled.

Talav stopped to sniff the dust-disturbed air and caught a whiff of something that smelled suspiciously like—uh oh. Sulfur. Talav roared. The wily fire dragon Tienu had tricked her into releasing a pocket of magma. She should have suspected as much. The once-powerful dragon king had resorted to worse in the past. Being trapped in a lizard's body must've driven him to the edge. But at least he was awake. That meant one more Keeper to help reach the Awen.

The temperature rose quickly, and the fetid odor filled the small chamber. Talav couldn't stop it now. Tienu had best be ready to squelch any volcanic eruption, otherwise they would both be in trouble.

Of course, a little lava was nothing compared to what would happen if they failed to reach the Awen. Every moment delayed was one step closer to Earth's demise.

Gorilla Surprise

Brian zipped his coat to keep out the biting wind. The others were behind them on the path somewhere. Cu lay on the grass licking his privates, after sniffing every available inch of the general vicinity. Brian watched a band of male gorillas retreat up the hillside and couldn't help feeling sorry for them. It would drive him ape-shit crazy to be on display twenty-four-seven.

Giggling at his pun, he thought of Pindar and Ruby, the girls from school they'd seen earlier. He had hoped they would run into them again. Pindar was pretty, but when Ruby batted those big, chocolate eyes, things happened to Brian that he couldn't explain. Things that left him tongue-tied and out of breath—so much so, that he hadn't been able to introduce them to Lugh and Emily. It had been that way since his first day at Druid Hills Middle School, when Brian sat down beside Ruby in homeroom.

Kicking at a shrub, he stubbed his toe and hopped on the other foot. He searched for the grown-ups and spied them through the crowd, holding hands and smiling. Which was good because his uncle hadn't smiled much since Brian had come to visit. But the two were moving snail-slow. By the time they reached him, the gorillas had all but disappeared, hidden by an outcrop of stone.

"Where are they?" Lugh appeared and bumped shoulders with Brian.

He turned his uncle to the correct angle and pointed up the slope. "If you stand just right, you can still see them."

"Look!" Emily squealed.

The MacBrayer men wheeled in unison. A large silverback scooted down the bank of the adjacent enclosure, knuckle-walking toward them at a brisk pace. Several females followed him, one carrying an infant and two leading youngsters by the hand.

"Hey, look!" Brian yelled as Cu shoved past. Thrown off-balance, Brian grabbed the dog's tail to keep from falling. Cu yelped and swiveled to nip at him.

"Hey, don't bite me. You're the klutz!"

The dog snarled, teeth bared, and scurried to join Emily by the fence.

"My God," she was saying when Brian snatched up the leash. "Aren't they magnificent?"

The gorillas had assembled along the top of a deep trench, the females and their young forming a line on either side of the silverback.

Eyeing Emily with growing respect, Brian crowed, "Shit-a-mighty, Emmy, the gorillas are doing it, too."

"Shit-a-mighty, they are," Lugh agreed, flicking the back of Brian's head. "Don't say 'shit'!"

"OW!" Brian whined, rubbing his head.

Beside him, Emily bounced on her toes. "Look, it's Willie D, my birthday-twin. Look, oh look!"

The silverback toed the wide trench, careful to stay behind the electric fence. The others inched forward, tightening the semi-circle around the patriarch. The crowd moved quickly in their direction.

"People are coming," Brian warned quietly.

A deep voice boomed inside his head, "Greetings, Awen." It was the silverback, standing tall on hind legs, as did the others. All except the baby clasped in its mother's arms.

Brian could hear Emily's answer in his head, too. "Thank you, Willie D. I am honored to finally meet you." She bowed and straightened. "And your family, too."

"Hurry," someone yelled. The crowd was nearly on top of them.

"All hail Awen, Queen of the Druids," the deep voice guttered.

"Hail Awen," the gorillas echoed. Breaking rank, they danced about the hillside and burst into a chorus of grunts, hoots, and whimpers.

A wall of people rammed into Brian, shoving and clamoring to view the gorillas up close. He lost his footing and fell on top of Cu, who yelped and scrambled from the melee, then turned to lunge back into the crowd, parting it with his frenzied onslaught.

On the other end of the leash, Brian used his elbows and shoulders to keep from being trampled, then tripped and pitched into an especially-nasty fellow, only to be pulled to the side by Lugh. Emily gave them a quick once-over and declared Brian and Cu okay.

"Ahh-wen," came an eerie cry, as if from under the earth.

Emily's head shot up. There it was again. Her heart pounded. Then all hell broke loose.

A rumble emanated from the bowels of the earth and built in ferocity until a crackling explosion shook the compound. The gorillas squealed and ran for higher ground. For a breathless second, the crowd remained still. Then screams erupted over the earth's thunder and the people disbursed helter-skelter like ants. The roar grew louder and the ground shook.

"Earthquake!" Brian yelled, and the crowd picked up the cry.

Heart pounding and fearing for his life, Brian clutched the frantically-barking Cu's leash and reached for Lugh's hand. But the ground heaved from side to side, throwing him to his uncle's sneakered feet.

As he landed with a grunt, Brian thought of how he'd once bragged to his friends that an earthquake would be fun. Using his uncle's pant leg, Brian dragged himself up with skinned hands, vowing never again to say anything that stupid. Assuming they got through this.

Over the din of the tortured earth, Emily yelled what sounded like, "Hold on. Stick together."

But another tremor flung them shrieking to the ground. Hysterical now, the crowd climbed over one another to bolt down the paths leading away from the African Rain Forest. The frightened squawk of wild birds filled the air as they fled the disturbance. Panicked, Brian pointed to the retreating stampede.

"Shouldn't we follow?"

The earth rolled back and forth in an odd, wave-like motion that made him want to puke. Cu danced and strained at his leash. Legs splayed wide, Brian managed to stay upright, but heard the scariest thing yet—a booming, splintering crack somewhere in the vicinity of the Scaly Slimy Spectacular Reptile House. Horror paralyzed him as the jagged line traveled, lickety-split, toward the gorilla compound.

The three druids and Cu clung together with their backs to the chain-link fence, as the fissure ripped through the rainforest, cutting off escape and isolating them from the rest of the zoo.

When the heaving stopped, dust and debris filled the eerily-quiet air. Lugh laughed nervously, and pulled Brian close with one arm and Emily with the other. Cu whimpered, glued to their legs.

The relative calm was unnerving. From around the zoo, squawking birds and shrieking animals sounded injury and alarm. A large blue heron swooshed over their heads and gained altitude. Brian sagged against his uncle, legs trembling and nostrils burning from the thick, pungent air.

Cu whined and nuzzled Emily. "Foreshock? Main event?"

"Possibly either." She swiped at her face, smearing the grime into a mask. "If that was a foreshock, it was a big one."

"How about trying one of those spells?" Hamilton urged.

Confused, Emily hesitated. Then understanding dawned. "To calm the earth! Of course! Form the circle!"

When she reached for his hand, Brian did a double-take. Emily was different. All doubt was gone. All hesitation. Confidence sizzled through the filth on her face. She tilted it to the heavens and the fingers of terror constricting Brian's throat let go just a little.

"Hands everyone." Hamilton stood on Cu's spindly back legs to complete the circle. Brian gripped a hairy paw and Emily's soft, cool one. "Do it, Em, speak the spell," Cu barked.

A grating shriek erupted beneath them, like a saw shearing through rusty metal. It built in intensity, filling Brian's ears until the zoo disappeared and the world exploded in a gut-wrenching screech. Emily's lips moved, but the wailing earth swallowed the grand druid's words and filled Brian with renewed terror.

And rightly so. A spider-crack snaked away from the main rift, releasing pent-up energy. With a resounding explosion, it shattered and raced toward them. Emily shrieked as the ground in front of them ripped asunder.

On the opposite slope, greening poplars lashed from side to side and disappeared, as the chasm groaned and continued on through the gorilla compound. The earth shook violently. Brian heard another scream and realized it was his own.

Terror trumping shame, he clung to the fence. The gorillas ran further up the hill, but the fissure claimed a lagging female. Brian sobbed and hid his face under his arm.

The earth bucked, pitching and yawing like a seesaw gone wild. It slammed Brian against the fence like a ragdoll, wrenching his fingers free. He slid backward toward the chasm, sucking in dirt instead of air. Catching hold of a bush, he retched and scrabbled to his knees and belly. When he was close enough, Lugh caught hold of his sleeve and yanked Brian to the fence, where his frantic fingers locked around the steel wire.

Grunting and huffing, he dragged himself up to cling to the only thing keeping the group alive. If the fence gave way, they would all be slung into the widening abyss. Blood flowed from his uncle's forehead. Emily's legs dangled as she struggled to find a foothold. Her nose was bleeding, and a welt bisected one scrunched-up cheek. Cu was glued to the fence, legs intertwined with Lugh's.

Brian held tight and tried to yell to them, but nothing came out. His throat was raw and full of grit.

Then the quaking stopped.

Eyeing one other, they remained still until Cu untangled his long forelegs and shook his body. Chunks of dirt flew through the air. Then gravity took over, dragging Cu backward toward the maw. Brian yanked the leash, and Lugh leaned forward to grab the harness just in time.

Underlying Fault

Emily's backside dug into the fence, her senses as sharp as they'd ever been. She was in her element, surrounded on all sides by a natural disaster. This was what she did, and who she was deep down inside.

She assessed the situation, brushing dirt and debris from her clothes with one hand and clinging to the chain-link fence with the other. Emily and her friends were marooned on a tiny island of asphalt, anchored by the sagging fence and a prayer.

The earth had calmed for the time being, but the reek of sulfur wafted to her and a chill ran up Emily's spine. Worse was coming. Much worse. No wonder Cu and the animals had been anxious. She should have listened.

Untangling a twig from her matting curls, Emily tossed it in the air and watched it somersault toward the narrow chasm. Zoo employees appeared along the trail, shouting instructions and encouragement as they pulled people from the rubble.

She noted with a rush of gratitude that one searched for a way to reach her group. Zoo and civil defense sirens blared. A news helicopter buzzed overhead.

Emily fished a crumpled tissue from her pocket and dabbed at her bloody nose and brow. God, it was hot. The temperature was rising too fast. Sweat gathered on her forehead and under her arms and trickled between her boobs.

Cu panted, his long tongue dripping beads of saliva. Damp hair curled around the men's smudged faces, and their cuts and gashes oozed blood. Wisps of vapor rose from the rift, along with something else—the stench of rotten eggs.

Heat by itself was not good. Heat *and* sulfur? Very not good. Especially since Atlanta was perched atop the long-extinct

Brevard Fault. She needed to get to the edge to confirm her suspicions.

"No!" barked Hamilton, reading Emily's mind. "Even a slight shiver and you'll end up in the bottom of that pit. If it has a bottom. No way am I letting that happen."

Emily knew he was right, but still. "Da, I suspect we're on top of a volcano that's about to blow. Feel that heat? Smell the rotten eggs?"

They all nodded. Brian scrunched his nose. Lugh wiped sweat and blood from his brow.

"Take my hand," she told him with feigned confidence.

Lugh did, without hesitation, keeping his eyes glued to hers. "I trust you Emmy. You can do this."

His words filled her with resolve. She could do this. Lugh believed in her.

Slowly, she slid her foot toward the edge, and the earth shuddered. Only different this time. Like the wavy-gravy jiggle of liquefaction.

The chills broke cold along Emily's spine. Adrenaline pumping, she squeaked an alert and shoved them all sideways, away from their refuge toward the edge of the crevasse.

Seconds later, they teetered precariously, as the little patch of asphalt melted away and the chain-link fence disappeared. Close to her ear, Brian let out a blood-curdling scream as the earth disintegrated at their feet, heaving a mighty "WHUMP!"

Dirt and debris spewed high in the sky and rained down upon them.

Pelted by rocks and chunks of the park, they reeled in disbelief, clinging to one another as the fissure groaned and split in two, exposing the iron-rich underbelly of the earth. On the facing slope, a screaming gorilla let go of an uprooted tree just in time to be rescued by the Silverback, while the tree cartwheeled into the abyss.

But it didn't stop there. A new sensation vibrated beneath their feet.

The mangled fence shot back into view and kept on going, taking Emily and the others along for the ride. In slo-mo, the entire shelf on which they crouched rose into the air like an elevator.

Terrified, yet thrilled, Emily clung to Brian, Lugh, and Cu, as they shot into the air, higher and higher, atop the forming mountain. With a groan and a lurch, their perch finally reached its zenith and halted with a jerk, throwing them all to the ground.

Emily scrambled up, wiping grit from her eyes. Intent on finding the epicenter, she left it to Lugh to make sure Brian and Cu were okay. She peered through the thick, roiling dust.

From this vantage point, she could just make out a cloud of steam rising in the southeast near the reptile house. Beneath the plume, Emily recognized the red stream of doom—a rooster tail of lava spurting from the earth.

It was as she had feared. Beneath Zoo Atlanta was a volcano on the verge of eruption.

Civil-defense sirens caterwauled, loud and urgent, warning residents near and far of impending danger. Smoke billowed high in the sky. Zoo employees shepherded screaming patrons away from the pooling lava and the fires spreading in its wake. Helicopters circled overhead. The air grew thicker, hotter.

The building pressure would blow them sky high and the zoo would be inundated in molten lava inside a minute. And if the release-blast was strong enough? Atlanta and all its surrounding cities would be destroyed as well, vanishing beneath miles of flowing lava.

Emily glanced back at Lugh and Brian, and the wolfhound Cu, bearing the spirit of her father. Collectively, they had come to mean more to Emily in six short weeks than anyone ever had. She couldn't lose them now. She couldn't. She wouldn't.

Suddenly, understanding dawned. She thought of Lugh's words in the cemetery and related them to Einstein's adage for the first time. Knowledge is what *is*, and nothing more. But, imagination *creates* what is.

As the truth resonated within her being, Emily knew what to do.

Aóme still rode her right forefinger. She shoved the other hand in her pocket and clutched the Otter Stone. The lava plume grew larger, shooting from the epicenter to rain down on hysterical animals and people. Feeling their searing pain as her own, Emily raised both arms overhead and sent energetic roots into the earth.

Thus grounded, she called on the spirits of the elements—first Earth, then Fire, Water, and Air. Power sizzled through Aóme and the talisman burned in her fist. Emily closed her eyes to shut out the chaos going on around her, and her mother's face flashed in her mind.

"Stop your posturing, young lady. You'll never amount to a hill of beans."

The familiar slur cut Emily to the bone. All she could think of was escape. Her eyes flew open. She took one stride and realized she was trapped on a promontory with nowhere to run. Heart in her throat, the panic expanded until Emily trembled with certainty. She was going to die. Along with everyone else.

"What's wrong, Em?" Her Da's reassuring voice broke through the suffocating terror. "Try again, little wren. I'm here beside you."

She gasped for breath, sucking in the sulfuric fumes. The plume had grown larger still, and the wind blew the fouled air in their direction. Pandemonium reigned.

From the corner of her eye, Emily caught a flash and dropped to all fours, cringing in terror.

An enormous dragon, crimson and flaming, rose from the pooling lava and roared. Its red wings stretched wide, making it the largest creature Emily had ever encountered. She could feel its malice. And it was aimed at her.

Her friends surrounded her, but all Emily could see was the dragon in the fire. All she could hear were the screams of the dying and injured. Their anguish poured out and multiplied, pounding Emily into submission. She cowered, unfazed by Lugh's ministrations or her Da's exhortations. It was Emily and the dragon, and he wanted payback.

Bile rose in Emily's throat and the hotdog she'd eaten came back up, as gross the second time as it had been the first. She retched again and the dragon screeched. From below the earth came an answering roar. The earth shook and the Hum grew louder beneath their feet. Sirens screamed, approaching the zoo.

The hum morphed into a melodious voice in Emily's head, "Tienu, you promised. Bring Awen to me." Her quaking insides calmed just a little.

Then something let go, and Emily could see and hear again. The air was hot and thick with smoke and noxious fumes. Rescue workers sprayed water and foam on the lava and fires, ignoring the dragon. Could they not see him?

"Dragon!" she yelled as loud as she could. The priest and wolfhound loomed above her. Brian hung back, wringing his hands.

"Don't you see it? It's humongous!" she gasped, pointing.

Lugh and Cu wagged puzzled heads.

"No, Emily, there is no dragon," her Da said firmly. "Are you okay? You've got to pull it together."

Lugh helped her stand and stuck his nose against hers. "Focus, Em. You have to stop the volcano before it blows."

Emily looked out at the reptile house. The dragon was there, but it had crouched beneath the rooster tail in the middle of the lava pool.

The smoke haze cleared and Emily suddenly found herself on the side of a very different mountain—one covered in snow. Her heavy robe was made of fur pelts, her hair much longer. It whipped in the wind and stung her cheeks.

Against her right hip, Cu stood. Hope pressed against her left knee. Four dragons were bowed before Emily—one fiery red, the second a shimmering blue, the third glittered rainbows, and the last glowed silver with transparent wings.

Emily, as Awen, lifted her hand. Aóme glittered on her first finger, but on her ring finger, a chunk of sapphire threw multicolored sparks, and on her chest, a ruby pendant blazed. She raised her left hand and the dragons stood. From that forefinger, a brilliant diamond flashed, emitting a beam of light that split into three and connected with the other stones.

Power surged through Emily and a heavenly voice rang sweet in her head, "Now, Awen! Do it, now!"

She opened her eyes to find herself standing in the same position, arms overhead. Only, a holocaust surrounded her. Lava spurted, fouling the air with sulfuric acid that stank of rotten eggs.

Quickly, she spoke the simple spell from the night of the blizzard.

"Earth, Fire, Water, and Air,
I command you to calm and still foree'er."

Sparks flew from Aóme, with a brilliant green ray that shot from the emerald straight into the earth. The lava plume calmed to a slow trickle, then fizzled altogether.

Inside her head, a velvety voice whispered, "Well done, Emily Bridget. Well done."

Her legs gave way and Emily collapsed amidst the rocks and rubble, plummeting into a black, bleak world where she wandered alone; deaf, mute, and bereft of feeling. All, that is, except loss.

"Wake up, Emily, you did it! You did it!"

Brian's high-pitched voice pierced the sinister fog. Emily's eyelids fluttered and the teen chirped, "You did it, you did it. You saved us!" But she couldn't move, or speak.

Lugh kneeled beside her, face close to hers, "Emmy, are you okay?"

He shook her shoulder and she woke at his touch, filled with an ecstasy she'd known once before. She blinked eyelids that were heavy and full of grit. Lugh's dancing eyes gazed into hers.

With a start, Emily realized she was in a heap on the ground, with sharp rocks digging into her backside. She struggled to her knees with Lugh's help.

Brian threw his arms around her waist. "Thank you, Emmy, you saved my life."

Lugh wrapped his arms around both of them. "You saved my life, too. Thank you, Em."

"And mine," her Da barked, rearing on hind legs.

He propped a paw on Emily's shoulder and the other between Brian and Lugh. They lingered that way for a long time, clinging to one another, grateful to be alive. When they were done with their own private celebration, they slowly unwound and separated.

Below them, the lava had indeed stopped flowing. The firemen worked to contain the fires. Paramedics swarmed, treating injuries, and news crews gawked from copters overhead. The dragon was gone. The earth had calmed.

"It worked," Emily sighed. "I don't believe it."

"Believe it, dear one," her Da said proudly. "We all knew you could. Now you know, too."

Gentle, so as not to disturb her wounds, Lugh pulled her against him and laid his hands on either side of Emily's face. With deliberate tenderness, he kissed her in the way of the druid; forehead, nose, chin, eyelids, cheeks, and finally, Emily's mouth.

Cu and Brian cheered them on.

Brimming with pride and exhilaration, Emily melted into the dark priest's arms and surrendered to his magical kiss.

Below the new peak, near the Scaly Slimy Spectacular Reptile House, two red eyes blinked and sank into the cooling lava.

THE END

LEAVE A REVIEW

Reviews are an author's bread and butter.

Thank you for reading *Awen Rising*. If you enjoyed it, and I hope you did, please leave a review on Amazon, Goodreads, Bookbub, Net Galley, or any other site that accepts book reviews.

Be on the lookout for:

UPCOMING BOOKS BY O. J. BARRÉ

The *Awen* Series:

Book Two, *Awen Storm*, is slated for release in 2020.

Book Three, *Awen Tide*, arrives in 2021.

ABOUT THE AUTHOR

O. J. Barré hails from the lushly forested, red-clay hills near Atlanta, Georgia where this story takes place. From birth, O.J. was a force of nature. Barefoot and freckled, headstrong and gifted, she was, and is, sensitive to a fault. Books became her refuge as a young child, allowing O.J. to escape her turbulent alcoholic home on adventures to untold places and times. Her daddy's mother was a Willoughby, making O.J. a direct descendant of William the Conqueror. Her Awen series is a love letter to that distant past.

For access to O.J.'s monthly newsletter, go to:
https://tinyletter.com/ojbarreauthor

You can find O. J. online at:

Amazon Author Page:
http://amazon.com/author/www.ojbarre.com

Website: https://www.ojbarre.com

Blog: https://www.ojbarre.com

Twitter: https://twitter.com/ojbarreauthor

Facebook: https://facebook.com/authorojbarre

Pinterest: https://pinterest.com/barr4739/

LinkedIn: www.linkedin.com/in/ojbarreauthor

Made in the USA
Columbia, SC
22 September 2019